THE RISING HORDE

VOLUME ONE

STEPHEN KNIGHT

ALSO BY
STEPHEN KNIGHT

CITY OF THE DAMNED

THE GATHERING DEAD

LEFT WITH THE DEAD

THE RISING HORDE: Volume One

THE RISING HORDE: Volume Two

WHITE TIGER, with Derek
Paterson

PROLOGUE

The dead overran Europe in less than a month.

The plague of the moving dead started in Russia and spread outward like some sort of creature expanding its territory. At first, the Russians handled it in the usual way—they denied there was any problem, controlled all media, and refuted all claims that Russia was responsible, or even involved. But by the time a million corpses walked through one of the heaviest artillery bombardments in history and descended upon Moscow, the European continent was lost.

Despite the technological advances of most European societies and the ever-vigilant police forces in several of the continent's nations, with the fall of Russia, the dead spread through the European Union like unchecked wildfire. By the time the EU's leaders had determined that the carnivorous hordes were a threat of significant consequence that required an overwhelming asymmetric response, it was too late.

NATO was generally powerless to operate in the beginnings of the conflict, shackled beneath a command and control structure both burdensome and lackluster. Despite early warnings from the American military, the Europeans didn't want to face the problem. When it came time to push and shove, the Americans were already withdrawing. Other than a token force sent to Britain to assist in stabilizing the United Kingdom—the only European nation to take the threat seriously from the beginning—Europe had to face the horde alone.

And the European ineffectiveness was all the dead needed to proliferate worldwide.

1

McDaniels watched Boston Harbor grow closer as the Coast Guard cutter *Escanaba* cruised down the channel at a steady six knots, her bow knifing through the polluted water. It had taken the *Escanaba* almost eighteen hours to make it from New York to Boston, and it seemed that her engines were running full-out the entire time. He had never been much of a fan of Boston, but he was happy to see it after what he had endured in New York. From a distance, all looked well. But as the *Escanaba* drew closer to the shore, he could see flashing strobe lights, scores of helicopters in the air, and smoke on the horizon. Just off to the ship's starboard side, Logan International Airport should have been a beehive of activity, with commercial carriers coming and going. Instead, the only aircraft were military planes, which landed and took off in great synchronicity. McDaniels leaned against the deck railing and hung his head.

The dead were already in Boston.

Shipboard announcements were made, telling the crew to remain aboard while the ship was reprovisioned. McDaniels already knew a car would be waiting for him at the *Escanaba*'s dock, to spirit him and the precious Iron Key flash drive sitting in the ship's safe to a safe location, if such a place existed. The dead had a funny way of being able to turn even a fortress into a tomb.

As a tugboat linked up with the Coast Guard cutter, rifle fire crackled somewhere on the shore. McDaniels recognized the likely caliber, 5.56 millimeter, the same caliber an Army M4 would fire. The regular beat of the shots indicated one weapon firing on full automatic. So either the military or a law enforcement SWAT team had just gone to guns on something. McDaniels was certain he knew what that something was, and looking at the Coast Guardsmen who tended to their duties on either side of him, he saw they knew, too.

"Major?"

McDaniels turned. Regina Safire stood beside him, her green eyes turned toward the approaching shoreline. She regarded the curtain of smoke rising into the air with a haunted expression.

"They're here; aren't they?" she asked.

McDaniels nodded. "I think pretty soon, they'll be everywhere."

"Where are you going? After we get ... what do they call it? Put ashore?"

"Nothing's changed. I'm still going to the Rid." McDaniels had been charged with delivering Doctor Wolf Safire and his valuable research from New York City to the U.S. Army's Medical Research Institute of Infectious Diseases, also known simply as "the Rid." The fact that Safire was dead was largely unimportant. McDaniels was the appointed custodian of Safire's final research, and that was good enough for the government. He had been in contact with his commanders over his satellite telephone, and they had told him he would be met when the *Escanaba* made landfall. The only major change was that McDaniels had been instructed to bring Regina Safire with him, just in case the researchers at the Rid encountered difficulty with the files. She might be able to assist in deciphering some of her father's processes.

"You're coming with me," he added. "Big Army wants you in Virginia."

She nodded, then turned away from the lights of Boston and looked at him. "What about Earl and Zoe?"

McDaniels sighed. "They're... they're not persons of interest. They're free to go anywhere they want once we dock."

"I've been talking with Earl. He doesn't know anyone in Boston. He doesn't have any resources. Kicking them to the curb now is kind of cruel. Don't you think?"

McDaniels nodded. "I do. But there's not a lot I can do about it. I can maybe get him a room somewhere, but I don't have any credit cards or anything. Not even an ATM card, so I can't get him any cash—"

"I'll take care of that. But Earl lost his wife and oldest daughter almost back-to-back. And he has Zoe to look after. With everything that's going on, dumping him onto the street and wishing him luck just isn't good enough."

"I'll talk to the Coasties. Maybe they can help out. In the meantime, you should get ready to disembark. Once we're at the pier, we're gone."

"All right." She turned back to the railing.

McDaniels made his way to the bridge. None of the Coast Guardsmen on the deck challenged him, but Commander Hassle didn't look very happy to see him. Not surprising, since McDaniels had basically called the man a coward in front of his crew for not going back into New York City to rescue one of McDaniels's men. Once aboard the *Escanaba*, McDaniels had made radio contact with the last of his men, First Sergeant David Gartrell. At the time, Gartrell, who had acted as a decoy so McDaniels could get the civilians—and the Iron Key thumb drive—to safety, was on the run from the zombie horde and still very much alive, but McDaniels knew his ammunition had to be almost depleted. A single soldier, even an accomplished thirty-year veteran like Gartrell with decades of special operations experience, was simply no match for thousands of hungry stenches. Alone in the city, Gartrell was fast approaching his expiration date, and the only thing that might save him would be McDaniels and a handful of Coast Guardsmen. But Hassle had denied McDaniels the men, denied him the use of one of the *Escanaba*'s small boats, and had finally stripped him of his weapons. McDaniels had been incensed at what he perceived to be cowardice on the part of the ship's captain, but over the time it had taken for the *Escanaba* to return to sea and journey to Boston, he had slowly come to understand Hassle's position.

While McDaniels had been operating under a surge of emotion, Hassle had a crew to preserve and a ship to oversee. Those were his primary mission essentials. Launching what would almost certainly have been a suicidal rescue effort for one soldier just didn't offer enough returns for sacrificing several of his men. And when McDaniels had time to get it together, he knew the Coasties would be literally chewed up if they went ashore. Their training and experience simply had not prepared them for protracted overland operations in urban terrain.

Besides, Hassle had taken a big enough risk by sending a detachment out into the waters of the East River for McDaniels and the others. McDaniels was surprised they made it out of New York alive. Even with the *Escanaba*'s firepower, the horde had almost taken them down. The entire Special Forces operational detachment that had gone in with McDaniels and Gartrell had been killed, along with the soldiers from the 160th Special Operations Aviation Regiment who had been trapped with them in the city. The horde had peeled them off, one by one, until only McDaniels and three civilians remained.

Given what he had narrowly survived, McDaniels wondered how he could have even *thought* of going back. The Special Forces code required that no one be left behind, but it didn't specifically state that everyone had to die to retrieve one of their fallen. And that would have been the case had Hassle allowed it.

McDaniels approached Hassle on the bridge and saluted. Even though Hassle wasn't in the Army, he was still a superior officer. And McDaniels felt he should show the officer some respect to possibly repair some of the damage he'd done earlier.

Hassle returned the salute perfunctorily. "Major McDaniels. We'll have you ashore in about fifteen minutes."

"Thank you, sir. I was wondering if I could speak to you about Mister Brown and his daughter. It seems they have nowhere to go and ... well, it seems that maybe Boston might not be much safer than New York."

"I thought they were your problem," Hassle said.

"The Army tells me that only Miss Safire is going to accompany me. The Browns are basically shut out. And I figured since this is your town ..."

"You figured that the Coast Guard would be able to look after them, Major? I don't think there's anything I can do to help. Once you're off and we've been reprovisioned, the *Nob* heads back to sea."

"I see. So there's nothing any of the Coasties ashore can do?"

"You called it when you said Boston has some issues, Major. Those Guardsmen ashore have other things to worry about right now than finding the Browns a hot and a cot. Again, I'm sorry, but..." Hassle shrugged and spread his hands.

"I understand, Commander. I'll figure something out. Thanks for everything. And I'd like to apologize for the things I said to you before. That was not in keeping with the traditions of my service, and it was just plain rude. You have your own mission to worry about, and I was wrong to try and press you to the mat over my first sergeant."

Hassle took the apology well, and some of his tension seemed to ebb. "I totally understand, Major. You guys were under the hammer the entire time and losing another man at the end... well, I wouldn't want to stand in your shoes. I wish there was more we could have done, but you saw the size of the crowd at the shoreline. Even with the fifty and seventy-six, we couldn't keep them back long enough to get your man. We'd have lost the entire party if we tried."

"I know that now, sir."

Hassle nodded. "After we dock, I'll hand off that thumb drive to you. I'm told a government vehicle is already waiting at the pier to take you to... to wherever it is you're going."

"Very well, sir."

"Good luck, Major. Whatever that man Safire came up with, I hope it can help us straighten all of this out." Hassle jerked his chin toward Boston. "And I hope it happens soon because whatever bug can reanimate the dead and then spread itself through bite wounds is probably something real, real bad."

"It sure as hell is, Commander. Trust me on that one."

McDaniels found Earl and Zoe sitting with Regina in the *Escanaba*'s cramped crew galley. Zoe leaned against her father listlessly, her gaze fixed on the tabletop. She didn't look up when McDaniels stopped next to the table and asked her how she was doing. McDaniels frowned. She was totally shut down. The things she had witnessed in New York had completely overwhelmed her ability to cope. But she was still young, and McDaniels felt—hoped—she would be able to recover.

Her father, Earl, wasn't in much better shape. His eyes were flat and dull behind his glasses as he looked up at McDaniels. Seeing his wife become one of the walking dead and the death of his eldest daughter as she fell down a dark elevator shaft had taken a terrible toll on the man. Despite the fact he had no military or survival training beyond what he might have picked up on the streets of Harlem, Earl had managed to get his daughters to a place of relative safety amidst the carnage that had descended upon New York City. If McDaniels and the others hadn't arrived, perhaps the zeds would have overlooked the Browns' enclave completely. But reanimated members of Operational Detachment OMEN—the Special Forces team that had been chopped to McDaniels for the rescue mission—had come hunting for the surviving special operators. And the Browns had paid a terrible price.

McDaniels saw no hatred or malice in Earl's eyes, only loss, hurt, and despair.

"Any news?" Regina asked.

"Nothing good," McDaniels said. "Earl, you don't have any place in Boston where you could go? No friends, no family?"

Earl shook his head. "Nothin' that I can think of right now.

Had an uncle who lived up this way, but he died years ago, and I wasn't close with his family. You got some sort of plan for us, Major?" There was a hint of life in his voice, and he looked at McDaniels almost expectantly. After all, they were both men of color; Earl was probably hoping that McDaniels would help out a brother down on his luck.

"Miss Safire and I will be leaving the ship in a few minutes. We're going to be met by a car at the pier. You and Zoe will have to leave as well, and the Coast Guard says there's nothing they can do for you right now."

Earl grunted. "I saw the city from the deck. Same thing's happening here as in New York. It's just startin', but it's the same thing. Boston's gonna go down the same way, and this time, I don't have no building to hide out in." He shook his head and squeezed Zoe, but she didn't respond. "And what am I going to do with her?"

"We can't take them with us?" Regina asked McDaniels.

"We might be able to drop them somewhere along the way, but I very much doubt we'll be able to take them all the way to Virginia with us."

A voice came over the speakers, "Attention all hands, attention all hands—ship secure portside. Major McDaniels, you and your party are requested to disembark at this time from the main deck. All crew, remain at your docking stations until further notice."

Regina looked from Earl to McDaniels. "We need a plan."

"I know. Like I said, we might be able to drop them somewhere along the way, but I don't know what's going to be between us and wherever it is we're headed, which I guess will be an airport." McDaniels sighed and put a hand on Earl's shoulder. "We'll figure it out. The first thing to do is go topside and find out what transportation has been arranged for us, then find out where it's headed. We'll work on the next step after that. All right, Earl?"

"Yeah. Okay."

McDaniels stepped back from the table. "Then let's get to it."

The air was chilly on the main deck. A passerelle had been erected, connecting the cutter to the cement pier. Several vehicles were parked on the pier, and McDaniels tried to identify the one waiting for him. All were either nondescript sedans or trucks waiting to service the *Escanaba*.

Hassle met McDaniels at the passerelle and gave him the Iron Key thumb drive. Someone had wrapped it in plastic, probably out of an abundance of caution should the device go overboard, which made sense. The device supposedly held the recipe for saving mankind from the growing horde of necromorphs that threatened the entire planet.

"That's something you probably want to take care of," Hassle said.

"You got that right. Thanks, sir."

Hassle motioned to a crewman who stepped forward with McDaniels's MP5 and Mk 23 pistol. "I had the ship's weapons officer service and clean your weapons, and we've filled the magazines. I hope you won't need them anytime soon, but they're ready if you do."

McDaniels accepted the weapons, checked them quickly, then secured them. He nodded to Hassle. "Gosh, hot food, hot showers, laundry service, flushing toilets... I'm not so sure I want to leave, Commander."

Hassle smiled and pointed down the passerelle. "Well, I'm sorry to hear that. Just the same, get the hell off my ship, Army."

McDaniels and Hassle exchanged salutes, then handshakes. "Thanks for taking care of us," McDaniels told the taller, thinner man. "You came through where even Marines failed."

"I'll remember you said that."

"Take care, Coastie."

"Stay alive, grunt."

The enlisted Coast Guardsman at the end of the ramp pointed out a black Ford Crown Victoria with government plates sitting at the end of the line of parked vehicles. "Your ride's over there, sir."

"Thanks, son." McDaniels signaled for the others to follow him as he set off for the parked car. When he drew near, the driver's door opened, and a tall kid in battle dress utilities climbed out from behind the steering wheel. He glanced at McDaniels, then took a longer look at the civilians. His features were tough to read beneath the shadow cast by the bill of his patrol cap, but McDaniels was certain he wasn't thrilled to see more bodies than he had been told to expect.

"Major McDaniels?" the soldier asked, saluting McDaniels.

McDaniels returned the salute. "You got it, Private. What's the drill?"

"I'm Private First Class Ernesto, sir. I'm to drive you to Logan, where they're holding a plane for you and Miss Safire." He looked at Earl and Zoe, but said nothing further.

"The other civilians are with us for the time being," McDaniels explained, hoping that would be enough.

"Sorry, Major. My orders are to take you and Miss Safire only."

McDaniels stepped closer to the private. McDaniels stood at six feet flat; the kid before him could have been a forward on the UConn Huskies basketball team. McDaniels glanced at the patches on the private's shoulder; he didn't recognize them. "What unit are you with?"

"The Nine-Seven-Two Military Police Company, part of the Massachusetts Army National Guard. We should get going, sir." To accentuate his point, the private pulled open the rear passenger door on the driver's side. The interior dome light snapped on, revealing decidedly no-frills government-issue accommodations.

"Is Logan still open?" McDaniels asked.

"Only for military use, sir."

"Are there any car rental places still open?"

The private's expression didn't change. "I don't know, sir."

McDaniels nodded and motioned everyone toward the car. "Okay, let's mount up. Private, the Browns are coming with us, at least to Logan. You can tell your commanders you didn't want a Special Forces officer landing on you with both boots. Hooah?"

The soldier obviously didn't like it, but McDaniels had him outranked by miles. His curt nod was accompanied by a quick, "Yes, sir."

"Pile in, guys." McDaniels steered Regina toward the rear door, and Earl pushed Zoe in after her. McDaniels walked around to the front passenger door and slid inside the idling car.

The private reclaimed the driver's seat and pulled on his seat belt. He pulled the Crown Vic away from the pier, and McDaniels watched the *Escanaba* recede from view in the sideview mirror.

While McDaniels didn't have any personal credit cards on him, Regina did. At her insistence, McDaniels ordered the private to stop the car at a nearby bank ATM. The National Guardsman did as instructed without comment and parked the car in a handicapped space.

McDaniels and Regina got out, and he scanned the area. The street appeared to be deserted. In the near distance, sirens wailed, and there was a faraway taint of smoke in the air. It all seemed familiar to McDaniels, and he didn't like that they had stopped on an empty street. Even though the streetlights were on and the avenue was well-illuminated, he checked to ensure his night vision goggles were secure in the pack on his belt.

"Hurry," he said to Regina. He put a hand on the butt of his Mk 23 pistol and escorted her to the bank's locked door. She swiped her ATM card through the card reader there and the magnetic lock clicked open. McDaniels pulled open the door and let her inside. He kept the door open with his foot and stood sentry while she hurried to one of the ATM machines and did what she needed to do.

After a few moments, a dark shape stepped out of the shadows across the street and staggered toward the well-lit bank. McDaniels watched it approach and pulled the pistol from its holster, the dread growing in his chest. Was the approaching figure a necromorph? A person? He had no idea, so he held his pistol in both hands, attaining a low ready stance. He glanced into the bank lobby and saw Regina was pulling cash from the ATM.

"Hurry it up," McDaniels said as he focused his attention on the figure approaching him. All he could tell about the advancing form was that it was half-walking, half-stumbling toward him. Just like a stench. When the figure came within twenty feet, McDaniels aimed the pistol at its head.

"Yo, man. What the hell?" The man raised his hands, his eyes wide with surprise. The middle-aged black man had a wispy white beard and was missing some of his front teeth. His clothes were filthy, and the faint reek of urine clung to him like a cloak. "I just need a dollar, man! You gonna shoot a brother over a dollar?"

It's just a bum. Calm down. It's a wino or crackhead, not a stench. Just the same, his heart rate didn't slow, and he didn't lower the pistol.

"Get the fuck away from us," he said, putting the steel of command into his voice. "If you don't comply, I *will* shoot you... *brother.*"

"Yeah, okay." The bum took a few unsteady steps backward, then lowered his hands. He looked at McDaniels with disdainful eyes. "Give a nigger a gun and look what happens. No respect at all."

McDaniels jerked his head toward the street. "Whatever. Take off."

"What's going on?" Regina asked from the doorway behind

McDaniels.

"Nothing. Let's go." McDaniels stood aside and let her pass, then escorted her back to the waiting Ford. After she slid into the back seat, he sat up front. The driver wordlessly backed the car out of the handicapped parking space and accelerated into the night.

"Here, Earl. Take this," Regina said. McDaniels turned in his seat and watched as Regina reached across Zoe and pushed a wad of cash into Earl's hands. "The ATM would only let me take out a thousand. I'll see if I can get some more at the airport, but that might be all you'll have for a while."

Earl nodded meekly. "Thanks, miss."

"Earl, you don't have an ATM card?" McDaniels asked.

"My wife kept all that stuff. I didn't need it."

McDaniels nodded and faced forward as the car charged onto a larger street, which contained a traffic flow that seemed almost normal. The driver steered the car toward a tunnel, following the signs that directed traffic to Logan Airport. The route to the airport was almost empty; traffic heading for the Mass Turnpike was much heavier, and McDaniels asked about that.

"A lot of people are leaving the city," the driver said.

"Is it being evacuated?"

The driver shook his head. "No, sir. But after what happened to New York, no one's really going to sit back and wait."

"How large is the outbreak in Boston?" Regina asked.

"I don't know, ma'am. Not very large right now, but the National Guard is being called in to augment the city police. The larger outbreaks are to the north." The car emerged from the tunnel briefly and quickly charged into another one.

"To the north?" McDaniels said. "Isn't that mostly residential neighborhoods?"

"Yes, sir. I'm not sure why the outbreak started there. Maybe you can find that out later."

The military presence at Logan was sizeable, but it hadn't entirely supplanted the civilian workforce. McDaniels told the driver to pull into one of the first car rental establishments he saw. Regina exited the car as soon as it came to a stop and ran for the agency's brightly lit office.

"Earl, you can drive, right?" McDaniels asked.

"Yeah, but where to?"

"To wherever you have someone. To someplace safe. Where are your nearest relatives?"

"Uh ... got people in Long Island, New Jersey, and—"

"No, no. You have to avoid the New York City area. Those things are all over there. Where else can you go?"

"I have a cousin in Ohio that I'm friendly with," Earl said after a moment. "In Akron."

"That sounds good." McDaniels smiled. "You really saved our bacon back in New York, man. I know you've gone through a lot, but if it wasn't for you, things would have had a different ending. And because of you, we might have a chance at stopping all of this. Thanks for everything."

Earl sat in the darkened car, clutching his daughter to his side. Her eyes were closed, and her breathing was deep and rhythmic in sleep. McDaniels was grateful that she'd been able to escape the terror for a few moments.

"You're welcome," Earl said. "And thank you for doing all this for me and Zoe."

"Of course, Earl. Of course."

A radio crackled in the car, and McDaniels looked over as the driver pulled a walkie-talkie from his belt. He reported their position and stated they would arrive at the assembly area as quickly as possible. Whoever was on the other end of the radio wasn't thrilled with that, and he ordered the driver to leave for his target immediately.

McDaniels took the radio from the Guardsman. "This is

Terminator Six. We'll be on target as soon as possible. Expect us in approximately one-zero minutes. Terminator Six, out." He switched off the radio and placed it on the seat beside him.

The driver looked at it, a slightly frantic expression on his face. "Uh, sir—"

"Don't worry about it, Private. I'm armed, and you're not. Make sure your commander knows that."

"Uh... roger that, sir."

Regina returned to the car a few minutes later, carrying an envelope, keys, and a rental agreement. "There was another ATM inside, and I was able to withdraw another thousand," she told Earl as she handed him everything. She then pulled off her watch. "Take this in case you lose the cash, or it gets used up. You should be able to trade it for something useful."

"How the hell are you able to get that much money from an ATM?" McDaniels asked.

"I have a two thousand dollar per day limit," she said. "I'm kind of rich, you know. And rich people can get different banking structures."

If Earl had heard this, he didn't comment on it. Instead, he looked at the watch and frowned. "I don't know nuthin' 'bout watches, Miss Safire, but I'm thinkin' this one's worth a whole lot of money."

Regina shook her head. "Don't even worry about that, Earl. I can always replace it." She pointed at the papers and keys in his hand. "You're all set. I rented a Nissan Pathfinder, since I figured it would be better to get a four-wheel drive, in case you need it. It has a full tank of gas."

Earl regarded the items he'd been given and nodded to her. He even managed a faint ghost of a smile. "That's wonderful, ma'am. I really thank you for this."

"You're welcome."

Zoe woke up in the middle of the exchange and looked from her father to Regina to McDaniels and back to Earl again. "Where are we going?"

"Ohio, little miss. Ohio, to see your cousin Emma."

Zoe nodded.

"Major, we really need to go," the driver said. "They're holding a plane for you."

"Understood, Private." McDaniels shook hands with Earl and touched Zoe's face. She looked especially fragile at that moment, and his heart went out to her. He wished there was more he could do. "Goodbye, folks. And the very, very best of luck."

Regina handed Earl a business card. "My personal cell is on there. Please call me and let me know you're all right. Just leave a message if you can't get me directly. All right?"

"All right, Miss Safire. I'll do that." Earl paused. "I'm sorry about your father."

Regina froze for a moment, and McDaniels knew she'd been using all the frantic tasks of the past hour to keep memories of her own loss at bay. He hoped Earl hadn't just blown a hole through the dam she had built to hold back her emotions.

Regina nodded. "Thanks, Earl. And I'm really, really sorry about Kenisha and your wife, too." As she said this, she reached out for the girl. Zoe threw herself into Regina's arms and wept softly. McDaniels reached around the seat and put his hand on Zoe's back, feeling a surge of emotion. Chances were good he would never see these people again.

"Major," the driver said.

"Yeah, okay, boy, keep your pants on." Earl threw open his door and climbed out of the Ford. He walked around to where Regina stood, embraced her quickly, then took Zoe's hand. "Come on, baby. We gotta let these people get goin'. Major, Miss Safire, thanks for everything. We appreciate it. And I'll repay you, ma'am. You can count on that."

"No need to do that, Earl."

"I know. But I'll do it anyway." He looked at her and McDaniels for a moment, then reached down and brushed the tears from his young daughter's face. "You ready, sugar pie?"

"Yes," she said softly.

Earl straightened and nodded to them one more time. "Goodbye, folks."

He led Zoe away.

2

McDaniels was surprised to discover the plane waiting for them was a US Air Force C-21, the military version of the Learjet 35 business jet. He and Regina were led to the jet by other members of the National Guard military police unit their driver belonged to, including the driver's commanding officer, a narrow-faced captain with a prickly demeanor and a thick Bostonian accent.

"You took your sweet time, Major. You realize how much it costs the government to keep one of these jets parked here?"

McDaniels cocked a brow and smiled. "You realize just how very little I give a shit, Captain?"

The captain seemed to get the message and didn't say anything further.

The interior of the jet was cool and inviting, though not as luxurious as McDaniels had thought it might be. The headroom was less than five feet, so he had to bend over to enter the aircraft; Regina only had to bow her head. As soon as they were aboard, the Air Force copilot closed the cabin doors and returned to the cockpit after prompting them to buckle up. He pointed out the refreshment station on the way, directly across from the door.

The jet's engines spooled up as McDaniels and Regina fastened their belts, and a few minutes later, they were airborne.

The flight to Maryland took slightly more than three hours. Regina passed out almost as soon as they were wheels up, but McDaniels remained awake. Sleep eluded him, and the Air Force crew didn't seem to want to talk. With nothing else to do, McDaniels leaned back in his seat and stared out at the night beyond the cabin window.

Fort Detrick didn't have an airfield capable of recovering the C-21, so the jet set down at nearby Frederick Municipal Airport. As the jet taxied toward one of the fixed base operations that offered fuel and other aviation-related services, the copilot turned back to the cabin.

"Major, a UH-60 is waiting to take you and Miss Safire to Detrick. It's off to our left, parked on the ramp."

McDaniels looked out the window and saw the helicopter sitting in the darkness. As he watched, its anti-collision lights came on, winking in the night. "Roger, I have it. Thanks."

Regina didn't look very happy. "Another helicopter ride?" No doubt she was reliving the helicopter crash in New York City. They had gone down on a modified special operations Black Hawk after a necromorph had jumped off a building and smashed right into the helicopter's main rotor.

"Try not to worry about it. I've flown in helicopters hundreds of times and never had a problem until this last hop," McDaniels said. "I don't think we'll have the same set of circumstances tonight as we did in New York. All right?"

"All right."

The helicopter jump from the airport to Fort Detrick took less than six minutes, and the Black Hawk touched down on the pad at Detrick without incident. A single Humvee waited for them, and they climbed inside it.

"Where are we headed?" McDaniels asked.

The driver, a female with sergeant's insignia on her lapels, replied, "Straight to the Rid, sir."

"Fantastic." McDaniels checked his watch—ten minutes after eight. "Can you tell me what's been going on around Detrick? Is the area secure?"

"Yes, sir. Right now, the area is secure. There haven't been any reported instances of an outbreak here, but Baltimore and DC both have... um, infestations. That's the official description, I guess." The sergeant pulled the Humvee away from the idling Black Hawk. "Where are you coming in from, sir?"

"New York City."

The sergeant gave him a sidelong glance. "You kidding about that, sir?"

"Not at all. Why?"

"Because New York City belongs to the dead. The entire Tenth Mountain Division is trying to stop the stenches from getting off Manhattan, but it's not working. They're all over the city now, in Queens, Brooklyn, and Staten Island. I heard even on Long Island. If you were there, you're lucky to have gotten out alive. That's all I'm saying."

McDaniels nodded. "I know. The rest of the alpha detachment I was with wasn't so lucky."

A few minutes later, the vehicle pulled up in front of the Crozier Building, a structure that must have dated back to the 1970s, in McDaniels's estimation. The big sign on the manicured front lawn said it all: USAMRIID. A small group of people on the sidewalk turned toward the Humvee as it braked to halt.

McDaniels thanked the sergeant, and he and Regina exited the hardy four-wheel drive vehicle. The approaching group of people was a mix of Army soldiers and civilians; the military folks wore Class B uniforms and garrison caps, while the civilians wore business casual beneath their white lab coats.

"Major McDaniels?" A short, thin man with a carefully manicured mustache and receding hairline moved to the front of the group.

McDaniels saluted. "Yes, sir."

The colonel returned the salute. "I'm Colonel Jeffries, commanding officer of USAMRIID." He pronounced it as *You-Sam-Rid*. "Welcome to Fort Detrick." Jefferies looked at Regina. "And you must be Doctor Safire?"

"I'm Regina Safire," she said. "Good to meet you, Colonel."

"Hello, Doctor. Ah, my condolences regarding your father." The two shook hands before Jeffries looked back at McDaniels. He cocked a brow and smiled broadly. "Well, Major, we don't normally get you Special Forces types around here, and certainly not while fully manned up." He gestured at McDaniels's weapons and body armor.

"Sorry, Colonel. Didn't have much time to change into the usual duty uniform," McDaniels said.

"Not a problem. Do you have the research data on you?"

"Right here, sir." McDaniels reached into his pocket and pulled out the Iron Key thumb drive. He handed it to Jefferies, who in turn transferred it to one of the civilians, a willowy blond-haired woman on the high side of fifty.

"Doctor Kersey will take it from here. I understand the data is encrypted, Doctor Safire?"

"It is, but I have the password."

"Then, would you mind going with Doctor Kersey?"

Regina shook her head. "Not at all."

Jeffries turned to back to McDaniels. He looked as though he was going to say something, but then he looked past McDaniels's shoulder. McDaniels turned to see three vehicles coming to a halt behind the Humvee; a fourth hung back on the main road. The vehicles were LAV-25A2 amphibious reconnaissance vehicles used by the US Marine Corps. Fully armored, each of the eight-wheeled vehicles carried a turret-mounted 25 millimeter Bushmaster chaingun and two M240 7.62 millimeter machineguns. The weapons were currently manned. McDaniels found the presence of armed Marines on an Army reservation to be a bit odd.

McDaniels looked back at Jeffries. "Sir?"

Jeffries shrugged. "Got me, Major. The Marines are a tenant unit here at Detrick, but I'm not sure what they're up to."

Several Marines dismounted from the vehicles. They were all rigged for combat and had night vision goggles mounted on their helmets. They scanned the area, their hands on the stocks of their M4 carbines. One of them hurried toward the assemblage standing in front of the Rid, his eyes on McDaniels. He started to salute, then noticed Jeffries and saluted him instead.

"Good evening, sir. I'm Lieutenant Bonevich, Bravo Company, Fourth Light Armored Reconnaissance Battalion."

Jeffries returned the salute. "Good evening, Lieutenant. Colonel Jeffries, commanding officer of USAMRIID. What, uh, what can I do for you?"

"We've been told to establish a defensive perimeter around the Rid, sir. At least until some regular Army troops can take over for us."

Jeffries pointed at the LAVs sitting at the curb. "What, with *those?*"

"Yes, sir. That's what we have, so that's what we'll use."

"Is there a problem?" McDaniels asked.

"The Rid isn't particularly well-defended," Jeffries replied. "We have some good physical security, but there aren't a lot of armed tenant commands here. We're mostly medical and signals, and the Marines"—he nodded toward the waiting LAVs—"are pretty much the only combat component on the entire base."

"And we were ordered to supplement security at the Rid," the lieutenant added.

Jeffries checked his watch and nodded to Kersey. "Take Doctor Safire inside and start working on that," he said, pointing to the Iron Key Kersey held. "Start your analysis as quickly as possible, and make multiple duplicates of the data. The sooner, the better."

"I will," Kersey said. "Doctor Safire, if you'll follow me?"

Regina looked at McDaniels, and he said, "Go ahead, Regina. Make sure they can unlock the data." She nodded and followed the taller woman inside.

Jeffries dismissed the rest, and as the assemblage turned toward the building, the short colonel looked at the Marine officer. "Lieutenant, do whatever you need to do to protect the building," he said. "We have essential research about to start, and if the necromorphs show up, I'm hoping you can zero them."

"Count on that, sir." The confidence in the Marine's voice was almost palpable.

"You know how to do that?" McDaniels asked.

"Head shots, sir. Though a round of twenty-five mike mike will probably make do." The Marine motioned to one of the armored vehicles waiting at the curb.

"Probably not. You can blow a zed to pieces, and whatever's still connected to the brain will try and come after you. Even if it's just a head and shoulders, the stench will come at a chin-crawl. I've seen it, so believe it, Lieutenant."

"Where did you see this exactly, sir?"

"New York City."

The lieutenant looked at McDaniels for a long moment, then nodded. "Roger that, sir."

"Major, we need to get going." Jeffries adjusted his garrison cap and pointed at the Humvee that still idled at the curb.

McDaniels was surprised. "Where are we headed?"

"To the helipad. We'll get aboard that UH-60 that flew you in, and then we hit the Pentagon. It seems you have a cast of thousands to report to, and now that you've completed your mission, I'm tasked to get you to them."

"Don't you need to review the data on the thumb drive?"

Jeffries snorted. "Doctor Kersey is the expert here, Major. She'll be able to square that away probably before we're wheels down at the Pentagon. Lieutenant... I'm sorry, son, what did you say your name was again?"

"Bonevich, sir."

"You're good to go with whatever you need to do. Just try not to shoot any workers here at the Rid. Some of them might look like zombies, but they're just tired."

The lieutenant managed a ghost of a smile, then turned to his waiting men.

McDaniels followed Jeffries to the Humvee, but he didn't like it. He was getting tired of all the helicopter rides, but he couldn't keep the folks at the Pentagon waiting, especially the senior ones. And if they had dispatched a full-bird colonel to hand-deliver him, then McDaniels knew the senior folks would have lots of stars and stripes among them.

The flight from Fort Detrick to the Pentagon took less than twenty minutes. The helicopter was met by two captains who ushered Jeffries and McDaniels toward the slab-sided heart of the American military. Above the rotor noise, McDaniels heard automatic gunfire in the night, and he stopped and turned, his hand resting on the butt of his MP5.

"What's going on?" he asked the captain nearest him.

"New York wasn't the only city with a sizeable infestation," the young captain said. "Don't worry, sir. We're secure here."

McDaniels fixed him with a glare. "Son, don't try and blow sunshine up my ass. We are most definitely *not* secure if those things are anywhere nearby."

"McDaniels, we need to get moving," Jeffries said.

"And Major, we'll need to secure your weapons before we go inside," the other captain said.

McDaniels laughed. "Try and take them from me, Captain."

Both of the junior officers looked at Jeffries. The colonel rubbed his eyes and looked at McDaniels as if he was a difficult child. "Major, I know you Special Forces types are wedded to your weapons and all, but really—"

"Colonel, I'm not giving up my weapons. I know what those things are capable of, and I know what they can do. They're easily the biggest threat I've ever gone up against, and I lost an entire alpha detachment to them. If you, if *anyone*, thinks I'm going to give up my weapons just because we're supposedly 'secure,' then someone's going to be *very* disappointed. Are you reading me on this, Colonel?"

"Sir, security won't let you in while you're armed," the first captain said. His tone was conciliatory and reasonable, but McDaniels saw something in his blue eyes—fear. He wasn't

The Rising Horde: Volume One

afraid of McDaniels. He was afraid of what McDaniels had said.

"Then make it happen, Captain. Or have whomever I'm supposed to talk to come on outside to chat."

"Major McDaniels!" Jeffries was starting to get hot under the collar, and McDaniels glimpsed what kind of commander he was: a man who liked to lead by intimidation, not example. "Give up your weapons! Now!"

McDaniels fought to keep the smile from his face. "I'm sorry, sir, but I don't believe you're in my chain of command. You're not even in one of the combat arms, so I'm going to have to respectfully decline your order. I'm not giving up my weapons while this nation is under direct threat." He pointed toward the nearby doors, which were manned by armed police carrying assault rifles. "Go on in and tell whomever it is we're meeting that I disobeyed your orders and see how things work out. Otherwise, this show has gone as far as it's going to go. Hooah?"

Jeffries glared at McDaniels, then marched toward the building. He conferred with the police for a minute. The junior officers shifted uncomfortably and exchanged glances, but said nothing. Behind them, the Black Hawk spooled up and lifted back into the dark sky. One of the police officers manning the door spoke into his radio, and two other cops stepped out of the Pentagon and joined them. Their eyes were all on McDaniels, who stood at ease and tried to look as non-threatening as any fully armed special operator could. The cops conferred with each other and Jeffries, and then the radio squawked. McDaniels couldn't make out everything that was said, but the cops looked at each other in surprise. One of them shrugged and waved McDaniels forward.

"Major, you're clear to enter with your weapons. I can't believe it, but the word comes down from the very top."

"Are you satisfied now, McDaniels?" Jeffries asked, the irritation plain in his voice.

"Yes, sir. I'm practically slap-happy." McDaniels walked toward the door. He half-expected the cops to rush him once he got close, but they only watched him. Two of them did break away from the group and walk off in different directions. McDaniels knew what they were up to. If he turned out to be a crazy man, the cops hoped their disparate positions would prevent them from taking fire before they could neutralize him.

"Sirs, we've got to hurry," said one of their chaperones, and the two captains picked up the pace.

McDaniels followed them down a series of corridors that all looked the same. He hadn't spent much time at the Pentagon, and the vastness of the facility was almost overwhelming. It seemed to him that they spent more time walking and standing in elevators than they had flying in from Fort Detrick. Finally, they made it to a hallway guarded by police and soldiers. Men in business suits stared at McDaniels like hungry tigers, muscles coiled and ready to pounce. McDaniels made them to be members of the Army's Protective Services, which meant someone very important was inside the room.

Before McDaniels could reflect further on that, he was ushered inside a conference room. The room was dominated by a long, broad table flanked by eighteen high-backed chairs, nine on each side. Along both walls, more chairs had been placed; almost all of them were full, as were the chairs around the table itself. On either side of the rectangular room, large LED monitors glowed. One displayed a detailed map of the continental United States, while the second showed a more global view. McDaniels had just a moment to glance at the display of the U.S. and saw the eastern seaboard of the country was dotted with red pips. He knew what the pips designated.

Zombie infestations.

My God, they're everywhere ...

"So you must be McDaniels, the fellow who caused such a disturbance downstairs." A small-framed man seated near the center of the table pushed back his chair and rose to his feet. McDaniels recognized the man as Secretary of Defense O'Hara. On either side of SecDef O'Hara sat generals and flag officers, all of whom were turned in their chairs to stare at McDaniels. McDaniels recognized some of them: General Walter Dotson, commanding general of United States Special Operations Command; Lieutenant General Josiah Abelson, commanding general of Army Special Operations; Admiral Rennick, the Chief of Naval Operations. It seemed that the collective body and soul of the U.S. military had gathered in the conference room, and all eyes were on him.

McDaniels suddenly felt self-conscious. "Yes, sir. I'm sorry for that."

The SecDef waved a hand. "I'm not worried about it, Major. We've been expecting you. Have a seat."

When McDaniels started scanning for a seat along the conference room walls where the aides and lower-ranking officers sat, the SecDef pointed to an empty chair across the table. "At the table, Major. At the table." The SecDef glanced at Jeffries, then indicated another empty chair at the far end of the table.

Jeffries, suitably star-struck by such an august assemblage, practically scurried down the length of the conference room. McDaniels didn't exactly take his time heading for his designated seat, either. He pulled out the chair and waited until the SecDef sat again. The chair was not as comfortable as it looked.

"We'll go over the general status of the nation and our current posture before we ask you for your report, Major," the SecDef said. He ran a hand through his graying hair. His dark blue suit jacket was draped over his chair back, and his white dress shirt was somewhat rumpled. A leather-bound notebook and a Blackberry smartphone lay on the table in front of him. He opened the notebook and looked around the room. Behind him, the army of military and civilian aides rustled, readying their support material.

"Who's going to kick this off?" the SecDef asked.

"I'll take that, sir." The current chief of the joint chiefs, an

Air Force general named Shockley, got to his feet and indicated the digital map of the world. In one hand, he had a laser pointer; in the other, a remote control unit McDaniels guessed was tied to the conference room's audio-visual system. When the CJCS spoke, special microphones caught and amplified his voice.

"As always, everyone should know this session is being recorded. Things could get a little heated because all the services dropped the ball on this one. I've already been through this with the rest of the service chiefs, so I hope we can keep our tempers under control and save the blame game for another day." Shockley looked around the room for a moment before turning to the map. "We've known about the so-called necromorph infestation in Europe for almost a month now. As far as we can tell, it started in the city of Kirov in the Russian federation, west of the Urals. Kirov was a leading biochemical center for the Soviet Union; they manufactured and stored not only weapon precursors, but completed biochem weaponry. Of course, after the dissolution of the Soviet Union in the early 1990s and the end of the Cold War, we were assured that the Kirov facilities had been idled and then dismantled. And that may have been the case. Our intel folks are split between classifying this as the work of a terrorist group, or an accidental release. It doesn't really matter at the moment, as it appears that whatever happened couldn't be controlled by the Russian government. If it was one of their weapons, they either never made an antidote or had destroyed it. Russia went dark two weeks after the first reported cases of, uh, zombieism caught our attention." On the map, red pips multiplied throughout Russia and began an inexorable surge westward toward Europe. A smaller surge went through the Ural mountains, heading east into Asia.

"The rest of Europe wasn't ready for what was coming their way, even though they'd had two weeks warning and had experienced isolated outbreaks in several cities, such as Berlin, Frankfurt, and Prague, anywhere infected Russians could travel. Quarantine procedures were implemented, but the initial implementations were extremely uncoordinated and very haphazard. At the last minute, Supreme Allied Commander-Europe tried to get involved and take charge of the situation, but it was too late. The Army didn't have the rolling stock for this type of mission any longer, not after the cold war came to a close. And without synchronized cooperation with the individual countries and their militaries, it was a lost proposition. Though we did make a great amount of progress in securing Germany, that all came to an end when the cordon sanitaires between Germany and Poland fell. There just wasn't enough manpower to hold back the zeds, and at that point, they numbered well into the millions. Conservative estimates say between twelve to fifteen *million* zombies marched into Germany alone. Once the defenses in Germany had been overwhelmed, the rest of Europe was just waiting for them. And as you know, Mister Secretary, at that time, all U.S. military assets in Europe were ordered to return to the continental United States. Regrettably, the lion's share of our assets were lost to the horde. We recovered a substantial number of Air Force and Naval assets, but most land-based elements were overrun." Red pips continued rolling through Europe. McDaniels noticed that, at the same time, flowers of pips started blooming in other parts of the globe: Saudi Arabia, China, India, Malaysia, Japan, Brazil, Australia.

"Understood, General Shockley. And as interesting as the cycle of events has been so far, I'm going to have to ask you to table the historical perspectives of your report and focus on the state of the nation," the SecDef said.

"Of course, sir." The electronic map behind General Shockley zoomed in to focus on the United States, with cutaways for Alaska and Hawaii.

McDaniels looked at the map closely. Clusters of red pips were all along the eastern seaboard; everywhere there was a major population center, red pips glowed. New York City, Long Island, Staten Island, and a good part of New Jersey glowed red.

A sprinkling of pips had made it into suburban Connecticut, and more lay in Boston. Down the coast, Atlantic City and Baltimore had outbreaks of their own. As he had already suspected, Washington DC was full of red.

"We're in pretty much the same boat as the European Union and most of Asia," Shockley continued. "We just weren't prepared at a national level for such a crisis. Our understanding of the transmission cycle was correct. The Russian virus is passed from host to host by a fluid exchange, such as from a bite. But we overestimated the time it takes for an infected individual to die and reanimate."

"Why is that? We had weeks of practical, real-time experience with Europe, including actual operational involvement," the SecDef said. "That we could be caught flat-footed doesn't make any sense."

"Mister Secretary, if I may?" Heads turned toward the other end of the table, and McDaniels was surprised to see Jeffries was the speaker. The Secretary of Defense looked at him for a moment, then back at Shockley.

Shockley nodded. "Colonel Jeffries is our man with the medical credentials."

The SecDef waved a hand. "Very well, Colonel. Go ahead."

Jeffries stood. "Sir, the reanimation cycle was clearly understood when the outbreak began burning across Europe. There was very little deviation—a person would be bitten or otherwise infected, and two days later, they would die from an uncontrollable fever and sepsis. Anywhere from one to sixty minutes after death, the victim would reanimate. Obviously, once an infected individual was identified, the two-day cushion gave us enough time to try and deal with their condition medically, or at least detain the individual until they turned." Jeffries paused and looked around the crowded conference room. "But the virus has mutated. Now, the cycle no longer takes forty-eight hours. It takes between four and twelve hours."

"Jesus Christ," the SecDef said after a long moment.

Shockley picked up the thread again. "And this is why we're having trouble, Mister Secretary. We can't find the infected persons quickly enough. They die, they reanimate, they go looking for food, they bite other people, and the cycle continues. We just don't have the number of troops necessary to break the cycle." He turned back to the map. "We lost every unit sent into New York City, and we'll likely lose control over Washington within the next day or so. And at this time, Mister Secretary, I'd like to recommend the president and senior government officials are evacuated from the area."

"The president has already left, General. For the moment, I'll remain at the Pentagon. Please continue."

Shockley nodded. "Miami has a substantial infestation ripping through the Cuban quarter of Little Havana that is, for all intents and purposes, uncontrollable by the Miami police department. We're getting some military assistance lined up for them out of Homestead, but it's going to take a while, and the reality is, we're probably going to lose Miami the same way we lost the New York City area. And speaking of that, the entire Tenth Mountain Division has been pushed back out of the Bronx and is withdrawing as the horde advances into Westchester County. We're back to the previous tactics we tried before: block as many streets and avenues as possible, start fires, and try to burn out the infestation.

"Baltimore and Charlotte both have outbreaks, but they are under control for the moment. There was a reported outbreak right here in Arlington, but that was put down by the local police. However, we're remaining vigilant. We have outbreaks that are growing in severity in Virginia Beach and Norfolk, and another in Richmond which is almost a full-blown infestation. You may have seen on the news that Richmond is one giant inferno now, and the stream of evacuees is so large that it's difficult to search every person for signs they've been in contact with the zeds. Infected individuals are getting past us, and there's not much we can do about it because we've got our hands full trying to contain the necromorphs. It would be of great help if the president were to establish martial law for at least the eastern half of the country, if not all of it. No reported outbreaks in Atlanta, Charleston, and Savannah at the moment."

"I'll bring it up. What else, General?"

Shockley referred to the map again. "The latest intel we have regarding outbreaks and infestations is that while the eastern seaboard is our current center of gravity, we do have outbreaks as far west as New Orleans. We're relying on National Guard units to do the heavy lifting that local law enforcement can't. But getting federal troops directly involved is going to help us gain ground. We have to move fast, Mister Secretary. If there's any change in the virus's transmission process, or if another city falls to the dead, then we're going to be far, far behind the eight ball."

The SecDef nodded slowly and then looked across the table at McDaniels. "Major? Tell us about New York, please."

"Everything, Mister Secretary, or do you just want the Cliff's Notes?"

"I want to know everything that you went through, and what happened to the alpha detachment that went in with you."

"Very well. I was assigned to oversee the extraction of a specific high-value asset, an individual named Wolf Safire, who apparently had data on the zed infection. There was talk of a cure, or some sort of inoculation. At the time I received my orders, New York City was already heavily infested. Telecommunications, including cellular and broadband, were no longer available on Manhattan. An under-strength alpha detachment called OMEN was on-post at Fort Bragg, and myself and a senior enlisted trainer from the Swick—ah, the Special Warfare Center at Fort Bragg—"

"I know what the Swick is, Major."

"Sorry, sir. Anyway, we were added to the team. The arrangement was that we would oversee the handling of the asset, while OMEN would provide security. I was not in charge of OMEN; that authority remained with the team executive officer, a warrant officer named Keith.

"We flew into Teterboro Airport in New Jersey on a C-17. We drove overland to the Upper West Side of Manhattan, secured the asset and a dependent he refused to leave behind, and then made for the Central Park assembly area, where transport helicopters were waiting for us."

"Why not just go back the way you'd come?"

"The reason we didn't return to New Jersey is that outbound traffic was badly snarled at the George Washington Bridge, and we didn't want to get caught in it when the stenches broke through the National Guard and NYPD blockades. Flying out of the city was the only option available to us."

"Very well. Sorry for the interruption."

"We made it to the assembly area without too much trouble, but before we could lift out, the assembly area was overrun. Most of OMEN Team was lost when their helicopter was overwhelmed by the necromorphs on takeoff. Our helicopter had a defective forward-looking infrared device, so we were forced to fly below the smoke layer—all of lower Manhattan was on fire, part of the process to try and stop the zeds from moving uptown. It didn't work, by the way. A zed managed to jump from one of the buildings and landed right on our Black Hawk's main rotor. The helicopter crashed in the Upper East Side, and we regrouped in an office building. We were secure there until ... until reanimated members of OMEN Team arrived."

The SecDef looked around the table. "Why is that significant?"

"Because OMEN Team retained its ability to respond to situations in a tactical manner."

An uncomfortable stir went through the room. The Secretary of Defense glanced first at General Shockley, then over at General Dotson, the top special operator in the room.

Dotson raised a hand. "Major McDaniels, are you saying that OMEN Team continued to function in an intelligent manner after its members had been reanimated?"

"I am, sir. At least four or five members of OMEN Team retained the ability to use their weapons, employ ambush tactics, and operate complex machinery."

Several people started speaking at once.

"That's ridiculous!" The booming voice of Admiral Rennick overwhelmed the rest of the chatter.

McDaniels said, "Admiral, it's absolutely true. Speaking as a soldier who was boots on the ground and danger close with the stenches, I recommend that you reconsider that assessment."

"Excuse me if I don't fawn all over you for surviving your encounter, Major. We've heard nothing to corroborate what you just said." Rennick glared, but McDaniels could see the fear in the man's eyes. General Shockley had said the U.S. was holding the losing end of the stick, and that was enough to scare the piss out of just about anyone.

"We *do* have corroboration." In counterpoint to the admiral's combative stance, General Walter Dotson's demeanor was placid, almost sublime. "We've heard from the commanding general of the Tenth that they've come under fire from fallen soldiers. And that other zeds are exhibiting characteristics that parallel rational thought. Most of the horde is just that: a mindless horde, incapable of thinking of anything other than feeding. But a very small percentage of the necros can apparently retain some skill sets. And some of those skill sets allow them to do things we hadn't expected, such as setting up ambushes."

Rennick shook his head. "You need to go back to that division commander and tell him that he's—"

"Quiet!" the SecDef ordered. "Admiral Rennick, get yourself under control, or leave this meeting. We don't have the time for this kind of back-and-forth. Pull yourself together!"

Rennick fell silent, his jaw set.

The SecDef leaned back in his chair, crossed his arms, and nodded to McDaniels. "Continue, Major. And tell us more about these, ah, these... do they have a name? These zombies that can apparently think?"

"We call them 'super zeds' at the moment, sir," Shockley said.

The SecDef nodded and motioned for McDaniels to continue.

"The team was killed when their Black Hawk crashed after takeoff. Several zeds jumped aboard before it broke deck, and we didn't hear anything further from them over the radio. But not all of them came back with intact skills, only a few. I can't explain why. But they used grenades to gain entrance to the building we were in, and then they engaged us with their weapons. They used weapons in a very conventional manner, with one notable exception: they shot to wound. I presume they did this to restrict our mobility, which would give them a better opportunity to... to feed."

The SecDef held up a hand. "Stop there for just one second, Major. Colonel Jeffries, could this ability of the zeds to retain skills and think be related to the mutation you spoke of?"

"In my opinion? Almost definitely, Mister Secretary. But we need more analysis of the virus in its current state to reach a conclusive determination. My team at the Rid is working on that."

"Let's come back to that. Back to you, Major McDaniels. How effective are these, uh, super zeds?"

McDaniels looked around the table, annoyed by the question. More people quietly entered the conference room, but he ignored them. "Mister Secretary, I went in with a Special Forces alpha detachment, augmented by myself and a senior Special Forces trainer with decades of special operations experience. We were additionally plussed-up by several ground control operators from the 160th SOAR. All of those people are dead. I'm the only one who made it out."

"Sorry to rain on your parade, Major, but that's not entirely true."

The voice struck McDaniels almost like a physical blow. He

bolted to his feet and looked toward the small group of people who had entered the conference room. All wore battle dress uniforms, but one of them—a man of medium height and lean build—wore BDUs that were absolutely filthy, covered with grit and soot, and a Kevlar helmet. His blue eyes gleamed among the grime that covered his face. And like McDaniels, he was the only other soldier in the room who was armed.

I must be fucking hallucinating ...

"Gartrell," McDaniels said, hearing the disbelief in his own voice.

First Sergeant David Gartrell nodded, and a ghost of a smile passed across his face. "Didn't think you'd be so pleased to see me, Major."

McDaniels turned back to the Secretary of Defense. "Sorry, Mister Secretary, I guess the first sergeant managed to escape New York after all." He looked back at Gartrell. "Though I don't know how that's possible."

"It's a long story. But I'm sure there are more important things to talk about." Gartrell's voice was flat and hollow, and any amusement he might have felt regarding McDaniels's sudden discomfiture faded like fog over a desert. He addressed the assemblage, "I'm sorry for the interruption, sirs. I was told to report here."

"Sounds like you should be a ghost, First Sergeant," the SecDef said with a grin.

"I pretty much am, sir."

The SecDef's smile faded, and he looked back at McDaniels. "Major? You were giving us an on-the-ground assessment of the zeds?"

McDaniels remembered where he was and what he was doing, and he slowly lowered himself back into his chair. "Uh, yes, sir. As I was saying, some zeds have the ability to do more than just stumble along and look for food. At least a certain percentage of them can retain memories—or at least skills—and use them against us in the field. I can't figure out the reason behind it, but it's true. Like I said, reanimated members of OMEN Team used firearms and other weaponry against us and used the appropriate tactics to try and fix us in place by fire." He looked at Gartrell. "First Sergeant Gartrell, anything you want to add?"

"Yes, sir. The situation can be more insidious. In my case, I was holed up in an apartment building after the major escaped, and a zed, apparently one who used to live in the building, actually used a key to get in the door."

The SecDef nodded. "I can see how that would be... *insidious*, as you called it." He looked toward General Shockley. "Are you aware of this change, General?"

"It came up the line just yesterday, though Major McDaniels is the first to give such a detailed report."

"So are we prepared to deal with these super zeds, then?"

"We are not." Shockley motioned to the map behind him. "The stenches have the momentum right now, sir. We need martial law declared so we can take the gloves off and get to work."

"You've made that point already, General." The SecDef looked back at McDaniels. "Major? Do you have anything else to add? Or you, First Sergeant?"

"No, sir, nothing further from me," Gartrell said.

"Same here, sir. Only to add that I don't think the military is going to be able to stop this all by itself. Just by looking at the map, the geographic diversity of the threat makes that unlikely."

"Colonel Jeffries? When will your analysis of this Doctor Safire's work be complete?"

"In just a few hours at the most, Mister Secretary. Quite possibly much sooner. I have my best people on that, and Safire's daughter is assisting us."

The SecDef turned to Dotson. "Do you need those results before we stand up SPARTA, General?"

Dotson shook his head. "No, sir, we do not. The sooner that starts, the better off we'll be. With General Shockley's blessings,

I've already socialized the plan with the rest of the service chiefs, and I don't think anyone has any misgivings." The burly four-star general looked around at his peers. No one questioned him, not even the Navy chief.

The SecDef nodded. "General Shockley, anything else from your side?"

"Nothing, sir."

"Very well." He checked his watch, then the Blackberry, and closed his notebook. "I'll need to leave now to meet with the president. General Shockley, General Dotson, you're with me. Thank you, everyone." The SecDef pushed back his chair, and the conference room came alive with activity. As he rose to his feet, he looked across the table and met McDaniels's eye. "Good work on getting that data out of New York, Major. I realize the cost was high, but it had to be done, and you did it. If things work out, this nation's going to owe you a great debt."

"Thank you, Mister Secretary. But the other soldiers did all of the heavy lifting."

The SecDef smiled as he pulled on his suit jacket. "I'm certain you did your share, Major." He looked at Dotson. "Are we ready?"

"We are, sir. McDaniels will be briefed by General Abelson."

"Good. Let's go." The SecDef nodded to McDaniels once again, then headed for the door. When he pulled abreast of Gartrell, he paused. Even though the first sergeant was absolutely filthy from his time in the field, the SecDef shook his hand and thanked him for his service.

Now there's a guy I'd vote for, McDaniels thought.

3

"Gentlemen, let's get this out of the way." Lieutenant General Josiah Abelson's tone of voice and demeanor were casual, not what you'd expect from the three-star general in charge of all Army special operations forces, especially when the nation was at war on its own soil.

"What's that, sir?" McDaniels asked.

"We need to go over an operations plan, and both you and Gartrell are involved." The general motioned Gartrell to the table and pointed at one of the high-backed leather chairs at the end. "Sit down there, First Sergeant. You look like you smell pretty damn ripe."

"Sorry, General. Haven't been able to cuddle up to my bar of Irish Spring lately." Gartrell pulled out a chair and sat.

"I know you've been busy, First Sergeant." Abelson's aides hovered behind him, but he ignored them and motioned to an Air Force officer standing two chairs away from McDaniels. The officer was just under six feet in height and wiry in build. His hair was graying and severely thinning, and a well-groomed mustache sat beneath his rather pointed nose. McDaniels noticed the man's blue uniform trousers were bloused inside his boots.

"This is Colonel Stanislaw Jaworski," Abelson continued. "As you can see, he's an Air Force officer, but we won't hold that against him, will we?"

Jaworski showed a faint smile. "Even though I'm a *Polish* Air Force officer, sir?"

"I'd make some Polish jokes, but you just wouldn't understand them. To your right is Major Cordell McDaniels, currently with the J-3 shop at USASOC when he's not pulling TDY on contingency missions like this one. Across from you is First Sergeant Dave Gartrell, one of the senior trainers at the

Special Warfare School at Bragg. Have a seat, Stas," Abelson finished, as Jaworski shook hands with McDaniels and, stretching across the table, Gartrell. The general pronounced the name as "Stosh."

"Pleased to meet you, gentlemen," Jaworski said, lowering himself into one of the chairs.

Abelson's two staffers went to work, presenting each man with a packet of documents. Abelson looked at McDaniels. "Cord, your wife is safe and sound at Bragg. The entire post is under lockdown, with troops from the Eighty-Second Airborne supplementing base security forces. We've had two outbreaks, but they were put down quickly—some returning troops that were infected during another contingency op. No word on your son, though. I've asked folks from Fort Hood to look into his disposition, but I haven't heard anything back yet."

McDaniels nodded somberly. Leonard McDaniels was attending his sophomore year of college in Austin, Texas. "That's mostly good news, sir. Thank you."

Abelson sighed. "Gartrell, we can't find your family. Your residence is empty, and gate security has them on video leaving the post. We found a note in your house, written on a whiteboard. It said, 'We're at the cabin.' I hope that means something to you?"

"It does. We have a cabin in the Smoky Mountains. Pretty remote, we need a four-wheel drive to get near it, and then ATVs to get the rest of the way. My family knows to go there if there's any real long-term danger."

"I hope they made the right decision. Bragg is currently as safe as it can be."

"They made the right call, sir. Believe me, when thirty thousand of the dead decide to go to Bragg, triple layers of concertina wire and the usual fortifications aren't going to hold them back for long." Gartrell's expression was flat, just like his eyes. "If the stenches are going to go for my family, they'll have to find them first."

"Very well, First Sergeant. Then let's get back to business." Abelson opened the first packet of documents, and the others mimicked him. "I don't want this to be a death by PowerPoint event, so I'll go over the highlights as quickly as possible. You are about to join Joint Task Force SPARTA, which will be commanded by Colonel Jaworski. This joint operation will be overseen by Special Operations Command in Florida. I will have provisional oversight and will be working out of MacDill unless there is an event in which SOCOM is compromised on the ground."

United States Special Operations Command was the highest-level component command overseeing all of the nation's special operations forces, and it was based out of MacDill Air Force Base in Florida. Every branch of service had a special operations presence of some type, and they were all tasked through USSOCOM.

"When this plan was originally established in baseline format thirty hours ago, JSOC was to have operational control. However, all tier one units are currently engaged elsewhere, primarily in protection of high-value individuals, such as members of the executive and legislative branches, as well as other assets of high intrinsic interest to the nation. As such, SOCOM will provide complete adult supervision.

"SPARTA itself is the designation given to a pharmaceutical facility located just outside of Odessa, Texas. The facility is owned by InTerGen, the corporation started by Wolf Safire. It's a top-level manufacturer of pharmaceutical supplies, everything from over-the-counter remedies to extremely specific medications used to combat all kinds of diseases. Safire sent his preliminary research to his associates there before New York went dark, so they've had time to review the building blocks and are pretty familiar with where he was going. Providing that Jeffries and his people at USAMRIID are able to deliver the full formulations, it's been decided that whatever medical regimen is required will be developed there.

The facility is fully self-supporting. It has an array of solar and geothermal power sources to keep it going even if the local power grid fails, and it's sufficiently remote enough that we feel it could be defended, with substantial investments in hardening. And as we speak, the Corps of Engineers is constructing additional structures to assist in that defense. On page three of this presentation, you'll find aerial photos of the facility and several maps of the general area.

"The facility will be fully militarized, but not to the point to where it is unable to complete its primary mission. Colonel Jaworski will oversee the internal operations of SPARTA and will head up the command element called Leonidas. McDaniels, you will assume operational control of the quick reaction force providing security for SPARTA, call sign Hercules. You'll also be joint task force executive officer. You are to be promoted by order of the president to lieutenant colonel, and Gartrell will accompany you as JTF sergeant major. Congratulations to both of you because you earned it the hard way."

McDaniels was surprised. "A promotion, sir?"

"It's not like you aren't in the zone, Cord. At any rate, I have your new insignia with me, and we'll go through the official frocking later. Returning to the topic of Hercules, the unit will be composed of three companies of Army Rangers from the 75th Rangers, alpha detachments from 10th Special Forces Group, and one troop of SEALs from Special Warfare Group One. Our vision is that the SEALs will be the long-distance maneuver element and will serve as forward area observers, augmented by the alpha detachments, while the Rangers will provide physical security for SPARTA itself. Additionally, two MH-47s will be made available from the 160th Special Operations Aviation Regiment, and they have already self-deployed to the area."

Gartrell flipped through his documentation. "Sir, it says here the SEAL team slice will come from Team Five, is that still correct?"

"It is," Jaworski said. "Is there a problem with that?"

"Negative, sir. Major McDaniels and I have dealt with them before, in Afghanistan." Gartrell looked at McDaniels. "Remember Hooks Johnson?"

McDaniels smiled ruefully. "How could I forget?"

"Do fill us in on that later," Abelson said, slamming the brakes on the nostalgia express. "You'll find the full TO&E under your oversight on page six, McDaniels. The SEALs won't report to you directly, they'll go through their own O-4, but you'll have OPCON of them through him. Not under SPARTA's direct control will be the 3rd Armored Cavalry Regiment and the 21st Air Cav Brigade, both out of Hood, which will provide area security and stability. 3ACR will act as the primary warfighting unit between SPARTA and the stenches, should they become a presence in the area. The regiment will in turn be supported by the 21st Cavalry Brigade, an air combat unit full of Apaches. SPARTA will be the regiment's center of gravity, but both it and the 21st will maneuver independently of Hercules. Colonel Jaworski will be in constant contact with his counterparts in both units."

"Is that your dream come true, sir? To be a ground-pounder?" McDaniels asked.

"At least by extension," Jaworski said. "And to think I might actually become an honorary cavalryman after this. The Air Force will never be the same."

"We don't know how long this posting will last," Abelson said, ignoring the side chatter. "I expect it will be weeks, if not months. All of that depends on how fast we can react to the spread of the zeds, and how effective we are at bottling them up and killing them off. My understanding is that Safire's wonder drug won't do anything to help us with the necromorphs; all it will do is possibly prevent those who are bitten from becoming the walking dead." The general snorted. "I can't believe I just said that. *The walking dead.* What a world."

"How long will it take to manufacture the drug, General?

Any idea?"

"None. I can only imagine that it will take some time. Colonel Jeffries will likely have that answer once he deciphers Safire's formulations. He said we'll know in a few hours."

"Can't the drug be develop at the Rid?" Gartrell asked.

"Perhaps. But in order to make enough of it to inoculate every person in the United States, we need a real, honest-to-God production facility. And that facility has to stay up and operational during the entire time the drug is being processed and manufactured. We still haven't figured out all the logistics behind it, mind you. Not only does the drug have to be manufactured, it has to be distributed, and the population has to be inoculated. The Rid can't do that, not on that scale. And besides..." Abelson pointed toward the electronic map of the United States on the wall. "...the Rid might not be around much longer."

McDaniels looked at the map and was shocked to see the number of red pips in the Washington area had *grown* in a matter of minutes.

Holy shit!

He turned back to Abelson. "When do we leave, sir?"

"Tonight. As soon as we're done here, you go to Andrews and catch a transport to Texas." Abelson put his hand on the stack of documents. "Everything you need to know is right here. You'll have all the resources you need. All the service chiefs are aware of the importance of SPARTA, and the president is going to be briefed on the plan by the SecDef and General Shockley shortly, but we're not going to wait for his approval. The plan is going forward because it's the only shot we have. The sooner we get things going, the faster we'll be able to save a good chunk of the American citizenry. And then, we'll be able to turn our full attention toward what we need to do. Which is kill every fucking stench in this country, and then on the entire planet."

Abelson sighed tiredly, then rose to his feet. He beckoned to one of his aides, who presented him with two small padded envelopes. "This probably won't be the most prestigious promotion ceremony ever, but at least the two of you will have a lieutenant general pinning on your new ranks, even if it's just on BDUs. McDaniels, Gartrell, let's get this done and get back to work."

McDaniels wondered if he would have a chance to fly in every aircraft in the military before the night was over. There was enough time for Gartrell to shower and get a change of uniform—somehow, even at that late hour, he was provided with a full set of BDUs that had his nametape—and then they hopped on a UH-72 Lakota back into Maryland. Colonel Jaworski was along for the ride, and the newly minted Lieutenant Colonel McDaniels felt they would be seeing a lot of each other in the foreseeable future. The Air Force officer was polite, but didn't seem to be in a very chatty mood, especially over an intercom system while strapped into a loud, noisy utility helicopter. McDaniels didn't begrudge him that.

Gartrell was also hushed. Even though they sat across from each other in the helicopter's cargo bay, Gartrell didn't make much eye contact; he simply looked out the Plexiglas window at the Virginia countryside. There was a lot of activity outside; other helicopters shuttled back and forth, and Interstate 95 seemed unusually full of traffic, given the hour. It took McDaniels a moment to notice that most of the traffic was heading out of the DC area and into Maryland; there was comparatively little traffic inbound.

Less than ten minutes after breaking deck at the Pentagon, the Lakota banked toward Joint Base Andrews, the large military installation shared by the Air Force, Navy, and Coast Guard. The aircraft pitched downward as it lost altitude, then flared above its intended landing zone. It vibrated as it passed through its own rotor wash, then landed with barely a bump. The ground crew pulled open the door, and McDaniels unfastened his safety harness and hauled himself out of the aircraft. Behind him, Jaworski and Gartrell did the same.

Another Air Force C-21 sat on the ramp. Its left engine was already spun up, howling in the night as the ground crew hustled the three men toward the aircraft. McDaniels allowed Jaworski to board first, then climbed up the short stairway into the waiting jet, dragging his pack behind him. Gartrell brought up the rear, and the ground crew secured the door as the Lear's number one engine spooled up. As McDaniels took his seat beside Jaworski, he noticed the C-21 was in better shape than the one he'd flown in previously. Gartrell sat all the way in the back, his backpack strapped in beside him. The jet's pilot informed them that they would make one stop for refueling, but that they could expect to be in Texas in less than four hours.

"What, you guys can't do better than that?" Jaworski asked with a smile.

"We might be able to burn up some time in the air, sir. We'll see how it goes." And with that, the pilots turned to their pre-taxi checklists.

"We'll be fighting some headwinds for a good portion of the trip," Jaworski told McDaniels above the mounting engine noise. "I checked out the weather, though; everything's pretty calm along our intended route. But there's no potty in this thing, so I hope you guys hit the latrine before we left."

"We did. It's practically Army regulations," McDaniels said.

"Then sit back and enjoy the flight, at least as much as you can on one of these things." Jaworski reclined his seat as far back as it would go, crossed his arms, and closed his eyes as the C-21 began to taxi. McDaniels looked back at Gartrell, who stared out the side window.

"How you doing, Sarmajor?" he asked.

Gartrell glanced at him. "Hanging tough, Colonel. Congrats on the promotion."

"Same to you, of course."

"Thanks."

Gartrell obviously wasn't interested in conversation. McDaniels didn't know what to make of that, but then, Gartrell had never been the most gregarious of sorts even when they'd liked each other, about a million years ago. He thought the senior NCO would have loosened up a bit after what they'd gone through, but Gartrell wasn't known for flexibility. It irked McDaniels at some level, but he shouldn't have been surprised. Gartrell was certainly consistent, if nothing else.

McDaniels leaned back in his seat and stared out the window while the jet taxied to the runway, powered up, and surged into the sky. As the jet banked away from Andrews, he was treated to a far-ranging vista of Washington, DC. At first, the city looked fairly normal, but then he noticed more and more flashing strobe lights from emergency vehicles, mounting traffic, and every now and then, fires. Even the residential areas looked busier than they should have been. McDaniels knew what was going down, and he was happy to be getting away from it.

After all, no one wanted to be in DC to begin with. Adding zombies into the mix did nothing to repair its lack of allure.

He found he couldn't sleep during the flight, so he spent the time studying the briefing materials. He paid close attention to the Mission Table of Organization and Equipment, known simply as the M-TOE. He would have a sizeable force arrayed under his command, if not directly, then by extension. It would be his first opportunity to command anything larger than a Special Forces detachment. He had always wondered if he would ever realize his goal of becoming a Special Forces Group commander, and his new mission would bring him one step closer. And it was a composite unit at that: a mix of Rangers, Special Forces detachments, Navy SEALs, and Air Force special operations. It was unusual for an officer with his modest track record to receive such a reward, and he was overwhelmed by it.

After all, the stakes were high, and in the back of his mind, McDaniels wondered just how hard the special operations community had been hit by the plague of the dead. For certain, they had been the first units called up when the stenches finally made it to America, and he knew of several encounters between US special operators and the walking dead in Europe. And no doubt, similar scenarios had been encountered in Asia.

He went through the list of equipment he could expect to have at his command. M1114 Humvees, up-armored and with suppression weapons. Four M1126 Stryker ICVs, wheeled infantry combat vehicles that were similar to the LAVs used by the Marines, which would provide limited external mobility for the Rangers. The Rangers themselves would come equipped with the newly-fielded Special Operations Infantry Combat System, an exoskeleton system that incorporated elements of the HULC and Land Warrior programs of the early 2000s. One hundred twenty millimeter mortars, heavy and light machineguns, mines, and enough spares and munitions to keep the units operating at a fair operational tempo for months. There were also plans to deploy a surgical hospital—under Jaworski's provisional command, he noted—but that would be a follow-on activity. All in all, SPARTA had some teeth to it.

But it was all so very conventional. If they were going against a human enemy, then the array would be nothing less than formidable. But the dead cared nothing about being shot. They didn't feel pain, so injuries didn't matter to them. They didn't even care about taking a round to the head that would result in complete lights-out. The dead were completely free from *fear*, the thing that usually kept humans from engaging in all-out combat. Aside from their increasing numbers, lack of fear was perhaps their biggest advantage. Zeds would do absolutely anything in order to feed, risk everything to try to satisfy that never-ending cycle of hunger.

McDaniels worried that even SPARTA's defenses wouldn't be strong enough. Because if they weren't, and the dead came to visit before Wolf Safire's wonder drug was developed and distributed, then the game would take an entirely different turn.

4

Things were not going well for the lightfighters of the 10th Mountain Division.

The necromorphs had pushed the entire division—or what remained of it—out of the south Bronx and all the way through the borough until the unit was ordered to reassemble in Yonkers. By that time, the division had been in contact with the zombies for almost twenty-four hours, and the tide of walking dead showed no sign of abating. Despite the heavy barrage the division's artillery batteries had thrown at the advancing zombie elements, even the punishing neutralization fire—a virtual storm of steel rain that would have reduced a heavy armor division to nothing—failed to do much more than delay the zeds. The first bombardment on Harlem lasted throughout the majority of the previous night, starting at eleven thirty and raging on until dawn at half past five the next morning. The division's small detachment of unmanned aerial surveillance systems weren't up yet—there was some sort of engineering glitch that kept the remote-controlled Shadow spy planes on the deck—so the word came down from the commanding general to mount up several infantry squads for movement-to-contact operations. The general just couldn't wait to discover how bad off the enemy forces were after weathering such an attack. Dozens of soldiers from the 1/87th Infantry battalion entered Harlem, both on foot and mounted on Humvees. For a while, things didn't go too badly. Fires were everywhere; the arty bombardment had perforated several gas mains, and entire buildings had gone up in furious explosions that left nothing behind but charred wreckage and thick clouds of black and gray smoke. The streets were cratered from the shelling; some had even collapsed into the subway tunnels beneath. As they made their advance, the light infantry troops found the remains of dozens, then hundreds, of stenches on the streets of Harlem. Most of them were still moving, even the ones that had massive deboning injuries that should have left them deader than doorposts. The soldiers were horrified to find even ghouls whose limbs had been amputated would come for them at a slow chin-crawl. Only shots to the head could make them stop moving.

As the smoke cleared and the sun shone brightly, the first elements of the zombie advance caught them out in the open. In the beginning, the lightfighters acquitted themselves well, but as the numbers of the stenches increased and the soldiers' ammunition began to run out, discipline eroded. Several of the squads fell off the tactical radio net, never be heard from again.

Others found relative safety in the subway tunnels, where they could use their night vision goggles to their advantage. That had been suggested by a single Army Special Forces soldier who had been trapped behind the lines, a first sergeant named Gartrell who had been successfully evacuated the previous evening. The recommendation had been a good one; it had not only saved Gartrell's life, but the lives of several lightfighters as well.

For the next few hours, anyway.

The dead finally figured it out as well, and they took to the tunnels in force. Perhaps not by design; there were just so damned *many* of the stenches on the streets that they had no choice. When that had happened, the 10th Mountain Division's tactical plan had to be changed. Subway tunnels were demolished to prevent the dead from using them, but at a great cost; every demolitions team was lost, and one subway line through Manhattan's Upper West Side was not completely closed. But by the time that had been discovered, the 10th's forces were withdrawing.

One of those redeploying units was the 1st Battalion, 87th Infantry (Light), commanded by Lieutenant Colonel Kent Royko, call sign Summit 6. Royko's unit had been the one to rescue the Special Forces NCO and pull him out from behind the lines. Upon recovering him, Royko had put him to work transferring his knowledge of fighting stenches to the 1/87th's operations team. Gartrell had gone in over twenty-four hours before, as part of the large-scale evacuation of high-value individuals from New York City, an operation that ended in total disaster when the helicopter assembly area at Central Park had been overrun by the zombies. Gartrell and his mission's survivors had found refuge in a skyscraper, but that hadn't lasted for long. Even though Gartrell's Special Forces team had taken all possible precautions, Royko was told that the zeds had managed to penetrate their defenses and take the building from them—because reanimated members of the Special Forces Operational Detachment had retained their military skill sets. Royko was from a steel-belt town in Ohio, and he'd considered himself a tough and hardy sort even before joining the US Army. But when he found that the dead could actually fight smart, he felt the bottom start to drop out. The stenches already had tremendous numbers on their side. If even a small percentage of them were able to interact with their environment in a meaningful manner—which meant acting against his troops in a measured, willful way—how the hell could the Army hope to bottle them up on Manhattan island?

The answer was simple. They couldn't.

More reports came back from the field, reports of not only reanimated soldiers using weapons against their former teammates, but of civilian stenches ambushing patrols and mounted elements. Vehicles were being used to ram armored Humvees to pin them in place so the dead could swarm over the mounted troops and consume them in minutes. The dead were jumping out of buildings and piling up on foot patrols, where the soldiers were ripped limb from limb. And the most sinister: reanimated children were used to lure troops into areas where their egress was cut off, and swarming stenches rolled in, overwhelming the troops' defenses. It was madness, utter madness. There was just no way to stop the zeds, not with a divisional element. On paper, it certainly *looked* as though it were possible. After all, the stenches had no real ability to conserve their forces, had no ability to reliably project force toward the division itself, but they were winning, through sheer numbers if nothing else.

Royko reported all of this to Mountaineer 6, the major general in charge of the 10th. His orders were to gather his remaining forces and retreat to an assembly area located at Yonkers Raceway and await further instructions. The order sounded so easy, but the fact of the matter was, almost all of Royko's forces were in contact, and pulling them back was no easy affair. It was chaos on the radio net, but when the orders to fall back were finally acknowledged, the soldiers standing between Royko's small tactical operations center and the zeds didn't just retreat. They *ran*.

Not that it mattered. The exodus of civilians out of the Bronx was far from orderly. Most of Royko's troops were pinned between the retreating civilians and the advancing stenches. He received reports that his own troops were gunning down American citizens so they could get past, in turn spawning more zeds. The Army had told Royko that only those bitten by the dead reanimated. Gartrell had already confirmed that if a person was infected with the whatever-it-was-called virus and they died, they would reanimate whether they had been bitten or not. The Army had passed it down that such was not the case; the infection was spread by contact with the dead, and that was that. It was a lie. Those who died without any contact with the stenches were reanimating.

Which means we're all infected already.

The four Humvees which made up the 1/87th's tactical operations center slowly moved northward through the night, followed by three M939 tactical trucks. The trucks should have been full of troops. Instead, they were mostly empty, each carrying only a few soldiers and several wounded. Royko had tried to ascertain exactly how the wounded had sustained their injuries, and it appeared none had been bitten. He was thankful for that, for it meant he wouldn't have to deal with a zombie uprising in what was left of his battalion.

After almost two hours of creeping north in bumper-to-bumper traffic, it was obvious the headquarters detachment would not be able to make it to the assembly area. The NYPD had not been able to close off Route 9A, despite assurances the roadway would be reserved for military-only traffic. And the reason for that was obvious: the NYPD was being broken down by resource constraints from having too much to do with suddenly too-few personnel. Royko knew the department was around thirty-five thousand strong a few days ago, twice the size of the entire 10th Mountain Division, but it still struggled to secure its home turf and provide enough stability for the lightfighters to do their job. He ordered the headquarters element to pull off into a baseball field in Van Cortlandt Park. Until the traffic situation got straightened out, Royko would operate wherever he could. He notified the division command and requested a helicopter be dispatched to take his wounded. He was told that a Chinook had just become available and would make it to the park in less than ten minutes. Royko was impressed. The Army was running short on aircraft, but the decision had been made to extract the wounded whenever possible, and that was a good thing.

When the Humvees stopped at the designated setup point, Royko jumped out and personally surveyed the area through his night vision goggles. It was hardly secure. The Saw Mill Parkway was nearby, and it was a virtual parking lot. Through the trees, he saw cars and trucks sitting motionless amidst a frenzy of blaring horns and flashing lights. Nearby McLean Avenue was no better, and the pedestrian traffic was even more worrisome. Any one of those people could be a zed, and Royko wouldn't know it until one of them walked up and practically bit him on the ass.

Then, to the lieutenant colonel's surprise, a National Guard CH-47F was suddenly overhead, its blades slashing through the air. Before he could order any of his men to assist in securing the landing zone, the helicopter touched down in the park only a few hundred feet away. Royko watched as the twin-rotored behemoth settled to Earth in a clearing amidst a cloud of fallen leaves, twigs, and branches. Crewmen wearing night vision goggles leaned out of the aircraft on both sides and from its open tail, no doubt giving the pilots the necessary information to avoid taking the tops off any trees.

Royko turned to one of his soldiers and motioned toward the M939 trucks. "Get our wounded onto that Chinook! I want 'em out of here immediately!"

"Hooah, Colonel!"

Royko ran back to the Humvees as they pulled into a diamond formation, with the rear of each vehicle pointing at the diamond's center. Tailgates were opened, radios and infrared lights mounted, and maps unrolled.

Royko pushed his way into the center of the activity, his eyes on the maps. "Major Fisch, where are the rest of our troops?"

"Still trying to sort that out, sir," the S-3 reported. "Lots of fragmented reports, but most of our guys are MIA. I haven't been able to raise a single full-strength unit, and those troops I've been in contact with are either on foot and trying to make it to us, or they're trapped in traffic."

"That's bullshit. If they can't move with their vehicles, tell them to bail out and pound the pavement! We can get the machinery later. Let's get the troops! Pass that down right now!"

"Roger that, sir." The S-3 reached for one of the field radios and relayed the order.

Royko pulled one of the maps toward him and studied the graphics written all over it in wax pencil that reflected the infrared light so the icons could be seen through his night vision goggles. To the uninitiated, it would look like a two-year-old's errant scribbling. To Royko, it was anything but. The 1/87th's disposition was written right there for him to see, and he didn't like the picture one bit.

"Are these graphics correct?" he asked.

"They are, sir," an operations NCO answered. "I've tried to keep them updated as carefully as possible, but it's been a bitch. A lot of our guys no longer have reliable commo, so I will admit to writing down some guesswork." The NCO was a master sergeant, and if he had any fear of invoking the ire of Summit 6, he didn't show it.

Even though he'd been in the TOC for well over a day and hadn't even had time to take a piss, Royko only had eyes for the maps. And what they showed was that, out of his entire battalion, only around thirty-six troops could be accounted for, beyond the headquarters staff.

"How many troops have you been able to account for, Master Sergeant?" he asked, even though it was written right in front of him.

"Thirty-six positive, sir."

"I see no number here for killed in action. Explain that."

"I haven't received a KIA status in over seven hours, sir. We presume the rest of the battalion is just NORDO, but the reality is, a fair number of them are probably zombie chow." The master sergeant's voice was cold and mechanical, and he displayed no discernible emotion on his face behind his NVGs when Royko glared at him. At first, Royko had thought the man was a hard-core professional, but then he realized the senior NCO was shocked silly, and he just couldn't respond in any other way.

"Colonel, dismount orders are out. All units who can't maneuver are abandoning their vehicles," Major Fisch said.

"Master Sergeant, send them a pulse to get a headcount," Royko said. "I need to know how many we have. It *can't* be just thirty-six!" He tapped the map taped to the Humvee's tailgate with his finger.

"Roger that, sir." The master sergeant turned to the radio, and the major handed him the handset.

Royko looked back at the operations officer. "Major, that man's got the thousand yard stare. I'm not sure he's very reliable right now. If he isn't, I want you to replace him with someone who is. Are you with me?"

"Yes, sir. One hundred percent. But who would I replace him with, sir?"

The question pissed Royko off, but he took a moment to rein in his emotions. He elected to ignore it. "I want you to redouble your efforts to gain situational awareness at the operational level. If this battalion has been rendered completely combat ineffective, I need to know that right away. I can't be standing around playing games of pocket pilot when division is tasking me with orders I can't possibly commit resources to; you understand?"

"Yes, sir." The major's response was barely audible as the Chinook powered up. Royko glanced over at it and watched the big helicopter climb into the sky. His remaining soldiers hurried back toward the 1/87th's vehicles, their M4 carbines slung, but close at hand.

Royko turned back to the waiting major and started to ask him to look into what other units were in the area when the honking horns from the Saw Mill Parkway suddenly reached a crescendo. He heard shouts, then screams of fear and pain. Engines revved, and the sounds of crunching metal and cracking fiberglass cut through the air. Royko looked off in the direction of the parkway, but it was on the other side of Van Cortlandt Park, and he couldn't see what was going on from where he stood. Several popping noises cracked through the air from beyond the trees. Gunfire.

"Colonel!" one of the soldiers said. His voice was almost a shriek. Royko turned and saw the soldier standing beside one of the Humvees. His attention wasn't oriented east, toward the commotion from the Saw Mill; he looked southerly, across the dark baseball field. Royko's view was blocked by one of the Humvees, so he hurried forward and looked over the soldier's shoulder.

Shapes emerged from the tree line and moved into the baseball field. At first, it was only a few figures; then, as Royko watched, dozens—no, *hundreds!*—more came forward, leaving the comparative cover of the trees behind them. Most shambled, some trotted, and a few even bolted across the baseball field, like guided missiles heading directly for the Army vehicles, their lifeless eyes fixated on Royko and his troops.

"Mount up!" Royko shouted. "Pack it up! We've got to get the fuck out of here *right now!*" He unslung his M4 while the soldiers behind him exploded into a flurry of activity.

The Humvee parked with its grille pointed into the baseball field was outfitted with an M2 .50 caliber machinegun. A soldier climbed into the vehicle and emerged from the cupola. He grabbed the .50, yanked back on its cocking lever, leaned into the weapon, and fired. The .50 cal thundered as it spat its heavy projectiles downrange, and the bullets glowed white-hot in Royko's NVGs. The first few rounds hit nothing more than the field itself and kicked up great gouts of sod in front of the advancing zombies. The gunner got his weapon under control and walked the next flurry of rounds through the runners sprinting toward the TOC. The big bullets blew off legs and arms, and blasted bodies into putrid wreckage... but the ghouls kept coming. Another .50 opened up, and Royko frantically stuffed his yellow foam hearing protectors in his ears, then shouldered his M4 and cracked off three rounds at an advancing zombie. The first two missed, the third hit the zed in the breastbone, driving it back a few steps. It started forward again, but went down as a .50 caliber round blasted through its head, exploding it like a melon filled with gray-black oatmeal.

Royko glanced behind him and saw the radios had been secured and the tailgates of the Humvees were being slammed shut. Overhead, the CH-47 returned, thundering through the air as it passed by off to Royko's right. The aircraft added its .50 caliber firepower to the fray, peppering the field with rounds, striking the approaching zeds from the side. Several zombies went down, but not for the count; even missing arms and with great, gaping holes torn through their abdomens, they slogged back to their feet and continued their advance.

Unreal... simply unreal. Royko couldn't rationalize what he saw, and as he watched the ghouls surge forward against the withering firepower, he realized why his troops' discipline had been sorely tested. The stenches were relentless.

"Sir, we gotta go!" Major Fisch shouted from behind him.

Several other soldiers joined the fray with their personal weapons, firing at the advancing horde as Humvee engines were brought to life. But they were shooting as they'd been trained, aiming for the center mass of the approaching enemy; their rounds did nothing to stop the zeds. Royko shouted for the soldiers to mount up and move out. When they fell back to the Humvees, Royko sprinted for his vehicle.

He leaped inside the Humvee's front passenger seat and slammed the heavy, up-armored door shut. The staff sergeant behind the wheel put the vehicle in gear as another soldier took charge of the Mk 119 grenade launcher mounted atop the Humvee.

"Get us out of here!" Royko said. "However you can, just get it done!"

"Yes, sir!"

The Humvee surged forward, its tires spinning on the grassy field. The driver didn't bother to go around the chain link fence that surrounded the baseball diamond. He just drove right through it. But the traffic on the street was another matter entirely. As the rest of the Humvees piled up behind Royko's, he knew there wasn't a chance in hell they would get very far at anything other than a slow crawl. Civilian vehicles were all over the place, and he suddenly understood how some of his soldiers had been able to open up on them, just to get past in a frantic bid to escape the zeds.

"What do you want me to do, sir?" the driver asked as the Humvee accelerated toward the street.

"Hard right, up the sidewalk!" Royko answered.

The driver cut the wheel to the right. The sturdy vehicle bounced along the sidewalk, sending those civilians who had tried to flee on foot scattering in all directions. Royko checked the side view mirror and saw the rest of the Humvee-mounted TOC element coming up behind him, but the big M949 trucks were being swarmed by the dead. He knew the soldiers manning the trucks were experiencing a death worse than any Royko could dream. The Humvee bounced up and down subtly on its suspension, and the driver released a keening sigh. Royko faced forward and watched in horror as they drove over a woman with a baby stroller. The Humvee began to slow as it bore down on yet even more people. The crowd shrieked as they tried to get out of the way, but with the stalled traffic to their left and the approaching walls of several buildings to their right, the people had no place to go.

Royko put a hand on the driver's arm. "Stop here, son." To the rest of the soldiers in the Humvee, he ordered, "All right, dismount! Let's give these fuckers what-for!"

Royko threw open his door and leaped out of the Humvee. He pulled his M4 into position as the rest of the element braked to a halt. The Humvee immediately behind his was splattered with blood, having driven right over the poor people the first had mowed down. Even through his hearing protectors, Royko could hear the screams of the living and the never-ending moans of the dead. Zeds closed in on the detail, but the .50 calibers and the Mk 119 grenade launcher broke their advance. Royko was jostled by terrified civilians fleeing from the melee.

The master sergeant with the thousand-yard stare had shaken it off; he was in combat, and his training had kicked in. He barked orders at the rest of the enlisted men, organizing them into a fighting team.

Major Fisch ran around his Humvee and took a position on the other side, covering the team from the street. He started firing almost immediately.

Royko hurried forward, his M4's stock pressed against his right shoulder. He stopped behind the troops the master sergeant had organized into a skirmish line. They fired, some from a standing position, some while kneeling, sniping at the stragglers that managed to get through the .50 cal and grenade fire. One troop ripped off on full auto.

Royko smacked him on the helmet and shouted over the din of gunfire. "Semi-auto! Everyone, semi-auto only! Conserve your ammunition, and *shoot them in the head!*"

The Chinook thundered past again, so low that its rotor wash tore through the area like a hurricane, its own .50 caliber pounding down on the zeds. Several ghouls fell to the ground, flopping about, suffering incredible damage that would absolutely have killed any normal soldier. But the dead rose again to press on with the hunt. Royko opened fire, sighting on his targets through his rifle's scope, popping off round after round. He hit his targets in the head more often than not.

So many of them. So many of them, so few of us...

The machinegun on the rearmost Humvee ran dry, and the soldier manning it frantically wrestled with a new box of ammo as he tried to reload. Royko ordered the other soldiers to give him cover, but there was nothing they could do. The dead swarmed over the back of the Humvee and engulfed it beneath a tsunami of rotting flesh.

Royko sensed movement to his right, and he took a step back and looked at the Humvee beside him. The ghouls were on the other side of the vehicle, and the soldier standing in the back, manning the Mk 119, couldn't see them. The Humvee's doors stood ajar, and one of the ghouls shoved itself through the driver's side rear door. Royko shouted a warning and fired at the stench, hitting it in the shoulder. Its left arm flopped and hung limp, but the zed ignored the damage and latched onto one of the soldier's legs with its right hand. As the soldier shouted and kicked, the zombie bit into his calf. The soldier screamed and, for a moment, allowed the still-firing Mk 119's barrel to drop. He fired three grenades into the hood of the Humvee behind him, and the triplet of explosions tore the vehicle open and ripped through the idling engine beneath the hood. Diesel fuel caught fire as shrapnel pelted the rest of the soldiers, bringing them to their knees.

Royko fired at the zed in the Humvee twice more and finally killed it with a headshot. The soldier manning the Mk 119 let out a tortured cry—he'd been bitten, and he knew what lay in store for him—but he recovered his command of his weapon and resumed firing at the wall of gathering dead.

"Keep firing!" Royko told the rest of the men. His voice sounded shrill and loud in his own ears. "Get up. *Keep firing!*" He ran toward the Humvee and jumped inside as another ghoul appeared in the open doorway. He shot it through the face, shoved the corpse away from the vehicle, and slammed the rear passenger door. He reached around the front seat and pulled the driver's door closed. The fire from his troops had become erratic, unfocused.

"Keep firing!" he repeated, to the trooper manning the Mk 119 and any others who might be able to hear him. Royko pulled himself out of the Humvee and shut the door behind him.

Two of the soldiers were down, bleeding badly from shrapnel wounds, and the others had pulled away from the burning Humvee. The flames burned so hot and bright that they overwhelmed Royko's night vision goggles. One of the downed soldiers rolled over onto his side—the master sergeant still held onto his weapon, and his gaze fell upon Royko.

"Colonel, get that man out of here!" he shouted, pointing at the soldier who lay beside him. He pulled himself into a sitting position and gunned down a charging stench, a dark shape silhouetted against the billowing yellow flame rising from the stricken Humvee.

Royko darted forward and grabbed the back of the soldier's body armor. He pulled the man away from the burning wreck. "Troops, fall back! Fall back!"

The Mk 119 gunner tried to haul himself out of the Humvee. He never made it. Several shapes mounted the vehicle and pulled the soldier toward the street. He screamed and disappeared from view.

Then the burning Humvee exploded.

Royko came to a moment later, ears ringing, uniform and body armor smoldering. His M4 was trapped beneath him, and he rolled to one side, freeing it. The flaming wreck of the M1114 HMMWV generated an amazing amount of heat, and the vehicles behind and in front of the destroyed M1114 were aflame as well. Royko reached for his night vision goggles, but they had been shorn from their plastic mount and were nowhere to be found. The soldier he had been dragging away from the maelstrom groaned and slowly rolled onto his back. Royko knelt beside him and zeroed two stenches staggering to his position. Royko heard screaming from the other side of the wall of flames, followed by full automatic gunfire.

"Soldier, get on your feet! Sergeant Wilkins, *get on your feet!*" he screamed at the wounded soldier. Behind him, the last remaining .50 caliber machinegun suddenly fell silent, and Royko turned to see the Humvee *covered* with the walking dead as they fought to get to the lone soldier inside it.

God, where did they all come from?

Wilkins reached up and grabbed Royko's arm; his grip was slack and weak. Royko dropped another zed that came around one of the burning Humvees, then reached down with his left hand and grabbed Wilkins's wrist. He hauled the sergeant to his feet. "Come on."

Wilkins screeched and grabbed Royko in a bear hug, his dead eyes gleaming in the firelight. The newest zed hugged Royko and tried to bite him in the neck, but Royko shifted at the last moment, and the ghoul sank its teeth into the fabric covering his body armor. Royko yelled and tried to break the zombie's grip, but something crashed into him from behind, driving him to the ground. Royko screamed and fired his M4 into Wilkins's legs, but the zombie didn't even notice. As another zombie landed on him, followed by another and another, Royko reached for one of the fragmentation grenades clipped to his body armor. Before he could pull the pin, the Wilkins zombie found the soft flesh of his neck, and Royko's last thought was that he had never felt anything so painful in his life.

5

Wheels down in Texas.

McDaniels had been awake for the entire flight to Odessa Midland International Airport. He looked through the window at the black landscape of western Texas, and what he saw seemed to be a reflection of his own bleary state of mind: dark nothingness, broken here and there by a shining light or two.

Jaworski stirred, stretched, and yawned. He had awoken only briefly during the trip, when the Lear had set down to refuel. He had fallen back to sleep before the plane had finished its landing roll and remained that way throughout the refueling operation and the following takeoff. He rubbed his eyes and looked at McDaniels. "Sleep well?"

McDaniels grunted. *Now I know why the zoomies always look so rested and refreshed all the time.*

Behind them, Gartrell stirred and started checking his pack and other gear. "So what's the op once the door opens, sirs?"

"Well, I figured we'd take a moment to defuel our bladders, see if there's any chow available, and then catch transportation to SPARTA. There's supposed to be a van or something waiting for us." Jaworski looked over his shoulder at Gartrell. "Already leaning forward and raring to go, eh, Sergeant Major?"

"The sooner we accomplish our mission, the sooner all of this is over, sir." There wasn't any hostility in Gartrell's voice, but it wasn't full of warm fuzzies, either.

Jaworski shrugged and faced forward. "I like that you have your priorities straight, Sarmajor."

"He always has," McDaniels said.

The jet came to a halt at the taxiway ramp, and its engines spooled down.

"I've got the door," Jaworski told the pilots, and he

unfastened his seat belt and duck-walked to the plane's closed Dutch door.

"Thanks, sir," one of the pilots said as he looked back into the jet's narrow cabin. He appeared to be momentarily put out, and McDaniels presumed it was unusual for a superior officer to be doing that kind of work.

"No problem, and thanks for the lift." Jaworski opened the door, and it split horizontally across the middle, with the lower half forming a brief stairway to the tarmac, while the upper half acted as a weather shield. Jaworski put on his garrison cap, grabbed a flight bag, and stepped out.

McDaniels and Gartrell followed more slowly. The aisle between the seats would have been tight for a six-year-old, and for two grown men wearing weapons and gear, it was a bit of a challenge. McDaniels found the air outside the aircraft decidedly less humid than it had been in either Virginia or New York, and he was grateful for it. The breeze was a bit chilly, but he was relieved to be standing outside after spending hours cooped up in the C-21.

"All right." Jaworski pointed at a soldier in BDUs waving at them from the door of a nearby FBO. "Looks like our ride is here. Let's get the show on the road."

They followed him across the tarmac and found the soldier was from the 3rd Armored Cavalry Regiment. He had a van parked at the curb in front of the FBO, and he led them directly to it after the men had hit the latrine. The van was a rental, and while it was decidedly no-frills, the interior was more luxurious than the rather workmanlike appointments about the C-21. Jaworski took the front passenger seat, and McDaniels half-expected him to fall asleep again as he and Gartrell loaded onto the rear bench seat.

Surprisingly, the Air Force officer managed to stay awake. "So where are we headed?" he asked the driver as the sergeant started the van and backed away from the curb.

"Direct to SPARTA, sir. There's already quarters

provisioned, and a headquarters element has already been erected. It's, uh, kind of rustic right now, and things are still moving along, but—"

"Not a problem, son. I know I'm Air Force, but I wasn't expecting a Holiday Inn." Jaworski paused, then added, "Though that would have been nice."

"Yes, sir," the sergeant said.

"Sergeant, have any other forces arrived yet?" McDaniels asked.

"I don't think so, sir. Only a few of us from the regiment are there, as the advance team. When I left to pick you up, the Rangers were still a couple of hours out. They'll be coming in to the same airport, but they're bringing their own transportation. We have some Humvees and tractor-trailers and some Strykers, but that's it for the moment."

"Well, at least we didn't get tossed into a Stryker," Gartrell said.

"Oh no, Sarmajor. We wouldn't send one of those for the task force commander and senior staff," the driver said.

"I know that, Sergeant. Was just busting your stones a bit."

"Yes, Sarmajor."

"Who's the officer in charge of SPARTA right now?" Jaworski asked. "And how are we getting along with the civilians?"

"Captain Chase is temporarily in charge of the troops at SPARTA, sir. And if you don't mind me saying so, the civvies are a pain in the ass. The Corps of Engineers is already tearing apart their campus, so I guess they have a reason to bitch, but you know..." The driver shrugged. "Anyways, Captain Chase can brief you once we get there. Should be in about thirty minutes. This place is kind of remote, but it's all highway, so it's not too bad."

"Well, every place in Texas is about a day apart, as they say," Jaworski said. "So tell me, why are there engineers tearing up the civilian campus?"

"To build defenses, sir. Right now, they're leveling everything out."

"Okay, I can live with that. So thirty minutes, right?"

"Yes, sir, about thirty minutes." The sergeant guided the van onto Interstate 20.

They headed westbound, toward Odessa. The only other traffic sharing the freeway with them were the long-haul trucks that bolted up and down the interstate.

Guess zed hasn't made it here yet, McDaniels thought.

"Well, wake me in twenty-five, if you don't mind." Jaworski closed his eyes and went to sleep.

McDaniels finally nodded off as well.

"Here we are, sirs."

McDaniels snapped awake as the van slowed and bumped over what felt like a curb. He sat up in his seat while Jaworski roused himself in front. Light poured into the van, and McDaniels blinked against its intensity. The van approached a guard post consisting of three Humvees, one Stryker, and several soldiers who manned what seemed to be a portable metal barricade that was stretched between two of the Humvees. Above them, halogen floodlights gleamed. Behind the Humvees, a generator was encircled by a ring of sand bags. A spider web of cables connected it to the pole-mounted floodlights. The driver slowed, and after a quick discourse with one of the sentries, he passed through the checkpoint. The van pulled into a large office park, one of those rambling kind of places surrounded by a sea of cement parking lots broken up by pools of landscaped greenery. McDaniels wondered how much water was wasted on the shrubbery, since the office park was located in the middle of the Texas desert.

A collection of trailers and temporary shelters had been erected in one parking lot, near the entrance to the park's main building. Construction equipment was everywhere, a lot of it still in use under the harsh glare of more generator-powered lights. Backhoes and bulldozers were digging trenches all along the office park's perimeter, decimating probably several hundred thousand dollars worth of high-end landscaping in the process. A pall of dust hung in the air, and the cacophony of controlled pandemonium reached McDaniels's ears through the van's closed windows. No wonder the civilians in charge of the office park were pissed.

The van stopped in front of the complex. McDaniels and the others got out, and Jaworski looked around as he straightened his garrison cap.

"Well, it looks like it *used* to be a nice place," he said.

"Top-notch," McDaniels agreed. "Looks like Uncle Sam is going to have to pay through the nose to restore it once this is all over."

"Here's hoping, because the alternative isn't looking so hot."

McDaniels smiled. "Yes, sir, I guess you're right about that."

They followed the driver toward a collection of temporary shelters. A pair of semi-truck trailers stood in the center of the shelters. The trailers were studded with antennae and had dedicated diesel generators hooked up to them. The printed sign on one of the trailers told McDaniels all he needed to know:

TOC/JTF SPARTA
RESTRICTED ACCESS

"This is the temporary tactical operations center, sir," the driver said. "Trailer one is for command staff; trailer two is for support."

"Great." Jaworski mounted the temporary wooden stairway that led to the closed door in the side of trailer one and pulled it open.

"Thank you, Sergeant," McDaniels told the driver.

"Sure thing, sir."

McDaniels returned the soldier's salute and mounted the stairs. Jaworski held the door for him and Gartrell. One side of the trailer was loaded with electronic equipment, mostly radios and small computer workstations. Only two people were inside, one enlisted man and one gigantic soldier who likely smacked his head every time he passed through the door. Both men looked over at them as they entered. The enlisted man rose from his chair and saluted, and the taller man mirrored the action.

Jaworski returned their salutes. "You must be Captain Chase?" he said to the tall man. "I'm Stas Jaworski, Leonidas Six."

"Pleasure to meet you, sir. Captain Larry Chase, 66th Military Intelligence Company." Chase extended his huge hand, and Jaworski shook it.

"Ghostriders, right?"

"Yes, sir, that's right."

"Fantastic. This is Lieutenant Colonel Cordell McDaniels and Sergeant Major David Gartrell. McDaniels will be heading up Hercules; Gartrell will be the QRF senior NCO."

"Great. Colonel, Sarmajor." Chase shook their hands and motioned to the enlisted man beside him. "This is Corporal Wang, one of our ELINT guys. I've got another twelve troops assigned to me, but they're off until zero six hundred. Have you gentlemen been set up with quarters yet, sir?"

"We have not, but we'll get to that in a bit. Can you give us a rundown on what's been going on for the past few hours, or is it too early for that?"

Chase turned and motioned to one of the monitors on the wall. CNN was tuned in, and the talking head featured there looked tense and drawn. The news ticker scrawling across the bottom of the screen was full of updates regarding the spread of stenches along the east coast. McDaniels wasn't surprised to see that one of the bits read, *"President evacuated from White House."*

"Not much to tell you, sir. We only received our deployment orders less than twenty-four hours ago. We're still setting up, and most of the units that are supposed to join us aren't on-station yet," Chase said.

"Tell us what you've got, then."

"Sure thing. We arrived on-station yesterday morning. We already have a team standing by with everything ready to go, what we call a silver bullet unit. It's configured for rapid OCONUS deployment, so pushing it out into the same state was no big deal. My unit, the 66th, was only a small presence, but we plussed it up with several staff members and brought along some extra gear—encrypted radios, terminals that can receive unmanned aerial system telemetry and images, that kind of stuff. Everything else was provided by the Cav regiment. We motored down here and set up after a bit of a pushing match with the civilians, but they let us position our gear where we wanted in the end."

"What was the problem?" McDaniels asked. "They didn't know you were coming?"

"Oh no, sir, they knew. They just wanted to keep this parking lot open for their employees. Once we made it clear to them that this facility is about to be completely militarized, I guess they figured out it was probably wise to listen to the guys with the guns."

Jaworski sighed heavily. "Captain, you *do* realize we need these people, right?"

"I'm told that we need them, sir, but I had a mission to complete, and that was to get SPARTA's initial presence up and operational. I did try to negotiate a settlement, but the folks here wanted it their way one hundred percent, and I just couldn't give them that."

"All right. Go on."

"The first elements of the Corps of Engineers arrived yesterday afternoon. Between them and myself, we hammered out a rough idea of how SPARTA would form up—nothing too fancy, we decided to keep everything in a grid pattern. That way, the layout is nice and logical, with straight avenues of approach. The big thing was keeping it secure. We're still working on that one. Doesn't look like these zombie things are very impressed by firepower, and the only thing that kills them is a shot to the head. Is that right?"

McDaniels nodded. "Other than completely destroying the entire corpse, that's right. A shot to the head is what's required to put them down."

"Then we're still trying to figure out the best method to use. We can set up miles and miles of concertina wire and fencing with zones of antipersonnel mines to give us some additional defense-in-depth, but other than that, we're kind of drawing a blank. Since normal suppression techniques won't work, we're kind of reinventing the wheel here."

"Passive defenses are what we'll need, sir," Gartrell said. "High walls with battlements. Trenches to make it more difficult for them to get to us. And yeah, lots and lots of concertina wire—that way, they'll get hung up, and we can snipe them." He paused. "We're probably going to need a hell of a lot of bullets, since a lot of our guys probably aren't going to be full-on snipers."

Jaworski nodded. "I like the way you think, Sergeant Major. Captain Chase, you mind if we let Sergeant Major Gartrell run with the security configuration around SPARTA?"

"Hell no, sir. If the Sarmajor has some input that'll be useful, I'm all for it. Whatever you need, Sarmajor, I'll make sure you get it," Chase said.

Gartrell jerked his thumb toward the tall captain. "Now *this* is the kind of officer we need in this man's Army," he said. "I guess we got the only one, huh?"

"Seems like," McDaniels replied. "Captain, what about supplies? Munitions, food, fuel, lubricants, spares, maintenance facilities ... the whole nine yards. Are we close to becoming self-sustaining for a while?"

"Initial shipments of class five, six, and nine supplies are already here. There's a road movement from Hood right now bringing the rest of the goods our way. We expect the first shipments to be here by morning. We'll have ten HEMMT tankers with fuel alone for the vehicles, and we'll transfer the fuel to blivets. And aviation fuel, too, which will come by Chinook later in the day. But we need to establish the airhead for them first, before they can start making their drops. Here's what we have so far." Chase turned to a map table a few feet away and flipped on the lights over it. An aerial photograph of the site was there, transferred to a clear film that allowed him to mark it up with a grease pencil. The photograph was illuminated from below by a series of LED lights; above the table, a camera recorded the changes and sent the digitized pictures to a computer for storage.

Chase pointed at one of the parking lots, located to the northeast of the pharmaceutical complex. "This is where we want the aviators to set up, but we don't have any of them here to make the final decision. So we have to wait for them to bless it. I think we're getting some units in from Fort Campbell, right? Chinooks? Yeah, then we should wait for them to determine if the lot is useable. We have some light poles here and here." Chase pointed them out on the map as he spoke. "And they might have to come down, but I don't want to tear 'em out of the ground just yet. The nights get pretty dark out here in west Texas, and light might be a welcome commodity if things go south and we find ourselves cut off from the rest of the country."

"How many generators do you have?" McDaniels asked.

"Six, sir. All of them are in use. We have more on the way, of course. But just so you know, the facility itself has a very robust backup power solution. Geothermal and solar powers supplement the electricity delivered from the power grid, and then there's a bank of generators in this building here, with a smaller bank in this building here." Chase indicated the appropriate buildings. "I haven't been inside to verify that, but I'm told the gensets run off a buried series of liquid propane tanks somewhere around this field here." He circled his index finger around a patch of real estate between the two northernmost parking lots.

"Let's verify that and make that a no-fire zone," Jaworski said. "At least, nothing we want to shell indefinitely. It would be a shame to go up in the blaze of glory by blowing up one of our contingency power sources."

"Roger that, sir." Chase made a notation on the photo.

"All the accommodations set for the moment?" Jaworski asked. "Does everyone have a cot and place to have a hot?"

"Yes, sir. Quarters are here, dining facility is here, latrine is here, but we have access to the facilities inside the building. There's a full cafeteria, workout facilities, and bathing areas."

"All right, but let's think about keeping our use of those areas off-cycle from the civilians," Jaworski said. "For now, our numbers are relatively small, so it probably won't be a major issue, but once the rest of the troops arrive, we'd better stick to our own areas. The civvies will have a lot of work to do, and they don't need us getting in their way. Keep that in mind, Captain Chase. We're here because the nation is depending on these folks doing their job."

"Hooah, sir."

"Pass that on to the rest of your troops, and keep that thought close at hand. We'll need to continually reinforce it to keep friction to a minimum."

Chase blinked. "Sir, if you're making a reference to my decision to set up the TOC in this parking lot—"

"I am not," Jaworski said, smiling. "Sometimes, we need to do what we need to do, and setting up our initial footprint is one of those things. But going forward, we need to consult the facility's management before we do something to annoy them. We're their partners in this, not their superiors. Look at it this way. We handle the tactical aspects of the mission; they handle the strategic elements. That's how it should be played."

Chase nodded. "Roger that, sir."

"Great. Okay, what else?"

Chase walked them through the rest of the proposed plan to consolidate SPARTA. McDaniels paid close attention to the areas where Hercules would assemble and launch in the event the facility came under attack. When he had been briefed in Washington, he had thought the forces made available to him were sufficient for the task, but seeing just how big the complex was, he realized securing it would need more troops, which meant that SPARTA would have to grow even more.

He started to bring that up to Jaworski, but the Air Force colonel stopped him. "Whatever you want to do, just write down all the details, and I'll try and get it done. But listen, Cord, getting more special operations forces assigned is going to be pretty tough. All the tier-one assets are spoken for, and a lot of remaining manpower is filling the void they left behind."

"Forts Hood and Bliss are in the neighborhood, sir," McDaniels responded. "We don't need special operators to button this place up. Regular troops should be good enough, but we'd need at least a full battalion."

"A battalion's what, about five hundred people?" Jaworski asked.

"Yes, sir."

Jaworski snorted. "Well, if the people here were getting annoyed by just this small presence, imagine what they'll do when a full battalion of horny infantry guys show up."

"We'll be keeping them busy, sir," McDaniels said.

"Okay. Write down the exact specifics and give me the list before twelve hundred tomorrow. After that, I'm not so sure it's going to be easy to dial home and get reinforced." Jaworski pointed at the monitor showing the CNN feed.

Washington, DC was on fire.

Oh shit, McDaniels thought.

"Let's get back to business and finish this up, Captain," Jaworski said. "It's going to be a long day tomorrow, so the sooner we can get to quarters and square ourselves away, the better."

Gartrell must have made a face McDaniels didn't see, because Jaworski suddenly looked up and addressed him directly. "I only joined the Air Force because of the light schedule, Sergeant Major. All this traveling and all these briefings and PowerPoint presentations have taken their toll."

Gartrell nodded. "I didn't say a word, Colonel."

6

The next day came mighty early. McDaniels awoke to the sound of roaring diesel engines, and he slowly sat up on his cot. Gartrell was already gone, as were the rest of the troops who had been snoring away when they'd bedded down last night. He checked his watch—0553 hours. The sun wasn't even up yet. He swung his legs over the side of the cot and rubbed his face. He felt stubble on his chin, and his eyes burned as if someone had attacked them with sand paper.

The joys of military life.

It was slightly chilly, so he pulled on his BDUs and wondered where he could find a shaving kit—his was lying somewhere along 79th Street in Manhattan. He was supposed to receive replacement gear, but the how and when hadn't been spelled out, so he would have to figure out how to manage until then. Gathering the remains of his gear, he left the tent and found a soldier who directed him to SPARTA's nascent quartermaster activity, currently running out of an eighteen-by-thirty-two foot Modular General Purpose Tent System like the one he had just vacated. It was located near what would eventually be the motor pool, and McDaniels was surprised to find it staffed by a sleepy-eyed Army specialist wearing 3rd Armored Cavalry Regiment "Brave Rifles" patches on his BDU blouse. The specialist nodded when McDaniels inquired about a personal hygiene kit and rummaged through the tent for a moment before he produced one. He then handed over a requisition form for McDaniels to fill out.

"Still have to account for everything, huh?" McDaniels said.

"It's the Army way, sir."

With that bit of business taken care of, McDaniels hit the latrine and found the field showers set up in an array of modular tents known as TEMPERs—Tent, Extendable, Modular, Personnel. The array consisted of two thirty-two-foot TEMPERs joined by a connector; one tent was for changing, the other for showering.

Stepping into the changing tent, McDaniels found Gartrell getting ready to exit. "Sarmajor," he greeted.

"Colonel. Feeling rested?"

"Not so bad. Yourself?"

Gartrell shrugged. "So-so. I've gone through worse."

McDaniels grunted and looked around. "Any place around here to store my weapons?"

"No, sir. I'll watch over them if you're not going to take a Hollywood shower."

"A quick shower and shave, and I'm done," McDaniels said. "Ten minutes, max."

"Five," Gartrell said.

"You're on." McDaniels removed his weapons and placed his gear in a nearby locker.

Gartrell checked his watch. "Clock starts now, Colonel."

"Damn!"

McDaniels made it through in record time, running surprisingly hot water over his body, lathering up, rinsing off, and scraping his new, virgin razor over his chin. After toweling off, he wrapped the wet towel around his waist and returned to the changing tent. He found Gartrell heading for the entrance flap.

"Done here, Sarmajor," he called.

"Fantastic work, sir. You're a minute late. I'm headed for the mess tent," Gartrell said, automatically dating himself. The term *mess tent* had been assassinated years ago by *dee-fac*, or dining facility. McDaniels was almost certain the crusty senior enlisted man wouldn't kill anyone if they were uncouth enough to bring up the fact that he was one of the Army's last remaining dinosaurs.

McDaniels dressed quickly, verified his weapons were still

in fully operational condition, then set out through the gloomy light in search of the dining facility, which was quite easy to find, as it was almost directly across from the showers. There weren't many troops in the facility just yet, which suited McDaniels just fine, as there were only eight tables, each complemented by six chairs. Half the tables were already full, and McDaniels put his helmet on one, officially staking a claim. He acknowledged a chorus of "sirs" as he made his way to the serving line. Gartrell was just finishing up there, so McDaniels grabbed a tray and watched as the serving staff—civilians, apparently—filled it with plates of scrambled eggs, French toast, bacon, hash browns, and even a small container of oatmeal complete with fruit topping and brown sugar cinnamon. By the time he made it through the line, McDaniels barely had any space to balance a cup of coffee on the tray.

Gartrell had already sat down at the table McDaniels had reserved. McDaniels joined him, and the senior NCO glanced over at McDaniels's full tray.

"You know, you might have left something for the rest of the troops. Just sayin', Colonel."

"Let them eat MREs," McDaniels said, complete with phony French accent.

Gartrell snorted and turned to his own breakfast, consisting of a single serving of eggs, bacon, and coffee.

"You get in touch with your family?" McDaniels asked.

"Affirmative. We have a satellite phone. My wife was able to call me when I was sitting in one of the 87th Infantry's TOCs giving the lightfighters some lessons in killing zeds. Everyone on my side is fine. What about your people?"

"Talked to both wife and son earlier today from the TOC. Wife is freaked out being confined to Fort Bragg, but it's probably safer for her there than anywhere else. She has no survival skills to speak of, so I told her to make a nest in the attic of our house and fortify it as best as she can. If it was safe, I'd tell her to get out of Bragg and try to make it to my son—he's over at the University of Texas. But I'm worried that she'd never make it."

Gartrell grunted. "Might be a better choice than staying at Bragg, Colonel. Once the stenches make up whatever passes for their minds to move on the place, there aren't going to be enough guns around to hold them back. It's not like the entire 82nd isn't going somewhere else, and the garrison forces will be, what, three hundred guys? Five hundred? Not enough to secure an entire reservation."

McDaniels started eating, even though he was no longer hungry. "I know. But she's not the hardy type. My son, though, is a different story. He's thinking about heading north to get her. I told him to stay put, that it would be better that way, but the boy's got a mind of his own." He chewed some French toast and looked around the tent that housed the dining facility. "I have to get a new cell. Mine's fragged."

Gartrell tossed his phone on the table. "Need to make a call? You can use mine."

"I'm good, thanks. I just need to get one for later."

Gartrell shrugged and pocketed his phone, then went back to eating. McDaniels watched him for a moment, wondering how to best approach what he wanted to discuss. Was it even a good time? Both men would be up to their necks in work in a very short time, probably the instant they stepped out of the DFAC tent.

"What's on your mind?" Gartrell asked suddenly. "If you have something to say, say it, Colonel. You staring at me from across the table is making me feel really weird, and not in a giddy schoolgirl kind of way."

McDaniels laughed. "All right. Gartrell, you should have had a hero's death in Manhattan. What the hell happened?"

"Why, Colonel McDaniels, you sound disappointed."

"The day's not too early for that to change, Sergeant Major. What happened in New York? Because whatever it was, it's kind of fucked you up." Gartrell looked up at that, and

McDaniels looked back at him calmly as he sipped his coffee. "You aren't the same soldier who went in, and I've been trying to figure out what kind of soldier you are now that you've come out."

"Sir, I spent a couple of days fighting off the walking cannibalistic dead. If I seem a little off-key, it's probably because of that."

"I think that's what you want me to believe, Gartrell. But that isn't really the case, is it?"

Gartrell's eyes narrowed. He took in a deep breath, held it, then released it in one long sigh. McDaniels held his angry stare for as long as he needed to, maintaining an outward façade of calm.

Eventually, Gartrell resumed eating half-heartedly. "I hooked up with a family, a lady and her boy. The boy was autistic. Not really controllable."

McDaniels sipped some more coffee. "You leave them to the stenches?"

Gartrell looked up again, and his eyes were unreadable. Just the same, McDaniels thought he detected an undercurrent of surprise run through the otherwise imperturbable sergeant major.

"I thought about it," he said finally. "But no, Colonel McDaniels, I didn't leave them to die. But I somehow managed to deliver them to the stenches anyway."

McDaniels didn't know what to make of that. "So you, what? Tried to get them out of the city?"

"The lady's not-so-deceased husband showed up. Used his fucking house key to get into the apartment building we were in. I was in contact with the 87th Infantry, and I got us some top cover while we boogied out of the apartment building and hit the subway tunnels. I still had my NVGs, and it was the only chance we had."

McDaniels noticed the soldiers at the other table were listening. They were trying to be discreet, but one of them looked away suddenly when McDaniels glanced over. He glared at the soldiers for a long moment until they got the hint, finished up, and left the area.

"I agree. The subway tunnels would be the best way to try and get out. Didn't the lightfighters try to come for you?"

"No helicopters available to evac us until after the stenches made it into the building, and I wasn't going to camp out on the roof with a lady and her special-needs kid waiting for a National Guard Chinook to show up. What if something happened and the bird got delayed, or retasked? The last thing I wanted was to be trapped on a rooftop with no other option than throwing myself over the edge to escape the dead." Gartrell drained his coffee and stared into the cup for a long moment, his blue eyes hollow, as empty as the vessel he held. "So yeah, we managed to get up the street and down into the subway system. The poor kid was going nuts from all the shooting, the explosions, the darkness, and obviously from being confronted by fucking zombies. The zeds were able to track us through the tunnel. Hell, a busload of 'em followed us down, and I couldn't take down each and every one. They caught up to us eventually, and by the time they took out the kid's mother, I was down to two rounds in my pistol."

McDaniels remained quiet, waiting for the rest.

Gartrell hung his head. He roused himself suddenly and looked across the table at McDaniels with those oddly empty eyes of his, and he smiled. The gesture didn't even approach looking realistic. "I rode you pretty hard about not killing that kid in Afghanistan," he said. "I know now that I was fucked up to do that. Making that kind of call, being responsible for something like that, well... I wouldn't have wanted to be in your shoes because I thought it would be an easy decision to make. I was wrong about that."

"What happened to the kid, Gartrell?"

"I popped him. Two fucking seconds before a squad from the 87th showed up on the opposite track, hauling all sorts of firepower. They wiped out every zed in the tunnel, but only *after* I'd put a round through the kid's head. Talk about ironic, huh?"

McDaniels didn't know what to say. Which was funny in a way, since he actually knew *exactly* what it felt like to carry around that kind of guilt. He'd been carrying it inside himself for almost a decade after losing five men whose lives might have been spared had he instead ordered Gartrell to kill one Afghan boy, a boy whose only crime was to discover the Special Forces team's hide site.

"I'm pretty sure you didn't have a choice at the moment, Gartrell. And it sucks that the kid had to die right before the cavalry rode up, but life is like that." McDaniels placed his elbows on the table and leaned toward Gartrell. "And at the end of the day, Gartrell, God forgives all our sins."

Gartrell snorted humorlessly. "God's a fucking asshole." He pushed back his chair and got to his feet. "I'll be stopping by the TOC to check on things, sir, if that's all right with you."

McDaniels nodded. "I'll be there directly. We'll need to start devising ways to defend SPARTA if the zeds show up."

"Hooah. I'll wait for you there." Gartrell picked up his tray, dumped the trash in a nearby garbage can, and left the DFAC.

McDaniels sighed and turned back to his breakfast, which had become cold and unappetizing. He forced himself to eat it anyway. He would need something in his stomach, and it gave him something else to do other than worry about just how far unhinged Sergeant Major David Gartrell had become.

7

Colonel Marcus Jeffries, MD, stared at the computer display as the modeling program ran once again, charting out the bug's various biochemical properties. It was a tough bastard, immune to almost everything a human host could throw at it. It outlasted barrage after barrage of white blood cells, shrugged off every antibiotic available, and continued to flourish even when exposed to temperatures above 112° Fahrenheit, a fever far more likely to kill the host than the virus itself. And when the infected subject eventually succumbed to the fever, the virus changed again... into something the wizards and bug masters at the U.S. Army Medical Research Institute of Infectious Diseases simply couldn't understand. And neither could the Army's counterparts at the Center for Disease Control. Whatever the virus transformed into had the ability to jumpstart portions of the recently deceased's brain, providing enough biochemical juice to get the brain operating again, albeit at a substantially degraded pace.

After days of examining the virus, Jeffries had concluded that there was no chance at reversing its effect after the infected patients had died. And while the rate of infection seemed substantial—the Rid had already isolated the virus in almost every one of its staffers, and Jeffries himself had it in his own blood—it only caused a small percentage of those infected to die. Of course, the dearly departed then reanimated, anywhere from minutes to a few hours later, and they in turn would attack and feed on living humans. The attacks resulted in a fluidic transfer of the new, mutated virus, which would then induce the cycle all over again in those bitten. That was where the virus was proving to be absolutely dastardly. In its original form, it was almost benign, causing no harm to 99% of those infected. But a bite from the reanimated dead resulted in a mortality rate that approached almost 100%, and the infection vector was growing almost exponentially.

And of course, the dead would rise again, unless sufficient trauma was introduced to the brain. The only way to keep the corpses still was to shoot them in the head, or otherwise destroy the brain before it could reactivate.

Even though he and his staff had been on the virus since the very beginning, spending days at a time without sleep, they'd made absolutely no progress in figuring out how to impede the virus's progress. It wasn't until Wolf Safire—a brilliant, truly gifted researcher and virologist if ever there was one—had determined there was no effective method to kill the virus that the first real breakthrough had occurred. Safire's work had centered on preventing the virus from bonding to healthy human cells by way of short-circuiting the phosphotransferase process, wherein the virus's as-yet unidentified proteins would adhere to the cellular walls of the host and multiply at a fantastic rate. Safire had determined that without the bonding, the virus was essentially harmless; it needed to be able to nest itself inside the host's cellular structures and tap the DNA to fuel its incredible expansion throughout the body. By utilizing a kinase inhibitor, the virus would be denied its anchorages, and would begin to die within twenty-four to forty-eight hours. While hardy and almost indestructible if it could harvest cellular tissues, the virus lacked enough "body fat" to live for very long without being able to contact the host's DNA.

That characteristic was the only flaw Jeffries and the rest of the staff at the Rid could think to exploit. Viruses were notoriously hard to kill, since they were living organisms, complete with complex proteins and either their own DNA or RNA. The zed virus which Safire had dubbed *Rex Articulus Morte*, the walking dead, was no pushover, but they had found its Achilles' heel, and the only thing left to do was to exploit it. The required inhibitor still needed to be synthesized; Safire had presented the appropriate formulations, which Jeffries's senior scientist Joanna Kersey had verified. The formulation had been packaged and distributed to every medical research facility in the world with which the Rid was still in contact. Most of Europe was off the map, but there were facilities operating in France and England, and those in Japan, the Philippines, and Singapore had not yet come under unrelenting threat.

Automatic weapons fire rattled outside, and Jeffries looked up, distracted by the noise. The stenches were coming to Fort Detrick in greater numbers than the post's security teams could reasonably control. Jeffries had already been notified that he and his senior staff would be evacuated—to where, he did not know. But the ruckus had only been increasing, and the Marines guarding the Rid had their tracked vehicles moving constantly. The pounding pulse of the 25 millimeter cannon mounted on their LAVs was something Jeffries had almost grown used to.

Jeffries went back to the computer model and ignored the sounds of gunfire as best as he could. He still needed to submit his report to the Army Chief of Staff's office, where it would go on to the Secretary of Defense and, he supposed, the president and the rest of the national command authority. He popped another antacid and wiped the sheen of sweat from his brow. He felt like complete garbage, and if he hadn't been running for days without sleep, he would be worried that he was succumbing to the virus in his bloodstream. But exhaustion was his foe, something everyone in the Rid was struggling against. Even though the keyboard grew blurry before him, Jeffries only rubbed his eyes and soldiered on. He had to get his work done. He heard more gunfire. And a distant shriek.

From inside the building.

Jesus, have the stenches gotten inside? He didn't stop typing, but his heart hammered in his chest and his breath grew short, as if he had just run a marathon. Panic gnawed at the edges of his consciousness, seeking a way to unravel his discipline and derail everything. Jeffries held it at bay as best as he could as his fingers flew across the keyboard.

"Colonel, we have to get out of here, sir."

Jeffries looked up from his computer screen, and it took a moment to register that the Marine standing in his office doorway was packing full battle rattle—body armor, weapons, helmet, goggles, hard pads on his elbows and knees. Outside the glass-walled office, another Marine lurked, a virtual clone of the first.

Jeffries went back to typing. "What's the situation, Corporal?"

"It's not too good, sir. The post is overrun. The cops can't hold the zeds back, and neither can we. Several buildings have already been compromised, including this one. It's time to go, sir."

"Just a minute," Jeffries said. "What about the rest of the staff? Doctor Kersey, her people, and the Safire woman?"

"All accounted for and being relocated to the roof, sir. Just like you should." More gunfire sounded, and the second Marine shouldered his M4 carbine.

The Marine corporal took a few steps into the office. "Colonel Jeffries! It's time to go, sir. Let's move it!"

Jeffries saved his document, dropped it into his e-mail, and sent it off to the Army Chief of Staff's office. He grabbed his helmet—all the military members of the Rid had been instructed to change into BDUs and combat gear if possible—and slipped it on as he rose unsteadily to his feet. The room blurred and swam, and he felt vaguely sick to his stomach.

Come on. Keep it together. Pretend it's an all-nighter with the boys.

"All right, where are we headed? To the helipad?"

The Marine corporal looked at Jeffries as if he had just released an explosive fart. "Sir, the building's already compromised, and there are *hundreds* of stenches outside trying to get in. We're going to the roof. We'll be extracted from there. Now, if you don't mind..." The corporal grabbed Jeffries's arm and hustled him out of the office and down the hall. The second Marine followed, guarding the rear, his M4 at ready. The Marine leading him along set out at an aggressive pace, and Jeffries stumbled a bit as he tried to keep up. He felt light-headed.

What the hell is wrong with me?

The Marine led him straight to the elevator and pressed the *Up* button. The elevator arrived a moment later, and the Marine corporal visually cleared it before he pulled Jeffries inside and pressed the button for the top floor. As the second Marine made to follow them, a door at the far end of the hall flew open. Several zombies emerged into the corridor, moaning when they saw the Marines and Jeffries entering the elevator. They shambled forward, but most of them were far enough away that they would never make it before the elevator door closed.

Except for the three of them that could run.

"Oh, fuck!" The Marine outside the elevator squeezed off several shots and struck the zombies as they ran toward him, but not one round hit any in the head. The stenches pressed on, arms outstretched, reaching for him even as he backpedaled and flipped his weapon over to automatic. He fired several bursts, and one zed went down, its skull blasted apart, leaking dark ichor onto the white tile floor.

The first Marine corporal shoved Jeffries into one corner of the elevator and raised his rifle. He fired past the other Marine's shoulder after shouting warning, and drilled another zombie in the forehead. It collapsed to floor, practically right at the second Marine's feet. Jeffries was almost deafened by the rifle reports, and as such he did not hear the Marine outside the elevator scream as the last runner slammed into him and drove him to the ground, but he could imagine it. The corporal next to him continued firing at the rest of the approaching zombies, dropping two more. He leaped out of the elevator and ripped the zombie off the fallen Marine, but it was too late. The Marine had already been bitten on the face.

"Colonel, get to the roof! The helo will pick you up there!"

the corporal shouted as the elevator doors closed. As the lift lurched upward, Jeffries heard more gunfire over the ringing in his ears and his own frantic breathing.

My God, those zeds were in uniform.

The elevator reached the top floor. Jeffries stood to one side as the door slid open. He couldn't seem to get his wind back, and his face and hands tingled. He slowly stuck his head out the elevator and looked up and down the corridor beyond. He saw nothing other than vacant offices and empty conference rooms. He stepped out of the elevator and turned left, heading to where he thought the stairs would be. If he remembered correctly, the only way to access the roof was from the stairway. Though the way his legs were trembling, Jeffries certainly wished there was another way to get there. He found the stairwell door and pulled it open. Gunfire echoed from below, then the gunfire abruptly ended. Were the Marines moving to another fighting position, or had they been overrun? He slowly stepped onto the stairway landing, still gasping for air.

Below, a door opened and closed. Jeffries heard movement on the lower stairs. When he heard the first moans, he realized stenches were climbing toward him.

A sharp pain in his chest caused him to wince, and his heart rate accelerated. He lunged for the handrail and mounted the stairs to the roof. It was only one flight to the roof door, which was already open; morning light and fresh air entered the stairwell. Jeffries climbed toward it as if he wore cement boots. As he broke out in a fresh sweat, he recognized that he wasn't just suffering from the effects of sleep deprivation. Something else was wrong, and if he remembered his medical training correctly, he was having some sort of cardiovascular episode.

Not the best time to have a heart attack, he thought as he continued up the stairs. He was gasping loudly, as he just couldn't get enough air. Overhead, he heard approaching rotor beats.

The stenches apparently heard the noise as well because

they surged upward, moaning.

"Jesus Christ." He was only halfway up the stairs. The zeds would be on him in no time.

Above, a figure stepped into the gloomy stairwell. It was another Marine, the lieutenant Jeffries had met just last night. The lieutenant looked down at Jeffries, a puzzled expression on his face. The puzzlement fled the second he heard the moaning zombies below, and he bolted down the stairs and grabbed Jeffries's arm.

"Come on, sir. You really have to move some ass!" The lieutenant tugged Jeffries along, and Jeffries followed as well as he could, stumbling on the steps. Finally, he emerged into the light of a crisp, early Virginia morning, propelled through the doorway by a very anxious Marine.

A UH-60 Black Hawk hovered thirty feet away, its landing gear only inches above the roof. Jeffries knew that was as good as it was going to get; the helicopter was far too heavy to settle on the roof. The helicopter's crew chief was helping several people to board—Jeffries's senior staff, along with Wolf Safire's daughter.

The Marine lieutenant slammed the stairwell door closed and dragged Jeffries toward the hovering helicopter. Jeffries found he could barely move; he couldn't draw enough air to speak, couldn't even shuffle along the roof. He felt dizzy and nauseous and feared he was about to vomit. The pain in his chest radiated down his right arm and up to his jaw.

I'm having a fucking heart attack!

"Colonel, you still with me?" the Marine shouted over the rotor noise.

Jeffries fell to the roof. Another intense jolt of pain shot through his chest, and then the world went black.

***

Regina Safire was lucky to have a seat on the helicopter, and she knew it. The medical personnel at the Rid understood that she had some value, since she was familiar with her father's work and his thought processes, and therefore, she was able to go... well, wherever the Rid's staff was headed.

She had just buckled herself into the Black Hawk's bench seat—*Not another helicopter, please, God, don't let this one crash too*—when she saw the Marine drag Colonel Jeffries out onto the roof. Regina didn't like the way the small Army officer looked. He was quite pale and appeared almost cyanotic as he struggled to follow the Marine to the helicopter. And then, he collapsed. The Marine slung his rifle and pulled Jeffries onto his shoulders.

The roof door popped open again, and zombies boiled out of the stairwell like a swarm of African killer bees.

The Army crew chief that had been helping his passengers secure themselves said something over the intercom system and pulled a rifle from a nearby compartment. It was too late. The zombies slammed into the Marine from behind, driving him to the floor. Jeffries flopped to the side and lay unmoving. The zombies tore into the flailing Marine, savaging him with their teeth.

Some of them continued past the melee toward the hovering helicopter, including one that could run as fast as a track star. Regina felt the helicopter pull in power and start to climb out, but the zombie launched itself at the aircraft and caught the bottom of the door frame. Doctor Kersey, who sat closest to the door, screamed, but the sound was drowned out by the wail of the Black Hawk's turboshaft engines. The crew chief stepped forward and fired a single shot from his rifle. The zombie fell as the helicopter climbed away from Fort Detrick, Maryland.

The body that had once been known as Colonel Marcus Jeffries stirred and twitched, then sat upright in the bright Maryland sunlight. It saw several Others nearby, feasting on their shrieking meal, their rotting bodies dappled with sweet, warm blood. Dead Jeffries could smell it, sense it, almost taste it, even from where it sat. The sudden urge to feed struck, and Dead Jeffries rose to its feet and pushed its way into the group, scrabbling for some chunks of warm flesh. But the exposed areas of the U.S. Marine's body had already been ravaged; Dead Jeffries unlaced a boot, pulled it off, and sank its teeth into the exposed foot. It ripped off toes with its teeth, crunching down on the morsels, feeling bone shatter and break in its mouth as it chewed. Most of the Others stared at Dead Jeffries stupidly, unable to comprehend what he had done, how he had found more food when the Marine's thighs and calves and arms had been stripped almost bare. Dead Jeffries shoved an Other out of the way and repeated the process with the Marine's other foot. The rest of the group reacted, and they reached out for the newly-exposed flesh; Dead Jeffries fought them off, striking them in their heads, driving them back. It devoured the appendage swiftly, teeth tearing flesh from bone, flesh it swallowed almost convulsively. But it wasn't enough. Not nearly enough.

Dead Jeffries pulled off the Marine's body armor, ignoring the man's screams as it ripped open the battle dress blouse beneath. Dead Jeffries sank its teeth into the soft, warm flesh of the Marine's abdomen and tore away a great chunk. Blood welled from the wound, shining brightly in the light. The Others crowded Dead Jeffries away then, overwhelming it by sheer mass alone as they descended upon the Marine, their seeking hands and teeth ripping apart his abdomen. Dead Jeffries fought against them, but there were too many. Dead Jeffries was losing out on the only meal around.

Something, a vague, dreamlike memory trickled through Dead Jeffries's brain, like sand down a funnel. Dead Jeffries crawled along the roof until it found what it was looking for: the Marine's assault rifle. With its dead, numb fingers, Dead Jeffries pulled the weapon toward it and, after a long moment, held the weapon's butt-stock against its shoulder. Turning toward the feasting Others, Dead Jeffries pulled the trigger and shot them all. One. Two. Three. Sometimes Dead Jeffries had to shoot an Other more than once, but eventually, their corpses fell to the rooftop, lifeless again, forever inanimate, as dark ichor leaked from the bullet holes in their heads.

Except for one. One of the Others looked at Dead Jeffries with eyes that weren't quite as lifeless, that still held a vague sparkle of something different, something unique. It backed away from the still-twitching Marine, its face and chin covered in a sheen of blood. Dead Jeffries watched it for a long moment, then fell to its knees and attacked the Marine. Dead Jeffries ate and ate, until the Marine shuddered his last. And then the meat was no longer what Dead Jeffries wanted, for the Marine had become a new Other. The reanimated Marine moaned, its dead eyes casting about, looking for food it could not effectively hunt; its legs and arms were mostly gone, devoured by the rest of the group.

Dead Jeffries rose to its feet and looked across the rooftop. More of the Others milled about, searching for more prey. Dead Jeffries did not join them. Dead Jeffries somehow knew there was no more prey there. As it watched, one of the Others must have sensed the same thing, for it walked right off the roof and plummeted to the ground.

Something thundered in the sky overhead. Most of the Others ignored it, but Dead Jeffries turned its face upward. A helicopter flew high in the sky. Dead Jeffries watched it for a long moment as it headed away from where it stood. It headed away from the columns of smoke that rose into the air from the east. Sounds echoed in the near distance: sharp, harsh reports. Gunfire. Dead Jeffries listened to the staccato blasts for a moment, and again, another trickle of something occurred in Dead Jeffries's brain.

Memory.

Intelligence.

Dead Jeffries knew the food was moving. Dead Jeffries already wanted to eat again, which meant it would have to follow the food. Dead Jeffries slowly walked toward the open rooftop door, not noticing that the Other—the one who had backed away from the food—followed.

Dead Jeffries kept the rifle.

The rifle could help Dead Jeffries get food.

8

"Hey, Roche. Did I show you my tattoo?"

Staff Sergeant Jorge Roche sat in the truck with half of 2nd Platoon, A Company, 1st Battalion, 75th Ranger Regiment, as it bumped and trundled its way down some Texas highway. The six-by-six's engine and the noise its knobbed tires created as they rolled down the thoroughfare were loud, so loud that Roche had figured even Sergeant Wally Dobbins, or Doofus, wouldn't be able to talk. Regrettably, that was not the case. Nothing shut up the Doofus.

"No, you didn't show me your tattoo, and I really don't want to see it," Roche said, raising his voice over the din.

"Man, check this out," the Doofus from Roofus, Kansas said. He pulled up one of the sleeves on his BDU blouse and exposed a series of Chinese characters.

Roche had to admit they looked kind of cool. "What's it say?"

"It says 'killing dragon,'" the Doofus said proudly. "Fuckin' awesome, huh?"

"Hey, Shin!" Roche yelled to the Ranger sitting across from him. Staff Sergeant Kent Shin didn't stir, and his head lolled forward, bobbing from side to side. Roche kicked Shin's boot. "Hey, Shin, check this out!"

Shin raised his head. He was an indecently handsome guy, and Roche thought he should have been acting in Hong Kong chop-socky movies. He looked like a younger, more intense, less round-featured Chow Yun-Fat. But Shin had told Roche over a zillion beers one night that he'd always wanted to be a Ranger, ever since reading about what the Regiment went through in Somalia. That kind of shit created real men, and Shin wanted to know if he had what it took.

"What the fuck do you want?" Shin asked.

Roche pointed to Doofus, who held out his arm proudly. "What does this shit say?"

Shin leaned forward slightly and looked at Doofus's tattoo. He threw his head back and laughed, long and hard.

"Hey, what the fuck?" Doofus said.

"Doofus! What the hell did they tell you that said?"

"It says 'killing dragon,' man!"

Shin laughed again. "You asshole, it says 'soy sauce!'"

"*What?*" Doofus stared at the tattoo as if he could suddenly read it himself. "Are you shitting me?"

"Totally not shitting you," Shin said, leaning back against the bench seat. "Where'd you get that done?"

"Off-post at Rising Ink. That old guy, the 'Nam vet—"

"Murray Watts." Shin nodded. "I know him. He knows Chinese better than I do, man, and he totally fucked you up. You're a labeled condiment, Doofus."

"No fucking way! You're just jerking me around, man!" Doofus yanked down his sleeve.

"Dude, do *you* know Chinese? Did it even occur to you to look around on the Internet to see what 'killing dragon' written in Chinese would even *look* like?" Shin asked.

"Watts said that's what this said!"

Roche chuckled. "Doof, Murray Watts is a pothead and known prankster. I heard a command sergeant major with third battalion went in a few years ago to get a tattoo that said, 'I Love Mom,' and he walked out of there with a tat that said, 'I Love Men.' Watts got the shit kicked out of him, but he laughed the entire time."

"You guys are full of shit!" Doofus shook his head.

Shin shrugged and closed his eyes. Doofus was seething.

Roche nudged him and tried to smooth things over. "Take it easy, Doof. If Shin's not fucking around with you, it can be removed. But we'll run it by Jimmy Tang. He's from Taiwan; he knows more about this shit." He jerked his thumb toward Shin. "Shin's a Korean. He probably doesn't even know how to read a takeout menu from a Chinese restaurant in English."

"I like numbah sixty-nine, gang-raped pork!" Shin said, screwing on a thick, glottal accent. Kent Shin had the ears of a bat, could hear practically anything.

"You're a fucking prick, Shin!" Doofus said.

"Ah, fucking plick numbah fifty-one, lound eye!"

Roche kicked Shin's boot again. "All right, all right, knock that shit off, man." Doofus was starting to get really wound around the axle, and he didn't want him getting too hot under the collar. They still had a few hours to go before they got to wherever the hell they were going, and the last thing he needed was for Shin and Doof to spend the entire trip sniping at each other.

"Yeah, yeah, all right," Shin said.

Doof made an indignant sound and leaned back against the seat, his arms crossed over his chest. He looked away from Shin, and some of the other Rangers in the truck smiled at his discomfort.

Roche figured it was good to have the distraction. Anything to take their minds off rampaging zeds was a good thing. No one wanted to think about that shit. He wondered how the family guys were holding up. He looked around the truck and looked at them: Harrison, Pfeiffer, Gupta, Chavez, Alberts. They all looked as ready as anyone else, total Rangers to the core. Roche was happy he wasn't married and had no kids. He didn't know how he'd be able to stay mission focused if he had that weight to carry around, too.

Thank God for the little things.

McDaniels and Gartrell met briefly with Colonel Jaworski, the commanding officer of the Army Corps of Engineers unit on-station—a major named Guardiola—and his senior staff, which included civilian and enlisted engineers. Also in attendance were the commanding officer of the aviation detachment from the 160th Special Operations Aviation Regiment, Major Carmody, and his appointed liaison, a chief warrant officer four named Billingsly. Held in the TOC trailer, the meeting was mostly a meet-and-greet session, where the officers and enlisted "heads of state" would be introduced to Jaworski's command philosophy and what the CO considered to be mission essentials.

"Basically, I want us to survive anything that's going to come our way," Jaworski said after the initial round of introductions. It was tight in the trailer with all the meeting attendees in addition to the staff from the military intelligence company, and a lot of people were standing as opposed to sitting. Jaworski was on his feet, having abdicated his seat to McDaniels. "There's a lot of bad stuff going on out there in the world right now, and it's headed for this country. We need to make sure we're ready, and if we need something—anything—we'd better get our arms around what it might be and ask for it now, because you know what? In just a few days, we might be on our own."

Major Guardiola, a short, solid man with a shiny bald head and vaguely sleepy features that belied the fact he was completely alert, looked at Jaworski with a puzzled expression. "Sir, aren't you maybe reading a bit too much into this?" Guardiola had an unusually deep voice, like that of a radio talk show host. "I know what happened in New York is happening all along the East Coast, but it's going to take a long while for those things to make their way here."

Jaworski turned to the towering Captain Chase, who stood at the far end of the TOC. "Chase, can you put up that satellite data on this screen over here? I want to show these guys what's happening." He pointed at a large LED flat-screen monitor over the briefing area table.

"Yes, sir. Do you want it to cycle through, or—"

"Yeah, yeah, cycling through is fine, I'll do the narration."

A moment later, the screen came to life. The legend on the bottom indicated that the footage was from a satellite, and the territory under examination was the Texas/Mexico border where Mexico's Nuevo Laredo and the Texas town of Laredo faced each other from opposite sides of the Rio Grande. The border had been effectively closed by the Texas Army National Guard a week ago, and the military presence on the American side of the Juarez-Lincoln International Bridge was substantial. The National Guard presence was spread out all along the American side of the Rio Grande River, and it looked as if every tree, every bush, every blade of grass had been razed so the Guardsmen had unobstructed fire lanes.

On the Mexican side of the border was a buildup of a different kind. Thousands upon thousands of Mexican nationals had been bottled up at the entrance to the bridge by the Mexican military and police. Even if they hadn't been stopped, the mass of vehicles at the base of the span had created an impassable blockage. There were people—or perhaps *bodies*—floating in the river. Several of those bodies were surrounded by a dappled halo effect, and it took McDaniels a moment to figure out those figures were under fire from the shoreline.

Zeds.

"Here's what happened yesterday at the U.S.-Mexico border," Jaworski said. "As you can see, there's a rather impressive mass of humanity just waiting to get into the country, since for the first time since day one, the border's been effectively closed. It only took the zombie apocalypse to get that done, if you'll pardon my sarcasm. Take a look at the bottom of the display where the Mexican citizens are massed behind the vehicles."

The image changed slightly. More people suddenly surged forward, caught in a still frame, but McDaniels could see the difference quite clearly. Hundreds of people had shifted position, hurrying northward, running between the stalled motor vehicles on the bridge.

The next image, with the timestamp a minute later, showed thousands of people on the bridge, running over cars and trucks, trampling their fellow citizens, leaving broken and bloodied bodies in their wake. And at the southern portion of the picture, a mass of new figures had appeared, figures that were blackened and dull, almost as if they'd been drawn in with a charcoal stick. Stenches. Thousands and thousands of stenches.

Another frame. The civilians were gunned down by the Mexican military and police on the bridge, but that did little to stop the tide of humanity seeking escape from the walking dead. More zeds flooded into the picture, overwhelming the civilians at the base of the bridge, swallowing them beneath a wave of filth and rot.

Another frame. The Mexican authorities fled across the bridge for the fortified American presence to the north. They didn't make it. American fire pulverized them and the civilians behind them. Fires erupted as Mexican Army vehicles exploded, sending tufts of black smoke into the air.

"Here's where it gets interesting," Jaworski said. "You seeing this all right, Major Guardiola?"

"Yes, sir." Guardiola's voice was soft, hushed.

Another frame. Half of the Juarez-Lincoln International Bridge was suddenly *gone*. The entire half of the span that extended from Mexico across the Rio Grande River had disappeared, reduced to nothing more than great chunks of debris that emerged from the muddied river beneath a cloud of dust and haze. Bodies—hundreds of bodies—were in the river. On the Mexican side of the waterway, the stenches continued to amass, swarming over the warm bodies lined up along the Nuevo Laredo shoreline, chasing them into the river, ignoring all but the most precise actions of defense. Streams of smoke pointed from the American military presence back into Mexico. The National Guard was opening up with the big guns, from artillery to tanks and infantry fighting vehicles to squad automatic weapons.

"They'd rigged the bridge a few days ago, before things got seriously out of hand," Jaworski said almost conversationally. "Kind of a last ditch attempt to keep the zeds at bay. Of course, it didn't really seem to work all that well..."

Another frame. Thousands of zeds emerged from the turbulent waters of the Rio Grande, advancing toward National Guard units, ignoring the absolutely hellacious amount of firepower directed their way. The Guard had decided to rely on its size and composition to protect the Texas border, not precision and quality of fire. But the stenches just weren't impressed by M1A3 tanks, Bradley fighting vehicles, or Strykers or M249 light machineguns.

McDaniels knew how things were going to end up. Another frame proved him to be correct. Laredo was inundated by a flood of the walking dead, a flood that rose up from Mexico.

"So in Laredo alone, there were about eighteen thousand Guardsmen and other reserve component units. They were due to be reinforced today by additional active duty units out of Fort Hood. Obviously, that's probably not going to happen now, and the focus is likely going to shift to our immediate south." Jaworski paused to take a drink from his mug.

"To our south, sir?" Guardiola asked.

"San Antonio," McDaniels said. He turned away from the screen and faced the Army engineering officer, who sat directly across from him. "Major, I want you to complete that trenchwork by nightfall, and I want you to bust up the driveway that connects the facility with Route Three Eighty-Five and replace it with a mobile bridge that we can drop if the need arises. The bridge needs to be able to accommodate not only civilian vehicular traffic, but fully loaded Strykers and HEMT tankers."

Guardiola started to say something, but McDaniels pressed on without giving him the opportunity to speak. "Once the trenches are complete, I want a dirt berm as high as you can make it completed overnight. The berm needs to surround the entire complex. Tomorrow morning, I want HESCO barriers on top of the berm as our first stage defense system. And I'll expect you to start building observation towers as well, as soon as you can."

"Colonel, I'm sorry to interrupt, but we don't have any HESCO concertainers here," Guardiola said.

Concertainer units, designed and built by HESCO corporation, enabled the construction of rapid and efficient engineered fortifications with dependable protection characteristics. Used in a wide variety of configurations, they could form a simple perimeter wall to a more complex unit of bunkers.

"Sounds like someone has an item for their wish list," Jaworski said. "If I were you, Guardiola, I'd put out a request for as many HESCO units as you can get, because I think McDaniels is right. A lot of resources are going to be thrown into San Antonio, and you might want to get whatever you can right away."

"Yes, sir." Guardiola opened a notebook and scribbled in it furiously; in counterpoint, his attending NCO typed on an Apple iPad. "What else, sir?" Guardiola asked McDaniels.

McDaniels looked at Gartrell. "Sarmajor, I'm going to defer to you on this, but I think we'd be better off going medieval here. Usual defenses aren't going to work, and we might have tens of thousands of zeds headed our way. Kill zones will be our best friends."

"Hooah. Major, maybe you and I should get together with your staff and hammer out some major shopping lists," Gartrell told Guardiola. "But instead of the HESCO units on the berm, we should maybe use CONEX units, starting with the ones we already have. They'll give us more elevation, and they're impossible to climb unless your name is Spider-Man."

McDaniels nodded. "Great idea. We'll need every container unit we can get, Major. Put that on your shopping list."

"I can transmit that now, sir." The engineering NCO waved his iPad. "HESCO and CONEX units. I've put down three bailey bridge sets which can be constructed, too."

"Baileys probably aren't what you had in mind," Guardiola said. "But mobile bridges won't be able to support the loads you intend to drive over them. The baileys can be made pretty cheaply and quickly and can be demolished fast, if needed."

"What about some old-fashioned draw bridges, then? I want to be able to get traffic across the trenches."

"That can be done. The more time, the better, though."

"We should have both," Gartrell said. "Raise the draw bridges, but keep the baileys as kill-zone funnels."

McDaniels nodded. "Very well. Major Guardiola, you have your orders for now. Any problems with getting things straightened out?"

Guardiola looked at Jaworski. "Colonel?"

"McDaniels is the XO and commander of the QRF element, and his mission is to keep SPARTA secure," Jaworski said. "So feel free to follow his orders. Immediately, even."

"Yes, sirs. Colonel McDaniels, I'll see to those details you need taken care of. Someone will have to discuss this with the civilians. If I pull the driveway before we can set up a bridge, no one will be getting in and out unless it's by foot."

"I'll tend to that," Jaworski said. "Good point, let's hold off on that last one for as long as we can. We need the civilians to be able to access this place. Cord?"

McDaniels nodded. "Absolutely, until other arrangements can be made. SPARTA needs to function. But if the zeds make it here in substantial force, having a concrete path leading to us isn't going to be very helpful."

"I'll make sure to pass that on," Jaworski promised. "Anything else for the engineers at the moment?"

McDaniels shook his head. "Negative."

"Major Guardiola, you're good to go for now. We'll send Sergeant Major Gartrell over to you once we're done here.

Where can he find you?"

"I'll be at the DTOS. That's the big white and blue box truck that has 'U.S. Army Corps of Engineers' and 'Emergency Operations' written all over it," Guardiola replied.

Gartrell nodded. "I know exactly where that is, sir."

"Aviation, you guys need anything from the engineers?" Jaworski asked.

Major Carmody exchanged glances with CW5 Billingsly. Despite his rank, it was pretty obvious that Carmody was the junior member of the pair. When Billingsly shook his head, Carmody repeated the gesture to Jaworski. "We're good, sir."

Jaworski nodded and glanced at Guardiola. "Okay then, you'd better get moving, Major."

"On it, sir." The two members of the Corps of Engineers left the operations center.

Jaworski motioned for Gartrell, who was leaning against a wall, to sit down. When Gartrell declined, the tall Air Force colonel took the chair.

"Okay, let's talk some more nuts and bolts. We figure we've got a few days until the first wave of panic-stricken civilians starts heading our way from the south. Right behind them will be the stenches. We need to figure out how we're going to handle that." Jaworski turned to Carmody. "What's the situation with your unit? You have all the assets you need? Fuel? Other consumables? Maintenance and spares? Your aircraft are on a hardstand, right?"

Carmody nodded. "We have all our aircraft at the northern parking lot, and we dropped sandbags across its entrance to keep out other vehicles. We also took down several light poles, with the help of the engineers. We have enough space to do what we need to do, and more fuel is on its way from Hood. They're sending HEMT tankers and trucks full of M500 blivets, which are fine for us, since we have two fuel pumps we can use to transfer the fuel. And if we need to, we can use one of the Chinooks as a fat cow and offload its fuel into the other aircraft."

"Weapons?"

"Both Chinooks have M134 miniguns up front and fifty cals in the rear. We tripled our normal ammo loadout. The AH-6s are reconfigurable, but we deployed with two M134s and two M260 rocket pods per aircraft, so they have the full loadout. They have short legs, but we'll be able to provide close air support if things hit the fan."

"They will," McDaniels said. "By the way, in New York, a lot of your guys went the distance for us. Pass it on to your commanders that all of them are recommended by me for silver stars, and two of them are going to be put in for the DSC." The Distinguished Service Cross was the Army's highest award for valor, only one step removed from the Medal of Honor.

"You have their names, sir?" Billingsly's tone was flat and expressionless, just like his face. His silvering hair was set off by his pitch-colored eyebrows and mustache.

"I do." McDaniels pulled his battered notebook from one pocket, opened it, and pushed it across the table.

The warrant officer looked at the handwritten list for a moment, then pursed his lips. He pushed the notebook back to McDaniels. "Thanks for that, sir. I'd like to add some more names to the list if you don't mind. A lot of other aviators went down with ROMEO."

"Hell, yes. Give 'em all to me, Mister Billingsly. Everyone gets their due."

"Thank you, sir."

"I'm sorry," Jaworski said, looking at Carmody and Billingsly. "My condolences on the 160th's losses, but we do need to move on. I don't mean to be insensitive—"

"No problem, Colonel. We get it," Carmody said.

"Yeah, well, just the same, you guys have my respect. And more importantly, it looks like you have that of Colonel McDaniels and Sergeant Major Gartrell."

"You got that right, sir," Gartrell said.

"Thanks, guys. We appreciate it," Carmody said. Billingsly only nodded stiffly, but McDaniels could almost see the roiling emotion beneath the man's stern demeanor.

"Okay, back to where we were. If aviation's good, then I guess we can move on to other things. But just the same, you saw what happened in Laredo. If you guys need to pull anything else in, then do it soon. Especially spares. I'm an aviator myself, and I'm really worried about spares for your Chinooks. We'll probably be using those things more often than we can plan for right now."

"I think we should probably send a pulse to the AVUM," Billingsly offered.

"Agreed." Carmody pulled out his own iPad and typed a note.

Am I the only Neanderthal without a damned tablet device? McDaniels wondered.

"AVUM is our unit maintenance facility," Billingsly said when Jaworski asked about the acronym.

"Ah, thanks. Again, Major Carmody, I really want you and Mister Billingsly here to go back, talk with the rest of your guys, and figure out what else you'll need. Definitely get more ammunition. From what McDaniels has told me, we'll be going through that like it's water. Hell, even ask for some water, now that I think of it."

Carmody laughed. "We'll do just that, sir."

Jaworski checked his watch. "The rest of the elements will be moving in today. I got word that the Rangers are on a road movement in our direction from Midland, so we should expect them in the next hour or so. Cord, you'll probably want to synch up with their battalion commander and find out what he needs to make his troops fully combat effective. I get the idea that Rangers travel light, correct?"

"Correct, sir. Rangers are the light infantry of the Army special operations community. I'm hoping they at least brought some vehicles with them, but other than that, we've already got everything they need. We just have to secure the post and make it as zed-proof as we possibly can."

"Ah, sirs, I'd like to add something with regards to vehicles and transportation," Gartrell interjected.

Jaworski looked up at him. "Go right ahead, Gartrell. What's on your mind?"

"Humvees, M949 trucks, maybe even HEMTs are not the best things to use for transportation through the zeds," Gartrell said. "On the open road? Sure. But to tell you the truth, when the stenches are in full force, those things are so damned thick that even a Stryker would have trouble getting through them. That was one of our biggest issues in New York, the overland escape. We had a beefy four-wheel drive van, and it still wasn't enough."

"So what are you asking for?" Jaworski asked. "Tanks? Bradleys?"

"MRAPs," Gartrell said.

McDaniels slapped the table. "Damned straight!"

Even Jaworski nodded in appreciation. "Anything that could survive IEDs in Afghanistan and Iraq is probably going to be able to take anything the zeds can throw at it. Which, happily, is mostly just other zeds. But still, those things aren't the most maneuverable things on the market. High off the ground, easy to roll..."

"But even if one did roll over, there's not a great chance the zeds would be able to get inside it," Gartrell said. "Survivability is the key here."

"And it's not like that's an asset that's going to be heavily resourced," McDaniels said. "MRAPs are very specialized. We should be able to get some delivered from Hood, or Carson at the farthest. Good call, Sergeant Major."

"My only job is make officers look more amazing," Gartrell said.

"Keep that up, and we might get out of this yet," Jaworski said. "All right, let's add MRAPs to the list, and anything else you can think of. Let's get it all while the getting's good. What else?"

"How about something a little less pedestrian?" McDaniels looked at the Air Force colonel directly. "The rules of engagement aren't entirely clear."

Jaworski seemed puzzled. "What do you mean? We kill as many zombies as we can if they show up."

"A mass of humanity's going to show up ahead of the zombies, Colonel. We could have thousands of civilians outside this facility, looking for safety. If we don't give it to them, they'll eventually try and get inside any way they can. That's going to put the entire task force and the facility itself at risk. We need clear instructions on how far we take this. We can't build another city out here, and if we could, there's no chance we could fortify it to withstand dedicated assaults from the stenches. Not that we have that circumstance well in hand yet, either. But the time's going to come when we're going to have to face down fellow Americans in extreme danger and either bail them out or turn our backs."

"The ROE's not unclear at all. We defend this facility and hold it at all costs. That's what we were told at the Pentagon, and that's what the operational orders say." Jaworski didn't seem uncomfortable, but something in his eyes told McDaniels different. No one had stopped to think, to *really* think, about the potential toll that might be looming just over the horizon. Everyone had been fixated on stopping the stenches, but no one had taken the time to factor in the human element.

"Colonel ... sir, think about this for just a second. There's a housing development just up the street, on the other side of three eighty-five." McDaniels pointed over Jaworski's shoulder. "A lot of the people who work here live there. Their families are there. How can we expect these people to work and do what we need them to do if their families are food for the zeds?"

"So what are you recommending, Cord? You just said yourself we can't build a big enough facility to house those people."

"We can probably house the families of the employees here, if they want to come inside before the walls go up," McDaniels said. "I'm thinking mission essentials here, sir. We do need to keep the people who we're depending on to come up with Safire's proposed treatment safe, and we need to keep them focused on that, which means we'll need to do something to improve the security of their loved ones. That is something we should plan on doing, which means we'll need to add that to the to-do list and see it actioned. But the bigger question remains—are we going to ask our soldiers and sailors and airmen to open fire on refugees? Because as soon as people figure out there's a sizeable military presence here, they'll come. And we have to prepare ourselves for that."

"And maybe more importantly, we need to prepare ourselves for what's going to happen when some of our troops can't commit to that action." Gartrell's voice was oddly subdued, and he had that semi-haunted look in his eyes that worried McDaniels. "In New York City, it wasn't that tough. We were on the run, and we had to think on our feet. Here, we'll be dealing with a stream of refugees who are desperate, people who will do anything to save themselves or their kids. And some of our troops will help them. Discipline's going to break down, and we all have ringside seats. It's not going to be pretty, Colonel. We can order the troops to deny the civilians access, but some of them won't be able to go along with that, even if they are special operations forces. Look at it this way." Gartrell pointed at McDaniels. "Colonel McDaniels has a son in college in Austin. What if he shows up here? How could McDaniels lead the QRF and not try to save his own son?"

Jaworski looked at McDaniels and shifted in his seat. "Your son is here? In Texas?"

"He is," McDaniels replied.

"Well, I can solve that. Let's get him here. Let's take that circumstance off the table right away."

McDaniels struggled with how to take that offer. If he could get Lenny there with him... "I appreciate that, sir, but it still doesn't really solve our dilemma," McDaniels said, tabling the issue for the moment.

"I know that. Jesus Christ on a rubber fucking crutch!" Jaworski leaned back in his chair and ran his hand over his face. He stared at the display on the wall for a moment, then looked back at McDaniels. "We have to do what we have to do. We can't house a massive displacement of civilians. If they try to get in, we stop them. Passive measures would be best, so we should look into getting some of that stuff here. Tear gas, electric fencing, whatever will work. And if they try to force their way in ... well, we'll have to resort to deadly force. There just isn't another way, unless you guys know something I don't."

"No, sir, I can't think of anything that would be as effective as we need it to be." McDaniels looked at Gartrell, and the sergeant major slowly shook his head. "We just have to be as prepared for that particular shit storm as possible. We'll have the best troops on hand, but..." He shrugged. There just wasn't much more he could say.

Jaworski nodded and checked his watch. "All right. I have to meet with the company CEO and his staff, and I'm sure the Rangers are going to show up any minute. You guys keep doing what you're doing. Cord, you have the authority to requisition anything that we're going to need, so don't wait for me to bless your shopping lists. And I'll seek guidance from the top about what we just discussed. I doubt they'll have anything very helpful to add, but we'll see what they come back with."

9

"Where are we going?" Regina asked Doctor Kersey as soldiers—or airmen, or whatever they were called—pulled the USAMRIID team from the Black Hawk after it had landed.

"Texas," Kersey said. "We're going to join your friend McDaniels and continue to work on the vaccine there. It's the safest place for us to be right now."

"What about the CDC?" Regina pulled abreast of the older woman and matched her long, bounding stride. "They have suitable facilities. Wouldn't it be better for us to relocate there?"

"The Centers for Disease Control isn't any more secure than the Rid was, Doctor Safire. You're right. It would make some sense to go there; after all, they have access to the same systems and technology. But if it should fall, we might not be able to find any transportation out of there. As you can see, things are a bit hectic right now, and this is only the beginning." Kersey weaved around the Air Force base, which was a beehive of activity.

Transport aircraft taxied about and formed long queues for the runways, their big jet engines wailing. But over the din, Regina heard the *crack-crack-crack* of gunfire from the base's perimeter. As the Army Black Hawk lifted off behind them, more helicopters swooped in and landed on the ramp. At the far end of the airfield, even more helicopters descended from the sky, separate from the rest of the pattern. Regina recognized them after a moment. They were the president's helicopters, but instead of just one, there were several and all identical. The choppers landed in an area secured by armed Humvees and other vehicles. Not far from their landing area sat the huge bulk of Air Force One. The president was obviously leaving the chaotic

Washington area, and Regina didn't blame him one bit.

It's all happening so fast.

"Where in Texas are we going? To the pharma facility by Odessa?"

Kersey nodded. She glanced over her shoulder as the gunfire reached a crescendo in the distance.

Regina looked back as well, and for a moment, she was almost overwhelmed by their circumstances, so similar to what she had faced in New York's Central Park only days ago. When McDaniels, Gartrell, and an entire Special Forces team had come to evacuate her and her father before the great metropolis fell to the gathering dead. When her father was still alive.

"There's your plane," one of their military escorts said.

Ahead was a fairly large jet, like one of the business jets her father's company had used. The jet's engines were already running, and a female flight attendant stood at the base of the air stair, watching them approach. She didn't wear a uniform, so Regina supposed the aircraft wasn't operated by the military.

The flight attendant directed them aboard while the two airmen escorting the group of scientists took position on either side of the air stair, their hands on the butts of their pistols. Regina joined the rest of the team as they settled inside the Gulfstream's sumptuously-appointed interior. Kersey buckled herself into one of the seats on the right side of the cabin—what the flight attendant called "the principal's seat"—and Regina took the seat across the aisle from her. As soon as the last person was aboard, a pudgy virologist named Adams, the flight attendant retracted the aircraft's air stair and closed the boarding door. The jet started its taxi before Adams had even made his way to a seat.

Regina looked out the large oval window beside her and watched as a Humvee drew abreast of the Gulfstream G450 and shadowed it. A female trooper stood in the vehicle's gunnery hatch, holding a rifle; another troop sat in the front passenger seat with a rifle across his lap. Regina supposed they were Air

Force personnel since they were on an Air Force base, but she didn't know enough about the military to be sure.

The flight attendant spoke over the cabin address system, just as if they were on a commercial airliner. She explained that the jet would take off as soon as it was cleared to do so, but there was substantial congestion on the ground, which would delay their departure. Also, aircraft were still returning to the base, and those aircraft had to be managed on the ground as well. She promised to update the passengers as more information became available.

"I guess the president isn't really bothered by all the ground traffic," one of the Rid scientists said from the back of the plane.

Regina turned to her right and peered through the window on Kersey's side of the airplane. Air Force One was already accelerating down a runway.

"So much for him being just like us," another researcher said. "There's some change I can believe in."

McDaniels was going over the placement of trenches with Gartrell and the engineers when the first of several M949 six-by-six trucks appeared. The vehicles turned into the InTerGen facility parking lot and, after a brief pause, were waved through the first checkpoint. The trucks continued, then ground to a halt near the Army Corps of Engineers emergency response vehicles.

"Looks like the first of the guns are here," Gartrell said.

"Looks like." As McDaniels spoke, he heard the growing thud of an approaching helicopter. He looked toward the northwest and saw an MH-47 Chinook heading for the landing zone that had been established by the 160th. Behind the first chopper, a second twin-rotored behemoth followed along a quarter mile back. He pointed out the helicopters to Gartrell. "Rangers get bragging rights. They beat the Special Forces guys to the area of operations."

Gartrell grunted. "Well, even mangy dogs have their days."

Major Guardiola looked from the trucks to the helicopters and back again. "Things are starting to get exciting."

"Wait until the zeds show up," McDaniels said.

"I'm hoping to be gone by then, sir."

"Better hope not. By the time you're done here, this is going to be the most heavily fortified installation outside of Cheyenne Mountain."

Guardiola grunted. "We'll do our very best to see that's the case, sir."

McDaniels looked at Gartrell. "Sergeant Major, we should synch up with the Rangers and the SF guys. Any further guidance for Major Guardiola here?"

"If you can't get enough shipping containers, use those sixty-foot trailers." Gartrell pointed at several semi-truck rigs that had been hired to ship goods from Fort Hood to SPARTA. "They're not as strong, but they're the right size, and if we bury their wheels in dirt and maybe fill up the trailers to weigh them down, they might be a suitable replacement."

"We'd already thought of that. We'll have to brace them so we can mount heavy equipment on top of them, such as gun emplacements and the like, but we're thinking it can be done."

"Outstanding, sir."

"Thanks for your help, Major," McDaniels said. "Keep up the good work. You think you'll get most of the trench work done by...?"

"Tomorrow night, Colonel. We've got a contractor on his way here with some heavy equipment to get that started, and at the same time, we'll start that berm."

"Great. Sarmajor, let's go hook up with the Rangers, and then we'll have a quick how-do-you-do with the Special Forces."

"Hooah, sir."

McDaniels headed toward the incoming M949s as the big, dun-colored trucks came to a halt. Soldiers dismounted immediately, leaping from the enclosed beds. The men were armed and wore full battle-rattle. Most carried M4 carbines, but some were outfitted with Mk17 SCARs, a "next generation" assault rifle that had gone through a lengthy acquisition process initiated by Special Operations Command. Initially procured as a replacement for the M4 SOPMOD the rest of the Rangers carried, the Special Operations Forces Combat Assault Rifle— for which the acronym SCAR was the official diminutive— proved to be less than advertised by the time they made it to the actual operators. McDaniels had tested the 5.56 millimeter Mk16 version in Afghanistan and Iraq, and the experience had ensured he would never be a fan of the weapon. The Mk417 was an upgunned version, chambered for 7.62 millimeter rounds, and its reputation was only marginally better than the original offering. But it would be preferable to the M4, which McDaniels had finally had enough of after his last one jammed during an engagement with the dead.

"Gartrell, do you think you can get your hands on some HK416s or 417s?" he asked, as they approached the Rangers.

"I'll add them to the list. But if you're hoping to get enough to replace those SCARs I see up ahead, you can forget it, sir. They're a Tier One weapon with the D-Boys."

McDaniels shook his head. "No, just get three or four if you can. One for me, one for you, and two spares."

"I'll try, sir, but I'm going to hook myself up with another AA-12."

McDaniels grunted. "Good call. Get another one. I might change my mind about the HK later."

"Roger that, Colonel."

Several Rangers broke away from their assembly and marched toward McDaniels, their movements as perfectly synchronized as any machine. The one in the lead was a lieutenant colonel, and McDaniels knew he would be the battalion commander. Since they were the same rank, McDaniels extended his hand as opposed to saluting. "Cord McDaniels."

"Ralph Haley," the Ranger said. "Call me Bull." He was

much shorter than McDaniels, probably only five foot eight or so, but he was built like a linebacker for the Green Bay Packers. His face was vaguely simian, his features blunt and hard, and he walked with what McDaniels thought of as "the Ranger strut," as if he were the undeniable the cock of the walk. His gray eyes were sharp and probing, and his grip was strong. There was no pretense to Lieutenant Colonel Ralph Haley. What you saw was what you got, and that suited McDaniels just fine.

"Good to meet you, Bull. I go by Cord. We've got plenty of GP medium tents that aren't occupied at the moment, so your troops would probably be better off getting set up as soon as possible. We'll be getting more boots in the zone throughout the day, including a detachment from Special Warfare Group One. So if you want to lay claim to some quarters, now's the time to do it."

"Understood. Whereabouts would you recommend?"

McDaniels pointed to a row of tents on the other side of the Corps of Engineers' area. "That row right there would probably be pretty good. It's close to showers and the D-FAC."

"I like the way you think, McDaniels. You're in charge of Hercules?"

"I am."

"Have we ever worked together?" Haley asked.

If they had, only Haley would remember it; black Special Forces officers were a rarity, whereas white officers were the established majority. "You tell me," McDaniels said.

Haley allowed a ghost of smile to cross his face. The expression seemed foreign to him. "I don't think we have. I'm sure I'd remember. Who's the CO?"

"Commanding officer's an Air Force colonel named Jaworski. Seems pretty competent. Super laid back though, and likes to sleep a lot. But other than being well rested, I think he's a sharp one."

"Heh. The zoomies always did have it good. So you mentioned a SEAL detachment is coming in? I guess this is going to be another great exercise in jointness?" The American special operations community was used to interacting with companion units from other services on a fairly regular basis, which made sense. That way, each service could leverage the skills of another service's area of expertise without any undue operational friction.

McDaniels jerked a thumb over his shoulder at the landing Chinooks. "We have a few alpha detachments from Tenth Special Forces dropping in too, to keep the SEALs occupied. I figure between us Green Berets and you Rangers, we should be able to keep the Navy and Air Force in check."

"Roger that." Haley glanced at Gartrell.

"This is Sergeant Major David Gartrell, my senior NCO," McDaniels said.

"Sergeant Major Gartrell," Haley said, returning Gartrell's automatic salute upon being recognized. "Heard you were in New York."

"We were," McDaniels replied. "Gartrell overstayed his welcome by another day, though."

"Is that so, Sergeant Major?"

"That is a fact, sir."

"Huh." Haley looked as close to impressed as he likely ever allowed. "Then I guess the two of you might have some pointers as far as the best way to take down the stenches, if they show up this way."

"We do. And they will," McDaniels said.

"They're moving on San Antonio now," Gartrell added.

"No shit?"

"No shit," McDaniels said. "We just saw the intel a little while ago. A freaking tsunami of dead meat crossed over from Mexico into Laredo." He turned and pointed to the row of antenna-studded trailers near the center of the camp. "See those antennas over there? That's where the TOC is located. Why don't you see to your troops and get them squared away, then meet us with your senior staff over there at"—McDaniels looked at his watch—"ten forty-five hours. Gartrell and I have to welcome the Special Forces and get them situated, as well as take care of some other odds and ends. Colonel Jaworski is meeting with the civilians in the office park, but he'll be back to introduce himself."

"Roger that."

McDaniels shook Haley's hand again. "Welcome to Joint Task Force SPARTA. I hope you brought more ammo than you thought you needed, because when the stenches get here, we couldn't possibly have enough."

"Cheery thought," Haley deadpanned.

10

"Colonel Jaworski? I'm Bob Blye. It's good to meet you," said the short man with the slicked-back hair and deep tan. His accent sounded as though he hailed more from southern California than southwestern Texas. He looked comfortable enough in a yellow Polo shirt, freshly pressed tan slacks, and brown loafers without socks. His handshake was firm, and his blue eyes were piercing, alert.

"Same here. Stas Jaworski, U.S. Air Force. I'm the man in charge of destroying your working lives, as well as your corporate campus." Jaworski wasn't joking. While Blye shook Captain Chase's hand, Jaworski looked around expensive corporate lobby.

"I hope it's not going to be that unpleasant," Blye said. "Let's go up to the conference room. Several people are waiting for us up there. We've also got some coffee and pastries and the like, in case you're hungry." Blye's obsequiousness automatically bugged Jaworski.

"We've already had breakfast, but the coffee's probably better here," he said, though in actuality, the cup he'd had earlier had been pretty damned good.

"Follow me, if you would." As Blye walked to an elevator bank, his loafers clicked on the shiny tile floor. Jaworski and Chase followed, while arriving employees openly stared at them. Most were just curious, but some were some obviously annoyed at the changes occurring.

The conference room was a sumptuous affair befitting a Fortune 100 company in New York as opposed to a pharmaceutical outfit in the Texas desert. Jaworski was motioned to a leather chair, and he slid into its soft embrace.

Coffee, croissants, and breakfast pastries were positioned at various intervals along the table, and Jaworski helped himself to those in front of him. Chase kept his broad hands on the table until Jaworski nudged him and told him it was all right to dig in.

"Folks, this is Colonel Stanislaw Jaworski from the Air Force, and—I'm sorry, your name again?—Captain Chase from the Army," Blye said. "Obviously, the nation is under a severe threat, and Colonel Jaworski is here to tell us what our part in countering this threat will be. Colonel, this is my senior staff, including the company's top researchers and engineers, all of whom are accomplished biochemists, physicians, and clinical researchers. Most of them were hand-picked by Wolf Safire years ago, and they in turn are responsible for assembling some of the very best minds in the pharmaceutical world." Blye waved a hand. "We're here to help you do whatever it is you need to have done. We've already received a preliminary heads-up from Washington and, of course, from Doctor Safire before New York... um... went down."

Jaworski swallowed a bite of pastry. "And I thank you for the invitation. Has your engineering staff been able to go over Safire's formulas?"

"We have, and we received more information from the Army as well. As it turns out, there was already some advanced research available on this particular type of virus."

Jaworski looked at him, surprised. "There was?"

Blye looked around the table for a moment, then back at Jaworski. "I'm sorry. You didn't know about that?"

Jaworski turned to Chase. "Did we know about that, Captain?"

"All I know is that *I* didn't know anything about it, Colonel."

"Consider us ill-informed and please enlighten us," Jaworski said to Blye.

Blye looked nonplussed. "Uh... Andrew, would you be so kind?"

"Of course." An overweight man seated at the far end of the table leaned forward slightly. His dark brown hair was thinning, and his round face was partially hidden behind a full beard. Unlike the others in the conference room, he wore a suit and tie. "Colonel, my name is Andrew Kerr. I'm with an organization out of Los Angeles, and I'm the individual who did the earliest assessment of RMA."

"RMA," Jaworski said. "The name Safire gave to the virus, right?"

Kerr smiled. "Wolf wasn't that original, actually. I'm the one who named the virus, though a slightly different variety."

Jaworski was gobsmacked. "You mean there's *another* version of this virus?"

"A *related* version. A precursor, if you will. The Soviets apparently modeled this version—which is now known as RMA 2, but the way—after the first. They substituted a different protein, one that was apparently synthesized in a lab somewhere, but the final effects are somewhat related."

"And just how long ago did you identify...?"

"What's now called RMA 1? I'm afraid that's classified." The big man's attitude and demeanor were passive, and Jaworski didn't sense he was the kind of man to play a bunch of silly power games.

"Does anyone else in this room know the specifics of your past research?" Jaworski asked.

"They do not," Kerr said. "As I said, it's classified information, and I haven't been cleared to disclose anything further."

"Classified by whom, sir?" Captain Chase asked.

"The Department of Defense, Captain." Kerr looked back at Jaworski. "At any rate, Colonel, my findings aren't specifically relevant to what we're facing here. If they were, you would know about them. I only mentioned it to ensure you and everyone else that Wolf's findings have been corroborated and vetted as much as possible."

"Okay. Thanks for that." Jaworski leaned back in his chair and regarded the pastry selection. He was no longer hungry. "Is there anything else related to that topic?"

"I think we're good on that," Blye said. "I think we'd all feel better if you were to give us a rundown on the situation, Colonel. Can you do that?"

"Certainly. As you might have noticed, your office park and manufacturing compound is in the process of being hardened against possible necromorph attack." Jaworski pulled his secure iPad from one of the pockets on his BDUs and placed it on the table. As it was outfitted with a privacy screen, he went ahead and switched it on so he could pay attention to any alerts that might be flashed to him from the TOC. "This is going to take several days, maybe even several weeks. I'm sorry, but it's going to be extremely intrusive. We'll be doing a lot of work, and almost all of it will impact access to the facilities. We're starting by digging a series of defensive trenches and using the soil to stand up several tall earth berms, on top of which we'll add additional security structures. More troops and engineers will be arriving from several services, and by the time we're done, there will be over five hundred soldiers, sailors, airmen, and contractors onsite. I realize this is going to be a huge imposition, but the government has identified this facility as a national asset. As such, Joint Task Force SPARTA is designed to protect it."

Blye held up a hand. "Colonel, we've all seen the news. We know what's going down, we know what's happened to Europe, and we know what's happening on the east coast. If you have to tear up every bush, tree, and parking lot to keep those things at bay, then you have my blessing. I'll even pick up a shovel and help. But I saw on the news today that they're in Texas now, down in Laredo. That's not exactly right next door, but it's a lot closer than New York."

Jaworski nodded. "That's true. We expect them to continue moving northward. I don't have any real information on those developments, but I would expect communities in their path will be evacuated to the north, where it's a bit safer."

"Colonel, *San Antonio* is in their path," Blye said. "Do you mean to tell me the authorities will evacuate an entire city?"

"I don't know what they plan to do, Mister Blye. All I know is they probably have two choices—leave, or barricade the place and stay. Which one they'll choose, I don't know, but we can expect substantial refugee traffic headed this way over the next couple of days. And that's one of the things I want to talk to you folks about. Do most of your employees live nearby?"

"Yes, of course. Almost everyone lives in Odessa. I know it looks remote from where you might be concerned, but Odessa is just a few miles up South Grant Avenue." The executive pointed out the window toward the four lanes of regional highway bordering the office park. "Why do you ask? Are our families in immediate danger?"

"No. Not yet. But you should plan on danger coming our way, sooner rather than later," Jaworski said. "I and the rest of the task force senior staff were wondering if it might make more sense to relocate your families here in the near future, provided they don't elect the leave the area, which might be the wisest choice. Obviously, you all have a lot of important work to do, and if the necromorphs arrive in force... well, I wouldn't want to be worrying about my immediate family if I had to concentrate on what I was doing."

Blye nodded. "I see what you mean."

"If dependents do decide to come inside, we'll assist you in any way we can in that," Jaworski said. "We're obviously very focused on hardening the site, making it as inaccessible as possible while we constitute our forces. So moving your families in isn't our number one priority right now, nor is it likely to be. But it is an option you might want to offer your employees. And it would be good to get me the number of potential dependents so we can start ramping up the logistics. Of course, all those people will need to be housed and fed. Even though the office park seems pretty well appointed from what little I've seen, I'm sure it wasn't built to support several hundred people twenty-four-seven without a little help."

"No, it wasn't. We have some excess space available, but not enough to accommodate the numbers we're probably going to see." Blye looked down the table at an older man with deeply tanned skin and a face that had seen more than its share of the hot Texas sun. "Ed, what do you think?"

"Personally? I think we're gonna get wallered down somethin' fierce." Ed's accent was Texas. "If'n the colonel there says we should think about gettin' our kin inside whatever walls he's gonna throw up 'round the place, we'd better get on that. Colonel, I'm Ed Wallace. I'm the facility manager here. I've already met the engineers, but you and I haven't had the pleasure yet."

"Well, we can consider that done now," Jaworski said. "Good to make your acquaintance, Mister—"

"Pardon me for interruptin', but it'd be better if you were to just call me Ed, Colonel."

"Ed it is. Anyway, if you can maybe take some time to talk to Major Guardiola—he's the head engineer—and Captain Chase here, we could probably start getting some kind of action plan put together. Like I said, we can't start paying full attention to relocating folks just yet, but it is an action item."

"Will do." Wallace looked back at Blye. "In the meantime, Bob, I'm going to start sending some of the boys into town to bring back some extra helpings of everything we can get our hands on. Food, water, all kinds of consumables. We'll start a stockpile in the basement, if you'll authorize the expenditures."

"Let's get a list together first," Blye said. "I'm sure you know what you're doing, but we can't just start buying up half of Odessa."

"Not so sure waitin's gonna be a good thing to do," Wallace said. "We're not the only people to think of this, and a lot of folks in town have probably already noticed Colonel Jaworski's people passing through and settin' up camp here. I'd imagine a sudden military buildup is going to make some people nervous, and they'll start buying up whatever they think they might need while we dicker back and forth about it here."

Jaworski fought to keep a smile from breaking out across his face. *This is one old cuss who has his head screwed on straight.* "Mister Wallace—sorry, Ed—probably has it right, Mister Blye. If you folks intend to start collecting an inventory of supplies, I wouldn't wait long. Buy as many perishable food items as you can and plan on eating those first, then move through the non-perishables. Buy batteries, propane, gasoline, flashlights. Hell, this is Texas, buy up all the guns and ammo you can, too."

Blye seemed overwhelmed by the turn in the conversation. "I-I'm sorry Colonel, but are we *really* at that point now? That we should start buying *guns* and bring them here? This office park is a designated gun-free zone—"

"Aw, like hell it is," Wallace threw in.

"—and I'm not sure the majority of our employees would feel safe if we, and by we, I mean the management, were to start stockpiling *weapons* on the premises—"

Jaworski raised his hand. "Whatever, Mister Blye. It doesn't necessarily matter to me. It was just a suggestion. But I wouldn't pass up the opportunity to protect myself, if I were you. You can never be too safe in these kinds of circumstances. But all of that aside, start planning to be cut off for the long haul. Communicate this to your employees, and come up with a plan that will allow everyone to relocate here in the event of an emergency. These zombie things, they tend to infest an area very quickly, so the more prepared everyone is, the better off they'll be. But this is up to you folks to decide. We'll support you in any way we can, but it's your call. You know what the government is looking for you to do, so that's got to be your focus. You have to develop whatever treatment Safire came up with, and then manufacture it in great enough numbers so we can start shipping it around the country."

"Yes, we get that," Blye said.

"Glad to hear it. Can I get a list of critical staff members who will be responsible for this effort?" Jaworski asked. "I don't care what their position is inside the company, but I want the names of anyone and everyone who will have a hand in the development, manufacture, and shipping of this drug."

"That's likely to be a long list," Blye said. "Why do you need it?"

"Because I need to know who's essential staff and who isn't. I need to know who's actually responsible for doing what we need to have done. And I'll want that list as soon as possible."

Bly gestured toward a Hispanic woman at the end of the table. "Geraldine? Can HR pull that information together?"

The portly woman pushed oversized glasses up on her broad nose. She didn't look at Jaworski or Chase when she spoke, but there was a substantial amount of disdain in her voice. "That's asking a lot, Bob. I'm thinking we would need to do a policy review before we can hand over a list like that. Normally, we don't share the personal information of our employees without it being thoroughly vetted. And Legal would have to weigh in on that, right, Malcom?"

She looked at a skinny black man sitting two chairs away. He looked at the Blackberry in his hands. "That's usually how we do it, yeah," he said, but there wasn't a lot of conviction in his voice.

Jaworski sighed. "Look, folks, the reason behind the request should be glaringly obvious. These folks are essential to completing the mission, and I need to know who they are. It's pretty simple."

"It might be simple for you, Colonel, but it's not as black-and-white for us," Geraldine said. "We have to be cautious about compromising the privacy of our empl—"

"Then let me make this real easy," Jaworski said. "No one leaves the office park until I get that list. I'll seal up the office park tighter than a bullfrog's ass, and no one will leave here until

I get what I need. And when do I need it? By five o'clock this evening, just in case anyone was curious."

Geraldine's eyes widened behind her big glasses. "You can't be serious!"

"Oh, I'm entirely serious. I realize I come across as a real laid-back kind of guy, but the truth of the matter is, I don't care about your corporate policies. The government doesn't care about your policies. The president of the United States, wherever he is at the moment, doesn't give a rat's ass about your policies, either. I want to know who these people are because they're vital assets, and if you don't tell me, I'll find out through other means." Jaworski held up a finger when Geraldine looked as though she would interrupt. "You can bitch all you want, but there's a new sheriff in town. And besides that, it's usually wise to listen to the guy with all the guns."

"Was that a *threat?*" Geraldine shrieked.

"Colonel, maybe you should let her go," Ed Wallace said. The skin around his eyes was deeply crinkled from his broad grin. "And maybe once you do that, you shouldn't let her come back."

"That's enough," Blye said. There was no humor in his voice. "Geraldine, you'll do what Colonel Jaworski has requested, and deliver that list to him no later than five this evening. All of the department heads will do whatever they need to in order to ensure that list is compiled properly and disseminated on schedule. There will be no delay in this. And Geraldine? This is a national emergency, and InTerGen has been identified as the only resource available to do what is necessary to save our country. I very much anticipate from this moment forward you will keep that at the front of your mind."

There was no misinterpreting what Blye's true meaning was, and the heavyset woman nodded instantly. "Of course, Bob. I'm sorry if I was being difficult."

Blye looked back at Jaworski. "Colonel, do you need anything else from us?"

"Not especially. Just keep things cool, and give us the latitude to do what we need to do. Parking is going to be a big problem for your folks since we're going to be taking up a lot of space with our own gear. We'll try and keep out of your way as much as we possibly can, but we already know that's not going to work to everyone's satisfaction. All I can ask is that your people try to stay out of the way, and listen to the engineers and other personnel when they give instructions. Things are difficult enough, and are likely to get even more so in the near future. We don't want any accidents."

"I'll pass on the word. What else?"

Jaworski was about to answer when his iPad emitted a ping sound. Chase's did as well, and both men consulted their devices immediately. Jaworski read the message that he been transmitted to him, then looked at Chase. The hulking captain sighed and leaned back in his chair. It creaked slightly beneath his weight.

"Is something wrong?" Blye asked.

"USAMRIID has been compromised." Andrew Kerr looked up from his Blackberry at Jaworski. "A good portion of the RMA 2 threat team made it out, but several did not. Most notably, Colonel Roland Jeffries, the Institute's commander." Kerr pursed his lips and put the Blackberry back in his jacket pocket. He spread his large hands on the conference table's immaculately lacquered surface and stared at them for a long moment.

"Did you know him?" Jaworski asked.

Kerr nodded. "A friend and colleague for many years."

"Ah. Sorry to hear that. My condolences."

Kerr sighed. "I'm no stranger to this kind of thing, Colonel, but thank you."

Jaworski glanced down at his iPad, then looked back at Blye. "Doctor Kerr is right; the Rid has fallen. The remaining members of Jeffries's team are headed this way. So is Safire's daughter, if that makes any difference."

"Ah, Regina. Yes, we know her, and she's welcome here," Blye said. "Is there anything else?"

Jaworski thought about it for a moment, then shook his head. "Not really. We all know where things are headed, so let's concentrate on working together to make sure we get along as well as we can. Sorry for busting balls over that personnel list, but I don't have a lot of time to dance around right now. And neither do you." He nodded toward Ed Wallace. "My two cents? I'd listen to what Ed there was talking about earlier. Start stocking up. It might be a very long winter."

11

By the time McDaniels and Gartrell made it to the north parking lot, the two MH-47G Chinooks had already landed, with wheels chocked and rotors halted. Dozens of troops exited each aircraft, all of them loaded for bear. Several Enduro-type motorcycles and four-wheel all-terrain vehicles were offloaded as well, and the soldiers assembled in a loose group some distance away from the helicopters. McDaniels was sweating in the rising dry heat of the Texas desert; what had been a pleasant early morning had been assassinated by a grueling midmorning sun. McDaniels missed the chill of the evening, and was glad he wasn't fully manned up. Lugging around an ALICE backpack in that kind of heat would be murder without a CamelBak to drink from.

If the rest of the Special Forces soldiers standing in the parking lot were bothered by the heat, they didn't let it show. Each man wore complete battle rattle, including weapons, CamelBak hydration systems, and whatever specialized gear their military occupational specialties dictated they carry. McDaniels looked from face to face and found he knew a few of them.

"I see Barney Rubble," Gartrell said. "And over there next to the last dirt bike, that's Dusty Roads."

"And there's Switchblade. He led Texas Eleven back in the day. Think he's feeling the heavy irony of his circumstances now?"

Gartrell grunted. "He should be thrilled to see you're an O-5 and have angel's wings while he's still an O-4. Mind if I watch you rub it in?"

"I'll be gentle about it."

"No need to dilute your efforts on my account, Colonel. I

can take it."

"You don't like Switchie, Sarmajor?"

"The Switch and I got along all right, sir. Unlike you and me."

McDaniels glanced at Gartrell as they marched through the bright sunlight. Gartrell kept his eyes focused on the growing group of Special Forces soldiers ahead, and if he noticed McDaniels looking at him, he didn't allow it to show.

The soldiers came to attention when they saw McDaniels's rank. Major Dale Lewis, better known as Switchblade due to his rail-thin physique and the ability to spring to his feet in one motion even while lying flat on his back, saluted McDaniels. "Sir, Operational Detachments Alpha Zero-Two-Two, Zero-Three-One, Zero-Three-Four, Zero-Three-Five, Zero-Four-Seven, Zero-Six-Five, Zero-Seven-Four, and Zero-Nine-Four reporting as ordered."

McDaniels returned the salute with a smile. "Damn, Switch, how long did it take you to memorize every detachment designation?"

"The helicopters flew real slow so I could get that under control, sir. Congratulations on the promotion."

"Thanks, Switch. I take it you're the senior officer here? The designated cat-herder?"

"Yes, sir, I am the designated adult."

"Outstanding. You might remember Dave Gartrell?"

Switch looked at Gartrell. "Hello, Sergeant Major. I see you got a nice nod as well. Shoot, if I'd known they were handing out promotions to go to New York, I would've volunteered. I'd be a damned brigadier general by now."

"I believe the younger generation would spell out L-O-L at that one, sir," Gartrell said.

McDaniels looked at the assembled Special Forces troops, nodding to the few he knew. "Dusty, how's it going? Barney! How's Betty?" he asked a short, broad-shouldered man with a big nose and a burgeoning double-chin.

The Special Forces weapons sergeant patted his sniper rifle. "She's doing just fine, sir."

"Glad to hear it. Switch, what's the composition of this element? I was told I'd be getting six alpha dets, but it looks like it got plussed up somewhere along the line. I'm seeing too many faces for the spaces."

"And you did get six ODAs, sir. You also were bequeathed myself and the bravo detachment I command to help you run the teams."

"Ah. Understood. All right, we've got an entire Ranger battalion on post already, and we're going to get a detachment from SEAL Team One any minute now. Once they're here, we'll be sitting down and talking about who's going to do what. I've got overall command of the QRF, which you guys will be part of, and I'm thinking the Ranger battalion commander is going to be the next in the chain of command. Questions?"

"Not at the moment, sir. Will there be a PowerPoint presentation?" As Switch said this, there were some guffaws from the SF grunts. McDaniels felt a flush of embarrassment. Switch's comment was obviously aimed at McDaniels's previous position as a staff member with the U.S. Army Special Operations Command's operations directorate, with whom he had been tasked to oversee PowerPoint presentations as part of his duties.

"There will not be, but if we do need one, I know who to turn to. Anything else?" McDaniels kept his voice as friendly and jocular as he could.

"No, sir. Was just kidding sir. Didn't mean to take a swipe."

"No problem, Major. Forget it. All right, let's get everyone over to the tent city and figure out where you're going to go. Rangers got here first, so they got the good seats. We'd better get you guys squared away before the Navy shows up."

"Hooah, sir!"

With the entire Padre Island National Seashore ordered closed to the public, the few park rangers on post had the rather dubious duty of driving down the park's one hundred nineteen mile length to shoo away the campers, who either hadn't heard the broadcasts or had elected to ignore them. Only three rangers were on duty, so that meant someone had to stay behind and turn away any people who might be tempted to take a walk along the shore. The rangers drew straws for it, and Bill Harrington, a silver-haired sixty-year-old with watery eyes shielded behind wire-rimmed glasses, had been the lucky winner. Harrington would stay behind and keep an eye out on the park's entrance, while Harlie Yates and Jessica Shaver took the F-150 SuperCrew down the beach.

Harrington felt guilty about pulling the winning straw, and he'd tried to trade with one of the women, but they had declined. Fair was fair, and the truth was, they didn't really want to deal with any clueless members of the public anyway. If they were dumb enough to come to the park after it was officially closed, then they'd probably try and bull their way inside by throwing around whatever weight they might have, and who wanted to deal with that?

Not that the campers are going to be any easier to handle, Harlie thought as she followed the broad-bottomed Jessica Shaver to the pickup. Jessica fairly waddled when she walked, and that was on the asphalt; on the white, sandy beaches of Padre Island, she could barely do even that. Where Harlie was short and slender, Jessica was almost six feet tall and probably close to two hundred and eighty pounds. Harlie wondered how far she was from that fatal stroke or coronary, and when it struck, would a beef brisket sandwich be found clutched in one hand?

Try to be a little more charitable, Harlie, she chided herself. *Just a little more, if you can stand it.*

The two women climbed into the truck, Jessica behind the wheel, Harlie riding shotgun figuratively as well as literally. While the rangers were not usually armed in public, these were unusual times, and the fall of Laredo had been all over the news. The Coast Guard and Navy were patrolling offshore, their ships in sight of the two rangers as they headed south down the island. There was talk of National Guard or regular Army soldiers augmenting the rangers, but so far, no units had materialized. Until that happened, the rangers were to keep close to their vehicles and keep their firearms on their persons at all times. The word had already gone out that the zeds could only be taken down by a direct shot to the head, something that Hollywood made look easy, but in real life was pretty darned difficult under most conditions. So Jessica drove because Harlie was a much better shot. Even though both women had marksman badges, Harlie was a dozen times more proficient with the M16.

"I'll do the drivin' and you do the shootin'," Jessica told Harlie.

"No problem." Harlie had the M16 slung over her shoulder and a .40 caliber Glock 23 on her belt.

Jessica wore her own pistol as well. They had left the shotgun with Harrington since he would be solo until their supervisor arrived from Austin, where he'd been visiting family. At least with the shotgun, Harrington had a chance of being able to deal with whatever might pop up, like a zombie trying to break into the ranger station to eat him.

They passed several vehicles on their way out of the park. No one flagged down the marked pickup truck, so it seemed these folks were in a righteous hurry to get the heck out of Dodge. Jessica reported the traffic back to Harrington over the radio and drove on, dropping the truck into four-wheel drive when the sand became looser. In the pickup's bed, several planks rattled. If the truck managed to get stuck, they would use the planks to free it.

The breeze was a constant refresher, rolling in off the green waters of the Gulf of Mexico, and there wasn't much seaweed despoiling the white, sandy beaches. Nor was there much oil either, which was always a welcome circumstance, though

Harlie figured the oil was preferable to the occasional swarms of Portuguese man o' war jellyfish that oftentimes washed ashore. While she'd never been stung by one, she had seen the effects of those who had stepped on tentacles with bare feet. The result of several hundred poisonous triggers injecting their payloads into human flesh was never a good thing.

After twenty or so miles into the four-wheel drive portion of the beach—only the first eight or so miles of beach were specifically tended to so passenger cars could get in and out—they came upon their first campers. The people were packing, but moving at a snail's pace. When Jessica braked to a halt beside the red shell tent and two ATVs, the deeply tanned young man and woman looked at them with desultory eyes. A pair of boogie boards were already strapped to each ATV.

"I know what you're gonna say," the man said as soon as Harlie rolled down the window. "We're already getting ready to move out." He wore red board shorts and no shirt.

"We're sorry about this," Harlie said, "but it's for your own good. There really isn't much protection if those things make it up here."

"Well, it's not like they can swim or anything," the man groused. His long red hair flew around his face in the stiff offshore breeze.

"We don't know about that," Jessica replied. "You do yourselves a favor and maybe move a little bit faster, all right? The park's been closed for hours."

"We only heard about it from some other campers who were leaving," the girl said. She wore cut-offs and a halter-top that showed plenty of cleavage. A red bandana was tied around her head, keeping her raven hair mostly in place. With the bandana and deep tan, she looked like an Indian squaw from a cheap 1970s television movie.

"That's all right, just so long as you're going to head out. Really, it's for your own good. And don't stop anywhere on the island. Keep going until you get to Corpus," Jessica said. Corpus

Christi was the nearest city, and it was already under a growing guard. The local police had all been called to duty, and the Navy and Army had contributed personnel to assist with securing the city. That was one good thing about being a military town, Harlie thought. There was always some muscle to be had from the government when things began to get a little wobbly.

"Yeah, well, we have to stop at the main lot to get my truck and load up the ATVs onto the trailer." The man favored her with a frosty glower.

"That's fine," Harlie said before Jessica could give him what-for over his pissy attitude. "You can get your truck. But keep going until you're across the bridge and in Corpus. It's not safe anywhere on Padre, and there's a mandatory evacuation for both north and south Padre anyway. Stop if you need gas or something, but otherwise, keep moving. And you might want to put some elbow grease into it. This is the real deal. Pack up and leave, folks."

The man sneered, but his companion put a hand on his shoulder. She nodded to the rangers and favored them with a thin smile. "We will," she promised. "Let's get the tent packed up, Roddie."

"Yeah, yeah."

"Thanks, and have a good day," Harlie said.

The man grunted and turned away from the truck, shuffling toward the tent. The girl waved and went to join him.

Jessica took her foot off the brake and slowly accelerated. "Well, wasn't *he* just a breath of fresh air?"

"Their vacation's ruined," Harlie said. "They don't look like they're from around here, so it's probably not like they have lots of opportunities to enjoy camping on the beach."

Jessica harrumphed and drove on. They passed more vehicles heading north, and while some folks waved—"*They* must be locals," Jessica said—most simply stared as they passed. They encountered some more tardy campers, including one family who hadn't heard anything about the park being closed, but had wondered about the sudden migration from the south. They'd spent most of the time fishing in the surf, and just watched the collection of four-wheel drive vehicles drive past their 1980s-vintage Chevy Suburban. Harlie urged them to leave as soon as they possibly could, and the family agreed. As they pulled away, the campers began to break down their two tents and pack up their belongings. Unlike the younger couple, they moved with alacrity.

The F-150 rolled further down the beach, its tires spinning every now and then whenever it hit a patch of unusually soft sand. Harrington reported in twice, confirming that beachcombers and campers were in fact fleeing the park. He asked how things were going, and Harlie told him everything so far had been a cakewalk.

"Hey, did a guy with long red hair and a girl come by on two ATVs?" she asked him.

"Roger, they came through about five minutes ago. As a matter of fact, they just got their truck trailer loaded up with their ATVs, over."

"Great, just checking on them. Over."

Fifty-four miles down the beach, they came across an old International Harvester Scout II sitting on the beach. The passenger door was open, and the vehicle's tailgate was up. As the F-150 drew near, Harlie leaned forward in her seat and looked at the battered four-wheel drive utility vehicle. It had Texas plates and a Padre sticker, so whoever drove it was a local. It looked as if the campsite around the vehicle was in the process of being broken down, but there was no one in sight.

"Well, ain't this a little odd," Jessica said. She continued driving toward the solitary vehicle, but took her foot off the accelerator. The F-150 slowed quickly in the sand.

Harlie pulled the M16 toward her and put on her wide-brim hat when the truck finally drifted to a halt about forty feet from the Scout. "I don't see anybody around," she said. "Let me get out and check around. Stay here. If you see anything fishy, lean on the horn."

"Uh, hold on now," Jessica said. "I'm technically the senior ranger here—"

Harlie laughed and flicked a strand of straw-blond hair from her eyes. "But if something goes down, which one of us can run back to the truck faster?"

"Good point," Jessica said. "So I'll just sit here in the truck and keep a watch on things."

"Cool." Harlie unfastened her seat belt and threw open the F-150's passenger door. The wind was constant, moving across the beach at around eight knots or so, a relatively stiff breeze, and it carried with it spray and salt from the surf, which she tasted immediately.

Harlie closed the door behind her and turned a full 360 degrees, the M16 in her hands. She walked around the idling truck, looking toward the surf, then back at the dunes that faced the Gulf. There was no sign of life beyond a gaggle of seagulls floating overhead. Harlie slung the rifle over her shoulder and walked toward the Scout. The vehicle had a sizeable lift kit installed and large, knobbed tires. It was painted black over primer, and the chrome work fairly gleamed in the sunlight; apparently, the vehicle's owner was restoring it. Since she was something of a truck girl herself, Harlie allowed herself a moment to examine the Scout with a critical eye. Through the open passenger door, she saw the interior of the vehicle was still ratty and unrefined, with torn seating that exposed yellow-orange foam. Continuing to move around the vehicle, she came to the open tailgate. A tent had been hastily shoved inside, and it hadn't been properly collapsed; one long swatch of weatherproofed fabric streamed out of the Scout and whipped and snapped in the wind. A plastic bottle of juice lay in the sand, and half its contents had spilled from its open mouth. The fluid spill was still vaguely damp. Two polyester and canvas camping chairs sat nearby. One of them had been folded neatly, but the other lay on its side. The heel of a pink flip-flop peered out from beneath the fallen chair.

Harlie felt something tickle the back of her neck, and she did another 360 degree turn. She spotted vague, almost indistinct footprints in the sand, several of them, emerging from the waterline and advancing toward the camp. She turned toward the dunes and saw two sets of tracks heading off into them. Looking down, Harlie saw the prints were all around the Scout. And they continued on into the dunes in erratic, unusual tacks.

Harlie adjusted her sunglasses and looked back at the F-150. Jessica watched her from behind the wheel, eyes unreadable behind her own sunglasses. Turning back to the rise of dunes, Harlie contemplated what she would do next. *Something* had obviously happened, but exactly what, she wasn't sure.

Overhead, the gulls continued to hover and squawk. Harlie looked up at them aimlessly for a moment, and noticed they were slowly sliding into position over the dunes. Harlie pulled the M16 off her shoulder and flipped off the safety. Glancing back at the F-150, she pointed toward the dunes, then marched that way. She heard the F-150 trundle forward, and a glance over her shoulder confirmed it stopped just short of the abandoned Scout.

The gulls became excited, honking back and forth to each other as they bobbed up and down in the breeze. Firming her grip on the M16, she powered herself up the face of the dune and slowly, *very* slowly, crested it. Without realizing it, she had brought the M16 to her shoulder. The gulls cried louder overhead as Harlie stepped across the dune's soft summit and peered into the trough on the other side.

A half-dozen shapes moved, gray shapes dotted with splashes of dark red. More red was spattered across the back of the dune. Harlie saw what looked to be a dismembered, disemboweled corpse at the bottom of the trough. It had been an older man, and the corpse's eyes stared up at her without seeing. Then, the eyes moved, and the head tilted to one side. Its dead gaze suddenly locked with hers, and it opened its mouth. With no diaphragm, it couldn't take any air into its lungs, so it just opened and closed its mouth. Even then, it took Harlie several seconds to process exactly what she was seeing. The rest of the figures surrounding the corpse were hunched over its remains, and those of a second corpse—what had been a fleshy woman who lay facedown in the sand. The woman's buttocks and thighs were almost completely *gone*, and the sand beneath her was stained the color of rust. The corpse suddenly twitched and shuddered, as if someone had just flipped a switch and turned it on.

One of the figures crouched over the remains of the man looked up. When its flat, lifeless, opaque eyes met hers, Harlie suddenly figured everything out.

Oh, my God, they're zombies!

Before the zombie released its first moan, the F-150's horn blared, long and loud. The rest of the zombies took notice, rising off their haunches and turning to look up at Harlie. Harlie shot one through the head, then another, and another. Behind her, the F-150's horn blared in strident tones. As the zombies below moaned and reached for her, she turned and ran back toward the beach.

Dozens of zombies were emerging from the Gulf, their gray, bloodless bodies glistening grotesquely in the bright sunlight. Even though the water was only up to their knees, they stumbled in the vigorous surf, and several of them went down, victims of the undertow. It was a horrifying sight, eliciting in Harlie a deep-seated terror she'd never known was possible. They were still well over a hundred feet out—the shelf of the Gulf of Mexico extended for a thousand feet at a very minor angle before suddenly deepening, one reason the undertow was so strong along Padre Island. Farther out, she saw heads breaking through the water's surface as more of the dead moved to the shore. *Hundreds* of heads bobbed up and down in the surf.

Oh, dear sweet Jesus—

Jessica kept leaning on the horn, and behind her, Harlie

heard a body fall to the sand. She didn't look back, she just sprinted for the F-150 as Jessica goosed the accelerator and brought it closer to her, its tires spinning for a moment, sending up a rooster tail of sand before they found purchase. Harlie reached for the door handle as Jessica screamed from inside the cab; she saw a spray of spittle fly from the heavier woman's mouth.

"Behind you!"

Harlie ducked to her left, and a bloodied zombie slammed into the side of the pickup with a grunt. Its head rebounded off the passenger door window, and it stumbled backward as it reached out for her. Its fingertips grazed the sleeve of Harlie's uniform blouse, leaving a small trail of sand-crusted blood on the fabric. Harlie backpedaled and raised the rifle as the ghoul steadied itself and came at her again. Its lips and chin were smeared with a heavy slick of dark blood, and when it opened its mouth, she glimpsed shreds of meat clinging to its teeth. The rest of the corpses tumbled and staggered down the dune, moaning above the constant rumble of the wind and surf. Harlie fired one round directly into the zombie's face, driving it back. When it didn't go down, she fired again, and the bullet slammed directly into its forehead. The zombie collapsed to the beach instantly, a thick ribbon of black-gray ichor funneling from its ravaged skull. Harlie pulled open the door and leaped into the F-150's passenger seat.

"Drive!" she shouted as she slammed the door. The F-150's engine revved, and its tires spun as it accelerated, weaving slightly in the sand. Most of the zombies moved slowly, barely shambling forward at a fast walk, but a few of them were fast. One of them jumped into the pickup's bed as the truck sped away, leaving the others behind.

"One of them is in the bed of the truck!" Harlie turned and tried to get the M16 oriented on the figure that hauled itself into a sitting position just on the other side of the F-150's rear window. The ghoul showed no fear, lurching forward and slamming its face against the tempered glass as it released a long, quivering moan. It slammed its fists into the glass, ignoring the fact that it was splitting open the skin across its knuckles.

"Hold on!" Jessica said, and she violently cranked the steering wheel back and forth. The pickup careened from side to side across the beach, and the zombie flew into the sides of the bed with great force. After a few evolutions, it was unceremoniously ejected, and it tumbled across the beach in an explosion of sand.

"That did it," Harlie said. "It's gone!"

Jessica was breathing heavily, and her face was flushed. She spoke between gasps. "We gotta go back. We gotta go back *through* those things to get back to Bill!"

"It's all right," Harlie said. "Most of them are dead slow. We can get past them, and if any of them get in our way and we can't avoid them, run them over!"

"More of 'em comin' out of the Gulf," Jessica reported. Fear was making her south Texas accent even heavier than usual. "Jesus! Lookit 'em all!"

Harlie saw. Dozens of zombies waded to the shore, trailing thick ribbons of seaweed as they stepped from the foaming surf. She'd grown up a Corpus Christi girl. The warm waters of the Gulf of Mexico had never been something to fear, even when the jellyfish were thick and the hammerhead sharks schooled right offshore. But the entire Gulf had become a doorway to Hell, transporting flesh-eating fiends to the bright, sandy beaches of Padre Island.

"Turn around, Jessie. We have to get back. We can't keep going in this direction." As she spoke, she saw a cluster of zombies a quarter of a mile down the beach swarming another campsite. She was too far away to make out exactly what was happening, but Harlie knew. The ghouls were feeding.

Jessica slowed the F-150 and brought it into a quick turn. Several zombies tried to catch it, but they were too far away. Even the fastest ones couldn't cover the distance as the truck sped away.

"You good to drive?" Harlie asked.

Jessica was sweating, and there was wide-eyed panic in her eyes. Not that Harlie thought she looked any better. She slipped on her seat belt and secured the M16. She didn't have to worry about the doors; they had locked automatically once the truck accelerated past ten miles per hour. Just the same, she hit the lock button anyway.

"I'm good," Jessica said. "Call Bill. Tell him what's happenin'. These things might be headin' for him right now."

Harlie picked up the radio handset and got in touch with Harrington as Jessica weaved the pickup around groups of zombies. The vehicle bounced once as one of the ghouls went down right in front of it. Jessica swore as the truck fishtailed in the sand despite the four-wheel drive being engaged.

"Are you girls joking?" Harrington asked over the radio after Harlie reported what was going on.

"It's no joke, Bill. You'd better get ready to go. Call the police, and keep that shotgun with you. We're on our way out, but maybe you shouldn't wait for us. Over."

"Ah, I think we're all—holy *shit!*" Harrington's voice cut off abruptly, and Harlie exchanged a nervous look with Jessica.

"Call 9-1-1, Harlie," Jessica said. She slalomed the F-150 through another gaggle of wet, shambling dead and then accelerated forward. The beach ahead was clear... for the moment.

"But what about Bill?" she asked.

"Sounds like he's got problems of his own." Clear of the zombies, Jessica sounded more in control, and she was breathing more normally. "Make the call, Harlie."

Harlie dropped the handset and pulled out her cell phone. The display only showed two bars of service, but that was all she needed. She got through to a harried-sounding operator, and she reported what had just happened. She added that there might be a problem at the park entrance, and briefly recounted the truncated discussion she'd had with Harrington. The operator didn't ask many questions, and told Harlie that police support would be at the park entrance as soon as possible.

"How long will it take?" Harlie asked.

"I don't know, ma'am," was the answer.

Harlie hung up, and just as she did, the radio crackled back to life.

"Sorry, guys. I had a bit of a problem here," Harrington said.

Harlie snatched up the microphone. "Bill! What happened? Over."

"Somebody came by who was bit," Harrington replied. "And then he died. And then he got up, but he was still dead. I had to put him down. I'm taking a handie-talkie with me and leaving the shack. There are still people coming out, but I'm going to go for my car. Over."

"Good idea," Jessica said.

Harlie nodded and depressed the *Talk* button. "Bill, roger that you're leaving the shack. Be careful, and if something goes down, just leave right away. We already called the police. Over."

"Roger, Harlie. I'm going off the air now. I'll contact you when I'm in my car. Over and out."

Jessica continued driving down the beach at a good clip, but not so fast that they were in danger of destroying the truck if they hit a soft spot in the sand. Harlie scanned the shoreline for any sign of more zombies making landfall, but all she saw was water. After a few minutes, Harrington reported in over the radio that he had made it to his car and had moved it to the middle of the parking lot.

"Keep your eyes open, Bill," Harlie said.

"Oh, you can count on that," Harrington replied. There was a quaking quality to his voice that Harlie found unnerving.

Funny how hearing that old Bill's scared is frightening me more than what we just went through.

"We're going to be okay," Jessica said, as the truck hurtled down the beach. Her voice was low and soft, and Harlie realized she was talking more to herself.

Not far from the turn off to the access road, a group of figures meandered up the beach, heading toward the vacant pier. As the pickup zoomed past, Harlie saw they were all zombies, at least six of them.

"They've made it down this far already," she said.

"No kidding," Jessica replied, totally deadpan.

Harlie looked in the side view mirror and watched as the zombies slowly reacted to the Ford's passage. It was almost comical. They reached for the truck as if it were candy, even though it was too far away to touch. "What do we do once we hook up with Bill? Wait for the cops, or—"

"Sweetie, I'm not waiting for anything." Jessica turned the truck onto the access road that led out of the park. The parking lot was almost empty except for a very few vehicles, one of them being Bill Harrington's and a single white Tahoe from the South Padre Island PD. Jessica stopped the F-150 on the other side of Harrington's car, and Harlie climbed out as the police officer in the Tahoe dismounted as well.

"They took out a couple of families on the beach," Harlie reported.

"Who took out what?" the cop asked. He was a young guy with a deep tan and a thick mustache. His hair was full of gel and formed into a dewlap at the front. His eyes were hidden behind his dark sunglasses.

"The zombies," Harlie said.

"Really." The cop didn't sound convinced. He pushed his sunglasses up on his nose and looked pointedly at her M16 before turning toward the beach entrance. He stood up a bit straighter when he saw the corpse of a zombie lying on the asphalt near the ranger shack.

"I shot that one," Harrington said as he rolled down the window of his idling Chevy Malibu.

"You *shot* someone? Why did you shoot that guy?" the cop

asked. As he spoke, he pulled his pistol and leveled it at Harrington.

"He was a fucking zombie," the older park ranger said, indignant.

"Get out of the car," the cop said. He reached for the microphone clipped to his shoulder and called for additional units to join him at the park entrance. He also reported a shooting. When he finished, he looked down at Harrington and waved him out. "Let's go."

"I don't think so," Harrington said. He pointed toward the beach entrance.

The cop turned, and Harlie did as well. A lone figure shambled toward them, stumbling past the ranger shack. Shirtless, its gray-white skin gleamed dully in the sun, marred by abrasions and lacerations that oozed a gray-black ichor. When it saw the group standing around the vehicles, it picked up the pace, heading right for them. Its eyes were a clouded white in color.

And behind the zombie, more came. They turned up the access road from the beach, and the wind carried their moans across the parking lot.

"Huh," was all the young cop had to say.

"Harlie? What are you and Jessica going to do?" Harrington asked.

"I think we're going to get out of here, Bill."

"Great idea," Harrington said, and he put his car in gear.

"Hey! Stay right where you are!" The cop grabbed the Malibu's door handle. "Put it in park! Right now!"

"Officer, are you an idiot?" Harlie asked. "Do you *not* see what's headed our way?"

"This guy shot someone. I don't care if he's a ranger or not, it looks to me like he murdered—"

"You can't murder those things, boy," Harrington said. "Have you not been paying attention to the news? Haven't you heard there's a state of emergency all throughout Texas? The entire country?"

"You can't just go around shooting people," the cop insisted.

Harlie raised her M16 and fired three shots at the approaching lead zombie. All three rounds hit it in the chest, but the zombie didn't even stumble.

The cop yelped, pulled his sidearm, and pointed it at Harlie. "Put the gun down!"

"Look at the zombie," Harlie said. "I hit it in the chest three times, and it's still coming!"

The cop glanced that direction. The bullet holes stood out on the zombie's pale chest as if they'd been drawn there with a Magic Marker. The wounds did not bleed, and the corpse seemed no worse for wear. It continued to advance, moaning, its open maw a black, featureless hole.

"Huh," the cop said again. "Yeah, you did hit him. Din'cha?" He sounded more than a little bit confused.

"Harlie," Jessica said, her voice very soft, "get back in the truck. We'll come back for your Jeep later."

Before Harlie could comply, another police SUV appeared. It sped toward them, lights flashing, and braked to a quick halt next to the young policeman's vehicle. An older policeman practically leaped out of his vehicle, holding his own M16. He glared across the hood at the younger cop, who kept his pistol trained on Harlie in a two-handed grip.

"Sanchez? What the *fuck* are you doing pointing your weapon at that ranger when fucking *zombies* are walking up on you?"

"One of these rangers killed someone!"

The older cop sighed, shouldered his rifle, and drilled a single round through the lead zombie. It collapsed to the parking lot. The senior policeman then fired off eight more shots, dropping six zombies. Harlie gauged that one of his shots had missed entirely, and the second had struck a ghoul too low to kill it, so it needed another round.

"Sanchez, have you not been listening to the radio?" the

older cop said. "I know you've only been on the force for three weeks, but these things are appearing all along the coastline. They're *real*, and we have to take care of them! Now get your rifle and start shooting, boy!"

"But... but what if they're *people?*" the younger cop asked, even as he ducked back inside his Tahoe for his rifle.

"Dude, take a look at them. Do they *look* like people?"

More dead appeared, this time stumbling over the tops of the dunes, kicking up sand. Several got tangled up in the vines and weeds, and they fell face-first. Those tumbled down the soft slopes to the firmer ground at the base of the dunes, got to their feet, and continued forward. Harlie shouldered her rifle and started firing. If the dead made it to the parking lot, they'd be more mobile, more likely to close the gap between them. She didn't want that to happen.

"Harlie, get in the truck," Jessica said again.

The older cop yelled into his radio, advising his department of what was going on as the younger officer reluctantly brought his AR-15 to his shoulder and opened fire. He hit the oncoming zombies in the center of their mass. His shots proved to be ineffective, whereas Harlie was able to drop five deadheads in rapid succession.

"Hit them in the head, guy," she shouted. Then her M16 went dry, and she reached for her fanny pack, where she had another four magazines, along with two for her sidearm. As she reloaded, her fingers moving with precision, she kept her eyes on the approaching zombies. She tried to count them, but stopped after getting to fifteen. She knew if she waited, more would come, drawn to the area by the gunfire, and she didn't have enough ammunition to make a protracted stand. She inserted another magazine into the M16 and cycled it, loading a round into the breech. She lifted the rifle to her shoulder and resumed firing, taking her time, focusing her efforts on the zombies coming over the dunes. From the corner of her eye, she saw Harrington climb out of his car, his shotgun ready.

"I'll take care of the ones that get too close!" he shouted. "You guys with the rifles, take 'em out while they're still at a distance!"

The older cop's weapon ran dry, and he ducked back inside his Tahoe for another magazine.

The first runner appeared, cresting a dune farther down. Harlie dropped another of the slower-moving zombies, then turned and fired at the runner from over the bed of the pickup. She missed with her first shot. She'd gotten used to plinking away at the slow-movers, and the fast one was a harder target. She fired again, but the round only grazed the top of the zombie's head, and by then, it had made it to the parking lot. It sprinted toward the idling F-150, only fifty feet away, snarling, its cold dead eyes fixated on Harlie. Jessica lowered the window and fired at the approaching zombie with her pistol. She wasted four shots, none of which hit the target. Harlie steadied herself and fired again, and the zombie fell sprawling to the parking lot, its skull ravaged.

Sirens wailed in the distance, growing louder above the gunfire. The bodies were starting to pile up. The younger cop had finally gotten his game on and was hitting the approaching zombies right in their heads. The older cop fired efficiently, scoring a hit almost every time. And then, as two motorcycle cops rode up, the last of the zombies fell to the pavement. Harlie did a quick count. They had killed twenty-nine of the walking dead.

"Okay, what are we going to do now?" Harrington asked. He looked at the cops, who looked back at him.

"Hey, man, it's your park," the older cop said.

"Four of us, four of you... I think we need some more guns." Harrington looked over the roof of his car at Harlie. "Fantastic shooting, young miss!"

"Thanks," Harlie said.

"Harlie!" Jessica shouted. "Get in the truck—now! More of 'em!"

Harlie turned. At the far end of the parking lot, more zombies massed, at least thirty, with more coming over the dunes. A moan from the beach entrance caught her attention, and she saw even more of the shambling dead moving up the access road. Several runners bolted toward them, their feet slapping the concrete, their jaws spread wide. The cops opened fire, dropping them, but one got so close that Harrington killed it when it was only twenty feet from the old cop's Tahoe.

"Guys!" Harlie opened up on the group advancing from the south. There were runners in that mix too, and she concentrated on them, the M16 kicking lightly against her shoulder as she squeezed off shot after shot. The zombies fell to the pavement with almost uncanny regularity, but each body hit the parking lot closer than the last one.

"We gotta get out of here!" Jessica yelled from the F-150's driver seat.

"Damn right, we can't hold 'em back with what we got!" the older cop said. "Let's go and regroup at the Sonic down the road!"

Harlie shot two more zombies, then threw herself into the F-150. Jessica wasted no time, and the truck's tires screeched as she stomped on the accelerator, heading for the park exit.

So many of them, Harlie thought, turning in the seat to look out the rear window. The zombies kept coming, over the dunes, up the access road. *So many of them, and so damn quick... like a swarm of bees.*

12

Gartrell walked into the tent that housed the Personal Communications Center, or PCC, where task force personnel were allowed to contact their loved ones as schedules allowed. Privacy partitions sat atop two rows of tables, resulting in narrow cubicles that provided at least a modicum of seated privacy. In each cubicle, an IP phone was connected to a laptop equipped with a camera. The goal was for the task force soldier to be able to view his or her family through the laptop, presuming there was a camera on the other side of the link. Gartrell knew there was no camera on his intended party's side, so he walked over to a bank of commercial satellite phones and pulled one from its charger. The PCC was empty save for one soldier making a call and the duty NCO who oversaw the center operations. Gartrell headed for the tent's exit.

"Hey, Sarmajor! You're not supposed to take those out of the tent," the duty NCO said. He was an E-5 with a pimply face and a large, hooked nose. Even though he was skinny and geeky, he apparently wasn't afraid to lay down the law with one of the task force's senior noncommissioned officers.

"Then I recommend you keep quiet about it, Sergeant," Gartrell said. He walked out of the tent and continued around the side, stepping over the tie downs that kept the structure rooted to the ground. He entered the narrow alleyway between the PCC and the next tent and punched a number into the satellite phone handset. It took a moment for the phone to link up with a communications satellite, but the delay was minimal, and he was rewarded with a ring on the other side of the link.

"Hello?" Laurie Gartrell's voice was subdued and cautious, even though only family members had the number for the satellite phone Gartrell had purchased for use at their cabin in the Smokey Mountains.

"It's me, hon."

"Dave? Jesus, Dave! Where are you? Are you all right?"

"I'm fine, sweetie. I'm in Texas right now. South of Odessa."

"*Texas?* What the hell are you doing there?"

"The government's bidding, as always. You doing all right? The girls are fine?"

"Yeah, we're all doing okay. We're secure. So far, we haven't had any problems, but when we left Bragg, they were going into lockdown. And from what I hear on the radio, things aren't so great in the world."

"Nope. Things are definitely going to hell in a handbasket," Gartrell said.

"When will you be able to come to us?"

"I don't know, Laurie. The mission I'm on... it's probably going to be kind of a long-term assignment. I'm with a JTF, and we've got a pretty big job to do. Listen, are you sure you and the girls are secure? You hid the ATVs? You've got all the weapons and food?"

"Yes, we're good here. No one's going to be able to find the ATVs unless they know where to look, and we've got all the guns and ammunition with us. Food's good; we've got a month's worth of supplies before we have to break out the freeze-dried goods. And the cistern is full, plenty of water for us."

"Any gunfire your way?"

Laurie paused for a long moment. "Yes. Every now and then, I hear some."

Gartrell didn't like that. "All right. In the cellar, you'll find a bunch of empty sand bags. Start filling them. I want you to block the doors and windows. Try and make the cabin as secure as you can. And if the zeds show up, don't engage them unless you have to. But if they see you, they'll come for you, and if they do, you have to shoot them in the head. You understand that, right?"

"I know, Dave. It's what they're saying on the radio. The only way to stop them is to shoot them in the head, or cause some sort of extreme brain injury."

"Okay. I just wanted to make sure you know."

"What do I do with the bodies?"

"What?"

"If they come, and we have to defend ourselves, what do I do with the bodies? Do I just leave them?"

Gartrell thought about that one for a moment. "Uh, I think it's all right to leave them. I haven't seen any indication that they even pay much attention to each other when they're walking around, much less after they've been shot. So if they come for you guys and you kill them, leave the bodies where they fall outside the cabin. Don't expose yourselves any more than you have to. And if they get into the cabin, barricade yourselves upstairs."

"All right. We will." There was a long pause. "You should probably be here with us, Dave."

Gartrell winced. "I know, hon. But the mission I'm on is directly related to what's going on. Can't cut and run right now."

"Are you still with McDaniels?"

"Yes. I've been promoted to sergeant major. I'm his CSM now. He heads up a quick reaction force down here in Texas."

"You were promoted?" Laurie laughed, and the sound was like music to his ears. "You mean it only took the zombie apocalypse for that to happen?"

Gartrell chuckled. "I guess it did."

"How are things going... between you and him?"

"We're not holding hands and taking long walks through the moonlit night, but things are better now."

"Really?" Laurie sounded amazed. "And just how did *that* happen, David?"

Gartrell thought about trying to explain what he and McDaniels had gone through in New York City, and what he had discovered about himself after staying behind in that city as it fell to the dead. Ultimately, he decided that it was just too much to go into over the phone.

"It's complicated. It's nothing too earth shattering, but I'll tell you all about it when I see you. Are the girls around?" he asked, changing the subject.

"They're right here. Which do you want to speak with first?"

"Both of them. Put me on speaker."

Gartrell spent a few moments talking to his daughters—Emily, seventeen and bookish, ignorant of her long-limbed good looks, and Alexandra, thirteen and awkward with her braces and her changing body. He tried to assure them that things were going to work out, that if they did what their mother told them and remembered what he had taught them, they would be fine. But it was difficult; they were so far away, and the satellite link did nothing to bring them closer. Gartrell wondered if it would be possible to have them relocated to Texas. They were already in a remote location. Would bringing them to the Texas desert make them any safer?

He checked his watch and saw he was perilously close to being late for yet another meeting in the Tactical Operations Center.

"Guys, I'm sorry. I have to go," he told his family. "I'll try and get a hold of you later tonight. Laurie, you and the girls make sure the place stays dark. Put the blackout shades in place and make sure they're secure."

"We'll take care of it, Dave," Laurie said. The girls said their good-byes, and Gartrell told them he loved them. Then, Laurie took the phone off speaker.

"How are they doing?" he asked.

"They're doing fine. As well as can be expected. They're worried about their friends, and of course, what's going on is... well, who could be prepared for that? I mean, really?"

Gartrell knew exactly what she meant. There was no way a person could fundamentally accept that *the walking dead* had become part of the American landscape. It was the stuff of fiction, not hard-edged reality. "I gotta go. I love you, hon. You and the girls are in my mind... always."

"Same here, Dave. Hope you can come back to us soon."

"I'll try." He disconnected the link, then returned the satellite phone to the charging cradle inside the PCC. And as he walked to the TOC, he wondered if he had his priorities completely straight: he was in Texas, and his family was holed up in a cabin in the Smoky Mountains in western North Carolina.

Something about that just didn't seem right.

"Sir? We've got zeds in Corpus Christi."

McDaniels was in the TOC, sitting at a small cubicle and working on his latest wish list on one of the center's ubiquitous laptop computers while waiting for the Rangers and the Special Forces troops to get settled. The SEALs had also arrived, and they'd brought all of their toys in the two C-17 cargo jets the Air Force had provisioned for the purpose. Adding to the menagerie of Special Forces vehicles, the SEALs had provided their Desert Patrol Vehicles, or DPVs. The lightly-armored dune buggy-like vehicles were faster overland than the M1114 Humvee, and since they were armed specifically for the occasion, they could prosecute tailor-made engagements that were usually beyond the purview of regular military forces. The arrival of the well-equipped SEALs left McDaniels feeling nice and rosy. The more gear that showed up, the less he would have to try to scrounge.

He looked up at the operations center NCO who delivered the news. "Corpus Christi? Isn't that somewhere on the Texas coast?"

"Yes, sir."

"So it would be, what, five hundred miles from here?"

"A little less than that, so it's not exactly right next door. But it *is* where all those CONEX containers you and the sarmajor requested are coming from."

Not good. "How many are we talking about?"

The sergeant pointed to one of the LED displays carrying a civilian news feed. "CNN's all over it, sir."

McDaniels pushed his chair back, turned to the bank of monitors, and found the one with the CNN feed. "Can you give me the volume?"

"I can put it directly onto your computer, sir." The NCO did something at his station, and the image from the screen appeared in a small window on McDaniels's laptop.

McDaniels raised the volume and listened to the report over the computer's onboard speakers. He leaned toward the display. The cubicle he sat at was so small that his broad shoulders contacted the partitions on either side.

"...confirmed reports of literally dozens of zombies stepping out of the Gulf of Mexico on Padre Island to the east of Corpus Christi. While authorities worked fast to clear the beaches, there are some reports of fatalities from swimmers and campers being taken down by the infected as they came ashore." The gussied-up male reporter wore a short-sleeved blue Polo shirt. He held a microphone and faced the camera with a somber expression on his tanned face, summoning up as much professional gravitas as any member of the media could. "But what's more telling is that now several other zombies have appeared here, right in Corpus Christi, emerging from Corpus Christi Bay where they were met by police and vigilant, armed citizens. We have some amateur video of one such encounter, and we'll play that for you now..."

The image switched from the concerned reporter to a choppy picture that showed several stenches climbing over a low-lying seawall. In the background, people screamed while someone, apparently the videographer, narrated the scene.

"They're coming over the seawall. Don't know how they got here. Must'a climbed up from the bottom of the bay. There's... let's see, one, two, three... four of 'em. God, just *look* at these things. They're just like what we've been seein' on the news in New York and DC."

The location graphic at the lower right portion of the screen read *Swantner Park, Corpus Christi, TX. Amateur video, recorded less than one hour ago.*

"Juan, get away from there, man! Some of those things can run!" cried a voice off-camera. A young Hispanic teenager appeared in the frame. He gestured at the zombies as they slowly crawled up the wall. One of the zeds made a beeline for him, and as McDaniels watched, he knew the man was doomed. Not all of the zombies moved at a sloth-like pace, and the one after the teen was a faster one. Before the boy could do more than take two steps back, the ghoul was all over him. It took him to the ground and slashed at his face and neck with its teeth; blood flowed. The teen screamed as uniformed police ran up, firing their pistols at the encroaching grotesqueries. Another policeman herded the small crowd away from the engagement, including the cameraman. As the videographer backed away, two Humvees rolled up, and troops in BDUs and body armor joined the fray. They zeroed the zeds easily enough, but not before the man they'd attacked had been infected. And one officer was bitten as well.

They're spreading faster than we thought they would.

As the report continued, McDaniels leaned back in his chair and looked at the operations NCO. "Okay, so they're in Corpus Christi, where our CONEXs are. How many containers do we have en route?"

"Not entirely sure just yet, sir. We had ten loaded on CUCVs on the way as of this morning, but more had been identified for transport. The Navy's taking care of that for us, since they have the most containers available. We also have some more stock coming in from Houston, but I haven't verified its disposition just yet." CUCV was military shorthand for "Commercial Utility Cargo Vehicles" and usually meant tractor-trailer rigs operated by private contractors.

"It's pretty important we keep track of what's coming in, especially if there's a chance the transportation network is going to be compromised," McDaniels said. "Do me a favor and start reaching out for some confirmation from the Navy that we're still going to get our stuff. If we have to make alternate arrangements to get what we need, we'd be better off finding that out *before* the stenches join us here, right?"

"Roger that, Colonel. I'll see what I can find out."

"Good man. And I'll have another list for you after my next meeting."

"Can't wait, sir."

McDaniels chuckled politely, even though he wasn't in a very jolly mood. He closed the media player window on his laptop and went back to work on his list, checking quantities and resources. He had only a few minutes more to work on it before the leaders of the Rangers, SEALs, Night Stalkers, and Special Forces entered the TOC—twelve troops in total. And following them was Gartrell, Jaworski, and Captain Chase.

"Okay, folks, let's get organized. We've got more personnel than seats." McDaniels turned to Jaworski. "Colonel, I'm thinking we're going to need to provision either another tactical trailer for us to meet in, or we're going to have to hold these little soirees in a tent."

"Already ahead of you on that, Cord. We've got two more inbound, Air Force units this time, from the 802nd Mission Support Group. They're already heading up from Joint Base Lackland. I figured I'd grab them now before the deadheads make it to San Antonio and things grind to a stop, since I'm pretty sure tens of thousands of zombies would make for interesting driving conditions." Jaworski looked at McDaniels and smiled vaguely.

"Well, that's what I call leaning forward in the foxhole, sir."

"I decided to try and take the initiative for once. Gotta admit, I don't much like it." Jaworski looked around the assembled military personnel. "So we have some SEALS, some

Rangers, and some Green Berets. Colonel McDaniels, maybe we should go through a round of introductions once everyone's settled down."

"Roger that, sir. Let's get squared away, folks."

Introductions were made, and Jaworski shook the hand of each officer and each enlisted man. McDaniels had no idea if any of the names were sticking with the task force commander; Jaworski was that difficult to read. It was easy to dismiss him as a pencil-pushing rubber-stamping kind of officer, but that couldn't be the case. He wouldn't have the job otherwise.

"So, Colonel Haley, it looks like you're the senior guy here after McDaniels," Jaworksi said finally.

"Yes, sir, it seems that way," Haley said.

"Good. I take it that none of you guys have any issues working together?" Jaworski looked around the crowded conference area. "Rangers and Special Forces, I think you guys probably interoperate fairly routinely, but what about the Navy?"

"Nothing to worry about as far as we go, sir," said the SEAL ranking officer, a lieutenant commander named Rawlings. "We always try to play well with our weaker sister services."

"Ha, ha," Switchblade Lewis said. "The only reason you haven't dropped your panties already is because you're holding out for some Marines."

"Well, they do tend to wear less body spray," Rawlings said. He was a narrow-faced man with a thin mustache and sandy-colored hair he wore in the usual medium whitewall fashion. Even though there was mirth in his voice, his pale eyes were emotionless. McDaniels rather thought that Switch's comment had annoyed him, but the Navy officer was covering it up. McDaniels made a mental note of that. The rest of the assembled warriors chuckled at the exchange.

Jaworski caught McDaniels's eye for a moment, then stepped back to lean against the wall Gartrell had leaned against earlier in the day. "Well, whatever your dating preferences might be, I think we can safely say no Marines will be joining SPARTA. Anyway, what we're here to discuss is how we're going to start operating. First things first, the stenches are closing in. Texas was pretty much in the clear yesterday, but now there are zeds walking out of the Gulf of Mexico and crossing over the Rio Grande. San Antonio and Corpus Christi are at some risk at the moment, and we don't see that risk diminishing in a meaningful fashion over the next twenty-four to seventy-two hours. SPARTA is a long way away from either trending infestation, but get this—the medical community says that at least eighty percent of the American population is infected with the first stage virus that started all of this. Only a small percentage of those infected get sick and die, so if everyone here is feeling all right, then we probably don't have anything to worry about in the short term. But Odessa, Midland, Killeen, Fort Hood, they're all fairly local to us, and we can expect someone to expire and reanimate any moment now. Obviously, the reanimated corpse will attack the living, and it will bite people and transfer the second stage virus directly. That infected individual *will* die from the encounter, and the cycle will begin again unless the brain is severely traumatized prior to the transition. So we're on some thin ice right now, and we need to start buttoning up this facility and keep it secure for the long haul." Jaworski pointed at McDaniels. "And that is where this man comes in. Colonel McDaniels is in charge of the QRF, call sign HERCULES. You folks will largely report to him, and he will in turn report back to me. I'll let him take it from here. You have the floor, Cord."

McDaniels turned to Rawlings. "So is Hooks Johnston still with your detachment?"

"You knew Hooks?"

"We had some interesting times in Afghanistan back in 2006," Gartrell said. "Around Samarra."

Rawlings glanced at his senior petty officer, who looked at Gartrell and McDaniels. "Before my time with the team, sir," the petty officer said.

Rawlings grunted. "Hooks was with the detachment up until about three months ago. He was released from duty. Pancreatic cancer. He didn't make it."

"Oh." McDaniels grimaced and exchanged an uneasy glance with Gartrell in the awkward silence that followed the declaration. "Damn. Sorry to hear that. We didn't stay in touch, but he was a hell of man."

"He was. I was under his command for two years. Best guy I ever worked for," Rawlings said.

McDaniels nodded. "You'll have to fill me and the sarmajor in on the specifics later. Getting back to business, our mission is to protect this installation and defend it against the zeds... and anything else that might come our way. I think you can tell from the various news reports that what's going down is taking a hell of a toll on the country. Just from what Gartrell and I saw in New York, law and order is going to be one of the first victims if an infestation takes hold in our area of operations, and we can expect a lot of very anxious civilians to come here looking for shelter and protection, which we can't really provide. To that end, any refugees that wind up on our front lawn are to be directed to Fort Hood. That's the closest evacuation center where there's a military presence."

"Going to be tough on resources if all of Odessa has to bug out," Switch noted.

"True, but that's not our problem. If the hammer comes down, I'd like to hope we can help out, but our mission is to protect this facility and keep it operational while the civilians develop whatever vaccine Safire dreamed up. We're far enough away from the action for now that maybe we won't have to make any tough choices, but we need to prepare ourselves for the eventuality that we might have to turn away Americans in need. All of you need to communicate that to your troops, because if someone isn't onboard with that and we allow infected individuals into the premises, we'll have a bigger problem."

"I agree that we don't want to be fighting the stenches on multiple fronts as well as our own rear area, but turning away Americans in need isn't exactly what my troops signed up for," Haley said. "That's going to be a tough sell, especially to soldiers who are from this area, and I've got plenty of locals in my battalion, Colonel Jaworski."

Jaworski looked at Haley. "I read you on that, Colonel Haley. But that comes straight from SOCOM, and they got the 'guidance' from Washington. No one here is going to like it if it happens, but it's what we have to do."

"So onward, Christian soldiers, is that it?" Haley responded flatly.

McDaniels thought back to what had happened in New York, when he had automatically ordered the Special Forces team he was with to abandon a woman and her child. Even if they had tried to help, it wouldn't have mattered; the zeds had taken both down before anyone could even step out of the Humvee to assist.

"We have some personal experience with what you're talking about, Colonel." Gartrell's voice was neutral, as expressionless as Haley's face. "I can tell you that when it comes down to it, the troops will make the right choice. There's no facing the dead and expecting them to give any quarter. We either defend this installation, or we don't, and if that means we have to turn our backs on Americans in danger, it's what we have to do. The dead, they're almost as dumb as a pile of bricks, but some of them, maybe just a *few* of them..." Gartrell tapped his temple. "...they remember. And if we give them an opening, they'll exploit it. You can count on that."

"I've heard that some of the dead can do things. That they can remember things." Rawlings looked at McDaniels. "You were in New York, Colonel. Is it true that some of those things really can... what? Plan?"

"We were ambushed by members of the alpha detachment we were with," McDaniels said. "They used vehicles and weapons against us directly, in both brute force attacks and in more refined circumstances, like fixing us in place with automatic fire. And Sergeant Major Gartrell personally witnessed a zed use its building key to gain entrance into an apartment building. So yes, some of them have the ability to do the unexpected. As if mass attacks weren't enough."

Rawlings seemed unimpressed. "Huh."

McDaniels moved on. "Anyway, I wanted to sketch out the force arrangement and go over some missions. I see the SEALs brought their DPVs with them, so let's put them to use. Rawlings, I'm envisioning your folks being the distance maneuver element out front, since you've got great mobility assets at your disposal. You can keep eyes out and let us know when the stenches start moving in our direction. I realize you can't be everywhere at once, so I want to backfill you with some Special Forces. Switch, we've got three SR teams in the mix, right?" SR was the abbreviation for Special Reconnaissance, a mission all Alpha Detachments were skilled in, but McDaniels could tell from the team designations that some were specialized in that specific operational art.

"We do. Zero-Three-Four, Zero-Nine-Four, and Zero-Seven-Four are the recon guys. Manned up with bikes and four-wheelers."

"Good. I want you and Rawlings to get them interoperable. You guys can work on that?"

Both Switchblade and Rawlings nodded.

"The rest of the ODAs will also spend most of their time outside the wire, but in a more civilized manner. They should keep eyes on Odessa, and watch for any signs of infestation. It might be worthwhile if they were to get synched up with local law enforcement so they can keep us briefed on what's going down in the city. And obviously, if any zeds pop up that the locals can't control, they should zero them right away. An ounce of prevention and all of that."

"Good copy on that, sir," Switch said.

"Since we've got more Rangers than anything else, we'll keep your guys close at hand, Colonel Haley. They'll be the internal security reaction team, but one platoon should rotate outside the wire and orient to our south. That way, if the stenches do wind up pressing north from San Antonio, they won't be able to sneak up on us all that easily. We'll have UAVs overhead, but they can't be everywhere all the time, so we'll need some mark one eyeballs out there, just in case."

"Roger that," Haley said. "You want to keep the mortar team inside the wire?"

McDaniels nodded. "Oh, yeah. Unless there's a reason to extend them?"

Haley shook his head. "None that would make any sense. We'll probably want them to set up someplace clear, and someplace where the helicopters won't be flying around. It would be a bad thing to bring down one of our own aircraft."

"I'm sure we can get that squared away. If nothing else—" McDaniels patted his iPad. "—I'm pretty sure we can use these things to read the relevant field manuals."

"Yeah, we'll probably need that," Hayley said, without an ounce of humor.

"So the nuts and bolts deployment is this: SEALs in what I call long-range security response; Special Forces and one platoon of Rangers as external security response; the rest of the Rangers as internal security response, along with whatever assets come our way. Lieutenant Colonel Haley will be the QRF XO, and if something happens to me, he will have full operational control over all elements. Commander Rawlings will be next in the order of accession. Rawlings, issues?"

"None," Rawlings said.

Something in the SEAL's voice rubbed McDaniels the wrong way. "Not hearing a lot of conviction in your voice, Navy. I'll ask again, issues?"

Rawlings looked McDaniels square in the eye. "And I'll say it again, Colonel. None. If I have any problems with what's going down, I'll let you know directly."

"Fair enough. I'll need an inventory of all consumables that each team feels will be high priority for resupply. Presume SPARTA will be cut off from the normal supply chains in three days. So anything you need, we need to push out the requests within the next twenty-four hours or so. Everyone should huddle with their senior officers and noncoms and figure out what it is they'll need. And I'm not just talking weapons and ammunition. We'll have a medical facility up soon, but presume that we can't rely on it full-time. So with that in mind, consider what medical supplies you'll need. Additional food, water, spares, fuel, etcetera, etcetera."

"Hell, just triple everything we already have," Switch said.

"I'd make it ten times as much," Gartrell added. "If the stenches show up in force, we'll run out of everything faster than you could believe."

"And given that we could find ourselves in the middle of two approaching elements, don't be shy when it comes time to asking for more of everything," McDaniels said. "We can probably count on something going down in Odessa, and the possibility of a good-sized contingent of the dead making their way to us from the south is pretty good right now."

"Going back to what you said about the ODAs camping out in Odessa, I think it would make sense to touch base with local law enforcement first, and then stay undercover," Switchblade said. "People start seeing uniforms with weapons inside the city, things might get a little uncomfortable for our guys. I realize no one in the city is the enemy, but I don't know if we want to openly advertise our presence."

"So what's your recommendation, Switch?"

"Plainclothes and civilian transportation. Or we have one or two of our guys serve as liaison with the cops, and the rest of the detachments hang tough outside of town."

"We'll actually have staff working in the liaison capacity," Jaworski said. "That's already in the works. It seems to me that having troops as specialized as Green Berets tied up looking over the shoulders of the police might not be the most efficient way to use them."

"That's actually part of what we train for," McDaniels said. "It's not all direct action and special reconnaissance for us. We actually *do* have some capability to interface with civilian and other government agencies to support our mission."

"Okay, but do you think this is how we should play this? If so, I have to agree with Major Lewis about keeping a low profile. I don't have my fingers on the pulse of the situation just yet, but I'd imagine the civilians are going to be getting pretty nervous right about now." As Jaworski spoke, there was a small rustle on the far side of the TOC. Jaworski glanced that way, and Captain Chase stepped away from the group. McDaniels heard him make some inquiries into what was going down.

Switchblade started to say something, but McDaniels held up his hand. "Hold that thought, Switch."

Chase came back quickly and looked at Jaworski. "Zeds in Odessa, sir. Police are going to guns on them. We don't have the details, but it looks like it started in some sort of housing project."

"Find out where and reach out to the police to see if they need our assistance," Jaworski said. "They're aware of our presence down here, but they might not know they can resource us in the event of unusual circumstances—like a bunch of flesh-eating zombies appearing in the middle of town."

"Yes, sir." Chase turned away from the conference area.

"Commander Rawlings, looks like you're up," McDaniels said. "Short notice, but I'm sure you have an element ready to go?"

Rawlings nodded. "One six-man team is already stood up. Give us a position, and we'll go straight there."

McDaniels turned to Major Carmody and CW4 Billingsly. "Aviation? I'm thinking we could use a couple of MH-6s right about now."

"You got it, Colonel," Carmody replied, while Billingsly and the Night Stalkers' senior NCO, a master sergeant McDaniels hadn't been introduced to, headed for the door. Rawlings's senior petty officer followed them.

"Hey, guys, no need to consult me or anything," Jaworski said. He gave McDaniels a quirky smile.

"Sorry, sir, didn't mean to get that far ahead of you. You want us to dial it back?" McDaniels asked.

"Negative on that, Colonel. I apologize. I didn't mean to indicate anything other than approval—lame attempt at humor on my part. This is your regime. You're good to go."

"Understood, sir." McDaniels picked up his iPad and got to his feet. "All right, let's end the meeting here for now. As would be expected, officers will present problems and issues to me, while the enlisted men will be represented by Command Sergeant Major Gartrell. We'll reconvene once the SEALs are back inside the wire. As of now, Hercules is officially active. Let's manage the engagement as best as we're able."

13

The two MH-6 Little Bird helicopters sprinted toward Odessa through the afternoon sunlight, their skids no more than thirty feet above the flat desert landscape. Four SEALs were strapped to the pods mounted on either of the helicopters, two men per side. The SEALs were fully manned up, outfitted for close-quarters combat with body armor, Heckler and Koch MP-7s as their primary weapons, and SIG Mk24 9 millimeter pistols as secondary weapons. One man in each element also carried an "Old Faithful," a meticulously maintained M4 carbine, a descendant of the ubiquitous, Vietnam-era M16 assault rifle. As each man was exposed to the elements—there was no protection to keep the SEALs comfortable during the ten-minute flight— they wore dust goggles to protect their eyes from dust and other hazards that might be encountered while flying to their designated area of operations. The most likely cause for significant eye damage during flight would come from insects; dust thrown up by the whirling rotors upon landing would be the second.

The unarmed MH-6 helicopters were escorted by two fully armed AH-6M Little Birds, each flown by two pilots and outfitted with two M134 miniguns capable of firing 7.62 millimeter bullets at a rate of over four thousand rounds per second. The attack aircraft also carried two cylindrical pods loaded with nine 2.75-inch rockets; the tip of each rocket carried a ten-pound warhead packed with high explosives. While the AH-6 team was unlikely to be resourced during the hop, they would nevertheless establish a combat air position over the engagement area by orbiting at an altitude of three hundred feet. From there, they would stand ready to provide close air support if things went to hell.

The four aircraft climbed higher into the sky as they approached the city of Odessa. In a usual penetration of non-permissive airspace, the Little Birds would have maintained nap-of-the-earth flight, rising and falling with the contours of the terrain. In the current circumstances, such operational stealth was not required. The local police were expecting the SEALs to be delivered by helicopter, and the zombies—if there were any—wouldn't likely be aware of how the SEALs were conveyed to the scene. The leader of the SEAL element—a petty officer third class, call sign Alcatraz 16—reported their progress through his personal comms gear to the SEAL command and control element back at SPARTA. When the helicopters drew nearer, the SEAL's reports became more frequent as he relayed more essential information, such as the number of police squad cars that surrounded a block of low-lying tenement buildings. At least ten police officers crouched behind the vehicles, sidearms and assault rifles drawn. One figure lay sprawled on the walkway leading to a shabby apartment building. Black fluid leaked from its ravaged skull, stark against the off-white concrete. More figures shambled out of the apartment building, and the cops opened up on them. As the Little Birds made a pass over the area, the SEALs and Night Stalkers watched as the zombies jerked and stumbled against the fusillade, but they didn't go down.

"Cadillac, this is Alcatraz One-Six. Local law enforcement is up against maybe a dozen stenches. Are we good to go for insertion? Over."

The answer came back immediately. "Alcatraz One-Six, Cadillac Six. You are go for insertion. Contact the lead on the ground, Sergeant Chavez, Odessa PD. Over."

Alcatraz 16 glanced over his shoulder at the Army pilot sitting behind him. The pilot nodded curtly and brought the MH-6 into a sweeping turn to the right. Alcatraz 16 looked down and watched idly as the Odessa neighborhood seemed to spiral beneath his feet.

"Cadillac, Alcatraz One-Six. Roger."

As the AH-6s climbed out and established their top cover pattern, the MH-6s descended to the street. They didn't land, but established a low hover in expanding clouds of light dust, their landing skids only a foot above the concrete. The SEALs hit the quick-release latches on their harnesses and leapt off the external personnel pods. They ran directly away from the helicopters, two men on each side; behind them, the MH-6s cranked up the power and climbed back into the sky. They exited the pattern, leaving the SEALs under the watchful eyes of their attack brethren.

"Cadillac, Alcatraz is on the deck, over."

"Roger, Alcatraz."

Alcatraz 16 signaled the rest of the SEAL element to form up on him, and they advanced toward the melee at a dead run. Some civilians stood in front of their ramshackle houses, watching the police firing at the zombies emerging from the apartment building. When they saw the helicopters drop off the SEALs, most of them returned to their homes.

"Looking for Sergeant Chavez!" Alcatraz 16 shouted as he pounded toward the cops. "Where's Chavez? Chavez!"

"Here!" a voice cried over the gunfire.

Alcatraz 16 turned and saw a frightened-looking police officer with a thick mustache and wide, dark eyes crouched behind a police cruiser. Chavez held a Glock in both hands and fired carefully at the approaching zombies. Despite his obvious fear, Chavez kept his cool and made his shots count. Every time the man pulled the trigger, a round hit a zombie in the head. The rest of the police weren't as proficient. Most of their rounds slammed into the face of the apartment house, shattering windows and piercing wood.

Alcatraz 16 wondered how many people they were killing inside the building. "You guys mind if we take care of this for you? You mind if we take out the zeds?" Alcatraz 16 waved at the apartment building. "Your guys are spraying lead all over the place. You're putting a lot of civilians at risk!"

"Ain't no one left alive in there," Chavez said. "But if you want to help out, go ahead."

"Have your people stop firing! We'll take it from here!"

It took a bit of yelling on Chavez's part to get the police to stop shooting up the place, but when they did, the SEALs went to work. They took out the first zombies from behind cover, placing well-aimed shots into each ghoul's right eye. The zombies fell to the dusty ground with great regularity, and within seconds, the immediate threat was neutralized. Alcatraz 16 counted fourteen bodies, including three children. All of them had been ravaged, as if they had been partially eaten. One woman was almost entirely disemboweled, and the stench of excrement filled the air.

Alcatraz 16 motioned the rest of his four-man element forward, while the second group held back and provided overwatch. As the SEALs advanced, the petty officer visually ensured each of the corpses on the ground had been hit in the head; he wanted no nasty surprises. He led his team to the apartment building's front steps and peered through the shattered lobby windows. More shapes moved inside, and Alcatraz 16 was disgusted to see a clutch of corpses feasting on the remains of another human being. A decapitated head lay on the white tile floor in a puddle of drying blood. Its eyes moved, and its mouth opened and closed.

"Okay, check that out," he said. "Everyone get a look at that. Even a severed head can still bite. Keep that in mind."

The zombies inside the lobby slowly turned toward them.

"They know we're here," another SEAL said.

"It's our voices," another said. "The gunfire didn't make them stop eating, but the sound of our voices gets their attention."

"They're predators, and like we've been told, they're always hungry," Alcatraz 16 replied. "Okay, let's do 'em."

Six shots took care of all six ghouls in the lobby. Alcatraz 16 preceded his element inside, and he took a moment to examine the severed head. Its dull eyes followed his movements, and its teeth clicked together as it opened and closed its mouth. It was trying to bite him, even though he was too far away and it couldn't move. All the SEALs wore lightweight video cameras strapped to their helmets, and Alcatraz 16 made sure he got some footage of the head before he fired a round through it.

Alcatraz 16 gave his orders: they would canvas the two-story apartment building, starting with the top floor and working their way downstairs. He dispatched one of the men to inform the police.

When the man returned, he reported the cops had been informed. "And SWAT just rolled up. They want us to pull out and let them take over."

"And what did you say?"

"I told 'em they transferred OPCON to us, so they're out of luck. They can take it back when we're done."

"Good man."

"Ah, one thing..."

Alcatraz 16 turned back to the SEAL. "What's that?"

"There's a cop out there who's been bitten."

Alcatraz 16 thought about that for a moment. "Not our concern. Let's execute." Speaking over his throat microphone, he tried reported the mission status to Cadillac, but received only a garbled reply. The apartment building was interfering with the radio. He hailed their top cover. "Highball Two-Two, Alcatraz One-Six. We're going to clear the building before we turn it back to civilian control. How long can you hold the high cap? Over."

"Alcatraz, Highball. We've got legs for more than an hour. You need us to relay that to Hercules and Cadillac? Over." The AH-6 flight lead was a high-ranking warrant officer Alcatraz 16 had known for years, and the sound of his friend's Mississippi drawl over the radio was strangely comforting. Even if it was coming from just another Army puke.

"Roger that, Highball. Mighty helpful if you did. Over."

"Will do, Razzmatazz," the pilot replied, intentionally using Alcatraz 16's nickname over the radio instead of the SEAL element call sign. "Happy hunting. We'll keep an eye on the ground condition while you're inside. Over."

The SEALs worked their way upstairs, alert for any noises over the buzzing of the helicopters orbiting overhead. They went through apartment after apartment, and found only two occupied by live people. All the others were empty, but showed signs of fantastic struggles. The SEALs advised those people remaining on the floor to stay inside their apartments, and that help would be on its way soon.

On the lower floors, zeds waited in several apartments. The SEALs were not taken by surprise. Every door had already been broken down, and the occupants had either been killed or managed to escape through the first floor windows. The men dispatched each zombie with care. There was no hesitation on the part of the SEALs, no fear, no anger, no disgust, just training and routine and almost mechanical responses. It was their job.

By the time they were done, Alcatraz 16 counted twenty-three dead zombies. He reported that to the Night Stalkers, who relayed the information to Cadillac. After making another circuit through the entire apartment building, they found no more stenches, only growing clouds of black flies. He led his element into the light of the waning afternoon and found that Sergeant Chavez had been replaced by a SWAT captain named Vasquez, who looked sharp and efficient in his black uniform and no-nonsense demeanor.

"I want to thank you guys for helping us out in this," Vasquez said. "We were on another call across town, and it took some time for us to get here."

"What call was that, sir?"

Vasquez nodded toward the bodies sprawled across the apartment building's walkway. He didn't need to say anything further. Alcatraz 16 looked into the sky. A news helicopter had joined the fray, hovering outside the AH-6s' orbit, its gimbaled camera pointing in their direction. Alcatraz 16 turned his face away from it. He saw an ambulance had rolled up, and a uniformed policeman was being treated for a bite to his arm. The man's face was a blank mask; he probably knew what was in store for him.

Alcatraz 16 pointed him out to Vasquez anyway. "Your problems are only just beginning."

Vasquez nodded again. "I know. We've been lucky so far, but today, there've been two outbreaks. We haven't been fast enough to contain them."

"You want help, have your superiors contact mine. No promises, but as long as we have the guns, we can try and get things squared away with you guys."

"That'd help. I'll pass that along." Vasquez hesitated. "What's going on down at the plant? Big military presence there." He looked up at the orbiting Little Birds. "Attack helicopters, Strykers, hundreds of troops... what's the deal?"

"Classified."

"Classified as what?"

"Classified as 'you don't need to know,'" Alcatraz 16 said. "Can I make it any clearer than that?"

Vasquez didn't seem happy, but he was professional enough not to belabor the point. "Thanks, I'm good."

"Call us if you need us. We have to get out of here now; choppers are running low on go-juice." It had been almost an hour since the element had entered the apartment building, and the Night Stalkers would certainly have to head back shortly.

"Thanks again, man."

"No problem." Alcatraz 16 turned away and headed up the street, where the rest of the SEALs had already secured a landing zone for the MH-6 transports.

14

"Severed limbs are hazardous waste," Anthony Lim heard a sergeant say as he walked past one of the troop fortifications. "You see something, you must bag it."

"You think I'm going to touch a dead arm? You *siao liao oreddy*? Who do you think is going to touch something like that?"

Lim stopped in his tracks and turned in the darkness. "Who said that?"

Three men stood inside the sandbag revetment. Two of them turned, while the third continued looking at the shoreline through light-intensifying binoculars. The pair who faced him were barely more than shadows in the dim light; Admiralty Road West was completely dark, part of the plan after the causeway connecting Singapore with Malaysia's Johor Bahru had been demolished just after sunset. All the government housing was dark as well; even though Singapore still had plenty of power, no one in the government wanted to advertise the fact.

Across the strait, Malaysia burned. And that was why the men had fallen suddenly silent. While he could see almost nothing of their features, the reflected firelight illuminated the subdued insignia on his battle dress, and the soldiers knew they were facing none other than the commanding officer of the 2nd Singapore Infantry Regiment. They saluted automatically, and called the third soldier to order. He turned and saluted immediately, silhouetted against the fiery maelstrom of Johor Bahru.

"I said it, sir. It was me."

Lim stepped closer to the man. He was an older individual, with a creased, weathered face and the rank of staff sergeant, which made him probably one of the senior enlisted men in the area. Lim looked from him to the younger man standing next to him. While the staff sergeant was obviously Chinese, the younger man was probably of Malay extraction. He was a lance corporal, and he stiffened when Lim's gaze locked with his.

"You said it," Lim said.

"Yes, sir, I said it. I'm sorry, sir," the lance corporal admitted.

Lim waved the apology away. "It doesn't matter. But you must listen to your superiors—anything that washes ashore should be considered hazardous, and it must be contained. This is something that all of us must take care of, from the most senior to the most junior."

"Yes, Colonel. I'm sorry, sir. I'll do as ordered."

Lim nodded toward the dark waters of the strait. "Return to your duties."

"Sir." The soldier turned and raised the binoculars to his eyes and resumed inspecting the water.

Lim turned back to the staff sergeant. "Staff, are we secure in this position?"

It had been hours since the causeways had been destroyed, and Lim was worried about the amount of zombies massing on the far shores of Malaysia. Kuala Lumpur was full of the walking dead, having fallen earlier in the day. Lim's darkest fear was that his own Singapore would follow suit. But the citizens of Singapore were vigilant; whenever a zombie rose, it was put down, either by officials or by citizens wielding machetes and clubs. Those individuals who had been bitten were quarantined and relocated to the Woodlands Civic Center, where they were kept under lock and key. A thousand troops had been moved into the area surrounding the civic center; most were Guards, the elite special operations force of the Singapore Armed Forces. Lim had no doubt that anyone who went into the civic center was going to die, and the Guards would ensure the infected were terminated by a bullet to the brain.

All of the city-state's 350,000 service members had been

mobilized, along with the island's sophisticated emergency management troops. Most of the force was comprised of conscripts, but over the past few days, citizens of every age had volunteered for service. There weren't enough weapons to go around, and there was no time to train everyone even if there were. Thankfully, Singapore had a healthy population of foreign expatriates, many of whom had formal military training. Lim had been surprised to find they were also eager to pitch in and help, and in fact, he had in his service several Europeans and Americans who were recent veterans of the conflicts in the Middle East. Just down the road, a former British SAS commando assisted in overseeing a heavy machinegun emplacement, and an American former Marine was advising one of Lim's counterparts with the 1st Singapore Infantry Regiment. Norwegians and Germans with the Singapore Navy were lending their own expertise to the littoral operations. The Singapore Strait was full of Navy vessels patrolling the calm waters, looking for any sign of zombies. Fairly often, gunfire crackled in the night as sailors aboard those ships fired on things in the water.

"We are secure right now, sir. An entire company is oriented in defense in that direction—" The older noncom pointed to the left of the emplacement. "—and we have a separate company in that direction. But you already know all of this." The staff sergeant adjusted his helmet. "Colonel, where is your escort?"

"I'm alone for the moment, Staff Sergeant...?"

"Chee, sir."

"I'm doing an informal inspection, Staff Chee. No need to have an escort. I'm among friends, and the entire second regiment is within shouting distance."

"I see, sir. Where are you off to next?"

Lim pointed up the coastline. "I intend to work my way to the docks to the north, then come back down."

"I'll accompany you, sir."

"Completely unnecessary, Staff."

"Completely necessary, Colonel. You can't be alone out here, not with those... those *things* in the area."

Gunfire rang out, and Lim looked across the dark strait. He saw muzzle flashes wink from one of the patrol boats, but there was something odd about it, something that didn't quite make sense. He figured it out when he stepped toward the line of sand bags and reached for the night vision goggles attached to his helmet. The sailors on the patrol vessel weren't firing at the water; they were firing at something *aboard* the boat itself.

"Staff!" The soldier holding the binoculars cried. "On the shoreline!"

The staff sergeant grunted as he stepped up beside the soldier. He switched on his NVGs and swung them in position over his eyes just as Lim did the same. What Lim saw almost made his heart come to a complete stop.

Thousands of the walking dead emerged from the water, sodden clothes clinging to their bodies. From well-heeled Malaysian businessmen to fashionable women to lowly *ah beng* boys and *ah lian* girls, the dead stumbled toward the shore. Many were horribly burned or gruesomely savaged, missing limbs or even disemboweled. One grotesquerie had been a pregnant woman who had apparently torn open her own belly to get at her unborn child.

"Sir, orders?" The staff sergeant's voice was flat, expressionless.

"Close and destroy," Lim said. He spoke into his headset and informed the combined tactical operations center located at the Marsiling Secondary School two miles away what was occurring. As he did so, the shoreline emplacements opened fire. All up and down the coast, machine guns and assault rifles spoke, including the 7.62 millimeter M240E6 Squad Automatic Weapon in the sandbagged position he stood in. The lance corporal squeezed off tight bursts, peering through the M145 scope attached to the weapon. The staff sergeant shouted orders to the men arrayed around the emplacement, and a dozen soldiers got to their feet, shouldering their SAR-21A assault rifles. Laser light flashed across the beach as target designators were switched on.

"Aim for their heads!" Lim shouted. "Remember, hit them in the heads!"

The staff sergeant relayed the order up the line in a harsh bellow, and more soldiers continued passing the order. A junior officer appeared and led one element of infantrymen forward as floodlights came to life, casting a glowing pool across one section of the narrow beach. The floodlights had been Lim's idea, intended to give the approaching zeds something to focus on while serving as a chokepoint. He hoped to bring all the ghouls into one area so they could be serviced by soldiers on either side of the illumination point. He was satisfied to see the tactic worked; the zombies shambled toward the radiant light, where they were put down by the soldiers.

What Lim hadn't counted on was that thousands of zombies would put ashore at almost the same time. Before he knew it, ghouls had penetrated the line, sensing the warm bodies of the soldiers beyond the blinding glare of the lights. Soon, dozens of carnivorous corpses stalked along Admiralty Road. An Army truck slammed through a gaggle of the dead, sending broken bodies flying through the air. Those bodies continued to move, to press on with the hunt, despite shattered limbs and bones. Lim pulled his own assault rifle into position against his right shoulder and gunned down several zombies, then assisted the lance corporal with reloading his belt-fed machinegun. Over the regiment's tactical net, he heard fragmented reports coming from the various units that made up the 2nd Singapore Infantry Regiment. Nearly every unit was in varying degrees of contact, even those on the far side of Admiralty Road. Overhead, rotors clattered as OH-58D Kiowa Warrior armed reconnaissance helicopters surveyed the area. On the water, gunfire from the patrol boats continued.

"Colonel!"

Lim fired at another zombie as it lurched through the night, then turned. Captain Horace Teo stood at the entrance to the emplacement, his rifle held at port arms. Behind him was an unarmed Humvee. The vehicle idled on the side of the road, its driver standing near the front fender, rifle at the ready, night vision goggles over his eyes.

"Teo! What are you doing here?"

"Colonel, they've been calling you on the tactical net! You need to come back to the operations center. The zombies are coming over from Lim Chu Kang in incredible numbers!"

"Lim Chu Kang..." Lim thought quickly, trying to remember the divisional deployment. "That's where the Fifth Infantry is located. It's not our area of responsibility."

"Sir, you don't understand." Teo pointed over Lim's shoulder, in the direction of Lim Chu Kang, a nearby district known for its wetland preserves and Singapore's only military live fire area.

Lim turned. A huge glow illuminated the near horizon, mimicking that across the strait in Malaysia. A tremendous fire had broken out. *When did that happen?*

"The Fifth has been overrun," Teo continued. "Estimates of twenty to forty thousand zombies have emerged from the water. They're headed this way."

Overhead, something shrieked past, first one, then another, and another. Brilliant explosions flashed, and the shockwaves seemed to hit Lim right in the chest. An airstrike, or perhaps artillery barrage, had just hit what he presumed to be the edge of the zombie element.

"We have to keep this beach secure!" Lim pointed at the zombies that continued to shamble up the beach, walking toward the lights. The bodies were already three feet high, and more gunfire raged from the darkness behind them. Men screamed in the distance, and Lim saw a soldier go down beneath a gaggle of hungry corpses. "You see what's going on? If we redeploy now, *this* area will become porous, and they'll be able to walk right down Admiralty to the Central Business District, eating everything in their way!"

"But General Singh has—"

"Is he here?" Lim waved around the area. "Do you see the general anywhere near this beach? Go back to the TOC and tell that patrician fool I'm staying with my regiment. The People's Defense Force is being held in reserve. My advice to him is to give them weapons, and let them loose!"

"But Colonel!"

Lim looked at Teo with hard eyes. He had always gotten along well with Teo, but it was their first time serving together under combat conditions. Lim saw the younger officer's fear, could sense it eroding his competence. Perhaps it was the type of combat. No soldier in the world had trained to fight legions of the walking dead, an enemy incredibly difficult to kill, an enemy whose response to debilitating injury was merely to keep attacking. If that was the cause for Teo's reluctance to return to the tactical operations center and inform the general overseeing them that the regimental commander had elected to remain with his troops, then Lim could perhaps understand it.

"When you're done with that, return here and assist with combat operations," Lim continued. "I expect you to report back smartly. Your job will be to oversee containment operations in our rear." He pointed into the darkness behind them, where muzzle flashes occasionally lit the area. The necromorphs were penetrating the Regiment's line, and secondary defensive positions were engaging them.

Teo turned and looked into the darkness, then faced Lim and saluted sharply. "Sir!"

Lim returned the salute, and Teo spun and ran back to his waiting vehicle.

Lim grabbed the senior sergeant in the firing position and spoke into his ear over the crackle of weapons fire. "Order your men into a skirmish line on the beach. We need to start killing the dead on the sand. Machinegunners will provide grazing fire and protective cover. Instruct your men to practice ammunition conservation. If they can't kill with one shot, they are to withhold fire until the proper opportunity presents itself. One shot, one kill, Staff. We are literally facing *millions* of dead. We must be disciplined!"

"Agreed, Colonel. I'll notify every company commander in the area and arrange the soldiers under my control into the element you ordered. You might want to consider getting on the radio and broadcasting that to the rest of the regiment, sir." The older man pointed to the tactical radio set up nearby.

Lim went over to the radio and snatched up the microphone. Broadcasting a Selarang Six—the call sign of the regimental commander—he relayed the same orders he had given the sergeant. Diesel engines roared, and he turned to see Singaporean Bionix II infantry fighting vehicles roll up. The vehicles lowered their boarding ramps, and more soldiers dashed out into the night, clutching rifles, night vision goggles down across their eyes. Over the roar of the machinegun to his left, Lim shouted for the infantrymen to get down to the beach and organize themselves.

The troops did as ordered without hesitation. Under the urgings of their senior noncommissioned officers, the soldiers raced past the sandbagged fortifications, killing the dead as they advanced. They organized themselves into a line on the beach, standing almost shoulder-to-shoulder. In less than a minute, over four hundred soldiers engaged the tide of the walking dead that shambled up the small beach.

Overhead, OH-58D helicopters dove toward the black water, firing .50 caliber machineguns into the strait. Lim surmised the pilots were able to see the dead in the water courtesy of the sensitive infrared components in each aircraft's mast-mounted sight. Occasionally, the helicopters would unleash a rocket, sending a thunderclap of fire and fury through the darkness. Further out, the patrol boats lit up the strait with their own fires.

Lim shouldered his SAR-21 and fired at the mass of wet bodies emerging from the surf. When he had told the sergeant the regiment would be facing millions of dead, he hadn't been wrong. Thousands of bodies rose from the black waters, climbing over rock and hard-packed sand, their waterlogged clothes clinging to their pale bodies like a second skin. Lim saw men, women, children, soldiers, nurses, doctors, teachers, and laborers. Lim knew he was witnessing the demise of Malaysia, and the thought of the same thing waiting for Singapore chilled him to the very bone. In the back of his mind, he worried about his wife and two sons, currently barricaded in their home in Holland Village. If he and his regiment fell, would his family be able to survive as the dead surged into Singapore like a tsunami of death? And even if they did survive the initial onslaught, who would come to their rescue? Malaysia and Indonesia were gone, and Australia was fighting the dead as well. Who would care about tiny, insignificant Singapore?

No one. With the answer firmly entrenched in his mind, Lim shouted orders into the radio, encouraging his troops to destroy the dead as quickly and effectively as possible. From behind him, the Bionix IFVs opened up with their 25 millimeter cannons, firing over the soldiers and raking the waterline. The zombies went down as the big rounds passed through their bodies, blowing off limbs and exploding chests and abdomens. The assault did not kill the necromorphs, but it did slow them and give the soldiers collecting below the machinegun position additional time to more closely coordinate their attacks. Already, hundreds of zombies lay across the small beach, their skulls ravaged by bullets. The dead emerging from the water had to pick their way across the motionless corpses, which slowed them even further.

Lim reported to the tactical operations center, advising General Singh of the 2 SIR's tactics and results. In the distance, someone fired a flare. Lim watched as the zombies turned toward the sudden brightness, and he could almost see their eyes tracking the flare as it slowly descended to the water. He had a sudden idea.

"Rainbow, this is Selarang Six. We need lights! The dead are attracted to lights. We can lure them into kill zones!"

No sooner had he made the report than a new wave of the dead rose from the water. Lim saw even more shapes making their way into shallower water. There were so many...

More flares shot into the sky. The moving corpses looked up at the light, their faces slack and dull. But for a moment, the dead stopped, as if hypnotized by the red-white flares floating in the sky.

The troops of the 2nd Singapore Infantry Regiment advanced, the fires from their SAR-21 rifles dropping the hypnotized dead like a ball rolling through wooden skittles.

Lim's heart leaped. The dead far outnumbered the living, but the living still had a chance.

15

As the days rolled by, the objective known as SPARTA was fortified with a speed so great that even McDaniels was impressed. Great trenches twelve feet deep and fourteen feet wide were clawed into the dusty earth surrounding the pharmaceutical facility in widening concentric rings. In the coming days, they would be lined with concrete to ensure their stability, and then they would be filled with either flammable fuel or acids to burn the dead, should they make it to the facility. At the same time, the dirt from the trenches was piled into several berms inside the ring. On those berms, the first CONEX containers were positioned. The containers were forty feet long, slab-sided crates of thick, corrosion-resistant metal. Originally designed for shipping goods across oceans, the containers were a principal storage and shipping device for all sorts of military gear, from vehicles to bombs. From atop the containers, the soldiers of Joint Task Force SPARTA would make their stand against the necromorphs. Concertina wire, floodlights, searchlights, flare canisters, low-light video cameras, and other high and low-tech solutions were added to the perimeter. Anything that could be used to deny the enemy access to SPARTA was resourced.

At the same time, more equipment showed up, much of it in the CONEX containers that went to the berms. Generators, tents, munitions, vehicles, fuel, laptop computers and personal data assistants, satellite phones, radio gear, antenna arrays, prepared meals and basic foodstuffs, cots, sleeping bags, water—everything the task force was likely to need—came in on lowboy trailers hauled by contractors. Most of the truckers were from the western states. Very few were from east of the Mississippi, and for good reason. The plague of the dead was leaving the eastern seaboard and moving across the nation.

Watching the televised news in the tactical operations center left McDaniels feeling anxious and worried. He had talked to Paulette three times in the past twelve hours alone. She'd assured him that everything at Fort Bragg was secure. The security was so tight that her movements had been curtailed, and curfews were in effect; anyone out after sundown stood a very good chance of being shot and killed. McDaniels wasn't surprised to hear that, but it didn't make him stop worrying about his wife's safety.

One bright ray of light came from his son. Leonard was studying at University of Texas in Austin. Like McDaniels, he had been speaking to his mother as often as possible, and he was just as unnerved at the set of circumstances.

"I think I should drive home to Mom," he'd told McDaniels during their first conversation.

"I think you should drive here to me," McDaniels said. "Your mom is as safe as she can be right now, but things are going to get rough where you are. The zeds are going to hit San Antonio soon, and when that happens, we might not be able to link up at all."

McDaniels told his son of the current siege taking place just south of San Antonio, where a sizeable contingent of the Texas Army National Guard and in-state Reserve forces were fighting to keep the city out of the hands of the dead. News coming from the area indicated that there was some progress to that end, but other reports showed even more dead streaming into southern Texas from Mexico. Corpus Christi had managed to control its outbreaks and annihilate the burgeoning infestation of the dead inside the city limits, but Padre Island was a total loss. Anyone who had been unable to evacuate the island was believed to have perished, save for those huddled in some obviously well-fortified homes.

San Antonio was where most of the action was. The dead

bearing down on the metropolis and its defenders numbered in
the hundreds of thousands. Despite withering attacks by the
U.S. Air Force, the stenches kept coming. McDaniels had no
doubt San Antonio would fall. While the military buildup
around SPARTA was tiny in comparison to that in San
Antonio, the troop density was actually greater, and the defenses
were more specialized, thanks to the Corps of Engineers.

"Dad, are you sure about that?" Lenny had asked.

"Lenny, I saw what happened to New York firsthand. So
yeah, I'm sure. The same thing could happen in Austin, too."

"The cops did find a few zombies here," Lenny said. "Two
of them were on campus."

"Not what I wanted to hear, son."

"Sorry."

McDaniels was silent for a moment, thinking over what
Jaworski had told him weeks earlier when he'd found out Lenny
was already in Texas. *Let's get him here. Let's take that circumstance
off the table right away.*

"Lenny, I want you to get in your car and get your butt to
Odessa," McDaniels said finally. "Do it now, while you can still
leave Austin, and before the stenches to the south have their way
with San Antonio. You'll be a lot safer here than on your
campus, believe me."

"You sure about that, Dad?" Lenny chuckled. "Maybe I
should just make tracks for Canada instead!"

"Maybe that's not a bad idea. But humor your old man and
come out this way, all right?"

"Can I bring some people?"

McDaniels thought about that. "No. Keep it to yourself. Tell
your friends to get someplace safe and start stockpiling food,
water, medical supplies, weapons, and ammunition. Shotguns
will be their best friends. Speaking of which, I want you to go
out and buy one right away. Twelve gauge, preferably an
autoloader if you can find one. You still have the AMEX, right?"

"Yes, sir. Though I can't believe you're telling me to go out and buy a high-end shotgun with it."

"Well, try not to go *too* crazy, but pick up something. A Mossberg 500, something like that. All right?"

"Um... okay, will do."

"And you're coming here, right?"

"Dad, what about Mom?"

"She's as safe at Bragg as she would be anywhere else right now, Lenny. Believe me, son, I know what I'm talking about."

"Okay. But, Dad, there's, um, there's this girl here. Her name's Belinda, and it's kinda serious."

Under normal circumstances, McDaniels wouldn't have been surprised. Leonard was a good-looking young man, smart, confident, but still lovably goofy at the same time, with a wry sense of humor and a keen wit. He'd never had any problems with girls once he'd moved out of his early teens and become more comfortable with himself. But Lenny had never had what McDaniels regarded as a "serious" girl.

"How serious is serious, Lenny?"

"Well, I was going to bring her home at Christmas."

McDaniels's stomach sank. "Jesus."

"Hey, come on, Dad. It's not like we *knew* the zombie apocalypse was going to happen, you know?"

"Just... just get over here, Lenny. As quickly as you can. Don't tell anyone else where you're going, or why. Just take your clothes, some food, all the cash you have, and your credit card. Buy the shotgun and as much ammo as you can. And get to Odessa." He gave his son the address of the complex, but told him he'd probably be able to find it easily enough, as it looked like an Army outpost in a hostile country.

Which it was.

Lenny had promised him he would do exactly as his father asked, and didn't mention anything further about his "serious girl." McDaniels knew that Lenny would show up with her in tow, and wouldn't be surprised if some of his son's other friends made it to Odessa as well. That didn't bother him. Lenny wasn't the kind to cut and run on his friends, and that was fine with McDaniels. He would smooth it over with Jaworski when the time came.

Every morning after breakfast, McDaniels and Gartrell drove around the facility in a golf cart and examined the fortifications. More helicopters were flying in and out of the landing zone established at the northern parking lot, including some slick-looking civilian jobs. Apparently, one of those aircraft had brought the team of researchers from the fallen USAMRIID, because when Gartrell whipped the little golf cart through the complex, McDaniels caught sight of Regina Safire as she and the others walked toward one of the office buildings.

"Let's go and say hello," McDaniels said.

"Sure thing." Gartrell steered the cart and braked it to an abrupt halt only a few feet from the group of scientists and researchers.

Regina looked over at them and smiled when she saw McDaniels. "Looks like we're together again, Major," she said.

"I'm afraid it's colonel now. You remember Gartrell, right?" McDaniels asked.

Regina looked at Gartrell, and her mouth fell open.

Gartrell managed a ghost of a smile. "Hello again, Miss Safire. Guess things stay the same the more they change, right?"

Regina launched herself at him and grabbed him up in a big hug, something that made even Gartrell bark out a laugh.

"I can't believe you're alive," Regina said. "I thought you died when you led the zombies away from us so we could get to the Coast Guard boat. Thank you for saving us in New York. Thank you, *thank* you!"

"Free of charge," Gartrell said. "Now if you don't mind, could you do me a favor?"

"What?"

"Stop choking me."

Regina laughed and released him. "Sorry about that." She looked at McDaniels. "So you were promoted?"

McDaniels nodded. "Both of us. I'm a lieutenant colonel, and Gartrell is now a sergeant major."

"If it sounds impressive, it isn't," Gartrell said. "And if it doesn't sound impressive, that would be correct."

"What happened in Maryland?" McDaniels asked her.

"Fort Detrick fell. The necromorphs seemed to replicate throughout the area at a phenomenal rate. I guess the, uh, authorities couldn't handle them. It was like New York City all over again." As she spoke, a haunted look descended upon her face. "We lost a lot of folks, including the Rid commander."

"How large a setback is that?"

The blond-haired older woman McDaniels remembered as Kersey stepped forward. "It was enough to hurt, Colonel. But we're here with all the research, and we're ready to pick up where we left off." She looked at Regina. "We really need to get going, Doctor Safire."

"Yeah, we'll let you get back to it." McDaniels checked his watch and nodded to Regina. "Good to see you again, ma'am. We have to head back to our operations center for a status meeting, but we'll catch you around campus, I'm sure."

"Hope so." Regina regarded him and Gartrell with a wry smile. "Looks like you guys can't be quit of me, huh?"

"That's the story of my life." Gartrell jerked his thumb toward McDaniels. "I've been trying to be quit of him for years, and look what happened."

Regina and McDaniels both laughed at the sergeant major's dry delivery.

Colonel Jaworski had his hands full running the task force. Even though McDaniels was supposed to be concentrating on the defense of the installation, as one of the task force senior officers, he had no choice but to get involved in the non-military issues confronting the operation. One of those issues happened to be a short woman by the name of Kensie Hobbes who represented the city of Odessa.

When the Corps of Engineers had dug the trenches, they'd had no choice but to tear up the rural highway in front of the pharmaceutical facility. The engineers had been reluctant to do it, but McDaniels and Bull Haley had been insistent. The trenches were designed to bottle up the zeds while they were still well away from the complex, which meant almost a mile away, not a few hundred feet. Jaworski had backed up his primary shooters, and engineers did as requested, though they did ask that Jaworski confirm that federal funds would be allocated to repair all the damage done to the highway. Jaworski received the confirmation on Department of Defense letterhead in the name of the Secretary of Defense himself.

The engineers set about chopping up the highway, but they built a wide extension to reroute traffic until the trenches could be filled in again. That had been a remarkable pain in the ass, for northbound traffic was steadily increasing as citizens fled the coming dead. Enough people complained, so Odessa sent Miss Hobbes down to find out just what in the hell the military was doing. Hobbes was short, pudgy, officious, and generally unlikeable, and McDaniels had a tough time keeping his cool while explaining that all damages would be covered by the DoD. Miss Hobbes claimed she was intending to sue on behalf of the city of Odessa and the counties of Ector and Midland, all of which depended on the well-being of Highway 385. McDaniels advised her that he wasn't a lawyer, but he was fairly sure the federal government, which had paid for the road to be built in the first place, could very likely do whatever it wanted with Highway 385 under the current circumstances. Miss Hobbes said she would return to the county seat and make her report, citing his personal intransigence and willing neglect, and that she had no doubt a local court would be issuing a cease-and-desist order. McDaniels noted that since SPARTA was technically a federal reservation, he doubted the papers could even be legally served. Miss Hobbes waved his dissent away and retreated to her Mary-

Kay-pink Cadillac STS.

McDaniels ordered the soldiers manning the newly built gate to deny her entry should she ever come back. He wasn't concerned about the legal action she had threatened, but he worried he might shoot her on sight.

The legality of such a lawsuit came up during one of the status meetings, and Jaworski dismissed the concern. "She can sue all she wants. Uncle Sugar owns the road. Besides, what are they going to do, send the local PD over to arrest us after we've been helping them take down stenches?"

There had been several more risings in Odessa in the past week, which wasn't surprising. If everyone was infected with the RMA 2 virus, then they would reanimate when they died, even if from an illness not associated with the virus. The area hospitals had armed security on staff twenty-four hours a day, just in case a critically ill patient crossed the line. The only way to deal with the eventuality was to shoot the recently deceased in the head. Two of the risings had required assistance from the SEALs, who were getting very good at eradicating the infestations before they spread. McDaniels had already decided to rotate other troops into the city if the risings continued, just so everyone could get some practical experience and to prevent the SEALs from being over-resourced.

"So does that mean I can't shoot her?" McDaniels asked. "I just got my Heckler and Koch, and I'd love to break it in on a live target." He slapped the rifle leaning against the wall beside him. When it had first arrived, he inspected the weapon, then took it to the range set up on the far western side of the area and zeroed it. After an hour, he had been hitting targets the size of a dollar bill almost six hundred yards away. He kept the HK417 assault rifle locked, loaded, and close at hand at all times.

"You'll get your chance. She'll probably come back as a stench," Jaworski said.

McDaniels grunted, then looked up as Gartrell nudged him. The sergeant major pointed to another enlisted man standing near the conference table.

"What's up, son?" McDaniels asked.

"There're an unknown number of stenches outside an elementary school, and the local SWAT team is tied up on another call."

"On it," Rawlings said immediately.

"Negative on that, Navy. Switch, stand up an ODA for this one," McDaniels said. "We need to start spreading the wealth before the rest of the zeds come this way."

"Roger that, Colonel." Switchblade left the conference table and hurried to another part of the TOC to communicate his tasking to the lucky alpha team.

McDaniels looked over at Rawlings and Haley. "And unless I'm totally off the wall, these uprisings have been happening a little more regularly lately. I think it might be about time for us to start deploying our external security teams on a full-time basis."

"Everyone's infected, Cord," Jaworski said. "And people die every day in a place as big as Odessa. I don't think there's anything more nefarious to it than that, but do you think we're at immediate risk?"

McDaniels shook his head. "Not just yet. Not from Odessa, anyway." He pointed at the LED monitor on the wall. San Antonio was under siege. The National Guard units had either been overrun or pushed back, despite the constant bombardments launched by the Air Force against the formations of the dead. Artillery had even been sent south from Fort Hood to add some steel rain to the fray, but it hadn't been terribly effective. Even neutralization fire was of very limited effect, as blast damage just didn't stop the dead the same way it did the living.

"We're looking at maybe five days until the first of the dead arrive in any numbers," Haley said. "I think it's a good idea giving the rest of the external security teams some time taking down the stenches. We should activate internal security as well, and make it a full-time occupation all around. My troops are ready to do something more than play Xbox and watch the engineers move dirt around."

"I don't disagree," McDaniels said. "Sarmajor?"

"No dissent from me, sir. But I do want to point out the Rangers have been plenty busy securing the perimeter, as instructed. We've got some excellent choke points in the process of being set up, so if the dead head our way, we'll be able to corral them into kill zones."

"Sounds impressive," Jaworski said with a smile.

"It's not as clean as it sounds, sir," Haley said. "A lot of troops are going to have to get their hands dirty disposing of the stenches once we've shot them. According to Cordell and the sergeant major, the rest of the stenches will just climb over the piles and keep coming, which means we have to figure out how we're going to get rid of the piles. We don't want to give them anything to hide behind, including mounds of dead zeds. Anything that disrupts our sight lines makes it more difficult to defend SPARTA."

"The company president told me they have some pretty volatile acids around that they use on occasion," Jaworski said. "Maybe we should check into that and see if they'd be of any use at breaking down the dead bodies. Hell, maybe when things get bad enough, we can flood one of the trenches with it. Let's see how many of them can make it out of an acid bath."

"There's an idea," McDaniels said. "We should probably look into that, sir. I don't know how practical it would be, but any defensive solution is worth considering."

"I'll see to it." Jaworski glanced at the monitor, which showed some of the city's outer communities ablaze. Images of the dead stumbling across the runways at Lackland Air Force Base made his normally affable expression harden.

"You know lot of folks there?" McDaniels asked.

"Sure." Jaworski didn't seem to want to pursue that conversation. "If the zeds show up today, what's our overall status? Are we good to go?"

"A lot of our planned modifications are underway, but none of them are fully completed," McDaniels replied. "Sure, we've zeroed out fire lanes, and the Rangers have popped off a few practice rounds from their mortars to make sure they're operational. Everyone is getting range time, and tons of munitions keep coming in, but we're still short on a lot of items, like guard towers and hardened observation posts, and physical deterrents like Alaska and HESCO barriers. We're way short on CONEX units to create the main walls. The trenches would slow them down, and the concertina wire will, too, but that's about all it would do. If they show up right now, the only thing between us and them are our guns. And our guys will have to rest sometime, while the stenches will just keep on coming."

"Add to that we haven't received a lot of the requested gear," Gartrell said. "The MRAPs won't be here until tomorrow at the earliest, and the armored cav regiment hasn't been fielded in our vicinity either."

"But they'll send some Apaches out our way in a day or so," Major Carmody said. "They have longer legs than the Little Birds, and can carry a lot more in the way of payload. I know they don't count for a whole lot, but it's an additional presence."

"The Apaches did fine by me in New York," Gartrell said. "Especially the thirty mike-mike cannons. The stenches aren't much of a threat if they've been blasted into twelve different pieces. But that was on a city street. The results might not be as spectacular out here in the big wild open."

"So how long do we need before we can say SPARTA is fully configured, defensively?" Jaworski asked.

"At least another two weeks," McDaniels said. "The supply chain from the east has been disrupted because there's a sizeable movement of zeds marching to the west. Why, we don't know. We don't expect them to get here within a month or so, but they're already making things more difficult for us."

"And for the rest of the country," Jaworski said. "Word

from my command is that our guys back east are going down for the count, and hard. The Army's sent several brigades against the dead outside of Fort Campbell, but they're not having much of an effect. They're stopping thousands of them, of course, but they need to be able to stop *hundreds* of thousands of them, and so far, they can't." Jaworski looked around the room. "So here's the big question of the day. Can *we* stop hundreds of thousands of stenches when they show up on our doorstep looking for their next meal?"

"So long as we're self-sufficient and can keep funneling the mass of their attacks into our selected kill zones, then yes. We can hold out," McDaniels said. "Bull?"

"Agreed," Colonel Haley said. "It won't be easy, since most of our weapons won't have the usual effect we've been trained to expect. But if we keep cool and keep hitting them in their heads, we'll be all right."

"Rawlings? Carmody?"

The commander of the Navy SEAL detachment and the officer in charge of the special operations aviators both responded affirmatively.

"Great," Jaworski said. "And forgive me if I'm a big downer here, but didn't you say the dead would start arriving in about five days or so?"

"That's only an estimate," McDaniels replied. "And it's a very optimistic one. We have helicopters and unmanned aerial systems that can keep watch to our south, so we can make sure we know where the dead are. But San Antonio is over three hundred miles away. If the dead are going after meat, they'll want to move on population centers, and the next one to the north is Austin." Even as he said it, McDaniels felt a twinge in his chest. Was Lenny all right? Was he doing exactly what he'd been told? Was he on his way?

Then, he heard the sounds of Little Birds passing overhead. He looked at Jaworski. "If you don't mind, sir, I'll want to plug in for the fight."

Jaworski nodded. "Roger that. You guys keep doing what you're doing. We'll go over status at twenty hundred."

McDaniels picked up his HK rifle and walked to the battle command desk in the operations center. Even though it promised to be minor, he still wanted to listen in as the Special Forces troops went to guns on the zeds.

16

The battle for Fort Campbell wasn't going in the Army's favor.

Despite the presence of thousands of war-hardened soldiers, armored vehicles, helicopters, artillery, and an understanding of what the enemy wanted—to eat human beings—it was almost impossible to stem the advance of the dead as they streamed into Tennessee and Kentucky from the east. There were hundreds of thousands of stenches, and they were like cockroaches. They seemed to be everywhere, and they were damned hard to kill, despite the best efforts of the entire 101st Airborne Division.

Artillery and aviation assets reached out and touched the advancing army of zeds while it was still dozens of miles away. Multiple-launch rocket systems pounded the enemy's advance elements with high-explosive munitions as the civilians fled; the first engagement occurred when the zeds approached Clarksville, Tennessee. The MLRS bombardment would have stopped a conventional army dead in its tracks and caused soldiers to seek cover and armored units to button up and move out of the engagement area. The zeds merely moved through the field of fire like some mindless beast, and forward observers reported the mass of walking dead didn't even seem to be *aware* of the bombardment. Even more chilling, the ones who lost limbs to the attack merely continued at a crawl as opposed to the usual shambling walk or loping run. The MLRS batteries continued firing for almost an entire day, until they ran out of munitions. But by that time, the artillery pieces had opened up, and tanks and infantry fighting vehicles had moved forward to engage the necromorphs directly. The artillery, the Army's "King of Battle," was as ineffective as the rocket systems had been.

Finally, one enterprising battery commander started firing smoke rounds. The dead's advance slowed. It seemed that even the zeds needed to see where they were going, and the fields of white and gray smoke caused them to become disoriented. The zed advance folded up, and the tanks, IFVs, and attack helicopters swooped in, using their thermodynamic optics, which saw through the smoke as if it weren't there. The zeds fell to the directed fires that hit them individually as opposed to as a single mass. In most instances, the rounds did not return the targets to death's embrace, but they rendered them immobile and unable to continue to hunt, which was the next best thing. But with the ability to kill from a distance taken away, the Army troops were at a disadvantage. While the soldiers numbered in the thousands and were well supplied, disciplined, and organized, the dead outnumbered them by almost a thousand to one by the time they swept over Clarksville.

One enterprising M1A3 Abrams tank commander found that, while his vehicle's weapons were mostly ineffective at stemming the tide, the tank itself was not. He ordered the tank's driver to roll right over the advance echelons of the dead, and the results were quite successful. Soon, every tracked vehicle in the area was rolling over the corpses, crushing them flat, leaving in their wake shattered husks that leaked black gore. Still, there were too many.

The armored vehicles couldn't be everywhere at once, and the stenches continued their march overland mostly unimpeded until they came upon the first sandbagged firing positions erected by the troops of the 101st Airborne Division. The troops hadn't had the luxury of a long wait. By the time their commanding officers determined that Fort Campbell was at a great risk, the troops had to be recalled from other missions to defend the base and the thousands of civilians who had sought shelter inside the fort's presumably impregnable defenses. But the dead were like no enemy the Army had ever fought, and their defenses were designed to keep living attackers at bay. The dead had no qualms about taking a few bullets, grenades, or even two-thousand-pound bombs. They merely existed to feed.

Despite their best efforts, the Airborne troops were pushed out of Clarksville and back into the southern half of Fort Campbell. Fighting from behind revetments and reinforced firing positions, the soldiers opened up on the zeds walking right into pre-ranged firing lanes. The firepower arrayed against the dead was awesome, and many a zombie fell to the ground, unable to continue. But for every one that fell, five more took its place. Soon, the zombies were climbing up the sandbagged positions. They ignored the firepower poured into them from close range and attacked the soldiers inside their fighting positions, overwhelming them in a series of swarm attacks.

Again and again, all but the most hardened positions fell to the horde, despite the crisscrossing helicopters and Air Force jets that hammered the necromorphs with a mix of precision and "dumb" weaponry. Those soldiers unable to retreat to another position met perhaps the worst fates imaginable.

The battle for Fort Campbell lasted six days. The military gave it back to the necromorphs as much as they could, saturating the enemy with withering firepower through layers of smoke and, wherever possible, white phosphorous munitions, which in heavy concentrations burned the necromorphs to the ground, reducing them to nothing more than smoldering smears.

Hour after hour, the Army was forced to collapse its perimeter and move it back to reconsolidate firepower. The military's area of operations continually shrank, becoming smaller and smaller. Tent cities set up for the civilian evacuees were abandoned, sometimes without enough time to transport the evacuees to another location. The dead fell upon them like hungry wolves, and those not consumed in entirety rose to join the legions of the necromorphs.

By the fifth day, the defensive positions had shrunk to encompass only the Blanchfield Army Community Hospital, just across the border on the Tennessee side. The defenders were supplied by helicopter from bases in northern Kentucky and southern Ohio, until those operations needed to be relocated.

Then, supplies came only from cargo airdrops. In most of the those cases, the Air Force cargo planes had to fly from bases in the Midwest, coming from as far west as Nebraska, Texas, and Oklahoma.

The air drops couldn't keep up with the frantic pace, and other areas of the nation's military and civilian infrastructure were equally threatened. On day six, the remaining commanders overseeing combat operations at Fort Campbell were told to bug out if they could.

They could not.

On the afternoon of the sixth day, most of the remaining munitions had been expended, and the necromorphs overwhelmed the fort's last defenses.

The fall of Fort Campbell was barely mentioned on the news, as entire cities were being overrun by the necromorphs. Even if it had been given a fair amount of airtime, Earl Brown had more things to worry about than the disposition of an Army base a few hundred miles to the south. He and Zoe had made their way across the country toward Ohio in the rented SUV Regina Safire had arranged for them, and Earl had managed to buy a shotgun and several boxes of shells when they picked their way across upstate New York. They were hardly alone. Thousands of other frightened people were starting to migrate west as well, and there were times when Earl feared he wouldn't be able to find more fuel for the car or food for them to eat. At his last fuel stop, he had filled a couple of two-and-a-half gallon containers with unleaded and put them in the trunk, then spent the next several hours worried that they might leak and cause an explosion as he drove down Interstate 90 through northern Pennsylvania. No such event came to pass, even when caught in bumper-to-bumper traffic outside of Erie. And it didn't take long to see what the holdup was. Erie, Pennsylvania, was on fire.

They're here, too, Earl thought.

"Daddy, where are we going to go?" Zoe had finally come out of the torpor that had descended upon her after the horrific events she had witnessed in New York City. She was hyperaware of everything and started at every unexpected movement on the road. Earl couldn't blame her, but her constant state of high alert led to more than a few false alarms.

"We're going to get off the highway as soon as we can and find our way to I-79," he said. "We'll follow dat down 'til we can find Interstate 80, and then we take dat into Ohio."

"How long will it take?"

"Don't know. Hush now, and try to relax."

Three hours later, he found an off-ramp that dropped them into a mostly rural backdrop promising little in the way of zombie interaction. Unfortunately, Earl wasn't the first to come up with the plan, and while traffic was a bit lighter than on the interstate, it was by no means smooth sailing. As Earl drove past the occasional broken-down vehicle, he saw more than a few hostile stares pointed in his direction. He wondered how long it would be until someone finally tried to take the car from them. Would they be shot? Could he shoot another human being in order to keep the vehicle and all it contained? He decided he could.

It took almost the entire night to make it to Interstate 79. Traffic finally thinned out, and even though they made good time, he was forced to abandon the highway early. He steered the car onto westbound Route 358.

"Daddy, where are we going?" Zoe asked, a tremor of panic in her voice.

"I need to get off the highway, baby. I'm dead tired, and I'm hopin' there's a place up here where we can get some sleep."

"No! Don't stop!"

"I have to, baby." Earl tried to keep his tone reasonable and reassuring. His nerves were frayed, and he noticed that even though they drove through mostly rural residential neighborhoods, traffic was thicker than it should have been at five in the morning.

"You have to trust me, Zoe," he continued before she could argue. "Your old dad's worn out. If I don't find someplace to sleep soon, I'm gonna fall asleep behind the wheel, and then we'll be in a whole *lotta* trouble. You get me?"

"Yes," Zoe said after a long moment. "I wish I could drive, Daddy. Then you could sleep, and we could keep driving."

"I know, hon. I know."

They came upon a small town called Greenville. Earl drove around until he found what he was looking for, and he parked the car on the street.

"Where are we?"

"Come with me, sweetie. Jus' keep cool, okay?"

He led her into a pawnshop where several overweight white men looked at him with blank eyes. They all looked related, with blunt noses and dark, porcine eyes that locked onto him and Zoe like a radar station locked onto an aircraft. All were armed with pistols on their belts, which they made no attempt to conceal. Earl didn't know if Pennsylvania was an open carry state, but he figured the times had probably changed enough over the last few weeks that such a thing no longer mattered.

"Help you?" the man behind the counter asked. He was broad of shoulder and sported the largest belly. He also looked to be the oldest, with steel-gray hair and a deeply creased face. He wore black, horn-rimmed glasses that Earl hadn't seen since the 1970s.

"I need a four-ten shotgun," Earl said. "Youth-sized. For my daughter."

The older man scowled down at Zoe. "You're lucky. No one's interested in the smaller gauges right now, but all the other stores are cleaned out. Even the Walmart up on Williamson—no guns, no ammunition, no food, no campin' supplies, no nothin'."

"We don't have much o' nothin' either," one of the younger

men offered.

"Hey, shut the hell up, Denny," the older man snapped. Denny sniffed and turned to look out the barred window at the front of the shop.

"Would you also have any ammunition?" Earl asked.

"Would you happen to have five thousand dollars?" the older man asked.

Earl blinked. "I'm sorry?"

"I have the gun you're looking for—a Mossberg 510, youth-size. I have twelve boxes of Fiocchi high-velocity ammunition. It's all yours, including a cleaning kit, for five thousand dollars or equivalent barter or trade."

Earl had to fight to control his outrage. "Five thousand bucks? Don't you think dat's a bit *high*, man?"

"It is what it is. If you can't afford it, get the fuck out."

"Daddy..." Zoe tugged at his hand.

Earl sighed. He'd been overcharged almost every step of the way, and of the two thousand dollars Regina had given him, he had only eight hundred left. The shotgun would normally have retailed for just over two hundred dollars. "I don't have five grand."

"Then get the fuck out. Denny, you and Larry see this man to the door."

"What would you take in trade?" Earl asked quickly.

"You tell me. And make it quick."

Early slowly reached into his pocket and pulled out the Cartier watch Regina had given him. He knew it was worth much more than five thousand dollars, probably ten times that much, but it was all he had. He held the diamond-studded watch out where the older man could see it, but not touch it. "Cartier, bought in New York City. Very high end."

"I can see that. That's a Captive model. Eighteen-karat gold band, diamonds, the whole nine yards. Where the hell did you get that?"

"That matter? I didn't steal it."

The older man held out his hand. When Earl hesitated, he said, "I'm not going to take it from you, boy, I just need to appraise it."

Boy? Earl gritted his teeth and handed over the watch.

The fat white man took it and laid it on the glass-topped counter, then pulled a jeweler's loupe from one pocket. He examined the watch closely, paying most attention to the diamonds set in the bezel. He turned it over. If he read the inscription on the back, he didn't mention it. He made a sound in his throat and put the loupe back in his pocket. He pushed the watch toward Earl.

"That's a true high-ticket item," he said as he crossed his arms. "I'd say that's a thirty thousand dollar item—on sale. Deep discount, fifteen thousand. That's worth a lot more than the goods you're asking about."

Earl blinked. "Not sure I unnerstand."

"I'm not a *thief*, damn it. If that's what you have for trade, I'll accept it at a face value of fifteen thousand dollars. And you're free to look around and see if there are any other items you might need that we have in stock."

"Really?" Earl asked, disbelievingly.

The old man scowled again. "The world ain't ended just yet."

With the vehicle loaded with more supplies, Earl and Zoe continued down the road until he found a small turn-off. The day was cool, but Earl still pulled the Pathfinder behind a thick copse of shade trees where he felt sure the silver SUV wouldn't be seen from the road.

Zoe sat up straight in the front passenger seat and looked around with wide eyes. "Why here?"

"I already told you; I need some sleep." Earl reclined the driver's seat, made the sure the doors were locked, the pistol he'd bought for six thousand dollars was close at hand in the center console, and that the shotguns were lying on the back seat next to the cheap tent that had cost entirely too much.

"I'm scared."

"And I'm tired. Just for a few hours, Zoe, then we're back on the road again."

She looked at him with eyes that had seen far too much horror. "You promise?"

Earl reached out and touched his daughter's cheek. "Promise."

The roads into Ohio were closed.

The traffic had backed up on every road Earl could find, not that there were that many in their slice of western Pennsylvania. The radio had finally come alive with news reports from the emergency broadcasting system, something that had only broadcast tests during all the years Earl had lived. There was a zombie force of some sort to the south, in Kentucky, and it had defeated the Army at Fort Campbell—Earl didn't know much about Army posts and whatnot, but he was certain that if an entire *fort* was overrun, then that meant the dead weren't just everywhere, but they were in great numbers. Worse, the dead were making their way north, while a smaller force of zombies was causing all sorts of hell in Cleveland.

Guess Ohio's off the list.

The radio announcement instructed all civilians to move to an emergency protection center outside of Pittsburgh, still over a hundred miles south. Earl didn't know what to think about that; if a bunch of zombies were coming up from the south, then he wondered how safe he and Zoe would be in an "emergency protection center," whatever that was.

But what choice did he have? The traffic pointed toward Ohio wasn't moving at all, and in the distance, he saw men in uniform on an armored vehicle of some sort forcing the traffic ahead to turn around and take a south-bound road. He ran a hand over his stubbled chin and watched the traffic slowly unwind. In the distance, somewhere in the woods to their right, he heard guns firing bursts on full automatic. That bothered Earl as well, since it meant there were probably zombies in the woods, zombies that could step out of the tree line at any moment.

"Well, looks like we're going to head south for a bit, baby girl," Earl said.

"Okay," was all Zoe said.

Earl patted her skinny leg and waited for his turn to pull out of traffic. He kept one eye on the trees to the right of the Pathfinder.

17

"Colonel McDaniels? We've got something going down at Gate One, sir."

McDaniels looked up at the young Army lieutenant standing next to his workstation. "What's happening, Lieutenant? A stench show up?"

"Nothing that critical, sir. If you'll open up cam two on your computer? It might be easier to show you than tell you."

McDaniels did as instructed, and a black-and-white window opened up on his screen. It was a direct feed from the camera unit at the gate. Every gate had four surveillance cameras, and camera two was a close-angle camera mounted right at the gate itself. Framed inside the window was the real-time imagery, which included armed sentries interrogating the driver of a white 2010 Mustang GT. The driver was a young black man in his early twenties.

"The man behind the wheel says he's your son," the lieutenant said. "Is that true, sir?"

"Yes, Lieutenant. That is in fact my son."

"We'll allow him through, Colonel. He'll have to go through decon just like everyone else, but they should be ready for pick up in about an hour." The lieutenant turned to go.

"*They*, Lieutenant? Who are the rest of them?" McDaniels asked.

The lieutenant turned back with a puzzled expression. "Well, your daughter-in-law and her parents, sir."

Daughter-in-law?

"Great. Thanks, Lieutenant. I appreciate it."

"No problem, sir."

McDaniels turned back to his workstation and looked at the surveillance camera footage. He could certainly make out

Lenny—calm, cool, and collected, even though his vehicle was surrounded by men with guns. Next to him was a blond-haired woman—girl?—who was less composed. The Mustang's rear windows weren't very large, so he couldn't tell who was in the back seat, but he was confident that some tortured souls were indeed trapped back there.

Oh, Lenny. What have you done now?

"Hey, Dad!" Leonard McDaniels almost shouted after he finally cleared the decontamination area. With him came a tall, slender girl with straw-blond hair. Like Lenny, she wore jeans and a T-shirt, but she carried a leather jacket under one arm. Behind her came what McDaniels could only presume were her parents. The father was rather squat and square-shouldered, an almost picture-perfect image of a redneck Texan. In his younger years, the man might have been a star of the gridiron. The mother was an older version of the daughter, only more faded, less vibrant, still attractive enough, but no longer a beacon of beauty.

"Leonard," McDaniels said. "Had I known you were bringing guests, I would have arranged for the good silverware to be brought out."

Lenny's expression became sheepish. That pleased McDaniels a bit. After all, Lenny was at the age when young men viewed their fathers more like pals than authority figures, so it was still a bit of a kick to see that Lenny hadn't made it to that point. Yet.

"Uh well, I did tell you about Belinda. Right, Dad?" Lenny asked as he approached. The others held back a bit, probably sensing the building disagreement.

"You did," McDaniels agreed.

"And these are her parents. She wouldn't leave without—"

"Lenny, forget about it. They're here." McDaniels grabbed his son and held him tight. He realized he'd missed Lenny terribly, and even in the middle of the dark night in New York City when he'd been fighting for his life, a part of him had still worried about Lenny. Seeing with his own eyes that his son was safe, he felt a sizeable chunk of stress dissolve.

Apparently, Lenny didn't feel the same way. He squirmed in McDaniels's embrace, and when he spoke, the embarrassment was clear in his voice. "Hey, Dad, I'm glad to see you too but all the soldiers are *looking* at us, man!"

McDaniels laughed and released his son, albeit slowly. "Well, let 'em look." But out of the corner of his eye, he saw Lenny was right. Several soldiers *were* looking at them, and most of them didn't seem very happy. It took McDaniels a moment to figure out what the issue was, but then understanding dawned. The soldiers didn't have their families anywhere nearby, but McDaniels had managed to get his own son to SPARTA.

Not too cool, Cord.

"Come on. Let's find a tent for you guys and get you squared away," he said, slapping Lenny on the shoulder. He looked past his son at the tall girl and extended his hand. "Hi, you must be Belinda? I'm Cord McDaniels, Lenny's father."

"Yes, sir." Belinda shook his hand, her grip firm and strong. "I'm very happy to meet you. And thank you for giving us permission to come here with Lenny."

"Of course." McDaniels turned to the couple. "And these would be your parents?"

"Jim Howie," the man said. His Texan accent was strong, and his handshake wasn't just firm, but almost bone-crushing. "Good to meet you, sir. Lieutenant colonel, am I right?"

McDaniels found he actually had to work to keep from wincing. "You are. Just recently promoted, actually. And it's good to meet you, too, Mister Howie."

"Please, it's Jim."

"Okay, Jim. I'm Cord." McDaniels turned to Belinda's mother, who extended her hand slowly, almost daintily.

"Colonel, I'm Jeanette Howie."

"Good to meet you too, ma'am. Can I call you Jeanette?" McDaniels shook her hand gently.

"I go by Jeanie, actually."

"Jeanie it is, then." He looked back at Jim Howie. "Did you folks have any possessions with you?"

"They're still in the car," Lenny said. "The guards wouldn't let us take anything out, and they took the shotguns."

"Procedure. Unauthorized weapons are confiscated, but we can get those back without much of a problem. And the rest of the gear, too. But Lenny, you might have to ditch the car for a while. Space is going to be at a premium soon."

"I understand," Lenny said, and he didn't seem to be all that broken up about it. "I figured since it's the zombie apocalypse, a Ford Mustang is probably going to rank pretty low on the vehicle survivability scale when things get rough."

"You got that right," McDaniels said with a grin. "Okay, we'll come back to that shortly. But in the meantime, let's get you quarters, and I'll try and familiarize you with the camp and get your gear returned to you."

"Thanks, Dad. I mean it. Thanks a lot."

McDaniels clapped his son on the shoulder again and ignored the barely contained disdain he sensed emanating from the nearby sentries. "You got it, kid. You got it."

Regina sat in the lab and added the precise amount of control agent to the samples of RMA 2 virus. All around her, a dozen research scientists did the same thing, using different combinations of the vaccine her father had invented. The goal was to narrow down which concentration would be the most effective across a mass spectrum. Whichever agent demonstrated the most efficiency in causing the virus to become incapable of binding to host cells would be the manufacturing candidate. Once the senior researchers had typified the agent and developed test batches for use on infected people, and if those results were positive, then the winning vaccine would go into immediate production. Already, the military had identified the aircraft that would fly the vaccine out to the west, where it would be replicated while the InTerGen plant continued manufacture in Texas. In fact, Colonel Jaworski had even requested another helicopter be brought to the facility for the express purpose of airlifting the vaccine out should the zombies surround the complex. No one was content to sit around and hope for the best while the world was going to hell. The zombies had already overrun San Antonio and were on the road to Austin. The news reports were full of coverage on all the flat-screen televisions in the conference rooms and breakrooms.

Not that she had a lot of time or inclination to watch them.

The test agent she worked with was one of the more successful ones. Almost immediately after exposing it to contaminated cells, the RMA 2 virus detached from the hosts. Free-floating in the plasma, the virus slowly undulated under the magnification of the electron microscope, seeking out new cells with which to bond. Regina watched as the virus particles came in contact with other cells in the batch and failed to establish a long-lasting bind. If the virus couldn't anchor itself to human cells, then it couldn't replicate. It needed the DNA in the cells to fuel its progression, and in order to harvest that, the virus had to be able to grab a cell and hold onto it.

It was a promising development.

When the sun started to slip past the western horizon, Regina took a break. After going through a bath of warm water and bleach, she removed her pressurized Racal suit and stepped through the two airlocks that finally deposited her in the ready room. Another batch of researchers was coming online for the day. Regina didn't know them, but they all acknowledged her presence with a smile or a nod.

Of course, I'm the former boss's daughter.

She left the research wing and headed for one of the breakrooms on the next floor, one she hoped be empty at that hour. It wouldn't remain empty for long. The company was moving in all the dependents of the employees, giving them some measure of security as the zombies inexorably drew nearer. In a few days, every building in the complex would be full of people. Things were going to get quite cozy over the next few weeks.

The breakroom was indeed deserted. She went to the refrigerator and pulled out a sandwich and salad she'd put there in labeled containers that bore her name and the date. She was happy to find that no lunch thieves had descended upon them while she had been working. She sat at one of the tables and looked out the third floor window.

The complex's transformation was impressive. In only a few short days, the military had effectively converted the property into defensive revetments and helicopter landing zones. The work continued throughout the nights, as more trenches were dug and bulldozers pushed the excavated earth up into high berms. Guard towers were being built, tall structures made from welded metal that promised to rise high into the sky. Helicopters came and went, but not all of them carried people and cargo; several were unmanned aircraft used to survey the territory around the complex. McDaniels had explained that one of the only ways they might survive the coming weeks and months was to find the enemy before it found them.

Regina felt comfortable with McDaniels, after all they'd gone through trying to escape New York City. All of the troops protecting her and her father had died; only McDaniels and Gartrell had made it out alive. McDaniels had tried to see to Earl and his daughter, even though there was precious little he could do for them, and that meant a lot to Regina as well. McDaniels had a heart, even with everything that was going down. He and Gartrell were the kind of men she could trust, and of all the people in the InTerGen office park, she knew what kind of threat they were facing. It was good to have people you could trust to do the right thing when everything started to turn into shit.

And shit is what's headed our way, she thought as she unwrapped her meal. *Slowly but surely, the stenches are coming out to play.*

On impulse, she reached into her lab coat pocket and pulled out her smartphone. To her surprise, she had a message. It must have come in while she had been in the research lab. Only approved electronic devices were allowed past the locker room, and smartphones were not on the official list. She dialed her voicemail and brought the phone to her ear.

"H'lo Miss Safire, this is Earl Brown. Ah ... me 'n Zoe, we're okay. I really appreciate everything you did for us. The Pathfinder's great. I did have to trade in your watch for some things. I'm sorry 'bout that. Didn't want to do it, but had to. Sorry. Anyway, me 'n' Zoe, we have to go to some emergency center outside o' Pittsburgh. We can't get into Ohio; the military has it blocked off. So um, I just wanted to let you know. We're fine. Hope you are, too. Thanks for everything. I'll try and get in touch with you later." There was a long pause, as if Earl had run out of things to say, then finally, "Bye now."

Regina tried to call him back, but the call went straight to voicemail. Regina left a message telling Earl to call her as soon as he could and gave him the switchboard number of the complex, so she could be paged. She very much wanted to know how Earl and Zoe were coming along, where they were, and if there was any chance they might be able to find their way to Texas.

18

After finding Lenny and his party a tent close to the civilian portion of the camp, McDaniels had precious little time to conduct anything even remotely approaching an orientation. He had meetings and other tasks to attend to, so he promised his son and the Howies he would return for them at around seventeen hundred hours. He pointed out the D-FAC on their way to the tent and advised them they could get some food and drink there.

"If anyone gives you any grief, tell them the deputy commanding officer has authorized you to use the facility, and if they have any issues, they can contact me directly," McDaniels told them.

"Will do," Lenny said.

"I'll have some troops bring your gear to you, or if you like, I can have them take you back to the car. Your choice."

Lenny looked at the others, then said, "I think I can find my way back to the gate, but maybe Mister Howie can help me carry the stuff back."

"Absolutely," Jim Howie said.

"Okay, I can arrange for that to happen. Give it an hour, and then head back to the gate. Bring your identification, but it shouldn't be any problem."

"Will we get our weapons back?" Lenny asked.

"I hope so because at seventeen thirty, we have gunnery practice."

"What does that mean?" Belinda asked.

Lenny smiled. "It means we're going to do some shooting at the range."

Leonard McDaniels watched as his father stripped down the assault rifle while explaining each and every part and what it did over the sporadic crackle of firearms. Several hundred yards behind them, the lights in the parking lots surrounding the InTerGen office park snapped on as the sun disappeared below the horizon, leaving behind a dusky glow. One of the soldiers started a generator, and floodlights flickered to life, bathing the impromptu shooting range in stark, harsh light. From the corner of his eye, Lenny saw Belinda run a hand through her long blond hair and look around as McDaniels continued breaking down the rifle.

"Belinda, are you getting this?" his dad asked without missing a beat.

Belinda focused on McDaniels quickly. "Yes, sir. I'm sorry."

"You need to stay tuned in to what I'm doing, no matter what happens around you," McDaniels said. "You should always be aware of your surroundings, but don't get distracted. Especially when you're supposed to be learning how to maintain a Heckler and Koch assault rifle."

"Yeah, pay attention," Lenny said, giving her a good-natured push.

"I'm with you," she said as she slapped his hand away.

McDaniels continued stripping down the rifle. There were more than a few parts, but Lenny was familiar with most of them already. The HK417 was little different from the M16s and M4s he had essentially grown up with, the major exception being the firing pin assembly.

"Do they jam often?" Belinda asked.

"The M4? Not as much as the first M16s did, but I had one with full mods lock up on me in New York City when I was danger close with the zeds. That's why I'm carrying one of these now." McDaniels slapped the HK417 slung over his shoulder.

"What's danger close? Sorry, I really don't know anything about military stuff."

"It means my dad was right there with the zombies, and his

rifle jammed on him. Danger close is where the bad guys are within spitting distance," Lenny said.

"That's right," McDaniels confirmed. A group of Rangers entered the range, and they set up a few benches away. One of them walked toward McDaniels and saluted. His father straightened and returned the gesture.

"What's happening, Sergeant Roche?"

"You mind if we set up over there, sir? We'd like to get in some gunnery practice before we get rotated outside the wall," Roche said.

Lenny thought there was something mild-mannered about the Ranger, and he sensed the change in Belinda's body language. The Ranger was also a handsome sucker, and Lenny felt a twinge of jealousy at the notion that Belinda might be attracted to him, even though he was at least ten years older.

"No, you guys go ahead," McDaniels said. "Your chalk's on the external security team? Call sign Badger?"

"Yes, sir."

McDaniels nodded. "Attaboy, Ranger. You guys tear it up. Just let us know if you're going to start lobbing grenades, all right?"

"No chance of that, sir. Thanks."

"All right," McDaniels said once Roche turned and walked back to his team. "This pretty much completes the tear down. Lenny, I want you to reassemble it first, then tear it down and do it all over again. Belinda, watch him. Once he's done, you're next."

"Okay," she said. "Cool, I've never done anything like this before."

"Prepare to be amazed, then."

The Rangers sighted on their targets and began firing; Belinda flinched at the sudden noise. McDaniels looked up and watched as the Rangers popped each man-shaped silhouette in the head, from ranges of one hundred feet to six hundred yards. Lenny noticed that the Rangers handled their M4s and Mk 17

SCARs with a precision that only a professional soldier could muster.

Glad to have them with us, he thought before turning his attention back to the Heckler and Koch assault rifle. He quickly replicated his father's efforts and slipped part into part until he held what he thought was a fully operational battle rifle. He held it up in his hands, then passed it to his father.

"How'd I do?" he asked.

McDaniels pulled back the rifle's charging lever, checked the breech, released the lever, then shouldered the weapon and pointed it downrange. He pulled the trigger, and Lenny hoped he heard a soft *click* in response. His father nodded and passed the rifle back to him.

"Excellent job. Strip it down. Belinda? Get ready."

"Yes, sir," she said automatically, and without even the remotest trace of sarcasm. It was tough to maintain the usual college sophomore façade of a peacenik when the world was falling down around your ears. Lenny was glad to hear that; while he'd always known his father would never turn someone away just because of their politics, he hadn't wanted him to have to deal with Belinda's admittedly annoying attitude. But she'd straightened up the second they'd arrived at SPARTA, and that was only a good thing.

"Lenny?" McDaniels prompted.

Lenny got back with the program and stripped down the HK. He didn't move as quickly and methodically as his father had, but he felt his fingers were moving with a purpose as they pulled a pin here, pulled a rod there. Soon, the assault rifle was reduced to its basic components, and Lenny took a moment to arrange things on the bench. McDaniels leaned over it for a moment, then nodded to Belinda.

"Okay, girl. You're up."

Belinda stepped up beside Lenny and reached for the stripped-down lower receiver. Her movements were timid, hesitant. Lenny knew it was the first time she'd ever seen a military weapon outside of the movies. He looked up at McDaniels, but his father shook his head slightly. His girlfriend was on her own for the moment. She tried to reassemble the weapon, but couldn't make the majority of the parts fit together. After several minutes, Lenny could tell she was getting frustrated.

"Here, let me help you out a bit," McDaniels said. Without taking over, he instructed her on how to reassemble the firing pin assembly and insert it back inside the rifle, and how to inspect it to ensure that it was properly seated against the recoil plate.

It took almost ten minutes, and sometimes his father had to shout above the racket the Rangers made, but bit by bit, Lenny could see that Belinda was getting it. When she finally had the rifle put back together, McDaniels took it from her, inspected it, and handed it back.

"Took a lot longer than you want, but good job," McDaniels said. "Now tear it down and put it back together, and let's send some rounds downrange. After that, we'll clean up and call it a night."

Gartrell sat at a table in the D-FAC, taking down a surprisingly tasty steak sandwich when two Special Forces NCOs approached him. They carried trays loaded with food and energy drinks.

"You mind if we dance with your dates?" Master Sergeant Donald "Dusty" Roads asked, parroting a line from *Animal House*. He'd even screwed on the urban black accent.

Gartrell had to smile at that. It had been a while since he'd thought about the boys from Delta Fraternity. "Have a seat, guys," he said.

"You sure?" Master Sergeant Rick "Barney Rubble" Forringer asked, even though he immediately pulled out a chair and plopped down into it. He definitely looked like a real-life

Barney Rubble—straw-blond hair, big nose, weak chin, small eyes—but that he looked like a living cartoon character was undercut by the fact he was one of the sharpest SF snipers Gartrell had ever known.

Roads was an intelligence operator, much taller and leaner than Forringer, and had looks that approached Hollywood handsome. Physically, they couldn't be more different, but personally and professionally, the two men worked well together.

"It's a free dining facility," Gartrell said, "but don't waste any time sitting down or anything, Barney."

"I gather no dust when it comes time to chow down," Forringer responded around a mouthful of food.

"The only thing he does faster than sit down to eat is lie down to sleep," Roads said as he put down his tray and pulled out a chair.

"Wow, you know how long it takes me to fall asleep? That's kind of creepy, man," Forringer said. He dug into his barbeque chicken without delay.

"Why's that creepy? I thought the two of you were engaged," Gartrell said.

Forringer frowned. "Please. I'm trying to eat."

"Like the commentary is going to throw you off," Roads said. "I figure half the Ranger battalion could be attacking you with a tube of Astro-Glide and you wouldn't even notice."

"Boy, do I miss the days of 'Don't Ask, Don't Tell.' Seems like Dusty's about to make a confession, Sarmajor."

"Try not to get anything on the walls, boys," Gartrell cautioned.

Roads grinned and started in on his own meal.

It had been a while since the three of them had broken bread together, especially since Gartrell had moved over to the Special Warfare Center and started training the next generation of Army Green Berets. Roads and Forringer had remained operational, though Roads had stepped out of the alpha det regime and worked directly for Major "Switchblade" Lewis as the senior intelligence NCO with the bravo detachment. Gartrell asked Roads how he liked working with the walking mountain known as Captain Chase, and was happy to hear a favorable review. Even though Chase was Big Army, Roads thought the huge officer was sharp as a tack and could read a situation for what it was without having to pull anything.

"All right, all right, enough foreplay." Forringer had finished his chicken, and his lips were smeared with barbeque sauce. He licked them clean and reached for a cob of corn. "We're here to find out the straight poop, Dave."

"Such as?"

"What happened to Keith and the rest of the guys in the Big Apple?" Roads asked. "I knew Rittenour pretty well; we were pods from the 90s."

"Ah." Gartrell finished the last bite of his steak sandwich and leaned back in his chair. "Keith's team handled themselves really well. Rittenour and Leary especially so—those guys were leaning forward in the foxhole the entire time. If not for them, I wouldn't be here right now. Or I'd have a different pallor and would be eating you."

"Did McDaniels screw the pooch again?" Roads asked. He and Forringer knew all about the bad blood between Gartrell and McDaniels. A lot of folks inside the community of Quiet Professionals had the inside line on that, since Gartrell hadn't been the most restrained of individuals in his younger days.

Gartrell took a moment to gather his thoughts. "I'm not sure that Bill Meadows himself could have done things any differently," he answered finally.

Forringer gaped at the invocation of one of the luminaries of the Special Forces universe. "You're mentioning McDaniels and Meadows in the same conversation? I think this qualifies as a 'what the fuck' moment, and it frankly has me scared."

"Try not to spot your thong," Gartrell said.

"You want to try and clear that up a bit, Dave?" Roads

remained fixed on target, which was what made him such an unflappable type of operator.

"Clear what up, exactly?"

"What happened in New York, and how McDaniels is suddenly a stand-up guy in your eyes."

Gartrell was annoyed by the questioning, but he tried not to let it show. He thought back to what he had gone through, both with McDaniels and after. The truth of the matter was, Gartrell had always prided himself on being able to keep his emotions in check. He'd always thought that he had the ability to suppress his personal desires and put the mission first. But if that was *truly* the case, then chances were good he never would have pulled a weapon on McDaniels and threatened to kill him over another disagreement on operational matters.

And then, there was the boy, Jaden. An autistic three-year-old boy Gartrell had tried to save by leading him and his mother through the black subway tunnels beneath New York City. A boy whose final moments in life were full of terror and pain.

"Dude, you all right?"

Gartrell looked up and saw Forringer and Roads studying him, concern on their faces. He wondered what they had seen in his eyes in that moment when he thought of Jaden and his mother, and the fate he had led them to beneath the streets of Manhattan.

"Guys, there's no mystery to it," Gartrell said. "I last worked for McDaniels in... what, 2007? A lot of water has gone under the bridge since then. Things change. People change. McDaniels has changed. And me, too. He did what he had to do in New York, and he accomplished the mission. Now Keith, Rittenour, Leary... all the troops who went in with us are dead. That's true, but it wasn't because of McDaniels. It was because of the fucking *stenches*." Gartrell pointed at the nearby TV, which showed a Stryker unit opening up on a gaggle of zombies ambling down a trash-littered highway somewhere in the middle of Texas.

"So that's it, then?" Roads asked. "Nothing more to it? Things change, and McDaniels is a stand-up guy again?"

"Dusty, do you want to ask him for yourself? I bitched about the move he made in Afghanistan, and I still have reservations about it, but in the end, it was his call. He has to live with the fallout, too. And right now, we've all got a pretty big fight to get ready for, so we need to put aside the petty shit and soldier like we're supposed to. We've got a butt-load of civilians in the compound now, and we have to protect them as well as this facility and preserve it so it can be used to accomplish its mission."

Forringer cackled. "Hah, this is the command sergeant major talking, right?"

Gartrell didn't smile. "Guys, I'm all about the mission. I'm the quick reaction force senior NCO, and I report directly to the lieutenant colonel in charge. We can discuss the guy's merits all night long, but in the end, he's the one calling shots. That shouldn't be a gray area, right?" As he said the last, Gartrell looked directly at Roads.

Roads shook his head immediately. "Not for me, bro. I'm good with it."

"Same here," Forringer said. "If anyone's interested, that is."

"Of course we're interested in what you have to say, sweetheart," Gartrell said. "But what was your name, again?"

Forringer shook his head. "I knew it. You're the kind who just won't respect me in the morning."

"Man, we don't even respect you now," Roads said.

"Damn you. Damn you all to Hell," Forringer said in his best Charlton Heston voice.

19

McDaniels awoke to the sound of sirens and the *bang-bang-bang* of gunfire from inside the complex. He rolled off his cot and snatched up his rifle as the rest of the officers in the tent sprang into action. Everyone armed themselves and made for the GP-Medium's entrance as the alarm system wailed and floodlights snapped on. Over the loudspeakers, which had just been installed the day before, he heard a voice that sounded suspiciously like Captain Chase's.

"Attention, internal security. Attention, internal security. Zed in the tent city. Armed reaction teams to respond. All civilians remain in place unless directly threatened."

McDaniels bulled his way through the tent's entrance and into the chilly night. Holding his assault rifle in both hands, he ran down the alley, dodging soldiers as they emerged from their tents, fully armed and ready for action.

"Hercules, coming through!" he shouted, and the soldiers stepped back to allow him to pass. McDaniels sprinted toward the tent city where the civilians were housed behind a series of revetments still under construction. Lots of people milled about in the semi-darkness. While the floodlights had been switched on, there were still wide swaths of area where the night remained impenetrable. McDaniels caught up to a group of Rangers, several of whom had their night vision goggles dropped down over their eyes.

"Rangers, what's the story?" he asked.

One of them pointed down an alley. "Right down there, sir. One zed, down for the count. Looks like someone died and came back."

McDaniels looked in the direction the Ranger pointed. Lenny shared a tent with Belinda and her family one alley over, so for the moment, his son was likely safe. When McDaniels started to enter the alley, the Ranger put a hand on his shoulder.

"Hold on for just a sec, sir. The area hasn't been secured. We have a chalk in there already checking out the site. Shouldn't be more than a few minutes."

"Just one stench?" McDaniels asked.

"That's what we've heard, sir."

Someone jostled McDaniels. "Aren't you supposed to be in the TOC, Colonel?"

McDaniels turned and found Gartrell standing beside him, his AA-12 in hand, helmet-mounted night vision goggles over his eyes. He was manned up in full armor and wearing his usual weapons load-out. McDaniels was running light, having only his assault rifle and sidearm. His night vision goggles were still locked in the upright position on his helmet.

"Aren't you supposed to be there as well, Sergeant Major?"

Gartrell shrugged. "Well, since the boss wasn't around, it seemed all right to bypass that specific destination in order to put eyeballs on target." Gartrell turned his head, panning his PVS-7's single light intensifier tube over McDaniels. "Sir, you don't have your radio."

Shit. McDaniels reached up and touched his left ear. Sure enough, his radio headset was still back in the tent, along with the lion's share of his gear. It was an amateur move, hurrying out before he was fully equipped to handle whatever the situation might dictate. *I need to get with the program and stay with it.* "Everyone has their moments, Sarmajor."

"Yes, sir." Gartrell looked back toward the darkened alley between the rows of tents, then started forward.

"Site secure, sir," the Ranger behind him said.

McDaniels nodded his thanks, embarrassed. If he'd had his own radio, he would have heard the report himself.

With Gartrell leading the way, McDaniels advanced into the tent city. Ahead, more Rangers stood outside a tent, weapons at port arms. Civilians stuck their heads out of several tents, and the Rangers waved them back inside without answering their questions. As they neared the secured tent, McDaniels heard the sounds of several people, including a crying child and a woman's raised voice. Gartrell stopped short and let McDaniels pass when they neared the Rangers' perimeter.

"What's the status here?" McDaniels asked.

The captain in command of the Rangers turned and saluted. "Had a rising in this tent, sir. Looks like a family member died somehow and reanimated during the night. We're thinking it was sudden, maybe a heart attack or something similar. We were in the zone already, and we heard it go down when the stench went on the attack."

"Injuries?"

"Two. One woman has a bloody nose. One kid has a, uh, bite wound."

McDaniels grimaced. "Damn it."

"Yes, sir." The Ranger captain didn't seem to like the set of circumstances either. "We were on it almost immediately, but..."

"Not your team's fault, son. We knew this was going to happen, and a lot of people are at risk until we can manage it. Any injuries related to your team's activities? I heard three shots."

"That's because three of us shot the zed at the same time, sir. We were on it so quickly we didn't have enough time to organize our fires, but every round hit the stench. No one missed, and all were head shots."

"Medical assistance is on the way?"

"Yes, sir. There's a team headed over right now from the main building." The Ranger officer pointed toward the main building in the office park, where the research facilities were located.

"Do me a favor. Tell them to reach out to Doctor Regina Safire. She's a pediatrician, and she's the one who should look over the kid."

"Hooah." The captain turned away slightly and spoke into

his headset's boom microphone.

McDaniels motioned for Gartrell to follow him into the tent. Gartrell held back for a moment, then slowly obeyed the nonverbal order.

The tent was in disarray. Several cots had been knocked over, and bedding lay everywhere. A boy sat curled on a woman's lap, cradling his wrist, sobbing in fear and pain. The woman spoke softly to the boy, but McDaniels saw tears in her eyes as well. At the other side of the tent, an older woman held a towel to her nose. She was tended by a Ranger, while another Ranger stood over the motionless body on the floor. A blanket had been thrown over the corpse, but McDaniels could smell the blood in the air, mixed with the acrid tang of cordite.

McDaniels knelt beside the woman with the crying boy. He gently reached out and pulled the boy's arm toward him. The kid had a bloodstained towel clamped to his wrist.

The woman looked at McDaniels with wet eyes. "He's been bitten. It's a big one."

"Medical help is on its way," McDaniels said.

"What's going to happen to me?" Tears streamed down the boy's face. He looked to be about seven years old. Did he know what a bite would do to him?

McDaniels thought that the kid probably did. He touched the boy's head and smiled as confidently as he could. "You're going to be fine, son. Just fine."

After the medical folks arrived and carted off the two women and the boy, McDaniels instructed the Rangers to stand guard over the tent to ensure no one entered. He wanted it quarantined until it could be decontaminated or taken down and destroyed.

"I've had zombie gore all over me, and I didn't get the bug," he told the Ranger captain. "But that's probably just pure luck on my part. Let's treat this as a lethal pathogen, and contain it as best as we can. Any biologicals should be destroyed."

"We'll treat it as a HAZMAT site," the captain agreed.

McDaniels nodded. "Hooah."

"Colonel?" Gartrell stepped toward him. "We need to get to the TOC. Jaworski and the rest of the senior leadership are waiting for us."

"Roger that. I'll need to stop by my tent and grab the rest of my gear. Can't believe I took off without it. Stupid."

"You were thinking of your son, right?" Gartrell asked.

McDaniels sighed and nodded. "Yeah. I guess I was."

"Not a big deal, sir. It's not like you were going over the wall into stench country with nothing on your back and no munitions on hand. But next time, you should take a second to pull it all together. Being unable to communicate at your level is bad juju." Gartrell tapped one of his radio's earphones.

"I hear you, Sarmajor." McDaniels paused and looked toward the main office building, where the injured had been taken. "You know, I'll guarantee you that kid's going to turn. Someone's going to have to put him down before that happens. Save him some pain and misery."

"Not me, sir." Gartrell's voice was small, almost inaudible. "Not me."

McDaniels turned to him. "I didn't mean you, Gartrell. I was just... thinking aloud, I guess."

Gartrell nodded. His night vision goggles were in the stowed position, and McDaniels could see his blues eyes in the tepid light of the floods two alleys over. Gartrell was still a hard-charger, but his gaze was distant. Haunted.

"Come on, let's get moving."

"Hooah," Gartrell replied.

McDaniels made his report to Jaworski and the rest of the senior staff, as he had been the senior officer on station. Both Jaworski and Haley were annoyed that the QRF commander had gone directly to the scene of an active engagement without notifying anyone in his chain of command, and that CSM Gartrell had mysteriously joined him there.

"That both of you were out of the TOC and in the AO is not a good thing," Haley said. "We have experienced troops who are entrusted to carry out the internal security mission. You and the Sarmajor running to the scene of an active engagement before the area was officially secured was reckless."

McDaniels almost laughed, but he managed to contain himself. Just because the Ranger battalion commander exhibited the usual alpha male pretenses during the operations meetings didn't mean the man was likely to run off into combat himself. He had been given command of a Ranger battalion for a reason, and approaching things in a levelheaded manner was probably one of those.

"I hear you," McDaniels said. "It was close enough that I figured I'd better put eyeballs on target. I brought the Sarmajor with me for some cover," he added, giving Gartrell an out.

Haley didn't respond, but Jaworski didn't seem to buy it. He looked at Gartrell directly and with no humor in his eye. "Is that so, Sergeant Major Gartrell?"

"It seemed like a good idea for us to head over there, since we were already close to the engagement to begin with, sir," Gartrell said. "We knew the Rangers were on-station, but we didn't know their exact circumstance."

"Hey, Colonel?" Switchblade shot Jaworski a winning smile. "Let's cut this stuff out, all right? We just had a rising in the middle of the complex. That's what we need to focus on. What the hell are we going to do about that kid who got bit? Will the vaccine the civvies are working on help him?"

"We were told by Wolf Safire that it didn't work that way," McDaniels said. "I haven't actually asked that question myself recently, but I've been operating under the premise that the vaccine is only useful if it's administered *before* the patient is bitten."

"I was informed that's still the case." Jaworski rubbed his eyes tiredly. "Okay. We need to manage that aspect more directly. What happens to the kid now? He's definitely been bitten, and we know what's going to happen. What do we do?"

"Simple," Haley said. "Lock him up somewhere, wait for him to turn, then put a bullet through its brain."

"Looks like the kid's mother is still alive," McDaniels said. "It was the father who turned, and he was one of the security guys for the office park. Another woman took a tap to the snot locker, probably while trying to save the kid. Everyone involved was taken over to the medical area in the main building for a full workup, but so far, only the kid's going to go over the fence. And as heartless as it is to even think about it, unless the scientists across the way can offer up something, the kid has to die."

Switch shook his head. "Damn, sir. And here I was thinking you were some sort of bleeding heart liberal."

"Well, I did vote for Perot in '92, does that count?"

"Who's going to do it?" Jaworski looked around the table. "Who's going to shoot that boy in the head?"

"We wait for him to turn, and *then* we do it, sir," Haley said.

"According to the news, dying from a bite is one of the most painful ways to check out there is," Jaworski said. "Cordell said the boy's mother is still alive. Are we going to make her sit and watch her son die in great pain over the next... what, twelve to fifteen hours?"

"Colonel Jaworski." Gartrell's voice was flat and unemotional even though he stared at the tabletop before him. "Do you mean to say that you prefer one of us to walk over there and shoot the kid before he goes into the final stages?"

"We should discuss it with the mother," Jaworski said. "We should lay it out for her and let her make the call. That's her kid. She probably needs to figure out what's best for him."

"I can't see a lot of utility in letting the kid go through that just so we can shoot him." McDaniels looked around the table. "This is something we might have to deal with more regularly as time goes on. We're going to need some sort of action plan. Shooting zeds through the noggin is one thing. Consigning people to die in great pain from the virus is another. I think you're right, Colonel. We should lay it out for the mother and see what she says. And we should loop in the medical people at InTerGen. They might be able to offer some alternatives."

"I'll do just that," Jaworski said.

"Better to let me handle that, sir." McDaniels rubbed the back of his neck. "I've already seen the mother. I know what to expect. And there's no need for all of us to go through this shit until it's absolutely necessary."

"You going to be able to handle that?" Commander Rawlings asked. "That's a lot for one guy to have to shoulder."

"You interested in the job, Rawlings?"

"No way, sir. Just making a point, is all."

"Someone has to do it," McDaniels said. "You guys are closer to the operational spectrum than I am, and I don't want something like this clouding your judgment when the chips are down. And this isn't that big of a deal, when you look at the big picture," he added, more for Jaworski's benefit than anyone else's. "I'll see to the boy's disposition. I'll be as humane about it as possible, but at the end, the kid won't become a threat to anyone else."

The assembled soldiers, airmen, and sailors looked at each other for a long, uncomfortable moment.

Switch finally broke the silence. "You're totally hard core, sir."

"There's nothing that we can do," Regina quietly confirmed outside the thirty-two bed Combat Support Hospital that had been deployed as part of JTF SPARTA. "Doctor Kerr is working on something that might be appropriate for these kinds of cases, but it's not ready and won't be ready for clinical trials for at least another two weeks." She kept her voice low because the only thing separating her and McDaniels from the infected boy was a small plastic partition. McDaniels looked past the curtain surrounding the boy's bed.

The kid lay on his back and stared at the florescent lights. His eyes were red, and his face was puffy from crying.

McDaniels thought the boy knew what was coming. "How's the mother?"

Regina snorted. "Her son has been bitten, Colonel. How do you think she is?"

McDaniels shuffled his feet and sighed. He grabbed Regina by the arm and moved her away from the small emergency ward. The CSH, or "cash," was just another assembly of interconnected tents, and the emergency ward was a single medium tent equipped with twelve surgical beds, a hard floor, and its own generator. It was staffed by one physician and four nurses. The doctor stood nearby, watching McDaniels and Regina as they walked away. He had allowed Regina to conduct the detailed medical workup since she was a pediatrician and the boy was only seven years old.

"Look, if there's nothing you can do, we can't have the boy turning," McDaniels said as they stepped outside. One of the nurses stood nearby, smoking a cigarette. McDaniels's nostrils twitched at the scent.

"I don't understand. What are you talking about?" Regina asked.

"I mean, that boy's in for a painful death over the next twelve hours or so. You know that, right?"

Regina nodded slowly. "Yes, I know. His body will begin to break down. Tissues will become necrotic and fuel an advanced sepsis through his abdominal tract, resulting in extremely painful cramps, vomiting, and bloody diarrhea. His temperature will go through the roof, and he'll start having convulsions in about six hours. It'll be twelve hours of hell, especially for the mother, who will see her son's body eject just about everything inside it before he dies." She listed the symptoms of the boy's coming death like some sort of a computer, brief and direct, without any kind of human warmth. Not even disgust or fear. McDaniels hoped she'd had a better bedside manner when she'd been a practicing pediatrician.

"So what can you do to spare him that?"

"Nothing. Short of putting him into an induced coma, that is."

"How would you do that?"

"With a dosage of specific barbiturates. Usually pentobarbital or thiopental, both of which could be measured to reduce the blood flow to the boy's brain and cause him to remain unconscious. But he'd still go through the same effects. The virus will still kill him in the same way. It would just be easier for him, I suppose."

"What if we were to overdose him?"

Regina looked at McDaniels oddly. "I don't understand."

"Yes, you do."

The nurse finished her cigarette and stabbed it out in a nearby ashtray before stepping back into the cash. The nurse had acted as though she hadn't overheard their conversation, but of course, she'd heard every word. McDaniels didn't care either way.

"If we overdose him, he goes from cardiac arrest, but he'd be unconscious and unlikely to feel anything. He'd go the same way Michael Jackson did, basically." Regina looked up at McDaniels. "I don't get why you're even asking. You know he'll still reanimate, right?"

"I want the kid controlled, and for his family's suffering to be over as quickly as possible."

Regina hugged herself in the cold, chilly air. Her breath fogged in the lights over the entrance. "So you want us to kill the boy."

"I want you to help me convince the mother that it's in her child's best interests, and to give her time to say good-bye to her son while he still *is* her son, before the virus takes him away from her."

"And after it's done? After the boy dies?"

McDaniels put his hand on the pistol at his hip.

Regina got the message. She half-turned away and looked back at the cash tent. "It's going to be very difficult to get her to agree to it."

"I know. I know."

The boy's name was Gregory Goodwin. His mother was Martha, and the older woman with the broken nose was Glenda, the mother of the man who had become a zombie. McDaniels and Regina consulted with the cash doctors, and all three of them were against the plan on ethical grounds, but the senior physician, a major, finally agreed to back up McDaniels.

"We know where this is headed, and if nothing else, it'll be better for the boy," he said. "So even though we all have strong feelings against this... euthanasia, we're prepared to move forward with it, since there is no treatment forthcoming, and the results of the boy's death would be... well, difficult to deal with as well."

"Then back me up with medical facts. That's all you need to do," McDaniels said. "I'll do the rest."

"Yeah, good luck with that, Colonel."

"Let me get this straight," Martha Goodwin had said twenty minutes later when she agreed to leave her son's side for a brief time to meet with McDaniels and the others. "You want to kill my son by giving him a drug overdose."

"There's no other way," McDaniels said. "There's no treatment available to stop the virus, at least not yet. It's underway, but there's not even an experimental trial to use. If we don't do this, then your son goes through a very long, agonizing death, and he still turns into a zombie. There simply aren't any good alternatives, Mrs. Goodwin. Every one we have involves your son dying, and the only difference is the method."

He nodded toward the Army doctors standing nearby. "They can make it quick and painless, and your son will pass with at least some degree of dignity. If not, then he goes out in great pain from bloody diarrhea and a burning fever."

Martha Goodwin closed her eyes and ran a hand through her graying blond hair. She might have been a good-looking woman once, but there were bags under her eyes, wattles under her chin, and saddlebags around her hips. She'd already watched her husband turn into a cannibalistic corpse, and McDaniels was asking her permission to terminate her son. McDaniels couldn't even begin to understand the pain she must be feeling.

"You don't know that," she said finally. "Greggy, he might be different from everyone else. He might pull through it."

"He won't." Regina's tone was gentle, but certain. "We've seen it dozens, hundreds, in some cases, thousands of times. There is no variation. When someone is bitten by one of the dead, an extremely potent version of the virus is transferred. This virus is different from the original. It's stronger, it breeds faster, and it causes incredible changes in the human physiology that we don't quite understand. And when the host dies, the virus is still alive. It does something to the body to make it animate again. And this is what will happen to your son, Mrs. Goodwin. He'll jump off that bed and try to eat you once he reanimates, and Colonel McDaniels here will have to shoot him through the head, like the soldiers did to your husband."

Martha squeezed her eyes shut. "Jesus. *Jesus.*"

"Mrs. Goodwin, if there was another way, I'd be all over it. A hundred percent all over it," McDaniels said. "But there isn't. Your boy will die, he'll turn into a flesh-eating zombie, and yeah, I'll have to shoot the body once it starts moving again. We can play it much more gently, but we need your permission, and we need it soon."

"He could be different," Martha repeated. "My son could be different from all the others."

"He won't be," McDaniels insisted. "I'm sorry, but he just

won't be. He'll be exactly like all the others."

The boy's mother was silent for a long moment, then she looked up at McDaniels, her jaw set. "You leave my boy alone. You let me and Gregory alone. He's not going to die. He's going to live, and he's going to be fine."

The lead Army doctor looked down at a manila folder in his lap. "Ma'am, his temperature has already spiked. The flesh around the bite wound is already turning necrotic. The pathogen is riding around his body, courtesy of his bloodstream."

"I'm not going to listen to this. What's wrong with you people? My boy is *not* going to die!"

"Is that your final decision?" McDaniels looked for support from the others, but he was met with empty gazes and minute shrugs.

"Stay away from me and my son, Colonel. I don't want you anywhere near us." With that, Martha Goodwin stormed out of the waiting area and hurried down the connector that attached it to the emergency treatment tent.

McDaniels sighed. "Well, that certainly sucked ass."

"I knew it would turn out this way, but I have to hand it to you, Colonel. You've got brass ones," the senior Army physician said. He rose from the stool and slapped the boy's chart against his thigh. "I guess we're going to be busy for the next twelve hours or so. Are you going to hang out here, or...?"

"I'll send a security detail to stand guard and take out the corpse once it's over," McDaniels said. "It'll be Rangers, maybe four of them. You'll know when the kid's going lights out, right?"

Regina nodded. "It'll be fairly evident. His pressure will drop, and he'll start convulsing. Tachycardia will be present, giving way to asystole, then his heart stops. Anywhere from two minutes to two hours later, the corpse will reanimate."

"So we'll have enough warning, then," McDaniels said.

Regina nodded. "Yeah. There should be enough warning."

"All right. I'll have the Ranger battalion commander make

the assignment, and we'll have a few extra Rangers in the cash at all times." He paused and looked at the senior physician. "But just in case, you might want to restrain the boy at some point."

The doctor nodded. "I agree and think that would be for the best."

Near noon the next day, a single gunshot rang out from the Combat Support Hospital. Gregory Goodwin had indeed succumbed to the virus, and his corpse reanimated fourteen minutes later.

20

The dead swept across the nation like a filthy tide, consuming all who got in their way. Mostly mindless—mostly—the legions lived only to feed, and in doing so, caused thousands and thousands more dead to rise, to join their ranks and the never ending hunt for food. They were like bipedal locusts, swarming from east to west. Humans were their main prey, but they would consume anything living—livestock, pets, any wild animals they came across who could not evade them. Because of that, the dead were preceded by a veritable flood of wildlife. Deer, bears, foxes, sheep, cows, horses, dogs, cats—all joined the humans and fled.

The military made several stands against the dead, using every weapon of war at their disposal. There was no easy way to kill the dead in mass attacks; in the end, it took soldiers, Marines, airmen, and sailors shooting the individual corpses in the head to stop them. While bombs, artillery, and other direct and indirect fire methods could disable the dead in some numbers, the maimed corpses were far from harmless. They would simply lie in wait for anything edible to come within range, then strike. And feed.

Some of the dead fought back. The military was surprised to discover that a number of the dead could use weapons, and in more than a few instances, the dead would bring down troops, injuring them so they couldn't flee, and then descend upon them and feast.

The military failed to stem the tide, and the dead progressed out of the east, walking down highways, wending their way around disabled and abandoned vehicles, making great progress as the dead had no need to stop and rest. Relentlessly, they continued the hunt, immune to exhaustion and the effects of physical exertion. Whereas the humans grew winded and needed to recuperate, the dead had no such constraints.

The deluge of evacuees fleeing the dead caused another set of problems. Resources, such as fuel and food, were consumed at such a rate they could not be replaced. Looting and violence became endemic as law and order broke down, even in the dozens of lightly defended refugee camps the government set up to shelter and manage the citizenry. The camps were exactly what the dead looked for; without any sort of credible defense and housing tens of thousands of humans who had nowhere else to go, the camps served as a kind of magnet for the dead. Intended to be sanctuaries, they became great, ghastly killing zones from which there was no escape.

And the number of the dead increased.

Dead Jeffries still wore the uniform of the United States Army, and still clutched the assault rifle it had taken from Fort Detrick. Like the thousands of dead surrounding it, Dead Jeffries continued to slog westbound. The only thing that passed for conscious thought in its mind was the desire to feed, to satiate the ceaseless appetite that could never be fulfilled. But as the army of the walking dead progressed, Dead Jeffries found it was compelled to turn southerly, where the weather was warmer, the roads less congested, and the territory more open. There was no deliberate awareness to this act, but as Dead Jeffries turned south, it was peripherally aware that thousands of Others turned as well. They followed Dead Jeffries as a pack of wolves would follow its leader. Most of the Others were the stupid ones, but many were like Dead Jeffries—able to use tools to help in the hunt, able to recall vague memories, able to anticipate the actions of the humans they hunted.

Dead Jeffries wasn't fully aware of why it was walking to Texas, only that there was something there that could threaten the dead. Something that had to be destroyed before the humans could complete it.

And then, the dead could feed on the entire world.

21

Two days after the dead arrived, Austin fell to the horde.

It was covered on the television, complete with breathless reports delivered by harried-looking reporters. Footage from orbiting news helicopters showed the progression of the dead through the city as they overwhelmed the defenders, swarming over them like great thunderclouds of rot. Evacuations had been in place, and the stream of fleeing humanity extended northward from the city, reaching places like Houston and the Dallas/Fort Worth area. The entire 3rd Armored Cavalry was arrayed against the dead to the south, and while they did a credible job at closing with the oncoming dead and decimating thousands of them, the numbers were just too great. The army of the dead was estimated to be almost five million strong, and growing at a rate of twenty thousand per day.

When McDaniels watched the report that mentioned the numbers of the dead, he quadrupled the amount of munitions he had requested and instructed the Rangers to work with the Corps of Engineers on modifying the buildings in the office park. It was no longer enough to harden the perimeter and fight point defense; if the dead numbered in the millions, they had to consider SPARTA would be compromised at one point or another, and they would need a place to fall back. But where? Where could they be safe and still continue their work while being pursued by an enemy as relentless as the gathering dead?

The answer did not come easily, but he knew one thing, even though he didn't want to admit it. If push came to shove, he would secure the scientists and researchers, collect their data and their trials, and ensure they were flown out on a Chinook to someplace safe. Even if it meant abandoning the civilians and the rest of the troops, he had to ensure the eggheads survived.

They held the key.

Jaworski had already anticipated that when McDaniels broached the subject. The Special Forces officer was heartened to hear that an evacuation plan had been put in place should SPARTA be compromised, and that there were redundant efforts underway to replicate Wolf Safire's vaccine, both in the United States and in Canada.

"It's not the people we need to save, so much as the data," Jaworski told him over another seemingly endless cup of coffee. "We should probably start collecting hard copies of everything and airlifting it out of here so it can be disseminated in case we lose broadband comms. As hard as it is to believe, the dead also screw up cable television and DSL."

"Simply shocking," McDaniels said.

"Get ready, it gets worse. Looks like the dead are turning this way." Jaworski typed a command into his computer and opened a few windows, then turned the display toward McDaniels. The satellite surveillance data showed a huge stream of the dead surging through the flatlands of Oklahoma. Thousands of cattle fled, visible in the imagery.

"Wow," was all the cold dread allowed McDaniels to say. When he saw the mass of dead darkening the landscape to their north, he felt his mouth go dry.

There are more dead there than in Austin. Ten, fifteen million, maybe more...

"Yeah, the numbers don't look so good," Jaworski said, as if reading his mind. "And check this out." He pointed at a cylindrical object amidst the dead, and scrolled through several photos. The object moved with the dead. "That's a tanker truck. Probably gasoline. And they're either bringing it with them, or the bodies are pressed against it so thick that they're just pushing it along."

"That's not so good."

"What do you think, Cord?"

"I think that if they're intentionally bringing it with them,

240

they intend to use it. But for what, I don't know."

"The Cav guys out at Austin report being engaged by stenches with weapons. Automatic weapons."

McDaniels nodded. "I had the same experience in New York."

Jaworski regarded the satellite imagery, a worried expression on his face. "If they come at us with weapons, that's going to be a bit of a game-changer. Especially if they use them in a sophisticated manner. Or start operating complex weapons systems, like tanks and bombers. Damn, could that be possible?"

"I don't know, sir. I don't think so, but I don't know. It would seem to me there's got to be a limit to what they can do, since they don't have their full faculties, but I'm just whistling in the wind here."

"We'll go over this at the twelve hundred meeting with the rest of the guys," Jaworski said. "But in the meantime, I want you to make sure every swinging Johnson and every engineer is working at a hundred percent. Because I'm thinking the hammer is swinging our way."

McDaniels got to his feet. "Yes, sir."

"One last thing," Jaworski said. "We're open to civilians for the next twenty-four hours. I've already told Blye that if he has more people to bring in, they need to show up by tomorrow morning. After that, SPARTA closes for business. The more people we have, the higher the chances of another rising, and that saps our resources. Our problems are almost unmanageable now, and while it seems heartless to do it, we have to remember our mission."

McDaniels nodded. "Understood, sir. I'll back you up a hundred percent on that."

Jaworski looked back at the computer monitor. "Thanks, Cord."

"Hello, Colonel," CW4 Billingsly said when McDaniels

drove up to where he stood in the northern parking lot. The MH-47G Chinooks were being lovingly tended to by their flight and maintenance crews, while the less sophisticated AH- and MH-6 Little Birds sat in a neat row several hundred feet away. McDaniels saw that four UH-60M Black Hawks had been invited to the party as well, though they didn't seem to be special operations birds.

"Those are from Fort Hood," Billingsly told him when McDaniels asked. "Not part of the 160th, but we're happy to have them since they've got more lifting capacity than the Little Birds, and aren't as maintenance-intensive as the Chinooks."

"Have you been in contact with your regimental command, Mister Billingsly?"

"Negative, Colonel. Once Fort Campbell went down, the Night Stalkers HQ went with it." If he felt anything about the event, Billingsly kept his emotions in check and hid them well away.

"Sorry to hear that, Mister Billingsly."

"I understand Fort Bragg is doing a bit better, sir."

"That seems to be correct. The dead are more intent on moving westward, but it hasn't been a walk in the rose garden." His wife, Paulette, had told him over the phone that were had been several pitched battles between the 82nd Airborne and the dead, but that the Airborne troops had managed to repel every attack. The dead were piled twenty deep outside the fort's perimeter, but their numbers appeared to be decreasing, Paulette thought. McDaniels had welcomed the news, though he wondered what it truly meant. Why leave Bragg alone? Why not slam into it as the dead had done to Fort Campbell?

"So, sir, is there something I can do for you?" Billingsly asked.

McDaniels looked around the tent that served as the 160th's headquarters. There was no sign of Major Carmody. "Just taking a look around. How are your troops doing, Billingsly?"

"Everyone's completely mission-oriented, Colonel."

"Things aren't tough yet. Is everyone getting as much sleep as they should?"

Billingsly frowned. "Sleep, sir? You're worried if the Night Stalkers are getting enough *sleep*?"

Something about the warrant officer's attitude had rankled McDaniels from the beginning. Perhaps it had been Billingsly's continual dismissal of his commanding officer, Carmody. Maybe Billingsly was just one of those people who didn't have a lot of interpersonal skills. Or maybe, McDaniels reasoned, he was one of those operators who thought his shit didn't stink.

McDaniels kicked over a nearby trashcan, and a flood of energy drink bottles tumbled out onto the floor. McDaniels picked one up, regarded it for a moment, then tossed it right at Billingsly's head. The warrant officer caught it awkwardly, and his brow knitted with anger. Before he could get a word out, McDaniels was in his face.

"Your attitude sucks, Billingsly. I don't require a sunny disposition from everyone under my command—and *yes*, you *are* under my command—but what I *do* require is that you respond to my questions immediately and without attitude. Because if you fail to comply, I will land on you with both boots."

McDaniels was aware of the rest of the troops in the headquarters tent paying close attention to the display, which was fine by him. He wanted an audience. He pointed at the empty bottle of Red Bull in Billingsly's hand. "If your guys are already reduced to sucking that shit down under our currently low operational tempo, then I have to wonder what the hell is going to happen when the shit hits the fan. I don't want your aircrews flying exhausted, and I don't want your maintainers overlooking simple maintenance items because they're tired. A lot depends on your aircraft and your ability to keep them operational in what's going to be a very demanding environment. You get me, Mister Billingsly?"

"Completely, Colonel."

"Good, because we won't be having this conversation again.

I'll have Carmody replace you with another aviator in a heartbeat. You get that, too?"

"Yes, sir. I understand everything you're saying," Billingsly said in a flat monotone.

"Outstanding. One other thing, have one Chinook and one of those Black Hawks ready to go on a trip every evening at eighteen hundred hours. We'll be flying out data to another site on a daily basis, starting with tonight. I'd rather use the Black Hawks for that, if possible, but have a Chinook on standby just in case."

"Yes, sir." To add some additional deference to the statement, Billingsly saluted.

McDaniels returned the gesture and left the Night Stalkers to their own devices. He hadn't come to the helicopter assembly area with the intention of kicking ass and taking names, but with the threat picture becoming a bit clearer, he wanted to ensure that everyone was on the same page. It bothered him that Billingsly didn't get along well with others, but the man must have skills his commanders had valued, otherwise he wouldn't be there. So long as he could ride herd on the rest of the aviators, it ultimately didn't matter.

He tracked down Major Guardiola of the Corps of Engineers and gave him a quick rundown on what his next taskings were. "We'll need to start fortifying the buildings next, once you're done with the perimeter defenses. People will need places to fall back to in case the walls come down."

"That'll take some doing, Colonel. We're running twenty-four-seven now. I'll do whatever you ask, but it would help if we could get some more work crews in here," Guardiola said.

"Don't you have contractors available?"

"A lot of them have vanished, Colonel. They all have families, and the dead are coming. No one wants to be here when they do. I can't say I blame them, but the contractors are running away like rabbits."

McDaniels sighed. "All right. I'll give Colonel Haley a

pulse; maybe he can have some of his troops give your people a hand. I can't promise they'll be any good, but at least you'll have bodies to move stuff around."

"If that's all we've got, that's what we'll use," Guardiola said.

"Outstanding." McDaniels turned to leave the emergency operations vehicle Guardiola used as his headquarters.

"Excuse me, Colonel?"

McDaniels turned back. "Yes?"

Guardiola sat behind his small desk and looked a little lost for a moment, but he snapped out of it quickly. "Uh, our headquarters in Dallas is closing up. I've put in requests for more men and equipment, but that's probably not going to happen. Seems like the dead are cruising through Oklahoma, and they're going to roll up on Dallas sometime in the next few days."

"I know."

"Colonel, my family lives in Arlington, a suburb in Dallas."

McDaniels looked at Guardiola for a long moment. "Are you in touch with your family?"

"Yes, sir."

"Tell them to load up and drive to New Mexico or Colorado or even Canada. Texas isn't the place to be right now. If you need to do anything more than that, you need to talk to Colonel Jaworski. I'm not giving you permission to leave your post, Guardiola. Is that understood?"

"Yes, sir." Guardiola didn't look very happy about it, and McDaniels couldn't blame him. He still felt guilty as he left the emergency operations vehicle. After all, he had his son with him.

"Looks like Hercules Six is looking for you, sir," Haley's senior NCO said as they toured the front gate area. Haley turned and saw McDaniels bounding up the metal ladder that had been welded to the interior side of the CONEX container Haley stood on. Haley frowned and checked his watch. They weren't due to meet for another hour and forty-five minutes. Below, outside the front gates, television camera crews had gathered. They were trying to get interviews with the Rangers or the other troops, and Haley had already conveyed everyone was to keep their mouths shut. As he watched, a van extended its satellite antenna into the air. SPARTA was finally attracting attention, and a small crowd of onlookers and would-be refugees were waiting outside the concertina wire.

"Well, it saves me the trouble of looking him up. Let's see what the Jedi Knight wants," Haley said, using the slang for Army Special Forces.

McDaniels made it to the top of the CONEX container a few moments later. He regarded the gathering crowd at the outer gate. Three deep trenches separated the first gate and the berm on which the container had been set upon, and the concertina wire and Alaska barriers had been built to resemble a funnel; that way, attackers would be driven right into the kill zones that had been preregistered.

"What the hell is that all about?" McDaniels asked.

"The media has arrived," Haley told him. "They want interviews, want to know our mission, want to know all about us and what we're going to do when the zombies show up."

"What have you told them, Bull?"

"Not a damned thing. I figure if the media found out about SPARTA, then it would only make things worse." He pointed at the growing crowd that his Rangers were trying to control. "But the bigger thing is that some civilians are trying to gain access, which you'd mentioned would occur a few days ago. Well, you were right, and a lot of those folks are starting to get unruly. They want us to protect them, and they see the InTerGen folks coming in and not leaving. They want their slice of the pie."

"Jaworski's guidance is this: No civilians are to be permitted inside the complex after tomorrow. The stenches are on the way. And they number in the millions now, Bull."

It took a long moment for that to register, but when it did, even Bull Haley felt a squirt of fear run through his body. "Millions, you said?"

"Millions," McDaniels repeated.

"Those things can be killed only by a very specific attack—a round through the head—barring something miraculous happening, like the Air Force napalms them all at once. I gotta tell you, Cord, we don't have the capability to fight off millions of those things. We'd need the entire Army for that."

"We have what we have," McDaniels said. "Jaworski's working on getting us some more muscle. The 3rd ACR got mauled trying to defend Austin, so we might not get them to act as our outer boundary defense, after all. But we will have attack aviation in addition to our organic assets, for whatever good they'll be."

"So no armored cav regiment guarding the front door? Well... okay." Haley didn't like it, as it meant the Rangers would probably be throwing their lives away trying to defend an installation they couldn't hold, but orders were orders. "What else?"

"We'll need to harden the buildings themselves, since it appears we might need additional fallback areas. I told Guardiola that your boys would assist him, since his contractors are cutting out. I hope I didn't overpromise?"

"We don't have a lot of slack in the chain, but I can make it happen."

"Keep your eye on Guardiola. His family's in the line of fire, and he's already hinted that he wants to boogie. I told him he would have to get permission from Jaworski, and he accepted that, but if his family is in danger, then he'll do what he has to do."

"Understood." Haley looked toward the crowd in the distance. Only about fifty or sixty people were out there, not counting the media jackals, but ten of his troops were already tied up enforcing the zone. Traffic was thick on the highway, most of it moving slowly northward, toward Odessa and

Midland. "On a related topic, what do we tell those poor souls out there? They need someplace to go."

"Fort Hood is an emergency evac site. They should go there. And they should go there now. Pass that on to your troops so they can make that known. Fort Hood is open for business, but no one knows for how long."

"Roger that," Haley said. "Is there anything else?"

"Negative. Just keep leaning forward, Bull. It might look like a forlorn hope right now, but who knows what the future will bring."

"Probably a lot of stenches," Haley said.

22

The gymnasium was packed full of frightened people who had nowhere to go, and no time to get there even if they did. The power had failed the day before, and the air inside the building was getting mighty ripe, especially since the water had gone out earlier in the day. The only lights available were from flashlights and battery-powered lanterns. Candles were forbidden due to the potential fire hazard. So over two thousand people sat in the stinking near-darkness almost shoulder to shoulder, many with weapons, most without. Earl Brown was happy to count himself in the armed group. Not that it mattered.

The dead had found them at nightfall.

The National Guard and Pennsylvania State Police that had been providing security for the evacuation site had tried to fight them off, but the zombies just kept coming. Sometimes in a horde, other times as a ragtag collection of individuals, but the stream had been constant and most unbroken. Earl had wanted to leave the second the first ones appeared, and he had even hustled Zoe out to the Pathfinder to do just that. He found the vehicle had been blocked in by other automobiles, and someone had siphoned almost all the gas from it. At first Earl wondered how that could have happened with all the cops and Guardsmen around, then it came to him. They'd done it themselves.

And in the near distance, Pittsburgh burned.

Earl and Zoe had no choice but to return to the high school gymnasium. By that time, the building was already packed solid, and it took them almost an hour to get back inside and thread their way through the crowd so they could get away from the doors. There were no windows in the gym, so when the doors were finally closed, total darkness reigned supreme, save for sparse islands of light. Gunfire crackled outside, and occasionally, an explosion tore through the air. The Guardsmen had hand grenades. One of them must have gone off close to the building because it shook and there was the sound of shattered glass falling.

"Those assholes just blew a hole in the plate glass windows outside," someone muttered.

Shoulda bought me some of those night vision goggles, Earl thought. But for what reason? So he could *watch* the dead come in and start eating people?

He found a very small space beneath the collapsed bleachers against the wall. Earl figured they were electrically-driven, so there was no chance of them being extended any time soon. He put his hand in the gap and felt nothing other than cold wood and steel. He pushed Zoe toward it.

"Daddy, what?"

"I wantcha to get in there," Earl said. "Take your shotgun and get in there, and don't come out until I tell you to. Unnerstand me?"

"Daddy ..." The plaintive whine in Zoe's voice stabbed Earl in the heart. He touched her face as his eyes burned. Outside, the gunfire was becoming more sporadic. Engines started, and men shouted. Earl knew the National Guard was mounting up and moving out.

And he heard *things* picking their way across the glass-littered floor outside the gymnasium.

"Go on, baby. Get in there, and don't come out until I tell you. All right?" Without waiting for an answer, he shoved Zoe toward the hole. She resisted at first, crying, but eventually she did as he asked and retreated inside the bleachers.

A pounding began on first one closed steel door, and then another. A collective shriek went through the crowd, and Earl damned them all. The last thing they should do was give any indication that there were live people in the building. The pounding at the doors redoubled, and Earl felt the mass of humanity in the gym push away from the entrances. People screamed as they were crushed against each other. Earl had a moment to prepare himself, and he pressed himself against the bleachers, his 12-gauge shotgun in one hand, his .22 caliber pistol in his belt.

"Zoe, hang on, baby. They're trying to get in!"

And then Earl was crushed against the bleachers by the crowd. Effectively pinned in place, he could do nothing but just try to breathe. Zoe remained silent, but he couldn't even draw enough breath to ask if she was all right.

Light suddenly flooded the gym when a door was forced open. Screams rang out, and gunfire crackled. Earl couldn't see what was happening, but he'd been through it before. The dead were in the gymnasium, where thousands of defenseless people were trapped. Some of the refugees still had weapons, and they used them, but the zombies had mass and numbers on their side.

Earl could hear shrieks of pain and agony as the dead fell upon the refugees and fed, tearing people apart in a flurry of slashing teeth and nails. He smelled the coppery scent of blood, followed quickly by the stink of perforated bowels. The din was so loud that he couldn't separate one sound from another; they all ran together in a horrible blend, a pounding cacophony that left him almost senseless, as if he were being physically beaten. He thought of his wife and eldest daughter, both dead in New York City, and mourned their loss anew. He mourned the coming death of his youngest, who was almost certainly going to meet her fate moments after he met his.

It took hours for the dead to make their way to Earl, and when the crush of bodies relaxed and he fell to the floor, he could glimpse their shambling, blood-covered silhouettes picking their way over fallen bodies, moving toward him. Earl firmed his grip on the shotgun and turned toward the small crevice in the bleachers where his daughter hid as the people around him fell before the advancing ghouls.

"Zoe! Can you hear me, baby?"

"Daddy!"

"Don't come out until I tell you, baby! Daddy loves you!"

He didn't have time to listen for her reply. The first of the dead reached for him.

Earl blew its head off with the shotgun, then did the same to the next one, and the one after that, and the one after that, until the shotgun was empty. He pulled the pistol from his belt and used that until the ammunition was gone, but the zombies kept pouring into the gym. Four of them attacked him at the same time, and he was torn asunder only feet from where his young daughter watched and wept.

"Doctor Safire? Regina?"

Regina looked up from her computer and was surprised to find McDaniels standing in the doorway to the small cubicle she used as a workspace. Another day was coming to a close; through the windows behind him, she saw the sun had already set, leaving a smear of yellow, orange, and red to bathe the desert in a diminishing glow.

"Hi. What's up?"

McDaniels looked around, then pulled a chair from another cube and pushed it into hers. He pulled his rifle off his shoulder and placed it across his lap after he sat heavily in the chair. Their knees were only inches apart. The Special Forces officer looked haggard, and he looked at her unhappily for a long moment.

"Colonel, what is it?" Regina prompted.

"Pittsburgh fell overnight. And the refugee camp Earl and Zoe went to... well, it belongs to the dead now. There are no reported survivors."

Regina looked at McDaniels for a long moment, digesting his words. She couldn't quite get her head around it at first, but as the seconds ticked by, she felt the sorrow slowly start to fill her. The emotion was unexpected; she barely knew Earl and his daughter, but together they had survived the crucible of the dead in New York City. Regina had blithely presumed that the

Browns would be able to handle any ordeals they might come across and had thought the camp they had found outside Pittsburgh would be safe. But the soft-spoken, almost painfully shy, yet resourceful janitor and his bright-eyed, intelligent daughter were...

"Are they dead?" Regina asked.

McDaniels sighed and crossed his arms. "Yeah. I think they have to be."

She put her hands to her mouth. She thought she might sob, but to her surprise, nothing came out. The sadness continued to fill her, but she could contain it. It hadn't turned to grief yet, though there was plenty of that to contend with. She still hadn't had enough time to mourn the passing of her father, who had died only two blocks from the East River and the Coast Guard cutter that had been sent to rescue them. The Browns had deserved better; they had endured so much. That they had become just another statistic was horrible, and she knew the time would come when she would weep for them.

McDaniels looked as though he was taking it hard. Regina felt the pain radiating from him, like waves of heat from a burning bonfire. His eyes were downcast, and when he unfolded his arms and grabbed his rifle again, she saw his fingers clenched it tight.

"It's not your fault, you know," she said.

He looked up at her and gave her a ghost of a smile. "I'm not that conceited. But the truth of the matter is, I could have made some waves and probably taken better care of them. I just... I don't know. I guess I thought they'd be all right once they made it out of New York." McDaniels rose to his feet and slung his rifle. He didn't look at her. "Anyway, I just wanted to let you know."

"Colonel... Cordell." Regina got up as well and put her arms around him. "It really isn't your fault. There's nothing you could have done."

McDaniels stiffened at the contact at first, then slowly

relaxed. He returned the embrace almost timidly. When he spoke, she heard the heartache in his voice.

"I could've done better. I could have. So many people are dead now. I should have taken a second and just *done better*."

"You did exactly what you could. And you're helping save the world, guy. This is what you need to do, and Earl and Zoe would have agreed with that." She pulled back and looked into his face. He looked away from her, but she saw his eyes were watery. She put a hand on his cheek and turned his face back toward hers. "I was a total bitch to you when we first met, because I thought you were just another military muscle head. But I know you care, even about the 'little people' like Earl and Zoe Brown. Probably more than I ever did, if I want to admit to that. We can't change what happened, so we just have to keep going. We don't have any other choice. But you're *not* responsible for what happened to them."

McDaniels looked at her for a long moment, then nodded. "Thanks, Doctor."

Regina smiled at him. "No problem, Colonel."

23

"Dudes, check this shit out," Roberson said.

"What is it?" Kelly asked. The sun was just rising above the horizon, and the air was frigid. The breath of the four Special Forces soldiers was visible in the brightening air, and a thin layer of frost covered their Enduro motorcycles and the one ATV that was used as a mobile sniping platform. Kelly was the nominal leader of the element, and he pushed himself up on his elbows, looking to see whatever it was Roberson was glassing through the binoculars. There was slow movement behind him, and he knew it was Estrada easing his M24 to his shoulder to peer through its scope. Kelly felt like a rube for trying to look downrange with the Mk 1 Eyeballs when he had a pair of binoculars sitting on the ground right beside him. He snatched them up and brought them to his eyes.

"Wow," Estrada said.

"Where the hell did *that* come from?" Gogol said.

Kelly scanned the horizon until he found what was causing all the commotion. There, silhouetted against the rising sun, one man-sized target stood alone in the desert.

"Is that a zed?" Roberson asked, giving voice to Kelly's unspoken question.

"Can't tell. Too much backlight washing it out," Gogol said.

"Crazy Hank?" Kelly kept the binoculars to his eyes, squinting against the brightening dawn as he struggled to make out the figure's features.

"I'm going to say yes to that," Estrada said. "One stench, about eight hundred meters out, just standing there like a store mannequin."

"But where did it come from?" Gogol asked again.

"If it came from your ass, you'd know," Roberson said.

"What're we going to do about it, Kelly?"

"Hank, can you confirm with a hundred percent certainty that's a zed out there?"

Estrada hesitated for a long moment before answering. "Not a hundred percent, no."

Kelly scanned the rest of the area, but found nothing terribly remarkable. The landscape was pancake flat, so if anything else was out there, they would have noticed it. "Can you make the shot from here?"

Estrada sounded offended. "What do you think, Kelly?"

"I think my eighty-nine-year-old grandmomma could make the shot, but I'm not so sure about you." Kelly got to his feet and dusted off his battle dress. "Okay, let's notify Hercules. We'll need to roll up on it to get a better ID. Roberson and I will head up, while Estrada and Gogol hold back. When we identify it as a stench, it's all yours, Hank. Do try to hit it on the first shot this time."

Estrada only snorted. He'd been servicing targets with one round for almost his entire military career as a Special Forces sniper. That was why he was called Crazy Hank; not because he was insane, but because he was able to make the craziest shots in the world and use only one round to make a kill.

Kelly called it in and briefed the operator in the TOC of his intended plan. It seemed to be only one stench, so the threat to the Special Forces element was low. Just the same, Hercules advised him that an aviation asset would be uncaged and onsite in less than five minutes, and that the remainder of Special Forces Operational Detachment Alpha Zero-Three-Four would be linking up with the element as a backup force. Kelly thought it was all overkill, but everyone wanted to take a swing at the piñata. So long as the 160th didn't send out a Chinook full of Rangers and SEALs to fastrope right onto the stench's head, it was fine by him.

He and Roberson rode on their motorcycles toward the figure while Gogol and Estrada held back, the latter stretched out over his ATV, ready to punch the target's ticket when the order was given. Kelly kept his eyes open behind his sunglasses, but didn't see anything even remotely threatening as the two Special Forces soldiers brought their bikes to a halt about fifty yards from the target.

Roberson made a face when he caught a whiff of it as the light desert breeze changed for a moment. "Christ, that fucker's ripe."

Kelly dismounted and gently leaned his bike on its kickstand; the dry desert soil was hard enough to support it. He walked toward the stench slowly, his modified M4 in both hands, ready to snap it up and fire at the first hint things were going to turn south. The zombie didn't seem to notice him, and there was a fairly good reason for that. It had apparently caught fire at some point, and its eyes were gone, as were its ears and a good amount of flesh. It reeked of cooked meat and rot, a combination that Kelly found to be incredibly disgusting. Obviously, the ghoul was so badly damaged that it couldn't sense him, and it apparently hadn't even heard them approach on their bikes.

"Tack Four-One, Tack Four-Six. Target is definitely a zed. You want to take it down? Over," Kelly said into his radio boom-microphone.

Estrada's answer was immediate. "Tack Four-Six, Tack Four-One. Roger that. Would be good if you were to halt your advance and hold your position. Over."

Kelly stopped and waved his left hand. "Tack Four-One, roger. You're cleared to engage—"

Before he had finished speaking, Kelly heard a slight *zip* as the rifle round sped past him and slammed into the ghoul's right eye. The zombie collapsed to the ground immediately as the seven-six-two millimeter bullet fairly decimated its skull. He sighed and turned back to where Estrada and Gogol waited in the distance and gave them both the finger.

"*Kelly!*" Roberson shouted suddenly, and he raised his rifle.

Kelly spun around and saw the desert floor shifting beside his right foot. A pallid hand reached up from beneath the dried earth and latched onto his ankle. With a grunt, Kelly half-jumped, half-stumbled away from the buried ghoul and brought his rifle to bear. As the stench clawed its way out of the sand, he fired two rounds into its head. Behind him, Roberson opened up. Kelly turned and saw two more ghouls rise out of shallow graves. He sensed more movement, and from the corner of his eye, he saw three more stenches emerge from the desert. As he ran for his bike, he spotted variations in the soil. At least a dozen stenches had buried themselves out there, and they were rising from their sandy hide sites with snarling moans.

It's a fucking ambush!

"Let's get the fuck out of here!" Kelly shouted to Roberson. He hopped onto his bike and fired it up, then yanked it around in a tight turn, kicking up a rooster-tail of dirt.

Roberson did the same, and he accelerated away with Kelly close behind. But then, the earth moved to Kelly's right, and before he could do anything further, a spindly arm lashed out and tangled itself in the aluminum spokes of his bike's front wheel. Kelly only had time to pop the motorcycle into neutral before he went flying over its handlebars.

McDaniels had just finished shaving in the latrine when he heard one of the Little Birds suddenly crank to life to the north, which meant something was going down. He wiped the remainders of shaving cream from his face, pulled on his BDU blouse, grabbed his gear, and hit the door as the Little Bird—an MH-6, the unarmed variant—buzzed past, bolting to the southeast. Soldiers and civilians alike emerged from tents, trailers, and buildings to watch the helicopter as it screamed toward the rising sun.

McDaniels pulled on his headset and switched on the radio. "Operations, this is Hercules Six. Is something going down?

Over." As he spoke, McDaniels struck out for the tactical operations center.

"Hercules Six, this is Operations. Sir, you'd better get over here. We have an engagement going down outside the wire. Over."

"Ops, Hercules Six. On my way."

Two minutes later, McDaniels pushed open the TOC door and rushed to his station. Gartrell was already there, as were Rawlings and Carmody. As he slid into his chair and traded his personal radio headset for the lighter version used inside the TOC, Switchblade and Jaworski ran in, followed by several other troopers.

"All right, talk to me," McDaniels said, looking around the TOC. "Internal Security?"

A first lieutenant with the Ranger battalion shot him a thumbs-up. "We're good. It's happening outside the wire, sir."

"Aviation?"

"One MH-6 has jumped out to provide recon for an ODA slice operating as ES, Colonel."

"Got that. External Security, give it to me."

Rawlings stepped forward. "A slice from ODA Zero-Three-Four reported a single stench, but couldn't establish complete VID. They rolled up on it to check it out, and something went south from there. We're waiting to hear what it is, Six."

"Somebody call the Green Berets and get it from them right now," McDaniels ordered.

Kelly hit the ground on his back and cartwheeled onto his face before he could stop himself. When he came to a rest, he was halfway on his knees with his ass sticking in the air and his face in the dirt. He didn't seem to be hurt, but he'd lost his rifle during his brief flight, and he couldn't see it in the scrub brush around him. Something cracked nearby, and Kelly shouted when a stench collapsed to the ground right next to him. He flipped over onto his back and pulled his Mk 23 SOCOM pistol. Just in time. Another stench ran toward him, and Kelly fired at it twice. He struck it in the chest both times, but the heavy impacts of the .45 caliber rounds didn't even slow it. The zombie fell to the desert floor when its head exploded, and Kelly heard the report of Estrada's M24 sniper rifle a moment later.

Roberson rode up and braked to a halt a few feet from Kelly. He shouldered his M4 SOPMOD rifle and took down two more zombies shambling toward them.

"Dude, are you hurt?"

Kelly felt a twinge in his left ankle, but he wasn't going to cry over it. "No, I'm good."

"Then get the fuck up and get on your bike. This is stench central, man!" Roberson fired three more shots, and Kelly flailed to his feet. He was totally disoriented. His bike gurgled nearby, and an armless zed crawled toward him, moaning, still covered with dusty earth.

"You must be the fuck who flipped me over," Kelly said. He put a round through its face, and the zombie fell motionless to the desert floor. He hobbled toward his idling motorcycle—yeah, the ankle was definitely messed up—and looked around for his rifle. He saw it lying a few feet away, and for a moment, he was torn between going for it or his bike.

"Come on! Move your ass!" Roberson shouted. He fired several shots in rapid succession, and Kelly heard a *snap!* as a round from Estrada's rifle flashed past.

An MH-6 made a high-speed pass at forty feet, practically right over Kelly's head, attracting the attention of the zeds. The zombies turned away from Kelly and stared after the aircraft for a moment as it executed a hard tight turn. He seized the opportunity to muscle his bike upright, mount it, and kick it into gear. Roberson spun his motorcycle around as well, and they accelerated away from the zombies.

Kelly heard Hercules calling the unit for an update, and in the near distance, two Humvees bounded across the desert, heading in their direction. Estrada continued to fire at the ghouls behind Kelly and Roberson, with Gogol peering through his binoculars, spotting targets for him. Kelly risked a glance over his shoulder and saw the stenches going down, one by one. Estrada was performing as expected—one shot, one kill, bang, dead.

McDaniels, Gartrell, Switch, and Rawlings went out into the field to inspect things first hand. Since the traffic on Route 385 was fairly impenetrable, they flew out of the complex strapped to the pods of an MH-6. That type of flight was a first for McDaniels, and though the ride lasted less than two minutes before his boots hit the Texas desert, he thought it great fun.

The traffic on Route 385 was horrendous. Moving northerly at a snail's pace, thousands of cars, trucks, tractor-trailers, and RVs rolled toward Odessa. Hardier vehicles, such as motorcycles and sturdy SUVs and pickup trucks had a better time of it; they departed the highway and simply charged across the desert itself. McDaniels was surprised to see one heavily laden pickup towing a boat through the middle of the desert. He pointed it out to Gartrell, who was strapped to the pod beside him. The sergeant major only shook his head.

As the Little Bird descended, McDaniels saw the Special Forces team walking through the engagement area in pairs. At least thirty bodies lay amidst the scrub brush, and the Green Berets were securing the area, making certain that all the stenches were combat ineffective and that no more lay in wait elsewhere. Then, the Little Bird's spinning rotors kicked up a cloud of dust, and McDaniels could see nothing more. He felt the tiny helicopter bounce on its skids, and he and Gartrell unstrapped and hopped to the ground. Joined by Rawlings and Switchblade, they hurried away from the helicopter as it lifted off again and climbed to establish a right-hand orbit over the area.

"Somebody want to fill me in on what happened?" McDaniels asked when he approached the captain who commanded the alpha detachment.

"Yes, sir. Sergeants Kelly and Roberson were physically on-scene when it went down, backed up by Sergeants Estrada and Gogol over there at the ATV. Hey, Kelly! Roberson! Get over here!" The young officer waved at two men standing near one of the dead zeds. They waved back and started walking over. One of them was limping, and his face was scratched up.

"Sir, that man there, did he come in contact with a zed? How did he get injured?" Gartrell asked, pointing at the limping soldier.

"One of the zeds hit his motorcycle, sent him over the handlebars and face-first into the dirt," the captain said. "He says he never came into physical contact with any of the necromorphs, and all of his injuries were sustained during his fall. It's just road rash and a sprained ankle, Sergeant Major."

The two soldiers saluted McDaniels. The Special Forces captain introduced him to the men,

Roberson, a light-skinned black man, nodded. "I know who the colonel is. I saw you speak during a formal dinner at Bragg on Martin Luther King Day. Good to meet you face-to-face, sir."

McDaniels snorted, remembering. "Damn, Roberson, that was like ten years ago."

"Yes, sir, it was. And at the time, you were the only black alpha det commander in the entire Army, if memory serves."

"Your memory is sharper than mine, Sergeant Roberson." McDaniels looked at the shorter white man who stood beside Roberson. His face was scraped along the left side, and if he hadn't been wearing his helmet and dust goggles when he took his spill, the damage would have been even greater. "You must be Kelly?"

"Yes, sir. Sorry, I must've missed the MLK shindig, but I'm sure you were awesome," Kelly said with a grin.

"You kiss ass," Roberson said.

"Oh, look who's talking."

"Guys, square yourselves away," the captain said.

"It's all right. Some good-natured bitching is part of the job," McDaniels said. "Okay, Kelly, you first. What happened here?"

Kelly retold the events from his perspective. The story didn't last long, as the engagement seemed to have been short. While the stenches had the element of surprise, they hadn't been able to sustain their momentum, and a combination of sniper fire coupled with precision fires from the rest of the ODA had ended the incursion within five minutes. Roberson corroborated the high points of Kelly's account, though he did add some color commentary regarding Kelly's impromptu attempt at flying.

"So both of you were danger close during the engagement?" McDaniels asked.

"Yes, sir." Kelly shuffled his feet and looked embarrassed. "Uh, I didn't do a proper area reconnaissance, sir. I should have noticed the variations in the soil where those things had buried themselves, but I was fixated on the zed itself. I hadn't been aware they could, uh, do ambushes and the like."

"In other words, you were complacent, which means you were stupid," Gartrell said in his best senior NCO voice. He speared Roberson with his gaze as well. "That goes for both of you. Tell me, did you curtsy for the zeds when they popped out of the ground like a bunch of prairie dogs?"

"No, Sarmajor," Kelly said.

"You're supposed to be special recon experts. You might want to keep your core competencies close at hand during the coming engagements."

"Yes, Sarmajor."

"The Sarmajor's obviously right," McDaniels said. "You guys got sucked into it like a couple of amateurs. Let's not repeat that, all right? Captain, that's something I expect you to see to personally," he added, ensuring at the ODA commander was on the hook as well.

The tall officer nodded, his face a blank mask. "Roger that, Colonel."

McDaniels turned to Rawlings and Switch. "Guys, anything from you?"

"I'm good," Switch said.

"We should take a look around, and see what we can see," Rawlings said. "Is anyone taking pictures?"

"Yes, sir, we're seeing to that." The Special Forces captain pointed up at the orbiting MH-6. "And the Night Stalkers are doing the same from the air."

"Great. Yeah, I agree with you, Rawlings. Let's take a look around," McDaniels said.

The necromorphs had buried themselves in the soil during the overnight hours in a vaguely circular pattern. The stench, which Kelly and Roberson said had appeared to be deaf and blind, had stood in the center of the formation. Tires tracks in the dust showed that one of the soldiers had ridden right over a buried zombie without realizing it. They had stopped twenty feet apart, with one of them—Kelly—closer to the center than the other. McDaniels walked to the center of the formation and looked down at the burned zombie, then slowly turned in a circle, taking in the entire area.

"Fucking bastards are getting smarter and smarter," he said to Gartrell.

"And our guys are getting dumber and dumber. This isn't looking so great for us," Gartrell said.

"I doubt they'll be making that mistake again," McDaniels said.

"How the hell did they get here?" Switchblade scanned the horizon through his binoculars. "Don't we have the entire area under satellite surveillance? And aren't we running the UAVs every two hours for local coverage?"

"They must have come in during the night," Rawlings said. "The necros don't show up very well on infrared unless there's a huge concentration of them. Thirty or forty zeds? They wouldn't even read. And if they'd buried themselves in between the UAV flights, I can see them getting close to us without anyone knowing."

"But the horizon's flat." To prove his point, Switch pointed toward it. "You can see a man standing up out here a mile away, and at night through night vision devices? Should be even easier to spot the silhouettes against the sky."

"They crawled in on their bellies," Gartrell said.

McDaniels looked at him. "How the hell do you know that, Sergeant Major?"

Gartrell looked at him evenly. "Because it's the only way they could have snuck up on the teams, sir. Remember, ODA Zero-Three-Four wasn't the only team out here during the overnight. And the SEALs made a rotation through the area at around twenty-three hundred, right, Commander?"

"Yep," Rawlings affirmed.

"Looks like things are getting a little hot," Switchblade said. "These things have enough advantages already, chief among them being that they're already dead and don't mind getting shot. But if they start using infantry tactics, that's going to change things quite a bit." He turned and looked at the corpses nearby, then called out to a pair of SF troops taking pictures of a zombie hide site fifty feet away. "Yo! Any of these things in uniform?"

One of the Green Berets pointed at a corpse near the edge of the engagement area. "Well, that one over there has a UPS uniform."

"I mean a *military* uniform. BDUs, anything like that?"

"Negative, sir."

Switchblade turned back to McDaniels. "Now *that's* just plain creepy. No obvious indication of specialized training in their previous lives, and they still knew enough to come in covertly."

"Let's not get that far ahead of ourselves," Rawlings said.

"I disagree. I think we need to start placing more

importance on the possibility that it might be the stenches that will shape the battlespace, and not us." McDaniels looked at the stilled corpse at his feet for a speculative moment and wrinkled his nose in disgust. "As unbelievable as it sounds—"

Horns blared from the highway. At the same time, the buzzing rotorbeats of the MH-6 changed in frequency, and McDaniels looked up to see the aircraft pulling out of its orbit.

Distant rifle fire cut through the air. All the troops stood up straight and pulled their weapons into firing position, looking for targets.

"Hercules, this is Hercules Six. We hear gunfire from the highway. Over."

"Hercules Six, Hercules Ops. Roger that, we have stenches outside the wire. ESRT is on it, but the stenches are mixed in with the civilians. Over."

"Roger that, Ops." McDaniels looked at the officers with him. "All right, let's figure out what the hell is going down."

24

McDaniels and the others caught a ride with the Special Forces team in their Humvees. The traffic on the northbound side of 385 had ground to a complete halt, and people were actively fleeing into the desert on foot, taking whatever they could carry with them. As the troops drew nearer, McDaniels felt that he had seen that particular movie before, and he wondered how long it would take for the zeds to make their special appearance.

He didn't have to wait long. One shambling monstrosity bore down on a woman who hobbled along on a pair of crutches. The stench was in pretty good shape, so it was overtaking her, its jaws spread wide and arms outstretched. Just as its fingers brushed against the woman's long brown hair, the top of the stench's head was blown off. The corpse crashed face-first to the shoulder of the road.

The Rangers strode through the traffic, moving quickly and efficiently. Each soldier wore a Special Operations Infantry Combat System, an exo-skeleton created from high-tech ballistically tolerant composites. The SOICS wasn't an elegant-looking piece of equipment, but its power lay in that it could allow a soldier to carry upwards of two hundred fifty pounds of additional gear without impeding the troop's mobility. On top of that, integrated tracking and communication gear were built into the system and made available to the soldier in a graphic format through a multifunction display projected on the soldier's helmet visor. Real-time information could be flashed to the SOICS-equipped soldiers, showing them the positions of all friendlies as well as OPFOR, the opposing force. A complex set of nanocomputers allowed the SOICS to mimic the actions of the soldier, so when the soldier ran, the SOICS would do the work for him and make him move three times faster. When the soldier jumped, the SOICS would translate the intended action into the desired result. When the soldier wanted to engage a target, the SOICS would designate the target—or any part of the target—on the soldier's visor display and assist the soldier in lining up his weapon with the designated receiver. It was an awesome piece of technology, but it had only been in the field for two years. It was McDaniels's first time seeing it in action.

The Rangers fanned out in a jagged formation and ran down the shoulder of the road, easily moving at ten to fifteen miles an hour. Civilians scattered, and McDaniels touched the shoulder of the Green Beret driving the Humvee.

"Follow the Rangers. They might be on to something."

"Follow the tin men, yes, sir." The soldier turned the wheel, and the Humvee cranked hard to the left, its diesel engine bellowing. The Humvees paralleled the Rangers from a range of thirty yards, and each vehicle's .50 caliber machinegun was manned and armed. The motorcycles and ATVs the rest of the alpha detachment used followed. Overhead, two armed AH-6M Little Birds crossed over the highway, then entered into a sweeping right turn.

Gartrell leaned forward and looked through the windshield at the small attack helicopters. "The Night Stalkers are establishing a high cap downrange."

"Herc Ops, this is Hercules Six. Is there a tally on the necromorphs? Over."

"Hercules Six, Herc Ops. Roger, necros are reported to be mixed in with civilian traffic approximately seventy yards south of the perimeter fencing. ESRT and attack aviation are on it. Over."

"Herc Ops, this is Six. Roger that, we're moving on it as well."

"Six, this is Hercules Ops. Ah, Leonidas wants you and your senior staff back inside the compound. Over."

The Special Forces captain in the front right seat looked back at them. "Colonel, you want us to halt here and wait for a

Little Bird to pick you up for transport?"

"Negative, Captain. I want to keep going. I want to find out how the zeds got here, and if there's any connection between them and the necros that tried to shag our guys in the desert." Into his boom microphone, McDaniels said, "Hercules Ops, Hercules Six. Pass on to Leonidas that we will be back inside the fence as soon as possible, but we're following a hot trail. We have enough protection to ensure our safety. Over."

"I guess Jaworski's a little anxious that someone important might get deep-sixed and leave him with a great big hole in his meeting schedule," Gartrell said.

McDaniels snorted. The Air Force colonel was very likely on the ceiling that McDaniels, Rawlings, and Switchblade Lewis were out in the field chasing moving stenches as opposed to looking at dead ones, which had been the original plan. Jaworski hadn't wanted them going outside SPARTA's defenses in the first place.

"He'll just order up some more special operations types to keep him company," McDaniels said.

"Stenches to the right, in the traffic!" the Special Forces captain said.

"Let's bail and go to guns," McDaniels said without hesitating. "Captain, you form your men into a skirmish line just off the shoulder of the road. We'll let the Rangers handle the initial contact, but I'm thinking their suits might not have been designed for fighting in bumper-to-bumper traffic."

"Roger that, Colonel." he captain said as the Humvee braked to a rough halt.

McDaniels threw open his door and leaped out, followed by the others. The Rangers pounded up, their SOICS units making tiny little whining noises as hydraulic and electric motors worked in concert to give them mobility. McDaniels turned and recognized the first Ranger—Sergeant First Class Roche.

Roche nodded to him from behind his tinted visor. "Six, what are you doing out here in Indian Country, sir?"

McDaniels didn't waste time with pleasantries, and he pointed at the traffic. Three or four zombies moved from vehicle to vehicle, trying to get at the occupants.

"Can your guys effectively fight and move in that kind of traffic?"

"It's going to be a challenge, sir. We don't have the same kind of lateral mobility in the suits that we would usually have," Roche said.

"Then take out however many stenches you can from out here. We'll go in for the close and dirty." McDaniels nodded to the Special Forces captain. "We're on."

"Sir, are you sure this is what you want to do?" the captain asked.

McDaniels didn't answer the question. He just started forward with his HK at his shoulder. Gartrell was right behind him, his new AA-12 at the ready. They'd played the game before and knew how to fight the stenches in close quarters. They led the Special Forces team and the other operators into the traffic, shoving aside civilians who got in their way. McDaniels yelled for them to get back in their vehicles and lock the doors; some actually heeded his commands.

"Colonel! Stench up ahead and to the left. Looks like it's gotten inside that Tahoe there!" Gartrell said.

McDaniels looked and saw the pewter-colored SUV just ahead. Its right rear passenger door was open, and the stench lurched toward it. McDaniels heard a child screaming. The zombie ducked inside the vehicle, and McDaniels fired three rounds into the stench's body. They were ineffective. He charged toward the vehicle.

"Get ready, Gartrell!" He slammed into the stench with his entire body weight, driving it against the door. The door's hinges shrieked at the sudden abuse, but if the zombie even noticed, it hardly reacted. McDaniels grabbed its filthy black T-shirt with both hands and yanked as hard as he could. He ripped the zombie away from the Tahoe and sent it whirling into a neighboring pickup truck. That got the zombie's attention, and it whirled toward McDaniels with a hiss. Its maw was as dark as a black hole might have been.

Before it could do anything more, Gartrell shoved McDaniels aside and stepped toward the zed. It leaped at Gartrell, arms outstretched. Gartrell slammed his fist into its face, driving it back. He then waded in and started beating the zombie with his hands and feet. McDaniels was shocked by the sudden display. Why didn't Gartrell just shoot the thing?

"Come on, you fucking piece of shit," Gartrell said as he punched it in the ribs with his gloved fists. "Come on. Show me just what the fuck you can do!" He smashed it in the face with a vicious punch that flattened its nose and sent the stench reeling. If it had been a live human being, it would have dropped right then and there. But it was a stench, and it had no problem with the beating. The zombie kept coming back for Gartrell, emitting a dry, dusty screech through its broken jaw. One of its arms hung at its side, and bone protruded through the forearm. Black, syrupy ichor oozed from the injury. Gartrell snarled and treated it to a vicious spin kick, booting it halfway across the Tahoe's hood. It rolled off and fell to the highway, then flailed back to its feet, its dead eyes focused on the rangy NCO. Gartrell cursed and kicked it in the face with enough force that he likely cracked some of its cervical vertebrae. The zombie fell onto its back, but then groped its way back to its feet. Gartrell stood over it, breathing hard, sweating in the Texas sun.

"Gartrell! Shoot that Goddamned thing!" McDaniels said. "You keep beating it, all you're going to do is tire yourself out, and then you're dead meat."

Gartrell glared down at the zombie with pure hatred as it rose up and walked toward him on unsteady feet. Gartrell spat in its face and pushed it back with the heel of his hand. McDaniels pulled his rifle to his shoulder, but before he could shoot, Gartrell finally snatched his Mk 23 pistol from its holster and drilled a single shot right into the zombie's forehead. The zombie collapsed to the highway and lay still. A thin puddle of black ichor slowly leaked from its decimated skull.

"Fuck you, you piece of shit," Gartrell said.

A thin cry came from inside the Tahoe. McDaniels spun toward the vehicle. A toddler wearing a bright white shirt and dark blue coveralls was strapped into a carseat. The boy's head lolled; the zombie had ripped a huge chunk from his neck, and blood trickled from his torn carotid artery in a weak fanning movement. They were too late.

"Oh *fuck*," Gartrell whispered. Something in his voice struck McDaniels, something he had never heard from Gartrell before. Pleading?

Other than the dying boy, the Tahoe was empty. Apparently, the child's family or caregivers had fled and left the boy behind. The boy was in deep shock and only moments away from death. Also, he had been bitten.

McDaniels raised his rifle and fired one shot, ending the boy's suffering then and there.

"Jesus, Colonel!" The Special Forces captain was right behind Gartrell, and behind him was Sergeant First Class Roberson. Roberson looked at McDaniels with horror in his eyes, and McDaniels wondered if he would ever hearken back to the Martin Luther King dinner where McDaniels had spoken at the Fort Bragg Officers Club with quite the same adoration he had shown earlier that morning.

"The kid was infected, Captain," Gartrell snapped. "What the hell did you expect him to do, let him turn into a fucking stench?"

Rifle fire rang out behind them. McDaniels pushed past Gartrell and shoved the captain back into Roberson. "There are more of them out there. Let's pull it together and find them!"

The captain nodded and turned away. He preceded McDaniels and Gartrell into the fray, where the rest of his men had found the apparent source of the zombie uprising: a battered, dusty blue Chevy panel van. Four more zombies emerged from the vehicle's half-open side door.

One of the Special Forces troops stepped up on the front bumper and peered in through its filthy windshield. "Just stenches inside!"

The fight didn't last for more than two minutes, and it was actually quite anticlimactic. Well-placed shots took out the zombies inside the van, and the Rangers managed to drop three others as they pursued motorists through the column of traffic. Overhead, the AH-6Ms continued to orbit, and their pilots reported negative visual contact with additional necromorphs. It wasn't even ten o'clock in the morning, and the forces from SPARTA were already getting a full run-up.

"Hercules Ops, Hercules Six. Let's keep top cover and the Ranger ESRT on-station for the time being until we can piece together how this outbreak occurred. Pass on to Leonidas that we had to take out an infected civilian, a minor who had apparently been abandoned. ESRT might have some video of that should it become a legal matter. Over."

"Uh, roger that last, Six. Over."

Commander Rawlings was already looking over the van. In the desert behind them, the Rangers waited in the exos, scanning the traffic column for any additional threats. High above the orbiting helicopters, a small fixed-wing aircraft flew at a thousand feet or so. It was one of SPARTA's unmanned aerial vehicles, looking for any evidence more zombies were in the area. Behind the Rangers, more vehicles pulled up: SEAL Desert Patrol Vehicles. Apparently, Rawlings had been in touch with his people and invited them to the party. That annoyed McDaniels.

"The SEALs were due to relieve the alpha det," Rawlings said when McDaniels looked in his direction. "That's why they're here, sir."

"All right." It made sense, so McDaniels locked away his annoyance and didn't pursue it further. Besides, he'd already had a pissing match and saw no sense in starting another. He moved closer to the van. Judging from the blood and assorted ripped clothing, many more bodies had been in the front. There were no windows in the back, which was separated from the driver's seat by a metal gate. That gate was padlocked shut.

"What was this, a delivery van?" McDaniels asked.

"Of a sort. We see this kind of thing in California on occasion. I'm pretty sure it's almost an unknown occurrence over at Bragg. What we have here is a coyote for hauling illegal aliens north for work." Rawlings regarded the bloodied interior of the van for a long moment. Flies were already buzzing in. "Looks like one or more of them were infected, got sick, died, woke up, and started chowing down. Must've infected all the others, too."

"That sounds pretty plausible to me," Switchblade offered. He leaned forward, peered into the van, and shook his head. "See, illegal immigration is the bane of this great nation. Now the Mexicans are starting anchor zombies."

McDaniels shook his head at the comment, but couldn't quite suppress a smile. Switch had always had a peculiar sense of gallows humor. "Let's get this thing pulled out of traffic and off into the desert. Then, unless the medical folks back at SPARTA have any requests to the contrary, let's burn it to the ground. This thing's got to be full of that virus, and I can't see any reason to leave it where it is."

"Roger that." Switch turned and hollered for the alpha detachment's commander to bring one of the Humvees up with tow chains.

As the Green Berets set about enacting the order, McDaniels moved to the shoulder of the road. A crowd of civilians had gathered, and McDaniels suddenly found himself face to face with a pretty female reporter dressed in the latest Banana Republic fashion.

"Hi, I'm Andrea Benenson from KWES in Odessa. Can I have a moment of your time?"

"You may not," McDaniels said.

"Are you in command here?"

"No comment." McDaniels noticed the cameraman had focused a professional-grade video camera on him, and he frowned behind his goggles.

The reporter ignored the rejoinder. "Can you tell us what's going on at the InTerGen facility up the road? Why has it been militarized? Does it have something to do with the zombie virus that's making the dead walk? Did they have something to do with its creation, or perhaps a cure?"

"Lady, even if I wanted to answer your questions, I'd have a hard time deciding where to start. You're all over the map."

"Just tell me what you're doing here." She held out her microphone.

McDaniels paused for a long moment, then said, "I've come here to chew bubble gum and kick ass, and I'm all out of bubble gum." With that, he pushed through the crowd and walked toward one of the Humvees.

Gartrell leaned against its rear quarter panel. "Did I just hear you quote a line from John Carpenter's *They Live*? If you're a fan, then I'm ashamed to confess we might actually have a common interest." Gartrell looked toward the line of traffic, the terrified civilians, and the almost bored-looking special operators.

McDaniels ignored the quip. "Mind telling me why you snapped your cap and went hands-on with that stench?"

Gartrell sighed and turned his gaze toward McDaniels. "When I saw it was a kid, I guess I kind of lost it. To tell you the truth, Colonel, after having to pop that kid in New York— well, it's left me kind of fucked up in the mental machinations department." He tapped the side of his head with one finger.

McDaniels leaned next to Gartrell. "I'm sorry that happened to you, Gartrell. But you couldn't have known the lightfighters were just around the corner."

"The kid was autistic. Couldn't even understand what was going on. He just wanted his mother, who was being eaten alive a few feet away from him. Thank God for the darkness, so he couldn't see it. His last moments were full of horror and pain. I'd kind of hoped, you know, that things might have ended up differently." Gartrell put a hand on the back of his neck and slowly moved his head from side to side. "Maybe you feel the same way about the kid in the Tahoe. Different set of circumstances, but the same result. At least the kid you shot was already on the way out and probably didn't know a thing."

McDaniels didn't know what to say, so he didn't bother trying to come up with something witty or pithy. And the truth was, he hadn't even really *thought* about the toddler before he raised his rifle and pulled the trigger. He obviously recognized the necessity of it—the child had been bitten, was within moments of dying from arterial bleed out, and would reanimate as a necromorph—so there wasn't a lot of internal debate to be had. He did wish it could have ended differently, but it hadn't. And McDaniels wasn't sure what that would mean for him emotionally once he tried to go to sleep later.

The two men watched as the van was towed out of the traffic and pulled out into the desert. The Special Forces troops went through it and pulled all the paperwork they could find, then tossed a white phosphorus grenade into the back. The blue van went up in flames, and it would blaze away for the better part of an hour.

"All right, let's get back to the camp," McDaniels told Gartrell. He waved to Rawlings and Switchblade.

Gartrell grunted. "Yeah, all this field work has made me suddenly grow fonder of Colonel Jaworski's rather adroit PowerPoint sessions."

"Give the man a break. He does use some really great clip art."

"Yeah, well, I guess everyone has to have a hobby."

25

Andrew Kerr studied the results of the latest trials through bleary eyes. All the staffers and consultants and virologists had been working around the clock for days trying to synthesize Wolf Safire's vaccine, and even though Safire had outlined the processes required, there was still a good deal of work to be done to realize the treatment. Kerr's own efforts had been the tipping point. Since he had worked with a bug that was very, very similar to RMA 2, he'd been able to make the conceptual leaps required to bring the process closer to fruition. And that had meant a great deal of declined sleep, something Kerr wasn't exactly used to. Adding to that, the noise outside the research building was reaching a crescendo. Helicopters came and went, vehicles entered and exited the compound, construction equipment rattled, and soldiers of all ranks scurried, further securing the objective called SPARTA. Kerr was used to working in a less harried environment, and he found the excess noise distracting.

Distractions aside, they had made fantastic progress over the past week and a half. Phenomenal progress, actually. Even though Kerr and Wolf Safire had been something akin to rivals, the portly scientist had to give the late virologist his due. He had captured the essence of RMA 2, managed to identify one of the three mysterious proteins that allowed it to work when exposed to living DNA, and his work had been the roadmap that led to the blocking of that protein from adhering to cellular walls. The results of over fifty scientific trials had proven that out, and even better, RMA 2 died in less than twenty-four hours if it couldn't interact with the host's cells.

In short, the folks at InTerGen had managed to formulate an effective vaccine.

He compared his analysis with that of Doctor Kersey, the senior scientist from the fallen USAMRIID. It took several hours just to go over the essential baselines and confirm they conformed to the standard testing practices, and then the rest of the day to validate the actual results. Kersey approached the work in a very pedagogic manner, reviewing each step in order to relate it to the results. But finally, after the sun had set and then risen again, she pushed back from her workstation and looked at Kerr with bloodshot eyes.

"Congratulations, Andrew," she said. "You did it."

"Actually, everyone else did. I just pushed things along here and there." False modesty wasn't in Kerr's arsenal of people skills. While he didn't devalue his own efforts, he hadn't done everything in a vacuum. "But let's not break out the champagne and caviar just yet. Let's get this thing into production." As he spoke, he heard the crackle of gunfire in the distance.

The zombies were coming.

The miles slowly passed beneath the worn soles of Dead Jeffries's boots.

It hadn't eaten in days, electing to forgo the hunt and continue walking westward. Behind it, thousands of Others followed, approaching the Dallas-Fort Worth metropolitan area. Already, flames and smoke reached into the sky, for ahead, over a million Others advanced before them, overwhelming all defenders and consuming all prey in their path. Soon, another great city would fall to the horde.

Dead Jeffries had a vague picture in its mind, an image of an office park it had visited in another lifetime.

That place was where Dead Jeffries and the Others marched.

There, Dead Jeffries and the Others would end their hunt.